WHEN KARMA COMES CALLING

A NOVEL

TOM BESTWICK

ISBN: 978-1-0685606-0-6

Cover and book design by Christian Storm.

To Nat and Lewie. My world.

To heal, we must first forgive...

and sometimes the person

we must forgive is ourselves.

MILA BRON

PROLOGUE

12 YEARS EARLIER

As Jonny McIntyre let the back door of his local boozer swing behind him, he was sure he was slamming it shut on the biggest mistake he'd ever made.

What Jonny didn't know, though, was his mistake was just a chapter in a story that spanned over two decades. He'd later find out it was just a mere bump in the road — a story that was driven by an obsession and a deep desire for revenge.

And he'd found himself entangled in it for what? Lust? To feel wanted again? To be wrapped up in the excitement of something new?

Right now, he was seeing it for what it was. He'd been weak and stupid and naïve. At first, it had been nothing but a bit of harmless fun. But as feelings had got in the way, the hole Jonny found himself in had only got deeper and deeper. His white lies had grown like a fungal infection and by the end, they were obvious and ugly, growing as they fed on his acts of deception and greed.

Nine months it had gone on for.

Nine months too long.

But now it was over. Or, at least, so he hoped.

That was what Jonny was thinking about as he flung himself into his beat-up Vauxhall Corsa, wanting to make a quick getaway. The weather had other ideas. The rain and cold had created a blanket of condensation that lay over his windows like layers of soggy paper. He turned the ignition, fired up the fans and got them working overtime to drive it away.

In the meantime, all he could do was listen to the rain that had swept in. It was heavy now, the type of rain that kept people indoors. The type of rain that comes as standard during the miserable British winter.

But like most folk, Jonny had conflicting feelings about this weather. On one hand, he'd be chief among the moaners if it fucked with his work on the construction yard. Yet, on the other, there was something ironically cosy and warm about it at this time of year, just before Christmas. Jonny would take pleasure in listening to the rain do its thing from a safe and dry place, zoning out to its taps against the window. It took him right back to his earliest memories as a child when his mum would read fairytales to him from the edge of his bed, the radiator humming away, the elements doing their thing against his bedroom window.

That was a long time ago now — a time when Jonny had no responsibilities, problems, or worries. A time when someone else would help him mop his troubles up.

Not like now.

Over the last few months, Jonny had really fucked things up, and no one was coming to save him. He needed to fix this himself.

As the condensation peeled away, he thought about how he didn't deserve Liz. She was too good for him. He'd always known that. There had been plenty of times he'd wondered what she was doing with him in the first place.

Because I love you, silly, she used to tell him when his insecurities got the better of him, more often than not when he'd had an ale too many.

And yet, Jonny had taken her love for granted. Betrayed it. He'd spend a lifetime trying to make up for it if Liz could truly allow him. No one would blame her if she couldn't.

That fear lingered as his windows finally cleared. Before setting off, Jonny scanned the pub's exterior one last time. As he hoped, the rain was keeping everyone indoors, including *her* — everyone except two silhouettes that were huddled together under a canopy, sharing a cigarette by the door that had slammed behind him.

Safe in that knowledge, he pulled away, the lights of his car cutting into the night.

You wouldn't be able to tell Christmas was just a matter of weeks away if you swung on to Wayborough Falls.

Aside from the Kings over at number 19, who put in a bit of effort with their external decorations, nobody else bothered. Not like those who live on Fenton Crescent, which was on the same estate as Wayborough Falls, but just a little further down the main road that was Bishops Drive. You couldn't miss Fenton Crescent, lit up like a Christmas show and tell every single year, which reminded Jonny of that Christmas film, Deck The Halls, with Danny DeVito and Matthew Broderick.

Instead, Wayborough Falls continued to live a plain existence. It was a far less fancy stretch of road than the name would have you believe, with its one and two-bed houses bunched together shoulder to shoulder, set back off a cracked and scarred pavement and streetlights that barely had enough energy to muster a flicker. Had Wayborough Falls been a person, it would have had a paper bag placed over its head.

It was for that reason, though, that it was so affordable for Jonny and Liz, who were barely out of their teens and trying to find their independence in the world. Their house on Wayborough Falls was their first step toward adulthood and living together as a couple. The rent was cheap. The location was ideal, handily placed just outside the town centre and a stone's throw from their family and friends.

It was a basic life, yes, but one they'd built together on their own — a basic life Jonny's actions had put in jeopardy.

As Jonny swung his Corsa onto Wayborough Falls and slipped down into second gear, a new thin layer of condensation started creeping across his view, fighting back against the fans he'd dialled down so he could listen to the Christmas songs on Capital FM. Jonny responded by whacking the fans back onto the highest setting, joining the wiper blades that were going as fast as they could to keep up with the ribbons of rain that pounded from the night sky.

Approaching home, Jonny slowed right down as he searched for a place to park. The cars lined up bumper to bumper, no surprise given it was so late on a Friday night.

There was a spot further up the road past his and Liz's place that would have to do.

"Fuck me," Jonny muttered to himself after locking the door behind him.

His shoes, the flares of his baggy jeans, and his coat were damp with rain, even though he had only been out in the rain for a matter of seconds after leaping from his car.

He carelessly dumped his work rucksack onto the hardwood floor and hung his dripping coat from a makeshift hook he'd stuck up himself. His keys went into the cracked pot on top of the shoe cabinet and, as he did so, he heard movement from upstairs.

First, there was a rustle from the bedroom, then a flick of a light being turned off. Elizabeth Stallard emerged on the landing, decked in cute nightwear that showed off a distinguished little bump belly. She tied her dressing gown closed over it as she made her way down to him.

Liz didn't look directly at him until she was at the foot of the stairs. Even then, Jonny could see it was taking everything she had to look into his eyes. Her face was cold and cautious. A picture of broken trust and betrayal.

"It's done?" She asked firmly, but quietly.

Jonny swallowed the hard lump in his throat. He didn't say anything, just nodded a couple of times as he sucked at his top lip.

"Ok."

Liz padded off towards the kitchen, stopping only to tap the light on in the living room. Jonny followed close by. She didn't acknowledge his presence as she turned the oven dials and then brushed past him to bend down and ferret around in the freezer.

"Here, let me do that," Jonny offered with a little too much earnestness.

"No, I've got it!" Elizabeth said with a snap.

Jonny backed off and let her do her thing.

Liz pulled out a couple of pizzas that are set on a couple of trays and slid onto the oven's top grate. She straightened out, taking a moment to gather herself again.

Then she headed to the fridge and pulled out a couple of drinks — a can of coke for her, a beer for him, clicking them both open. Rather than hand the beer to Jonny, she left it on the worktop and took herself off to the living room without saying a single word.

Jonny didn't follow right away. She asked for space and time and that's what he would give her. He took a long swig of his beer. He'd still be in the box spare bedroom and was becoming familiar with the cold shoulder he deserved. Jonny had resigned himself to the usual Christmas festivities being on pause this year. Well, until they put on the forced act they talked about when they visit Liz's parents.

Jonny accepted this was how it was going to be right now.

He wished he could make everything better and take it all back. His saving grace was that Liz hadn't kicked him to the kerb. He suspected the fact they were going to be parents in just under four months was a big reason why he wasn't ringing around his mates and crashing on sofas.

But he also hoped there was more to it than that, that she was giving him a chance to fix things because she wanted to. Not because she felt trapped by the life-altering change that was on the horizon.

And even if it took a lifetime, Jonny would do his damndest to make this up to her.

He would make this right.

PART 1

EYES A DARKER SHADE OF BLACK

WEDNESDAY

6TH NOVEMBER 2019

RHYS

A few weeks ago, Rhys McIntyre overheard a debate.

It was between a couple of older kids during one lunchtime in the St Andrews Academy library. They'd verbally jostled over what one superpower they'd all have if they could have any — all while they chowed down their sandwiches and packets of crisps.

For Rhys, the answer was simple. He'd loved nothing more than to go back in time. To change what happened in the summer. The thing that had changed everything.

He looked over at his bedside clock, knowing full well what was coming.

"Rhys, come on! Don't make me tell you again!"

He thought it wouldn't be so bad to be able to disappear, either.

Rhys dreaded his mum's final morning call every morning, a call that was laced with frustration and annoyance, signalling there was no more time to drain. Not another second. Not without really ticking her off.

Never poke the bear, his dad had told him once. Rhys sat at the edge of his bed, knowing he couldn't afford another poke.

And as he reluctantly pulled himself up, turning the TV off took all his willpower. It wasn't like it was Friday and he had just one more day to get through before the weekend. No, it was still only Wednesday. He wasn't even halfway through the damn week. Rhys had heard his aunty Esme shout 'happy hump day' on a Wednesday one time before in a cheery and sweet voice. Happy hump day, what was that all about? What was satisfying about the prospect of having to go to work — or school, in his case — for another three days before the weekend?

These thoughts were a sludge that filtered down Rhys' body, making everything require an extra ounce of effort.

"Have you got your PE kit, hon?" His mum asked. As Rhys slowly took the stairs one at a time, she didn't look at him. She was too busy gazing into a mirror, forcefully pulling a brush through dishevelled and straggly blonde hair. There hadn't been time to squeeze in a shower.

"Yeah, packed it this morning," he responded. Another thing done begrudgingly.

It hadn't always been this way. Rhys used to like school. But then, nothing had been the same since the summer.

His mum hadn't noticed that change in him. Instead, Rhys' mum was over enthusiastic about what he was doing at school, treating him the same now as she had when he came out of Primary School. So obviously trying to keep things like before. She wanted to know *everything* about what he got up to.

That was well and good when you've got friends, enjoy your classes, and was doing well.

It's not the same when school sucks ass.

The morning drive to school followed a similar pattern every day.

Rhys would climb up front by his mum. He'd wrap his headphones over his ears, crank the volume up on his iPod just enough to block everything else out and do his damnedest to avoid having to talk about the day ahead.

Sometimes it worked. Sometimes it didn't.

Today it didn't.

Rhys had heard his mum trying to get his attention as he watched his little corner of the world pass by out of his passenger window, watching the houses whiz by, each one drawing the academy closer and closer.

He rolled his eyes, hearing his mum again. All the while, he pretended not to. It was time to give it up.

"Sorry. Didn't hear you," he lied, slipping the headphones back around his neck.

"I'm not surprised with how loud you have those things on."

And so they did their usual routine. She asked Rhys her questions. He batted them back with simple, sharp answers. He couldn't tell her the truth. His mum had enough on her plate without him adding to it. As far back as he could remember, Rhys had always been taught the importance of not lying. There was no such thing as a good lie in her book.

But Rhys told himself he wasn't lying. Not really. He was just covering the truth from her, hoping that one day everything would get better on its own.

He reasoned she didn't need to know because there was nothing she could do about it, anyway.

The moment the car pulled up outside St Andrews Academy emphasised how differently Rhys felt about the day ahead compared to everyone else.

That familiar feeling of dread sunk into the pit of his stomach as the buzz of pupils meeting up with friends swirled, distorted beyond the car door. Everyone wore the same mask of excitement, a mask that everyone else, except for Rhys, appeared to own.

He stared bleakly out of the window, wishing for the day to be over before it had even begun. But as he did every morning, he turned to his mum, smiled, kissed her on the cheek, and told her he loved her. Once the car pulled off, that smile he wore for her vanished.

Rhys had trudged this path down to registration alone for the last couple of months. When he'd first started at St Andrews Academy in September, he'd done this trek with Danny Waldron, his best mate from when they were together at pre-school. It had been a friendship initially forced upon them as toddlers, by two mums who had hit it off on a new mum group and had met most weeks, two quiet and cautious toddlers in tow, for soft play and park dates. Rhys and Danny became as thick as thieves and had done everything together ever since.

But that friendship had eroded, not that Rhys could hold it against Danny, who had tried to keep their bromance alive. The academy had split them up into different classes. Danny made new friends quickly. There was Rob, Darlow, Coco, Bonnie, and Hazza. Maybe Danny got tired of Rhys not making any effort with his new mates. And as those first days and weeks passed by, it felt like the burning fire of their friendship dwindled into a flicker before it went out entirely.

Their eyes crossed this morning. Danny put his hand up. Rhys reciprocated. That was that.

Onwards towards registration. On his own.

Multi-coloured leaves — reds and browns and oranges — littered the path and danced in the wind, doing their best to avoid being crushed under some kid's shoe. Rhys weaved one way, then the other, navigating his way around clusters of students that all seemed to be much bigger than he was. The sharp roof of A-block and the English department came into view, stabbing at the dark clouds that had set in for the day.

Then came the familiar morning greeting.

"Look at the state of that fuckin' tie, lads!' Get over 'ere Maccie!"

Conor Wilkinson, or 'Wilko' if you were one of his boys, was your typical dickhead. To the point Rhys found this moron to be a strutting cliché: carefree attitude, arrogant, swaggering around like he owned the place. The type of guy who only made an effort to impress his buddies or make someone's life a misery just for a laugh. In recent weeks, it seemed Rhys had become that someone.

"Walking on your tod again, Maccie? Here, let me sort that tie out for ya."

Conor jumped from his perch on the wall, pushing a stray blade of his swept-back hair back into position behind his ear as he made his way over, brandishing a smile Rhys could only dream of wiping away.

Kyle, Charlie, and Gary — his entourage — followed, creating a wall behind Conor in case Rhys decided, stupidly, to run around them. He'd tried that once. It hadn't gone so well. And so Rhys now just took what was coming.

Conor grabbed at Rhys' tie at the top of the knot and tugged as hard as he could at the bottom. Rhys felt the loop squeeze and pinch around his throat.

"That's better isn't it, pal," Conor muttered, slick with the usual sarcasm. He accompanied the words with a couple of lazy slaps on Rhys' left cheek.

"Well?" He added, pushing Rhys to indulge him.

Rhys lifted his eyes off the floor, cautious not to even look at Conor in the wrong way.

"Aren't you gonna say thank you, lad?." His pals had smirks etched across their faces.

"Are you not grateful Maccie? Come on..."

Rhys yielded. He accepted there was nothing else he could do and it wasn't worth taking a punch to the gut for.

"Thank you, Conor." He sounded pathetic.

"That's alright, pal. It wouldn't be cool of me to let you go walking around with your tie looking like that. Christ. Did your mum get you ready again this morning?"

The final bell clanged, signalling the start of registration. Conor wrapped an arm around Rhys' shoulders and led the way, his entourage pacing closely behind like shadows.

Conor gave Rhys a final smack on the shoulder and sent him to his usual space at the front left corner of the classroom.

"See ya later, Alligator."

Free of the nob head's grasp, Rhys readjusted his tie. If he had his way, he'd remove the damn thing altogether. Mrs Johnson wouldn't have any of that, though. She was a stickler for the uniform and it was another fight never worth having. So he straightened himself out the best he could without a mirror. Conor waved at him from the opposite end of the room. Rhys took his seat and whipped out his sketchpad.

"Morning everyone. How're we all today?"

Mrs Johnson swept in, long ginger hair flowing and bouncing with each step, a bunch of folders hugging against a dark blue blouse. Mrs Johnson was one of the good ones. A good egg. A great class tutor class tutor but an even better teacher at the academy. Smart. Engaging. Passionate. She conducted her classes like a stage performance. Above all else, though, her best quality was that she didn't take herself too seriously. She could be silly and knew how to make a room laugh. Not like the others.

For more obvious reasons, she was also a hit with boys who were at an age where their testosterone levels were starting to fizz out of control, like Mentos dropped in a cola bottle. Not many days went by in this hell hole when some kid didn't make some kind of comment about how good she looked or, the age-old, how she'd get it.

And just as it did every morning, her arrival stopped the room's chatter dead. Aside from the odd sniffle here and cough there, Mrs Johnson's voice echoed as she called out the names of the students in front of her, ticking them off on a sheet as she always did, hunched over her desk.

She occasionally looked up to survey the room, flashing that sweet and bright smile around that made you feel warm inside.

"Rhys McIntyre?"

"Here."

She whisked her head around to the left. "Can I see you before you break for class, please?"

Again?

With his chin nestled comfortably in the palm of his left hand, he nodded.

"And... fabulous."

Mrs Johnson finished her list. She gave her pep talk and gave a last reminder about needing permission slips for the school trip to Hilltop Adventure Park next week.

At 8:55, the bell rang again. This time for the start of the first period.

"Right guys, chop, chop, chop. I hope you all have a great day. You all have my email if you need me for anything... now go on, get outta here."

The sound of chairs clattering and scraping almost suffocated Mrs Johnson's words. Like cars funnelling onto a busy motorway, Rhys watched as his class shuffled past her into a corridor that was already brimming. Conor smirked in his direction, nodding Rhys' way as he followed at the back of the line.

Rhys remained where he was, sheepish and awkward. He always felt the same when a teacher kept him behind, particularly as it had become such a frequent occurrence recently.

He caught Mrs Johnson's gaze without meaning to and turned away in an instant. She closed the door behind the last kid and made her way over to his corner of the room.

"I just wanted to check to see how things have been going, Rhys?" She rested a hand on the back of his chair.

"They're ok, thanks, Ms," he said, swallowing the lie down hard.

"You sure?"

Rhys wasn't daft. There were only two reasons why she'd be asking. It was usually to do with Conor or the other thing Rhys *really* didn't like to talk about. This time, he thought, it was likely to be the former, possibly about Monday, when Conor had left Rhys with a sore backside and a bruised ego after pulling a chair from underneath him before science class. It left the rest of the class in stitches. His cheeks had flushed and gone warm. And when Rhys' cheeks go warm, they turn horrible and blotchy. Got his mum's genes to thank for that. Mr Pulmer had held him back after class, again to ask if he was ok.

It was always attention Rhys didn't want.

"Rhys?" Mrs Johnson asked, catching him in a moment of hesitation.

"Yeah, sorry," he shrugged his shoulders, and looked Mrs Johnson in the eyes, playing it as cool as possible. "Everything's fine."

She nodded with an acceptance that the suspicious look on her face didn't reciprocate. Perhaps conscious that her doubt was on show, she quickly pulled her lips into a sweet smile. "Ok."

At least she didn't ask about the other thing. Well, she wouldn't have done had he not been so foolish and had his sketchpad out on his desk. The book was open to his latest drawing.

"What're you drawing there?"

Rhys cursed himself silently for giving her ammunition.

"Um... it's... it's just something I'm finishing for my sister."

Mrs Johnson stooped closer to inspect his work — a lotus flower that needed just the last tiny details, a dab of colour here and a bit more depth there. Three weeks it had taken to do, on and off. Three weeks of starting, ripping out, and binning sheets and starting all over again until it was just right. Rhys turned away embarrassed. No one else was supposed to see it, not until it was finished.

"Rhys, you've done this?" The question came out as sweet as sugar. "It's beautiful."

Rhys didn't say a peep. He felt a gentle squeeze on his shoulder that caught him off guard.

"Your sister will love it."

Rhys hoped so.

Thankfully, there wasn't time for Mrs Johnson to probe any further on the matter. Rhys felt relief sweep over him like a brush stroke as a knock on the door stole Mrs Johnson's attention.

"Can we come in, Ms?"

"Hey, Ellie. Of course, get yourselves settled down."

Rhys took the opportunity to quickly slide the pad back into his bag.

"You'd better get off to class as well," Mrs Johnson said, eyes training back on him. "I'll see you at the end of the day."

And Rhys couldn't get out of the room quick enough. He didn't look back but could feel his tutor's eyes following him like a nosey CCTV camera. He wormed his way through the oncoming traffic and out into the bustling corridor.

As he approached the first corner, he was met by a familiar face. A girl he didn't know by name. She was propped up against the wall, her hair tied into its usual neat bun.

Their eyes locked, just for a second. Rhys pulled away awkwardly, as he always did, as he scurried along to his first class of the day that he couldn't be less arsed about.

ELIZABETH

It was turning into a horrible day. Apt for the time of year, but horrible nevertheless.

The sky was dark with leaden and heavy clouds, and the wind stalked through the tree branches that formed an arch over Clopton Road.

As Elizabeth swung onto the street, she eased off the accelerator. The road was tight and pokey. That had always been the case. Cars aligned neatly against either side of the pavements, reflecting the light emitting from the streetlights that had tapped in for the night shift despite it only being two o'clock in the afternoon.

Thank God Ma and Pa had a drive that she could park in front of. That was one thing she never had to worry about.

She pulled to a stop and checked herself in the mirror, shaking her head at how tired and baggy her eyes appeared and how pale her skin had become recently. No angle made her look any better, and she puffed with disappointment. It hadn't been like this since Eevie was a newborn.

Elizabeth hopped out. The wind tugged her wiry blonde hair across her face. The Crossland locked on her press. As she made her way up the drive, she couldn't help but look over at the window of Mr Dorset's bungalow next door. More often than not, he was there, waiting to greet her with his beady and accusing eyes.

Sure enough, he was there today, arms folded behind his back, his frame buried under a heavy beige cardigan. Elizabeth assumed he was overlooking the street to make sure she wasn't parking anywhere she shouldn't. He was a one-man neighbourhood watch for Clopton Road, was Mr Dorset.

As teenagers, Elizabeth and her sister, Esme, had given the old man a hard time. They took the mick a little, playing dumb stuff like knock a door run whenever they got a chance. Threw eggs at his door one Halloween when they felt extra brave, too. Anything for a laugh back then. Anything to fit in. However, what Elizabeth had never told her sister — or anyone else, for that matter — was that Mr Dorset had scared the bejesus out of her.

She'd always been a big reader. Elizabeth had devoured every word of the Harry Potter books and had always thought of her neighbour as a carbon copy of Argus Filch, that miserable caretaker of Hogwarts School for Witchcraft and Wizardry. That association had never left her, even now, as she'd grown into a woman, a wife, and a mother.

Thankfully, now that she was in her early 30s, she found him less intimidating.

Elizabeth put her hand up to Mr Dorset weakly. He reciprocated the gesture. You'd never catch old Filch being so polite!

On she went. She felt the first spit of rain kiss her nose as she trotted up the steep incline of her Ma and Pa's driveway.

Elizabeth used her key and slipped inside quietly — just in case Eevie would be sound asleep — and instantly felt the warmth and scent of the familiar vanilla diffuser that she had always associated with this house.

She kicked off her ballet flats. Again, she always did, and wrapped her scarf around the bannister. She listened intently to a voice — singing. She could it hear coming from the living room further down the hallway.

She padded on down and peered through the door that was etched open an inch. Just enough. There she was — Ma — giving her best rendition of Old MacDonald Had A Farm, animal noises and all, totally off-key yet perfect at the same time.

Nana Nellie was singing to Elizabeth's little girl who rested peacefully on her lap, embracing a plush rabbit with her free tiny hand, sucking and nibbling at the ear.

Elizabeth's heart melted. She went for her phone but stopped. Once upon a time, she wouldn't have hesitated to have got her camera up and filmed a moment like this. The type of video she would have relived over and over.

But things were different now.

Lost in that moment's hesitation, her shoulder pressed a little too hard on the door. Its old hinges let off a wheeze, a creak. The singing ceased. Ma's eyes met hers through the gap.

Nellie turned back to the girl on her lap, her fingers tickling her tummy. "Oh, look who's here, Eevie."

Elizabeth's daughter didn't stir or respond. Not like she used to.

"You'd make a good cow, you know," Elizabeth said, letting herself into the immaculate living room.

"Ha. Ha. You hear this, Eevie? That's no way for mummy to talk to Nana now, is it?"

"Yeah, yeah. You stay silent if you disagree, honey." Right on cue, Eevie pulled away from the rabbit and began blowing raspberries with her freed lips.

Typical. Kids never do what you want them to do when you need them to.

Ma's response was obvious, cheesy, and sarcastic. Triumphant.

Elizabeth made her way over to the vacant single-seater in the far corner, Pa's seat. It was part of a twin set that had been here even before she and Esme had moved in all those years ago. *Christ, how long had it been now?*

"Where is he today?" Elizabeth quizzed.

"Over at the allotment," Ma squinted through her glasses to focus on the tiny clock sitting in the middle of the fireplace mantel. "He shouldn't be much longer. You want a drink?"

"I'll pass. Thank you. Gotta get Rhys from school."

"No bother at all." Ma's attention returned to Eevie.

"How's she been?" Elizabeth asked.

"Good as gold," she said, her voice taking on a raspy tone that came with years of smoking. She pointed a finger and began tickling Eevie's tummy. "We had a few tantrums here and there, but nothing we're not used to."

Tantrums. They had become the norm but it still disheartened Elizabeth to hear those words. Not that she'd ever say that's the case. She retained her brave, unfazed, face. The one expected of her.

"Tantrums, ey! You're lucky it's your birthday or there'd be trouble, missy." She joined in the tickling.

Elizabeth turned back to Ma and her lips straightened out. "Thank you for looking after her."

"There's never a need for thanks in this house. We always like to have her."

"Still, we know she can be a handful now."

And just like that, the conversation shifted, taking on a serious underbelly.

"How are you and Jonny?" Nellie asked.

Elizabeth gave her best who-knows expression and a swift shrug of the shoulders. "Ok... I think. Same old, same old. He started his therapy today."

"About time. Take it he's still off work?"

Elizabeth knew where the conversation was going and she was keen to shut it down.

"For now, yeah."

Ma's expression was always the same. A plastered on look of disapproval. She puffed out her bottom lip, nodding curtly, not buying what she was hearing. She never did. Elizabeth knew Ma wasn't Jonny's biggest fan. Ditto for Pa. They'd never hidden that fact either, always thought their little Elizabeth could do better.

"He should be helping you more if he's off. I mean, what does he even do with all his time?"

"It's not that simple, Ma."

"I just don't know why you put up with it. Your room is still set up upstairs. You and Rhys—"

"Ma, please," Elizabeth said. Her frustration burst right out of her. "I don't want to hear it. Not today"

Ma flicked a hand up and conceded defeat. That was the end of it.

Elizabeth flicked a glance at her watch — it was just after 2:30. It wouldn't be long before Rhys was finishing at school and there may well be an impromptu Costa trip on the cards, providing the roads were clear.

"We'd better be off. Come here, missy."

Elizabeth heaved Eevie up in her arms, faking a groan as she did. "Four years old today. We're getting a big girl, aren't we?"

Where had those years ago? She nuzzled into her neck and gave her a sloppy kiss on the cheek.

The three of them made their way back down the hallway. At the door, Elizabeth fumbled her scarf around her clumsily with her spare hand before sliding on her flats.

Ma held the door open ready for her.

"You be careful driving in this weather," Ma pulled her thick cardigan tightly around her. "That wind's a nightmare and it looks like it's going to bucket it down any moment."

"What're you talking about? I'm always careful."

"Who're you kidding? I've seen your driving!"

Elizabeth's face feigned hurt. She played her ace card.

"Well, you won't be wanting a lift tomorrow morning then, right?"

Her little sister, Esme, was up from London for her monthly visit. The three of them had made a habit of using the occasion to get the girls together. Give Ma a break of her own.

"Oh, you wouldn't make me get Ron to drop me off, would you?"

"I wouldn't dream of it. Say bye-bye to nana."

Elizabeth did the waving for her daughter, tugging at a droopy arm. Eevie looked tuckered out and ready for a nap. She rubbed her eyes the same now as she did as a baby. Elizabeth would try putting her down for a cat nap when they got home, a little earlier than normal. It would take her out of her normal schedule but Elizabeth wanted her to be awake and active for dinner and the little birthday celebration she had planned.

Elizabeth strapped Eevie into her car seat in the back passenger side, restraining her arms as Eevie fought being manipulated into position. There were no tears this time. That itself was a small win.

Finally clipped in, Elizabeth waved farewell to Ma. "See you tomorrow!"

She booted the Crossland up. Elizabeth couldn't help but have one last glance over at Mr Dorset's window. The old man was nowhere to be seen this time.

Apparently, he does have other things to do.

She swung the car off the drive and headed back down Clopton Road. She was desperate for her first gingerbread latte of the year.

JONNY

His mind had drifted into a fog until the rumbling of a passing Freightliner jerked him back to reality.

Startled, Jonny pinched hard on the bridge of his nose, feeling the dull ache right between his eyes. He took a moment to let consciousness seep back in as he slumped into his seat.

One of the many sleepy villages that littered this route had replaced the dreary picture of the desolate countryside and valleys and cliffs that stretched for miles. Disoriented, he couldn't figure out where exactly he was on his journey home. His eyes flicked to his watch. He'd zoned out for ten minutes, fifteen tops, he estimated. But, indeed, Jonny hadn't missed his stop.

There was a time, a few years back after a work exhibition in London, when he had done just that. The combination of a warm train and a few networking beers too many had finished him off. He had never forgotten it, never forgotten Liz's voice, as he had to call her, tail between his legs, after waking up and seeing his get-off vanishing in the distance. Boy, Liz was fuming when it was clear Jonny wasn't pulling her leg.

They had laughed about it later, sure, but he swore never to let it happen again, no matter how exhausted he felt. And right now, he was as tired as he'd ever known. He thinks he would do anything — *anything* — to recognise a moment's peace and be able to drift off and have a good night's kip. Or anything to at least not feel and endure that stinging sensation behind his eye sockets every day. Or have his mind racing like an unrelenting F1 car built without brakes.

It was why Jonny was on this train.

Liz had reached her breaking point with it all. His struggles to adapt to their new reality. She'd told Jonny he couldn't go on like this. But what was the answer? Hers was to visit the doctor, a suggestion Jonny had reluctantly agreed to. His brief 10-minute appointment with Doctor Kaimana last week led to him being referred to the Evolve Therapy Centre in the next town over. The doc had determined Jonny was showing mild signs of depression and anxiety — unsurprisingly so, according to her, after what had happened during the summer. Go figure.

While he might think it was a hopeless venture, at least Liz was happy and optimistic. Liz thought it was great the doc had referred Jonny to talk to someone, that it could help him, in her words, move on.

That was a sentiment that Jonny silently didn't share, mainly because neither his wife nor the doctor knew half of why he'd been the way he was.

Not that he could share that nugget of information. Christ, they'd both think he was as crazy as someone tucking into a soup sandwich if he told them what was *really* keeping him awake at night.

To that end, Jonny had also pre-determined a weekly trip to Evolve to talk to a Dr Nielson, who Jonny thought looked like a pretentious weasel when he looked him up on the website, someone that had never known a struggle in his life, would be a pointless exercise, that he wouldn't get anything out of it.

He felt he was making the trip more to appease his wife than to get help.

But what Liz didn't know couldn't hurt her, right?

And that's what Jonny was telling himself as he got out of his seat and got off the train a stop early an hour ago.

It wasn't because he was doing this more for his wife than himself. Or even that he thought he wouldn't get anything out of it that got him out of his seat and rushing out onto the platform.

It was all because of the eyes and hazy shadowy figures that followed him wherever he went.

They had become an inescapable presence in his life, materialising out of nowhere and vanishing without rhyme or reason.

There was no discernible pattern to them — no logic to their existence Jonny could grasp onto.

The first time he'd seen those abyssal black eyes outside of his nightmares, Jonny had dismissed it as a figment of his imagination, a trick of the light on a stranger's face. He'd chalked it up as an illusion, deeming what he'd seen as an impossibility.

That was a short few months ago. And yet, those impossibilities continued to occur, more and more. It began with those eyes.

Eyes that Jonny could only describe as a darker shade of black and radiated what he was sure was malevolence. They tormented him relentlessly, following his every step, just as a crow would keep its eye on a nearing presence to make sure it didn't get too close.

But soon there were the figures — black silhouettes, like shadows peeled off the ground, that appeared and vanished with the same will, leaving Jonny with a constant eerie sensation that he was being followed. He didn't need to see them to know they were there, waiting for him.

He just couldn't ever be sure where.

There was no logic to any of it and Jonny, since these impossibilities gatecrashed his reality, had been trying to do the only logical thing he could do and convince himself that it all had to be in his head. A byproduct of not being able to sleep.

It had to be. Didn't it?

As the train rattled along, Jonny massaged the small of his back, trying to alleviate the tension gripping his shoulders. He cricked his neck from side to side, hoping to find some relief from the discomfort. Three stops was all that separated him from the quick trip home.

The carriages were quiet. By nine, the early morning commuters had cleared out, leaving plenty of empty spots for Jonny to choose from. He pinched a secluded seat at the back of an end carriage, conveniently close to the conductor's quarters.

Sitting there, Jonny hoped for minimal interactions, avoiding the awkwardness of dealing with other passengers. As long as no one took the seat across from him, the only person Jonny might have to interact with before reaching his destination would be the ticket collector.

It had been a case of so far so good until he'd heard steps hobbling in his direction at the next stop.

Jonny shifted his body away from the carriage's centre, his eyes fixed determinedly out the window. Despite his efforts to avoid the newcomer, he couldn't help but notice a pair of worn brown leather shoes shuffling across the train's faded blue carpet. The man they belonged to wheezed as he settled into the seats opposite.

The familiar surge of apprehension took hold. Jonny's heart raced. The train's rhythmic chugging mimicked the frantic pace of his pulse. Heat flushed his skin and prickled.

Out of his mucky window, rows of houses passed in a blur beneath the darkening sky, disappearing almost as quickly as they appeared. Two stops to go.

But within that picture, Jonny couldn't help but notice the old man's reflection. While his features were indiscernible, Jonny could make out the tuft of white hair peeking out from under his beanie. The thick eyebrows above wrinkled and sunken sockets.

Just don't look. Don't look. That's all you have to do. Don't you fuckin' do it! Keep... your head... down. Jonny muttered inwardly as a silent plea, trying to maintain his cocoon of privacy.

But that was easier said than done.

He glanced once more. He did this a lot, trying to test his own theory that he was losing his shit.

But there it was, again — a flicker of hazy darkness, just below the old man's beanie. Jonny shook his head in surrender, grinding his teeth and squeezing his eyes shut.

"No... No... Nope," he whispered to himself, the words a desperate mantra. "Get a grip, man."

He listened to the whistling of his nose and absentmindedly scratched the corner of his lip. The train was approaching its next stop. Another set of footsteps echoed in the carriage.

"Any tickets, please," a woman's voice droned with disinterest. Jonny remained silent, hoping she would pass by, leave him be. But she drew nearer, politely requesting the ticket from the old man across from him. Still, Jonny kept his silence.

"Sir, can I see your ticket, please?"

Fuck.

His heart sank. Jonny blindly ferreted in his coat pocket, finding nothing. He tried the pockets of his jeans and got the same result. The woman hovering over him grew impatient. At last, he fished the ticket from his shirt pocket and held it out, but received no acknowledgement.

He creeped his eyes open enough to see the floor. She stood square to him. Unmoved.

"Is everything okay?" he stammered, unnerved by her silence. He stuck the ticket out an inch further.

He cautiously glanced up again, tilting his head slowly. But like the old man's, the ticket collector's eyes were dark and empty beneath a tightly pulled bun of blonde hair, set on a cold, expressionless face. Jonny tore his eyes away. He scratched nervously at the nape of his neck. They would disappear. They always did. He just had to ride it out.

And then...

"Thank you, sir."

She took the ticket, scribbled lazily on the corner and retreated, heading back the way she came. Across from him, Jonny felt a hand on his shoulder. "Everything ok, son?"

His eyes settled on the old man sitting opposite. His eyes were also normal under that tuft of hair, wide with concern under wrinkled bags that hung like melted candle wax, whites circling chestnut brown irises.

"Fine, thank you."

Up ahead, Jonny could hear the rattle of a cart, the soft calls by another woman to see if anyone wanted anything off it. Someone stopped her and asked her for a tea. Jonny listened to the click and clack of a laptop keyboard, the pages turning of a newspaper, the ping of a mobile phone. Someone talking loud enough for everyone to hear.

Everything around him felt normal.

But inside, Jonny felt anything but.

RHYS

Not for the first time in the last 30 minutes, Rhys looked up from his desk at the clock hanging in the left corner.

It was 2:57 (and 32 seconds, to be exact). How had only another three minutes elapsed since the last cheeky glance?

Mr Draycott stood at the front of the room. He readjusted his drooping trousers that were doing a poor job of tucking in a wrinkly short-sleeved shirt. A shirt that was obviously a size too small for his popping stomach, buttons fighting with every fibre to make sure it stayed closed.

He was *still* going on about databases and formulas.

Rhys had found he could get away with murder from his space at the back of the room during IT classes. Hidden behind a line of bulky desktops where he could let his mind wander into an entirely different, less boring place.

Most of the class clicked away, cracking on with the task at hand. Others attempted to find online games that the academy's firewall hadn't blocked. Rhys turned to his sketchbook and pencils.

Mr Draycott might be boring, but he was a pushover, too. He'd set his task for the day, talk through it from a textbook, and settle down for 40 minutes or so of peace and leave you to it. Much like the class, it appeared he didn't give much of a toss.

And here Mr Draycott was, running his last bit of monologue, pointing at the projector behind him as he did so. Rhys pondered that maybe Mr Draycott would be just as happy as he would be when the bell chimed and he could send everyone off on their merry way.

Rhys watched as the ticker went about its tick, teasing him with how slowly it hopped around the clock face, inching closer to pushing the other hand over the finish line.

Bag packed. Computer shut down. He was ready. If only everything else moved as quickly.

And... there it was. The bell clanged. The only thing Rhys had in common with anyone in this class was they all leapt out of their seats as quickly as he did.

"Righto, we'll leave it there," Mr Draycott bellowed. "Let's pick this up again later in the week. You've all got your homework, yes? I expect a full-page review of page 32 in the textbook on my desk before we start on Friday morning."

The rubbing of chairs against the hard carpet and frantic packing of bags had drowned him out, and within seconds, the room was empty.

He had only 15 more minutes to get through — the debrief and sign-out session back at Mrs Johnson's room. A pointless exercise created to trap the kids longer than necessary.

Rhys clung to his backpack straps as he weaved one way, then another, navigating around clusters of students catching up and having their own debriefs. He rounded the corner that connected

IT to English, hitting the home stretch.

It was then that he heard footsteps. A stampede of ugly and cheap school shoes clapping against the resin floor, heading right towards him.

Rhys thought nothing of it. Why should he have? It was just a bunch of kids fooling around. They'd race by him and that'd be that.

Except they didn't.

Instead, the clattering got louder and closer, barrelling straight into him. He jolted forward. The hefty shove sent him sprawling with a thud. A sharp throbbing pain just above his left eye took over the initial shock in his neck. Small raindrops of blood beaded on the dirty floor.

"So, the freak bleeds."

Rhys didn't need two guesses to know who was above him as he heaved himself up onto his knees and elbows.

Conor grabbed hold of Rhys' arm and yanked him back to his feet. Maybe it was instinct or adrenaline. Perhaps it was the stinging pain. Or it could have just been how fed up Rhys was with everything. Whatever it was, it possessed Rhys to slap Conor's arm away.

"Found some balls, have you, big lad?"

Rhys regretted it immediately.

A small group of kids within earshot of what was happening circled them. A couple whipped out their phones, anticipating, maybe even hoping, to see Rhys beaten to a pulp. Christ, the closest he'd got to any type of fight in his life was by playing Tekken and Mortal Kombat on a games console.

"Fuckin' do him, Conor!" someone shouted from the growing crowd.

Conor stood with that same smirk.

Dropped his bag without a care, taking a step forward.

Rhys had nowhere to run.

But Conor didn't get a chance to do anything else.

"You want to tell me what happened?"

Rhys did not. No matter how thankful he was that Mrs Johnson had stepped in when she did, he wasn't daft enough to blab and make the situation worse.

He also wasn't daft enough to think this was over. This was Conor, after all. Why did he have to push his arm away and create a scene? Why couldn't he have just got up, taken the usual crap, covered up his eye and gone home?

He'd only gone and made everything 10 times worse.

The crowd, baying for a punch up to talk about later, dispersed, unsatisfied and disappointed. Conor and his mates, likewise. After everything had settled, Mrs Johnson escorted Rhys to the nurse's room, located right across the other side of the school, with a slither of toilet paper clinging to the cut above his eye that stung like a bitch.

Ms Timpson, the nurse, sorted him out. She wore thick-framed glasses under a bob of grey and white hair which made her look similar to the old dude in the Pixar movie, Up. What set apart from him was the short-cut green uniform that showed off faded but pretty tattoos — a weird collection of flowers, hearts, snakes, and dream catchers riding her dry and scaly arms.

Ms Timpson didn't mess about and didn't have much to say either, just smiled here and there as she dabbed balls of wet cotton above Rhys' eye and sorted him out with a plaster. A waft of rose water cut across his nose whenever she stood in front of him.

She ordered Rhys to neck two capsules of paracetamol, pushed a cup of water into his hands, and watched until they were gone.

"You'll live. No need for stitches," she proclaimed as she made sure she was happy with her work before exiting.

Mrs Johnson stood by Rhys' side, her arms folded, her expression unusually stern — a side to his tutor he had rarely encountered before. She was not about to let this incident slide.

"Come on, Rhys. What's going on?" she demanded, her tone firm.

Rhys took a sip of water, using the moment to gather his thoughts, searching for words that wouldn't make his situation worse. "It was just an accident, Ms."

"Uh-huh," she responded, nodding sceptically. Her disbelief was evident in her eyes, as it had been that morning. "And was Conor involved?"

Rhys shrugged, feigning uncertainty. "I don't know."

"Did Conor push you?" she pressed further.

"What? No."

"Are you sure?" she persisted.

"Positive."

"Really? Then why did you push his arm away?" The question left Rhys scrambling for an answer.

Damn.

"I dunno."

"Rhys, I can't help you if you don't talk to me."

"I know, but nothing happened."

Rhys wanted to get away. He glanced over Mrs Johnson's shoulder, peaking at the clock hanging above the nurse's door. 3:24. The hive of activity that had been out in the courtyard after the final bell 10 minutes ago had waned.

Mrs Johnson noticed Rhys' gaze, checking the time herself.

"Your mum here to get you?"

Rhys nodded.

"Come on then, get your bag. I'll walk with you up to the gate."

Was there any greater humiliation than being escorted to the school gates by your tutor?

Rhys pondered this as he walked past the last smattering of students that still hung around, acutely aware of the conspicuous shiner he now sported, an unasked-for accessory that he would have to explain away to his mum. It was like the school's version of the Walk of Shame.

Mrs Johnson didn't accompany Rhys the entire way. She stopped a few yards from the school gates. "You going to be ok from here?"

"Yeah."

"You sure?"

"Sure. My mum should just be waiting up top."

And that was that.

His mum started with the obvious as Rhys hopped up front alongside her in the Crossland.

“What on Earth happened to you?”

“Don’t,” Rhys replied, in hope of avoiding the impending onslaught of questions he expected.

“What do you mean ‘don’t’?” She said with concern. “Do I have to go down there and ask someone else for the details?”

“Mum, come on. It’s nothing.”

Right on cue, Eevie had one of her ‘moments’. Rhys had once called them what they were: a mard — a full-on arm swinging, leg kicking, wailing, mard. Mum hated that word — mard — it had got him into a world of trouble a month ago when Eevie had a ‘moment’ in the middle of a busy coffee shop. That had been the mother of all mards, a real stinker. It’d ended with a smashed plate and his mum wearing a half cup of coffee on her favourite jumper. Despite the chaos that often came with them, his sister’s ‘moments’ often drew attention away from him.

Rhys did what he always did and joined his sister in the back to soothe her, using the opportunity to escape an interrogation all the way home.

“We’ll talk about this when we get home?” His mum conceded.

“Ok,” Rhys said, only to appease. He’d try to avoid that for as long as possible.

When they arrived back home, Rhys shot straight upstairs.

Out of sight and out of mind.

He hoped.

ELIZABETH

No sooner had Elizabeth yanked up the handbrake, Rhys was out the door and in the house.

Not even a chance to shout for him to wait.

Not even an offer to help with getting Eevie or her stuff in the house.

All Elizabeth had wondered the entire way home was why he was being so evasive. He'd never been like this. Rhys was an open book. He had always told her everything.

But for the first time that she can remember, she felt disconnected from what was going on with him.

With a tired and unpredictable toddler in the back seat, Elizabeth didn't have time to overthink things. She needed to get Eevie into the house, go through her routine, and put her down for a nap. She planned to talk to Rhys later, once everything had settled down — after the little birthday celebration she had planned became just a memory or, at the very least, a photo on her phone.

It'd be a low-key affair. Better than nothing. Still, it stung Elizabeth that she couldn't throw her daughter anything bigger than a night in, something for just the four of them, a takeaway from the local chippy.

It was her fourth birthday! Family and friends should have

been coming around, tucking into a big-finger buffet that she'd spent hours getting together, pulling party poppers, and playing games. Then at the end, they'd all get huddled together around a big cake and sing happy birthday while she filmed Eevie making a wish for something undoubtedly ridiculous and blowing out her candles.

Just as they had done for Rhys all those years ago.

That — all of that — would just be too much, though. Too overwhelming for Eevie now, who, despite appearing much more settled in her rearview mirror, was still grumpy and fidgety.

Well overdue for that nap.

The first thing Elizabeth heard as she struggled into the house were murmurs from the TV in the living room.

Jonny.

Parked in his recliner, jogging bottoms on, half a bottle of Beck's beer cradled against his midriff, engrossed in whatever garbage was on TV at just gone four in the afternoon.

Above him floated a pink Happy 4th Birthday balloon over silver and gold bunting. Seeing it now, Elizabeth wondered whether she'd taken her low-key approach too far and should have decorated more.

"How'd it go?" she asked, leaning against the door frame, trying to get a read for his expression.

"Yeah... it was ok," he responded, refusing to take his eyes off the damn telly.

"Just ok?"

"Just ok."

Someone else hiding things from her. Elizabeth wanted to probe more, but she didn't have time. She needed to get everything sorted.

"Ok, anyway... I've got to get some stuff out of the car. Can I leave Ee with you while I grab them?" Ordinarily, she'd have left it at that, but Jonny hadn't been the same since what happened a few months back. "Promise I'll be quick," she added for reassurance.

Not that they didn't stop Jonny tensing as he reluctantly agreed. He moved his beer to the nest of tables and shifted in his seat to take Eevie on his lap — without even looking at Elizabeth.

Was he cross with her?

Eevie was a picture of tired bewilderment: eyes drooping, mouth ajar. Looking like she was experiencing something for the first time, but couldn't enjoy it because she needed to sleep.

It was only a few months back that Eevie used to lap up attention from her daddy. Remembering that injected a shot of sadness straight into Elizabeth's veins. Sadness, though, that she refused to show.

"Won't be long," she reaffirmed, already turning on her heel, leaving the words hanging.

The wind started tugging at her hair again as soon as she was out the door, getting in her way as she loaded her arms up with bags from the boot, saving enough space on her forearm to balance the birthday cake she's picked up from Morrison's — a simple Madeira sponge, layered with raspberry jam, frosting, and decorations that created the head of a unicorn.

She double-checked it before taking it inside, making sure it had survived the car journey.

First things first, get that all packed away. Then she'd get started with Eevie's needs and settle her down for a nap before dinner.

RHYS

Rhys *never* bought anything for his sister's birthday.

He didn't want to pick up something tacky or something pocket-money cheap from the shelves of a store. He also thought buying something off the internet was the easy way out. Letting Google tell you the answer was cheating. And vouchers, well, they were the biggest cop-out of all.

No. Rhys wanted to give something unique that no one else could find.

That led him to drawing.

It had become something of a tradition, one that gave his passion for art a real purpose each year.

And once he started it — usually a few weeks before Eevie's birthday — working on it would become his healthy obsession.

For her first birthday, he'd drawn a field of sunflowers. That turned out ok, but not spectacular. When she turned two, he gave her a picture of a single pink rose standing tall and graceful in front of a snowy mountain backdrop. That had been better, but had still lacked depth. Last year, he'd drawn a lone castle tower decked in wisteria vines. That had been his favourite drawing. His magnum opus, his dad had called it. Rhys had to Google what that meant.

But his latest was his best yet.

Rhys scrutinised his latest drawing, squinting at the lotus in front of a foaming, rocky waterfall. His previous three pieces had relied on photos he found online, but this year he wanted his work to be entirely original, from idea to completion. That desire for uniqueness had sparked his interest in photography about a year ago, and he'd put it to good use.

Prior to starting, he knew he wanted to include a waterfall, but there was a slight problem with that: the McIntyres' estate, off urban Yorkshire, was far from any real waterfall. So Rhys had to improvise, which led him to the local garden centre.

When he asked his mum to take him one weekend, he knew what he was looking for. He found a pond full of pretty lotus' bobbing in front of rockery that lined the back of the fountain. He'd snapped a few different angles as they danced peacefully atop the ripples, shots right up close and others from a distance, capturing the light and the shadows that filled his shots.

It wasn't just that the drawing had to be done right; it had to be perfect.

And now Rhys' eyes danced from the photos he'd taken on his laptop screen to his sketchpad and back again, cross-examining the little details.

He felt satisfied. Better than satisfied. All it needed was the finishing touch.

Rhys hopped from his desk to where his bag sat at the foot of his bed. He fumbled around, his fingers grazing his Marvel pencil case. He dug out the specific pencil he needed.

Back at his desk, Rhys hunched over his drawing and carefully traced *Rhy-Rhy* and *1/1* in the bottom right corner.

Just as he did for every drawing for his sister.

He was called downstairs an hour and a bit later.

The family — all four of them — would eat together first. Birthday gifts and cake would come after. That was the part Rhys was looking forward to.

After finally giving his drawing of the lotus his seal of approval, Rhys had pried the page from the sketchpad binder, basking in the crisp rip that came with the slow and precise tear. It always made him feel more emotional than it probably should have. He'd cleared space for it on his desk, pushing everything else to the side to make sure the paper remained flat and untainted.

Making room for it meant more clutter on the bedroom floor, clutter that could wait until later. He killed the rest of his time waiting to be summoned downstairs by laying in bed watching video game streams on Twitch. Tidying up was always a future Rhys problem.

Before heading downstairs, Rhys stopped in the bathroom to survey the swelling over his eye, pushing it this way and that in the bathroom mirror. He'd got rid of any remaining flakes of dry blood around the plaster. The damage was well-covered, but there was no hiding from the pulse of pain it gave him, more so now the magic paracetamol Ms Timpson had given him had worn off.

Heading downstairs, the smell of chippy chips was instant. Waiting for him at the dinner table was his usual battered sausage, chips, and a small pot of curry sauce. There was a slice of bread on the side of the plate to mop the remains up.

The conversation was quiet as Rhys wolfed the lot down, the mood different from any other birthday that had been and gone before.

His dad sat opposite him, stuck in a trance and mind elsewhere. He'd been like that a lot lately — distracted. More so since he stopped working a month ago. Next to Rhys, his mum juggled feeding herself and Eevie. So calm and patient, even as Eevie coiled her neck in any direction to avoid a spoonful of mushy peas.

With the food polished off, plates and cutlery stacked ready to be washed, the four of them headed into the living room, which was decorated with more balloons and bunting than there had been that morning. His mum had been busy.

"I think we know who wants to give you their present first," mum said, settling Eevie down on dad's lap.

Rhys *always* went first.

He raced upstairs and back again. His heart swelled with a concoction of excitement and nerves, mixing together like juice being poured into a glass of water. He always looked forward to this, the final result, the wonder and awe in his sister's eyes. The front of his drawing faced his chest, concealed as though it were a hidden secret. He held the paper at both sides with a delicate pinch.

As he returned, Eevie was trying to claw at her dad's patchy stubble, reaching as high as the tip of his nose. She wasn't interested in Rhys or his picture. Not like she used to be. Selfishly, that hurt a little. It was stupid to think like that. Of course it was. But Rhys couldn't help it. This script wasn't playing out like it used to.

As though his dad telegraphed how Rhys felt, he set Eevie straight further down his lap, his face out of reach of her tiny fixated hands. Her body was turned towards Rhys. After losing interest in dad, she finally looked at Rhys with googly eyes, her jaw locked half open. She looked at him like she was wondering what the hell was going on.

This used to be the best bit.

Rhys looked at his mum. He wasn't sure why. Maybe for some encouragement. She looked comfortable sat upright in her checked armchair and gave him a sweet smile that egged him on.

Since what happened in the summer, everyone had adopted this child-like tone around Eevie. One that had grated on Rhys. He felt like it was patronising. Like she was a baby again. Like she wouldn't understand you unless you spoke in that tone. He wished everyone would treat her the way they used to. He couldn't — wouldn't — do that to her. And so as he carefully lowered himself onto his knees he spoke to her like her big brother. As he always had done. "Happy Birthday, Ee! Bet you can't guess what I've got for you."

Rhys turned the picture around slowly into full view of his dad and sister. The grand reveal. He rediscovered that same sense of pride he'd felt putting the finishing touches to it just a couple of hours earlier and, again, as he'd piled up the stairs to fetch it. Mum shifted awkwardly in her chair, hanging over the armrest to take a look herself.

This was more like it. How it had always been.

"Rhys," his mum said, hand coming to her mouth. "It's gorgeous."

Eevie reached out a hand and patted the centre of it — the colourful centre of the lotus, her fingers tickling around the foam of the waterfall. Encouraged, Rhys pushed the page in a little closer, inviting her to take it off him. He did so tentatively, just in case. Treating her like a cat that would scratch his hand rather than purr. She was that unpredictable.

"Isn't that amazing, Ee?" mum said, again in that infuriating child-like tone.

Rhys ignored it, looked over at his mum. He had every intention of mouthing thank you and giving her an honest smile. But something was wrong. Off. Her eyes had gone funny like they had been replaced by two black holes. The whites, her green eyes, consumed.

"M- mum?" His skin prickled. His chest tightened.

He turned sharply to his dad. He too had the very same leering endless black pits where his eyes should be. As did Eevie. All three of them stared right at him.

"What the f..."

Chills ran the length of Rhys' body. He stiffened. His fingers tightened around the edges of his drawing. He looked from his mum to Eevie and dad and back around again. His eyes darting, his mind...

"Rhys? Rhys? Honey, you ok?"

He heard the words. Muffled. Low. As though they were coming from a different room. His mum spoke through a mouth that didn't open.

Rhys felt a tug on his picture. His grip refused to relent. Another tug.

Rhys welded his eyes shut, wishing whatever was happening would end.

"Ee... Eevie... Rhys let go. Let go!"

And then he heard the rip.

His eyes opened. The first thing he noticed was that the black eyes he'd seen were gone. The second was the torn picture he held. A wild rip. The smaller piece Eevie had held was tossed in the air. His sister burst into a 'moment'. Her hands balled into fists. She welded her eyes shut and she began to bawl hysterically.

Dad brought her up his lap in an attempt to soothe her, but with her arms swinging in all directions, one of Eevie's fists whacked the side of his nose. Blood oozed down to his lips instantly.

And at that point, Rhys ran. His mum shouted after him but he climbed the stairs two at a time, the chaos unfolding downstairs ringing in his ears, chasing him.

He slammed his bedroom door behind him and slid down, his back to it, onto the floor, mind reeling.

What the hell just happened?

ELISA

I'm flustered as I arrive, the type that burns your cheeks.

It kicks in as I drive down the long stretch of empty road that is enveloped by a thick fog.

Then, in the distance, the dull red bricks of the hospital come into view. Shutter Island is one of my favourite movies and this building reminds me a lot of the outside of Ashecliffe Hospital — a home for the clinically insane.

But this building I'm pulling into isn't for the insane. It's exists to turn that moment you've been waiting your whole life for into a reality.

However, the only way I can experience such a moment myself is through this recurring dream.

I swing the car into a parking space. It's late in the day and there are plenty of spots to choose from.

Gregor, my husband, is already here, leaning near the entrance. Tall and relaxed. His eyes watch me as I pull into the car park and trot over in deep heels, which is bizarre because I hate heels. I rarely wear them at all.

There's a chill in the late afternoon air. The sky's always as red as blood. The people milling around the building — apart from Gregor's — are all faceless. A lump of pink skin, some smooth as silk, others smudged and pressed in like Play-Doh.

"I'm sorry I'm late," I said, ignoring the surrounding horrors. As though it was perfectly normal.

His lips curl at one end. He doesn't talk. He never does. But I can tell he's relaxed with his hands buried deep into the wide pockets of his favourite sand-coloured chinos.

I lead the way up the brick-paved path and push the door open.

The waiting area is tight.

Two receptionists — both female and, again, faceless — impossibly stare through me as I sign in. I fill out a questionnaire with pencil and paper, covering various related health questions. I fill it in on behalf of Gregor, too. He stands in the corner, nearby where I'm sitting. He doesn't like to sit. Never really did.

I finish up and pay for the scan I'm about to have on my credit card.

One receptionist then departs, leaving the three of us in silence.

The other receptionist sweeps a strand of ginger hair from where her eyebrows should curl and picks a book up she can't possibly read.

I know this place inside out now. Its labyrinth of walls, doors, and halls are identical to every other time I've been here. Yet I still find myself looking around this room, smiling as I take in the traditional blue and pink teddies decorating the shelves, cute clothes available to purchase, and little tokens to remember this moment by.

On the wall closest to me is a chart split into two tables — again, one-half blue, one-half pink. The results of every gender-reveal scan this Ashecliffe Hospital lookalike has completed this month, marking each one with a paper cutout of a baby's foot.

I picture a foot; it doesn't matter to me whether it is blue or pink, up there on that chart, representing my baby and try to imagine what it must feel like.

My leg jolts up and down as I wait patiently again. Like it's a puppet on strings. I lack patience, always have done. Another faceless couple walks in through the automatic door. I know which is the woman by the baby bump that I estimate is around the 20-week mark. Faceless or not, I imagine them smiling from ear to ear, rejoicing at the news they've just got.

The printer whirs behind the receptionist's desk and a photo of their scan is handed over to them.

I look on in envy.

The other receptionist returns and curls a finger towards me, beckoning me to follow.

Gregor lets me lead. From well-lit corridors, we're guided into a dark room. The sonographer is tapping away on his laptop as I drop my bags on the spare seat in the furthest corner that Gregor has no intention of using.

The sonographer doesn't say a peep. He's like the rest. A blank slate for a face. But he invites me with his hand to settle in on the chair. I do so with a polite smile.

Regardless of how many times I have been through this — and I truly have lost count — the magnitude of what's about to happen hits me like a wave crashing ashore.

I look at Gregor. He returns my gaze, carrying my hopes and dreams, but his face tells me nothing.

The sonographer is waiting on me, as though he knows that I'm aware of what comes next. I unclip my trousers and shuffle them down, just slightly. Just enough. I pull my top up and rest it underneath my breasts. The sonographer hands me a blue paper towel that I trap under my trousers. My hands come together as a gloop of cool ultrasound gel tickles my tummy.

I inhale the same deep breath

My eyes lock on the screen on the far wall as the transducer massages the gel into my skin. There's another deep breath as the screen begins to adjust and glide with every touch.

This is the moment that I should see the little pea that will grow and become my child.

But there's nothing. The screen only shows a black abyss, a bright light shining into nothing.

Like an endless deep sea dive.

It is at that point I wake, consumed by the same pain and loss of something that wasn't real.

I head downstairs and pull out the unfinished bottle of Sauvignon from the fridge. I empty it into a mug and I take my place on the sofa.

My laptop sits nestled in the corner spot and I pull it to my knee. After tapping in my password, I head straight to Instagram, tap the letter E into the search bar and click through to *her* profile.

I do the same thing I do most nights and doom-scroll through her life.

She hasn't posted for a while. Not for a few months now. It doesn't stop me looking, though. For a while, I looked at her Facebook as well, but she posts less frequently there.

Everything that has happened in my life comes right back to her.

I believe in Karma, believe that all our actions have a consequence. Like a debt that has to be repaid.

I've had to be patient while I wait for Karma to catch up to my sister.

Her time is coming, though.

I can feel it in my bones.

THURSDAY

7TH NOVEMBER 2019

JONNY

How had it got to this?

How had it reached the point that Jonny felt he had to take the largest kitchen knife to bed with him? Held in a vice grip, hidden under his pillow. Just to feel a degree of safety, but not enough to prevent him from relaxing and closing his eyes.

Because he knew full well those black figures stalked on the other side of the bedroom door.

How had it reached the point where they had branded him as depressed and were advising him to seek professional help? He was a big lad who worked in construction, for Christ's sake. The concept of therapy was foreign and unnecessary.

But worst of all, how had he become the husband whose wife was having to plead with him to spend time with her? How had he descended into a state where he felt he couldn't — shouldn't — be in the company of those he loved most?

Jonny, if he were honest with himself, feared their judgement more than the horrors he believed haunted him.

Those questions played out silently as he hid away in the shed at the bottom of the garden that morning, waiting for Liz to get the kids out the door for the school run, just as he had done every weekday for the last month or so.

The shed, a simple 12 by 12 kitted-out space, was supposed to have been the man cave Jonny had dreamed of having whenever he'd got a place of his own. It'd be a home for his inner child, his old consoles and games and posters and art. After the McIntyres were handed the keys to their new build on Sandon Mount, it had been Jonny's first passion project.

Yet it had become something more than just a place of solitude. It had become the only place he felt safe. Behind its door, Jonny discovered a fragile semblance of normalcy he felt nowhere else. A feeling he needed as much as a drowning man gasping for air.

That need to disappear into his own space — alone — hadn't been an issue initially, after what had happened, happened. In fact, Liz had probably appreciated that she, too, had her own space to read or do whatever she did when Eevie went to bed. But with each passing day, Jonny's need for isolation deepened as the illness — that's what the doctor called it — took a firmer hold of his life.

But that need had become a source of friction, a wedge between him and Liz.

So as Jonny had tried to slope out the backdoor last night after Eevie had finally settled and her weary eyes had closed, Liz had asked — well, insisted — that Jonny stayed with her for a change, that they should spend some time together, stick something on Netflix, curl up on the sofa.

Like they used to.

Before.

It hadn't been as bad as he'd anticipated.

After caving in to Liz's demand, Jonny managed to wrestle the situation to his advantage. He'd offered his lap for her to rest her head on and gave her a hair rub. Liz's let out a sigh of satisfaction as she snuggled down. He couldn't remember the last time they'd done this.

He dipped in and out of watching *Orange Is the New Black*. In the TV's reflection, he was sure he'd seen them, those hazy black eyes, overwhelming his wife's perfect olive colour, piercing his own. So he turned away, blocked them out. Squeezed his own eyes tightly shut and didn't take the risk.

"Everything ok?" Liz had asked at one point, as Jonny struggled to calm his breathing.

"Aye, just a bit of indigestion." If only that was it.

Just before 9, Liz said she was tired and ready for an early night. Jonny had said he'd follow her up a little later. She'd kissed him on the cheek and took the stairs quietly, avoiding the spots that creaked loud enough to stir Eevie. Jonny, indeed, followed a couple of hours later. He tried, he really did, to retain that normal routine, one as simple as going to bed with his wife, turning out the lights, giving her three quick pecks on the lips and telling her he loved her. But he would inevitably return downstairs in the early hours of the morning for two reasons: to escape his anxieties and not burden Liz with them, either.

She dealt with enough.

Jonny stood by the shed window, his hand involuntarily poking and prodding at his nose, which was still sore from the whack he'd taken from Eevie.

He waited for the house to clear.

Observing from a distance as the rest of the family went about their morning routine was a weird experience for Jonny. Just a few short months ago, he was the early riser, up and at 'em before the sun had even had a chance to rub the sleep out of its eyes.

Only a month back, he'd led a team at GW Construct, working jobs across the county, spending long hours on the yard and the road with the boys.

That was until a fuck up with some scaffolding — and a pretty big fuck up at that — had left Booner with a broken arm. The big boss, Georgey Whitedale, had no choice but to force Jonny to go off on the sick. For a man not accustomed to taking a break, this hit Jonny hard. He wasn't the type of guy that went off sick.

But that scaffolding had been the straw that broke the camel's back for Georgey, more commonly regarded around the local boozers as Gindale. To Jonny, he was more than a boss. Ol' Gindale had been a pal of Jonny's for years, right back to when they lived on the same rough estate together where everyone was just one wrong word away from a fistfight.

Even when Jonny was a prat, he was always cut some slack around the neighbourhood after his mum had packed her bags and left, leaving Jonny with a deadbeat alcoholic father and no one looking out for him. By 11 years old, he was bunking school, was on first-name terms with the cops, and was constantly reminded about his wasted potential.

The initial sympathy for his situation had waned with most on the estate. But not Gindale, who was several years older than

Jonny and had always looked out for him like an older brother would.

And when Gindale had set up his own renovations and extensions business, he gave Jonny a chance when no one else would.

Gindale got him the training he needed, took him out on the road, and showed him the ropes. Jonny had loved it. Fast forward 15 years and Jonny was still there now, practically part of the furniture and even talking about owning a piece of the company pie one day. Things had been rosy.

Until the summer.

However, his string of mistakes had ol' Gindale at a boiling point. It was bad enough that Jonny was costing him pounds and pence, but now he was costing him his workers, too. And Booner was a bloody good worker.

So things came to a head a month ago, when Gindale, abundantly conflicted by what he felt he had to, urged Jonny to take some time to get his head straight.

What did Jonny do? He'd told Gindale to fuck himself and slammed the door behind him before grabbing a bottle of something strong and drinking himself into oblivion in his shed.

But Jonny couldn't blame Gindale. Once the red haze — and hangover — had subsided, Jonny knew he'd left his oldest pal with no choice.

That was water under the bridge now. Gindale had since checked in once or twice a week to see how Jonny was getting on. He made offers to meet up for a coffee or to grab some lunch but Jonny wouldn't. Or rather couldn't.

So, Jonny was no longer the bread earner. Thankfully, money wasn't an issue. Jonny still had a packet of his dad's inheritance left over after his old man had died before Christmas last year. It was the only good thing his old man had ever done for him.

All that dosh came to Jonny and he immediately put a big chunk of it down for the deposit on a new build on Sandon Mount. Finally, he could get his family out of the tight shit tip on Wayborough Falls and into a shiny house that Liz had spent endless nights obsessing over and chewing his ear off about.

The remainder of that nest egg was still more than large enough to make sure Liz and the kids would be fine for the foreseeable. More than enough time for him to get this — whatever the fuck this was that he was going through — sorted and under control.

More than enough time, to get his head straight, as ol' Gindale had said.

With the coast clear, Jonny made his way back up to the house.

First things first, he needed pain relief. The usual dull morning headache was settling in and the corner of his eyes throbbed with it. The pain had a pulse of its own. He hurriedly filled a glass from the tap and downed it so fast some escaped down his chin. Immediately, he filled it again. He retrieved a packet of paracetamol from the medicine drawer and popped two capsules. The rest he stuffed into his pocket, reserved for when he'd undoubtedly need to fetch them out later.

As he finished the rest of his second glass, he gazed out into the garden. The sky, shrouded in grey, bore a light fog, and the rain had momentarily ceased.

On the dining table, Jonny noticed a couple of post-it notes, their edges curling upwards, beckoning for his attention.

> Taken Rhy to school, seeing Ma and
> Esme with E. Back about 4:30.
> See you later. Love ya xxx

The second was one of Liz's daily mini tick lists, the tiny sheet that brought order to the chaos.

> ~~Eevie's cares~~ (Liz)
> ~~Pack Rhys' lunch (Liz)~~
> ~~Put washing on~~ (Liz)
> Hang washing on airers (Jon)
> Slow cook beef – 10am (Jon) –
> bottom shelf of fridge
> Pick up a pack of bottled water – 12pk- (Liz)
> Eevie's meds – 5pm (Liz)
> Chill out!!! (Liz + Jon)

Liz loved a list. Even to cover the smallest of tasks. Jonny shook his head and smiled fleetingly.

He glanced over at the washing machine. It was still whirring away and would be for another 35 minutes.

He had enough time to squeeze a shower in.

The water cascaded over him, a cleansing torrent that Jonny wished would wash away more than just the grime of the past day.

Nestling his head comfortably into the crook of his forearm, that propped him up against the bathroom's white, veiny, marble tiles, he wished for the water to pull every thought, feeling, and fear he had right now down the plughole with the water, never to be seen again.

For the last ten minutes, Jonny had stood like a statue. Letting the hot water relentlessly pound the nape of his neck and shoulders, licking the tribal tattoos adorning both his arms and racing down his spine.

Time to move it, Jon.

With one last blast to his face, he pushed the excess water through his auburn hair that was overdue a cut before reluctantly shutting off the supply. Enveloped in a cloud of steam, he grabbed the towel resting atop the glass screen and wrapped it around his waist before stepping out into the cold. Immediately, he stopped dead in his tracks.

What faced him on the other side of the bathroom was a smiley face etched into the fog of condensation that claimed the feature mirror. Lines of water dribbled down from the corner, distorting the image that, initially, took him back to his days as a young boy when his mum used to leave similar drawings on the mirror during bath time.

And here they now were. Almost impossibly identical. Over two decades later.

That thought had made Jonny consider whether this was simply his mind playing tricks on him, a hallucination drawing on stored memories, capitalising on his lack of sleep to invade his reality.

He swiped it away, leaving a reflection of the broken man he'd become.

But there was no time to dwell on that observation.

His ears pricked up.

Amidst his heavy breathing, the final droplets of water from the shower head, the chirps slipping through the cranked-open bathroom window, and the distant hum of cars leaving the estate, he was certain he heard the creak of a floorboard.

Jonny stood in tense silence, his senses heightened as slow and deliberate steps approached the bathroom door.

Whoever — or whatever — was in his house stopped just outside. Jonny didn't move an inch. His eyes fixed firmly on the foot of the door, bracing for whatever might unfold.

After a while, the steps gradually resumed, meandering down the landing towards the bedrooms.

The sounds faded and then ceased entirely, leaving Jonny in a momentary stillness he knew he couldn't linger in.

He cracked the door open and cautiously scanned the landing. Nothing stirred. Nothing popped out to surprise him or say boo. Yet that daunting anticipation never left his side.

Taking measured and quiet steps, he searched each room anxiously, one arm wrapped around the towel, the other gripping the knife that went wherever he did.

But no one — nothing — was there.

Jonny was all alone.

RHYS

After convincing himself he'd ruined his sister's birthday, Rhys had been sure he was going to be facing the music the next morning.

He'd delayed the certain reprimand he'd expected by pretending to be asleep when his mum came to his room last night. He'd buried himself under the covers, like a kid hiding from the boogeyman. Unlike any monster, though, his mum had left him be and slipped back the way she came, pulling the door quietly closed behind her before her soft steps receded further down the landing towards her and dad's room.

But there'd be no avoiding her on the school run. Rhys had got tummy cramps just thinking about it, imagining all the horrible ways it could play out. Fake conversations turned in his mind like a washing machine. By the time he climbed into the back of the car, Rhys was fairly sure his breakfast was going to be sitting next to him in a puddle of gross bile.

He braced himself. *Any minute now.*

But it never came. And neither did the bile. Instead, once they were off the estate, his mum asked if *he* was ok. She looked at him with sad eyes through the rearview mirror. The way his dad had when... *No, no, no.*

"You want to talk about it?" she asked.

He did not.

And to Rhys' total surprise, that was the end of it. There were none of the usual questions about school. None of the usual enthusiasm. The mood in the car felt different. Heavier. Rhys watched his mum nibble away at her already short nails as they drove the normal route through town before looping back up the Balercrescent Lane hill towards the academy.

It was only when they pulled up outside the St Andrews gates his mum spoke again.

"You promise me everything's ok, don't you? There's nothing you need to tell me?"

Rhys hated lying to his mum. It wasn't just that he'd been taught the importance of not lying. Ever since he can remember, even the smallest of white lies had ignited a festering guilt that would pester him for days.

"You know you can talk to me about anything, don't you, sweetie?" Her hand rested on his, urged him to open up. Her face was so clearly riddled with worry.

If only it was that simple. There was no way Rhys could add anything else to her plate. He nodded, adding a smile, hoping it would be enough to appease her.

Before jumping out, Rhys reminded her he needed lunch money. There'd been no time for mum to make his usual pack-up lunch. Eevie having a 'moment' and chucking up her morning milk had seen to that. Dad was down in the shed, keeping his distance as normal. Nowhere to be seen. Leaving mum to deal with the morning chaos solo.

She dug around in her purse and stuck a wrinkled fiver in his hand.

"Don't go buying rubbish with it," she demanded as the tension wilted between them. "I know what you're like."

This was how a typical Thursday morning ran.

Registration would lead to Maths. Maths to History. History on to German.

German was a funny one. Rhys wasn't interested in learning a new language and given that he'd been learning it for three months now, it was pretty damning that the only two words that had stuck with him were Scheisse and Großvater. The latter was obviously popular because it sounded like '*gross farter*'. For the first few weeks of term, everyone was going around calling each other a gross farter, finding it hilarious.

Anyway, German was the last lesson before lunch. And while nothing topped the end of the school day, the bell for lunch was a comfortable second best. Admittedly, that's a low bar to meet. Rhys thought of lunch break as the same as when prisoners get their 30-minute break outside. Given a small rope of freedom that would end up yanking them back like a tethered spaceman right back to where they came from as soon as the bell clanged.

Unlike prisoners, though, at least Rhys went home at the end of each day.

During lunch hour, the kids dispersed to the familiar spots, sticking to the territory they had claimed for their own since the beginning of term. There was the lunch hall, tennis courts, the astroturf, the garden, B block (where you'd find the older kids), the athletics field (when it was open for the summer), and the library.

Rhys *always* headed straight to the latter. He enjoyed the quiet and the limited amount of people that milled around. There'd also be no sign of Conor and his band of idiots, who'd head straight for the astroturf or tennis courts. For one hour at least, Conor was someone else's problem, as bad as that sounded. For one hour at least, Rhys got a break from having to listen to being called a dick, or a retard, or a fuckwit, or a scrote, or a mute, or a short-arse, or a square. Or anything in between.

Today, there'd be a pit stop before heading to the library. Rhys made his way to the lunch hall, which was less than 100 metres away from where he was in the Foreign Languages block. He grabbed himself a Rollover hotdog and a fizzy fruit twist — a neat upgrade to the usual cheese and pickle sandwiches, salt and vinegar crisps, and bottled juice.

The only downside was that there wasn't a lot of change from the fiver to be pocketed for another day.

Scheisse.

It didn't feel like swearing when you said it in another language.

The school library was the size of two classrooms smashed together and had three-tiered wooden bookshelves sectioning off various subjects.

Among the book nooks, three iMacs idled, unused in one corner.

The usual faces dotted around. There was a small group of guys huddled around a table playing D&D, two older kids sat together with their heads in a doorstopper book while taking notes, obviously preparing for mocks or just revising. Ralph Steadman (who Rhys only knew as a kid in the same year) sat as normal with his head buried under his hood, a tinge of his green quiff sticking out, playing on his Nintendo Switch. Ralph looked up as Rhys stood at the mouth of the door, a mere glance before returning to whatever it was he was playing.

Poor kid got the crap teased out of him more than Rhys did.

To his left, Ms Ling manned the desk. She always looked the same. Dark hair cropped at her shoulders, cardigan over a blouse tucked into black trousers. She scooped up books and split them into two different carts, readying to take them back to their rightful home. She gave a faint smile to Rhys and brought a single finger to her lips. An unspoken understanding that he was welcome to eat there as long as his food didn't leave stains on the books or mess on the tables.

Rhys and Ms Ling hadn't spoken all that much since he'd started at the academy a few months back, but for whatever reason, Rhys thought Ms Ling had just got it. She knew and understood why he hung out here. There were no questions, and she didn't pry. She left him to his own devices and gave him a place to feel safe for 50 minutes each day.

Choosing a secluded table in a corner, away from the science books, Rhys laid his dinner out on the round table. The Rollover hotdog had gone lukewarm in the time it had taken to get from the lunch hall. Not that it bothered Rhys. He'd take it over soggy sandwiches any day.

With his mouth on autopilot, chewing away, Rhys' thoughts drifted, plagued by the weird events from the previous night. Of visions of those eyes, blacker than a moonless and starless night sky, claiming his mum, dad, and sister's faces. Shimmering and hazy.

Last night, as he'd struggled to sleep, he'd opened the laptop and scoured Google, attempting to find explanations. Frustration brewed as vague searches led him astray — Black Eyed Peas and remedies for actual black eyes weren't even close to what he was after. Even searches like 'Seeing black eyes' or 'Seeing black eyes in a person' yielded little. The closest he got was with a Quora thread that had hinted at a pessimistic life view and introversion, but it offered no concrete answers.

The only other commonality he'd found while exploring was their connection to dreams.

But what Rhys had experienced was no dream.

He was adamant. Absolutely no way.

Surely...

His focus was ripped back to the present by a girl's voice and a familiar face with tightly tied mousy brown hair, freckles decorating her slim face. She stood by the chair opposite Rhys, meeting his gaze with a request.

"Can I sit here?"

It turned out her name was Annie.

And Rhys had made his mind up that she was an odd bod.

Annie liked to stare and didn't bother concealing it. Direct, unflinching, most people would glance away once caught, but not Annie. She kept it up, observing him with those oversized eyes, leaving Rhys unnerved and feeling caught in a standoff he hadn't asked for.

Silence sat alongside them. Rhys continued to chow down the last of his Rollover. Annie's gaze unwavered.

She was all perfect posture, too. Not a slouch in her. Her hands hid under the table.

And while she was unmoved, Rhys wrestled with discomfort, weirded out by whatever was happening. He felt the need to do something, anything, to diffuse the awkwardness that had infiltrated his moment of peace.

Thank Apple for the iPod.

He thumbed through it, purposely taking his time to flick through his endless playlists to wedge open the tension that sat between him and this strange girl. Finally, he hit play on *It's My Life* by Bon Jovi.

The beat had hardly kicked in when Annie finally spoke.

"Are you always this odd?" she said ironically, leaning forward, elbows settled on the table like Alan Sugar preparing to shout 'you're fired'.

"Sorry?" Rhys said, hitting pause on the iPod.

"Are you always..."

"No, I heard you. Just... you've been staring at me since you sat down."

"Do I make you uncomfortable?"

"Kinda."

"Ok."

The silence fell back in. So did the staring. Rhys took a swig of the fizzy fruit twist, the cool bubbles tickling as they slid down his throat.

"Lean over here."

Rhys covered his mouth, stifling a burp.

"Lean... over... here."

At first, Rhys fumbled around with his words, trying to catch a response that wasn't forthcoming. Eventually, he caved in.

Annie leaned in, her pinched face just inches from his. After a second or two, she relaxed back in her seat. Her ruler-straight lips gave nothing away.

"Looks nasty. Why'd you let Conor get away with what he does?"

Rhys hadn't wanted to answer that. He wasn't sure why Conor had singled him out or what had set everything in motion. But part of him felt he deserved it. In a way, he believed Conor was his punishment for what had happened during the summer holidays.

"I don't know," he replied weakly, skirting around the question and shrugging his shoulder. "I guess I... No. No, I don't know."

"He's a piece of Scheisse, isn't he?"

Rhys couldn't help but grin.

Annie continued. "Want to know something?"

"What?"

"If Conor keeps on the way he is, his time will come."

"Whatcha mean?"

Annie smiled, a smug *I'm so glad you asked* kinda smile.

"I mean, every action and decision we make has a consequence that always comes back to us — good and bad," she said.

"You mean like Karma?"

"Exactly like Karma."

There was no doubt Annie was odd. Maybe she was one of those types who obsessed over star signs and tarot cards, faith, healers, and destiny. Thinks everything happens for a reason type.

Not that Rhys had anything against any of that. Each to their own and all.

He opted for a safe response. His dad had always told him never to poo-poo on other people's ideas and beliefs. "You believe in that?"

"You don't believe me now, Rhys McIntyre. But you will," she said. "You'll see."

At that moment, the bell clanged.

Annie casually got to her feet. Satisfaction painted her face. "See you around, Rhy-Rhy."

Rhy-Rhy.

There was only one person that called him that and hearing that name tumble out of Annie's mouth left Rhys frozen. His tongue tied up in a heavy knot and he felt goose skin crawl up his arms.

And off she went, gliding past the D&D gang who were packing up for another day and around Ms Ling who pushed a cart stacked full of tattered paperbacks along. After Ms Ling cut across her. Annie was nowhere to be seen.

Rhys scrambled to his feet and snatched up his bag. Made a beeline for the double doors Annie had headed towards.

He burst out into the B-Block courtyard and scanned frantically, but Annie was nowhere to be seen, lost in a mist of bustling kids and teachers making their way to the next round of classes.

Scheisse!

As much as he wanted to look for her, it'd have to wait until later. PE was calling.

Mr Stevens.

The only thing to know about him is that he's a bit of a dick. Scratch that. Rhys thought he was a royal asshole.

Mr Stevens was the type of teacher who got off making things difficult for everyone. Where most teachers were content with a figurative slap on the wrist or a scolding when students stepped out of line, Mr Stevens, the academy's Head of PE, fed off on taking his punishments to the next level.

His slaps on the wrist were endless laps of the gym or astroturf pitches. His scoldings ended with you doing push-ups. And if you *really* boiled his piss, you likely ended up doing both.

Didn't do it properly? Well, you'd just do it again.

Rhys had never been on the end of these punishments so far, and he had no intention of changing that anytime soon. That meant not being even a fraction of a second late for class.

The military single file line stretched out from the foot of the imposing double industrialised doors and snaked down by the side of the gym. Rhys arrived precisely on time, amid a sea of bundled-up students shivering in the chilly November air. Mr Stevens, all bulging biceps and calves in his standard navy t-shirt and shorts, stood out amidst the huddled masses, putting their big coats and thick hats to shame.

"McIntyre," he hollered, his voice thick and Brummie, juggling a basketball from one hand to the other up at the front.

"Sir," Rhys responded, catching the familiar sneer from Conor and his posse, as he trudged to the back of the line.

The routine unfolded predictably: get changed in cramped and sweaty changing rooms, work through half-hearted warm-ups and drills, and finish with a mini-tournament.

Captains got selected and teams got picked. What that meant for kids like Rhys was that they were the last to be hooked. He was never the last, though. That was often poor Evan Greaves, a little dumpy kid wearing a kit a tad too small and who spent PE constantly readjusting big square glasses around his downcast eyes.

Tossed a red bib that hummed with ageing sweat, Rhys lined up with Liam, Alfie (both starters on the school football team), Woodsy (a pal of the other two), and Simmo (fairly well-liked but whose bulging belly said sport wasn't his thing).

The rules were simple: first to shoot three hoops won and stayed on.

"Roight, quiet you lot!" Mr Stevens howled after a sharp toot on his whistle. "Let's have blues against yellows to start. Greens an' reds, on the bench."

Rhys followed his team to the benches that were so hard they sent his ass numb. The other four in the red squad chatted among themselves. Rhys perched on the end, a literal outsider, stuck on the team to fill a quota. Not that Rhys minded. Sport was hardly Rhys' thing either. He didn't mind football and understood it to a certain extent from watching a game or two with his dad. But basketball was alien to him.

Rhys doesn't get time to even try and settle in before the Reds are called to their feet. Blues won their game without breaking a sweat, shooting three hoops to nothing in what felt like a blink of an eye, even with Evan Greaves on their team.

Rhys wandered awkwardly and aimlessly onto the court. He looked from Liam to Alfie to Woodsy, waiting for some guidance or even a little clue — as to where they wanted him positioned. None was forthcoming.

Conor stood opposite, focused and ready, his tight blue bib hugging his chest. Rhys scooted over to the edge of the court to put as much distance between them as possible, trying to look busy.

The ball got tossed in the air and began to zip around left to right, back to front. The wooden gym floor screeched harshly under the tatty gym trainers.

The Blues got the first hoop. *What a shame.*

Liam took it badly, tossing his arms in the air, gesticulating, pointing fingers. One of them gets jabbed in Rhys' direction. "Maccie, come on here and fill this fuckin' space, will ya!"

"Any more of that and you're done, Liam," Mr Stevens says after another blast of the whistle. He didn't need to say anything else. Liam buttoned it.

The ball was tossed to Rhys from the restart. Like a dope, Rhys fumbled it, catching it on the second attempt. A blue bib rushed him, filling him with a panic that Rhys rid himself of by launching the ball as far as he could in the hope it found a fellow red bib.

It didn't. Not even close.

For his trouble, Rhys was shoved to the grotty floor by the blue bib who didn't hit the brakes.

"Up on your feet, Maccie!" Kyle snarled as he towered over him.

By the time Rhys was off the grubby floor, it was two to nothing. Liam was foaming, spitting as he vented sour frustration, shaking his head, face flushed. One more hoop and the reds would be sent packing back to the benches.

The ball whirled around again. Liam, Alfie, and Woodsy pop it between themselves, working their way forward. But they eventually lost it and rushed back to regroup.

"Rhys!" The shout came from Alfie this time. "Cover the space behind me."

He didn't get a chance to do as was told.

Rhys knew Liam was behind him. He felt a hand push sharply into his back.

Whether it was intentional or not, the shove sent Rhys stumbling straight into the path of the guy with the ball. They collided together and ended up in a heap on the floor.

The guy he fell into was Conor.

The moments after became a complete blur. Rhys instinctively curled into a protective ball, clamping his eyes shut and securing his hands around the back of his head as Conor lurched on top of him. The punches began to rain and there was nothing Mr Stevens' whistle could do to stop them.

ELIZABETH

Mother's guilt was simmering beneath the surface.

It always did whenever Elizabeth left Eevie in anyone else's care. Even if those hands were Ma and Pa's. She felt that unease now, bubbling like a kettle ready to hit peak temperature, as she rolled to a stop outside their house.

Elizabeth had only recently grown accustomed to entrusting her daughter for a few hours each week to her parents. She'd done so with great reluctance a month ago when they'd insisted they took her one day a week.

"You can't keep going as you are," Ma had told her on one of those afternoons when it had felt like anything that could go wrong had. "It doesn't have to be us pair, but you need to let someone help."

Their rationale was fair. Even if it was just a few hours, it would give Elizabeth a bit of R&R and a release from the 24/7 pressure.

"Get your head in a book. Go and meet a friend for a coffee. Go out with Jonny for a late breakfast. Just have some you time. You don't just get to be Elizabeth anymore," Ma had said.

But what good was 'you' time when it got consumed by worry?

Babysitting Eevie wasn't like caring for any other toddler. Not anymore. She came with a long list of instructions, a bag full of essentials and just-in-cases. She was demanding and unpredictable. It only took a moment for everything to spiral out of control — just as it had that one afternoon that set the arrangement in motion.

And because of that, Elizabeth spent most of her 'R&R' time clock-watching — even though the past month had passed without incident. She was still on edge, tethered to her phone, just waiting for the call to say something had gone wrong.

Elizabeth might have taken their advice and accepted their help, but she did so with a silent reluctance.

But today was different.

Because today, Elizabeth had an appointment she simply couldn't miss.

She held on to the handbrake after pulling into a tight space in the car park.

The time on the dashboard showed she was early. Elizabeth had always made a point of *never* being late.

She had told Ma that she was catching up with a friend she used to work with at the local Waterstones. Torey Willard. Ma would remember her and how close they were a few years back, back before Torey had left and started store-hopping across the region in her new role as a manager.

There was no meeting with Torey, though. Perhaps Elizabeth had subconsciously thought about Torey because there was a part of her that wanted to reach out and reconnect. That would need to wait, though.

Who she was making time to meet was more important.

As Elizabeth had arrived outside the Halton Haig Library, she wasn't sure she was entirely ready for what was to come. She'd chosen this location for a couple of reasons. It wasn't just because it would be quiet and there'd be no interruptions, but it was also far enough outside of town that she was unlikely to bump into anyone she knew.

Thinking about it in these terms, the secrecy shrouding it, made it sound like something out of a David Baldacci or Lee Child novel. Truth was she just wanted a bit of privacy.

Halton Haig Library was much like other libraries Elizabeth had visited — battered and worn down by years of neglect and insufficient funding. The chipped bookshelves were barely holding together, while the shabby carpet looked as if it hadn't been replaced since the day the library first opened. The place was on life support, kept alive by the older locals who'd been coming for years and the occasional group of kids from one of the nearby schools.

Once the former was gone, undoubtedly it would be time to pull the plug. The thought upset Elizabeth as she made her way across to a private space out of the way and took in the neglect that surrounded her.

She occupied a small table decorated with magazines that dated back to the beginning of the year, distinguished by creases and old coffee stains left by people who had sat in this very spot before her. No doubt they would have been here catching up with friends, losing themselves in a novel they hadn't read, or even just taking a moment for themselves.

Elizabeth ordered a large latte — her third of the morning already — and sat waiting, nervous, sucking at her top lip, trying to psyche herself up.

She checked the time on her phone, which she'd switched from vibrate to ring. Again, just in case there happened to be any issues with Eevie. She kept an eye on the entrance door, waiting in anticipation for it to open.

The butterflies kicked around. Her cheeks had undoubtedly already transformed from pink into their usual blotchy red.

The door opened and in walked the man she had been waiting for.

Walter Demick dressed like a man who was ready for the impending winter months.

Thick coat over a snug jumper. A big, dense scarf that clung to his neck. An oversized beanie hat that covered his ears.

Elizabeth recognised Walter from his old newspaper mugshot.

He'd been the guy who spent his life chasing the story, hooked on the adrenaline that came with running investigations into corruption and frauds and gang behaviour, working mostly as a freelancer for the nationals before spending five years working at Bellingcat, a website dedicated to international open source intelligence and fact-checking. He embodied a character straight out of Stieg Larsson's The Millennium trilogy novels that Elizabeth adored.

Walter was semi-retired now. He'd packed in the journalism beat a couple of years back and topped his pension up as a renowned private eye.

Elizabeth recalled watching him give an interview on the BBC, discussing the career transition. He'd emphasised a desire to help rather than expose. It wasn't surprising that someone of his stature had a month-long waiting list just for consultations.

Elizabeth had a lot going on in her life. The timing couldn't be worse for this meeting. But she had to make this meeting. She didn't know if she'd get another opportunity like this.

And here he was. At Halton Haig Library in the flesh.

Walter, a black man who was well into his 50s, was taller than she expected. His face didn't deny his age. He wore wide glasses that did a poor job of hiding tired eyes and the layers of bags underneath them that drooped like candle wax. Wrinkles held hands at the bridge of his nose. His stubbly beard was grey verging on white.

But Walter was a smiler. He had the look of a pleasant man as he surveyed the equally tired library looking for his latest client.

Elizabeth stood from her spot, pushing herself up with her hands tightly clasped around her knees as though she were preparing for a rollercoaster ride.

In some ways, she was.

Over he came. Walter shook her hand delicately and rooted himself in the seat directly opposite her, settling in and abundantly far more relaxed than Elizabeth was.

They made small talk while he shed his winter gear and ordered himself a flat white.

The chat was nice. Elizabeth felt at ease in Walter's presence. The raging butterflies inside her chest had calmed down, but hadn't entirely disappeared. There was still much to discuss, much of it not small talk.

Walter pulled out a weathered notebook from a beaten satchel and opened it on his lap, signalling the shift towards why they were really here in this worn and tired library.

"So, shall we get into it?"

A lot got covered over the proceeding two hours, ground that hadn't been uncovered for many years.

Elizabeth had needed breaks here and there. Reviving ingrained emotions and feelings that had been sleeping in a deep coma for years was harder than she thought it'd be.

She started at the very beginning, as far back as she could remember after her mother died of an aneurysm. They were on the sofa: Elizabeth, her mother, and her two sisters, Elisa and Esme. They were watching a film (she doesn't remember which one, it could well have been a TV show), picking at popcorn, cuddled up under a duvet, fire roaring across from them.

By the time the film was done, her mum was dead after collapsing at the bottom of the stairs while heading to the loo.

Elizabeth was only four years old. Little Esme was barely one and strapped in pull-up nappies. Thankfully, too young to remember.

There was no one else — no dad in the picture, no known grandparents, and no aunts or uncles willing to step in and raise the three sisters.

And so, inevitably, they ended up falling into the care system.

Childhood had been rough. The three of them spent a lot of it tossed around different orphanages. They were as inseparable as you'd expect three sisters to be in that situation. They counted their blessings because some poor kids were alone, isolated, and had no one in their corner when they needed them.

But things had happened, things that had led Elizabeth to this worn-down library to talk to a private eye.

She wanted to find her missing sister.

Elisa was the eldest. Esme was the baby of the trio. Three years separated each of them. As the eldest, Elisa adopted the adult figure after their mum was gone. She was the one who told Elizabeth and Esme that, no matter what, everything would be ok.

That the three of them would get out of the system and live a god damned normal life.

It didn't transpire that way.

Not for one of them, anyway.

Elizabeth held a tangled web of memories surrounding her and Esme's departure from the Aston Orphanage, an event that felt more like a rescue to her.

It was a passage of time that sparked both hope and regret.

The day they left was the last time Elizabeth saw Elisa — more than 20 years ago. Her last memory of her older sister was of her banging on the upstairs windows, silently screaming and struggling against two social workers as her two younger siblings got whisked away to start a new, shiny, and god-damned normal life.

That memory was a nasty rash that no amount of soothing could rid her of. Forgetting about it and hoping it would go away on its own accord over time didn't work, either.

The problems started when the three sisters first met Nellie and Ron Woodley — Elizabeth and Esme's saviours, the parents they'd been without for so long. Ma and Pa.

That was back in July 1996. Elizabeth remembered it all so vividly. Her eyes held back a dam that was ready to burst.

"Take your time," Walter said.

"Thank you. Honestly, you don't want to see me when this mascara runs."

While the words were intended as a joke, they also undoubtedly carried a serious undercurrent.

Elizabeth had liked Nellie and Ron from that first meeting. They were warm and kind and all smiles. They brought a couple of teddies with them to their first meeting. Elizabeth's had passed hers down to Eevie. She'd never been able to part with it, always associating that teddy back to when her fortunes changed.

Elisa was a different kettle of fish, though. She'd held reservations about the Woodleys that no one else could see.

"We can't trust them," Elisa had said.

Elizabeth remembered that moment being the first time she ever doubted her big sister. There had been a few meetings with Nellie and Ron over the forthcoming weeks — get-to-know sessions, things like that. That led to Nellie and Ron taking them out for the first time. They'd gone on a road trip to a local park. It was a glorious day, not a single cloud in the sky, a slight breeze hanging in the air, the grass green and full of life, the play area jam-packed full of kids. For the first time in a long time, the sisters were just like every other kid.

Nellie had packed a picnic, an enormous wicker basket full of savouries and sweets that sat on top of a couple of tartan blankets. The four of them ate, laughed, played games, and grazed under the sun's unrelenting rays.

"The four of you?" Walter asked.

"Elisa refused to come with us."

"You didn't try to... persuade her? Get her to see sense?"

"Of course I did. She didn't want to know."

"That must've caused more issues?"

"Like you wouldn't believe."

The lies and accusations began. All baseless. All skewered. All fabricated. All concocted by Elisa's imagination to achieve one outcome, Elizabeth thinks: to get the orphanage to block Nellie and Ron from trying to adopt them.

The worst, the most heinous and foul, of those lies was when Elisa accused Ron of grabbing and hurting her.

"It wasn't true at all and I told Ms Dickson that," Elizabeth said. "She was running the place at the time. I was in tears when they launched an investigation and called the police."

Fractures started to form between Elisa and Elizabeth. Esme was a pawn in their constant bickering, being manipulated by both of them. Elizabeth admitted how tough it must have been for her, having to choose between her two sisters who fed her polarising stories.

Those fractures turned into cracks, deepening and getting bigger, and just like an ice sheet, they began to split and drift apart.

Elizabeth remembered the night vividly. The one that finished them.

Split them.

"She was so mad I'd gone against her and told the police she was lying," Elizabeth told Walter.

She rolled down her sleeve to reveal a tiny scar left from that night. When her sister attacked her.

"I can't remember who it was at the time but the on-duty social worker had to drag her off me. I had blood pouring from my arm. Esme was curled up in the corner, crying. She was in hysterics. We were moved to a different room that night. It was the first time we were apart."

She continued. "For the first time in my life she... she scared me."

There's an unwritten rule that you don't split siblings up in the care system. You try and keep them together, wherever possible. However, it had become, what's the word, untenable. The situation had become irreparable and Elizabeth had a big choice to make.

"Me and Esme were called to Ms Dickson's office after all this. We were still young but she laid it out for us as plainly as possible. Nellie and Ron wanted to adopt us. Only us. They wouldn't be taking Elisa."

"God, that's tough," Walter said, taking a steady sip of his coffee.

"What else could I do? I'd have been cutting my nose off to spite my face, denying myself and Esme the chance of something good, something normal. I had to do what was right. We might have been kids, but you quickly realise good things don't come around often when you're in a place like that. Nellie and Ron could have been our one-shot. I wasn't going to let it slip through my fingers."

"So you took the offer?"

"Yes," Elizabeth said firmly.

The application process began as autumn turned to winter.

Elizabeth and Esme continued to see Nellie and Ron and every day with the Woodleys seemed to be a first. The four of them tripped out to the zoo. Esme petted and fed animals and played in the park. They saw the lions and tigers and marvelled at giraffes that took food right out of her hands.

They went to the cinema. The four of them went to go and see 101 Dalmatians. They threw popcorn at each other. Esme snuggled into Ron's arm, like a daughter with her real father.

Together, the four of them felt like a real family. Away from them, Elizabeth and Esme were counting the days, hours, minutes, and seconds until they were back with them, dreaming of what it'd be like to live with them all the time. In a normal home.

It was the happiest Elizabeth remembered her childhood after her mother died.

While progress was made, Elisa remained in the background at Aston Orphanage, blending in with the other kids Elizabeth had done anything not to be like when they were in the system: isolated and alone.

Elisa always sat in the same spot by the upstairs window when her two sisters returned from any trip out with Nellie and Ron. Like she was waiting for the two of them to run upstairs and tell her she was right all along.

But that never happened. It was never going to happen.

The adoption approval came through just after New Year, 1997.

"I dunno, maybe Elisa didn't think it would ever happen," Elizabeth said, her fingernails tussled with the frails seams of her jumper. "When she was told that everything was done and me and Esme would be leaving she just lost it. Some of the things she said were awful. Horrible. Things that no sister should say to another."

"Did things ever get. . . physical again? Violent?"

"Yes."

"Do you want to elaborate on that?"

"Is it important for this?"

"It could be."

Elizabeth leaned forward, her fingers locked together between her knees. "Then, yes. Me and her got into a fight and a couple of weeks before we were due to leave, she pushed Esme down a flight of stairs, broke her wrist."

"Why'd you fight?"

"She said mum would hate us. That she'd be disgusted. That I was a traitor and was splitting the family up. I tried to walk away but she wouldn't let me go. She hit me and I retaliated. It was so stupid, I know. She was much bigger than me and you can imagine how it went."

Then came the day Elizabeth and Esme left later that March.

The morning was conflicted. Pure joy fought against guilt and sadness.

Their suitcases, packed with their few belongings, were taken to the car. Elizabeth held Nellie's hand, Esme Ron's. Elizabeth couldn't help it. She looked back up at the window she knew Elisa would be standing at.

Back up at the sister being left behind.

The sacrifice for her and Esme to live a goddamn normal life.

It was the last time Elizabeth saw Elisa.

She never forgot the hatred on her sister's face.

She paused before continuing. "And that's why you're here, Walter. I just want to know what happened to her."

ELISA

1999-2000

I should probably preface this story with a disclaimer.

You know, like those disclaimers at the start of any good ITV or BBC drama.

Warning! Contains scenes that some viewers might find upsetting.

This story, though, was the making of me when my two sisters, the two people that I loved most in this world, left me behind to rot in a place that was my version of hell.

After that day, I made attempts to escape, but looking back now; they were half-hearted, poorly planned, and naïve. The longest I managed on the streets, with nowhere to go and no one to turn to, was just a couple of days before I got caught by the cops.

Every time.

The consequence of those failed attempts was iron bars bolted to the outside of my bedroom windows and my curfew cut to 7:30, my bedroom door locked from the outside when the lights went out. There were also times I went without food.

I might as well have been in prison. All that was missing were shackles around my ankles.

But, like in any good drama, prisons have the potential to be broken out of.

All I needed was the right moment and a proper plan. I'd learned that the hard way.

And my moment arrived at the start of the millennium.

Alfred Mongan used to be a shopkeeper in the local area and got brought in to help around Aston on a part-time basis, presumably as a volunteer.

On the surface, he seemed ok. A nice guy. Someone who would come and sit and chat with you if you were ever alone. He smiled a lot. Told shit jokes. Knew magic. You could say he had a way with the kids.

After a while, though, rumours started bubbling in the corridors that Alfred had a thing for the girls.

You hear rumours like that all the time in the system. It's not uncommon. Particularly with friendly folk. Kids in the system don't have a lot of trust for the nice ones. There is *always* an ulterior motive.

Most of the time, it's also bullshit, and I thought the same when I heard the chatter about Alfred.

But then I witnessed it myself. Well, rather I heard it for myself.

Alfred had been floating around Aston for a couple of months, getting his feet comfortable under the table, or rather getting himself in between the girls' legs. I remember waking in my room one night to the sound of squeaky springs penetrating my ears through the wall, the muffled moans and sharp cries from my neighbour, Jessica Thomas.

This happened for a while. Night after night. Some sessions were long, others short.

Then Alfred would silently leave, lock the door, and leave Jessica crying into her pillow.

I still think about it now. I still remember the bruises, purple and large on her legs. The other girls saw them, too. Yet none of us — not one of us — did or said anything about it.

There was no unified front. We were all just a bunch of kids that would do anything to get out of Aston. It was survival of the fittest and telling tales — especially about staff members — was a surefire way to set you behind everyone else.

My piss poor excuse, my reason for keeping quiet, was that Alfred was going to be my ticket out of Aston.

I just needed the right moment.

That moment came on New Year's Eve, 1999.

The day I realised Alfred had his eye on me.

I had stood against the wall around the back of the orphanage in the court area. We were all gathered there — the children and staff — to watch fireworks lighting up the sky from a distance.

As I mentioned, I was one of the 'vets' by this point. I saw Aston for what it was, but not every kid was like that. The young, fresh meat hadn't seen the place's ugly underbelly. You could pick them out on that night. They were the kids that stood with the staff, oohing, ahhing, at the bright colours and every crack against the sky, wearing a smile that wouldn't be there in 12 months' time.

It was during that night that I looked around and saw Alfred, totally uninterested in the fireworks. Instead, his eyes were being lit up by me.

I knew full well what was on his mind. His glare made me sick.

He nodded at me casually.

The clock was ticking.

It was a few days into the New Year when Alfred let himself in my room for the first time.

Alfred had a key. He used the excuse of being assigned to conduct a fresh round of welfare checks with me.

Checks, he claimed, he was doing with all the kids at Aston.

He touched my bare feet and the bottom of my calves as he spoke and quizzed me about all sorts. Nothing important. Every touch of his bony fingers sent shots of disgust coursing through my veins. Every fibre in my body repulsed and implored me to push him away.

But I couldn't. Not yet.

Alfred came back three more times during January. Each time, he'd got a little closer, his hand a little further up my leg. Each session, he got more confident that I'd fall in line like the rest.

And that's what I wanted — needed — him to believe.

I thought of Jessica a lot during that time. What she endured. What she must have gone through.

His time would be up soon enough. I just had to make sure I was ready.

Karma *always* has a way of catching up with you.

Sometimes it happens in an instant. Sometimes it can take time. Regardless, it always finds us.

For Alfred, Karma came knocking for its debt on Friday 11 February 2000.

He'd let himself into my room — as always, at lights out.

Unlike every other time, though, he sat at the base of my knees, not my feet. He stroked my cheek softly and kissed my forehead with dry crisp lips that were as rough as the scouring pads we used in the kitchen.

I just closed my eyes and sucked it up.

Alfred asked me to lay my legs out. "Such a pretty girl," he'd said.

More disgust flared in my stomach.

My legs mesmerised him. His hand had started on the top of my foot and he drifted it up towards my thigh and the elastic rim of my pyjama shorts.

This had been what happened to Jessica. This sick bastard, with all his promises of helping me, was only here for one thing: to strip me to my underwear and shamelessly do what he wanted with me.

Like I was nothing.

And when it happened once, he'd be back again and again until he was bored and moved on to his next victim — only this time it would be Jessica on the other side of the wall, trying to block out the springs, my muffles.

Only I had no intention of going down the same path as Jessica. I intended to make sure that Alfred never touched another girl again.

And so with Alfred drunk with visions and dreams of what he was going to do to me, I reached under my pillow and drew out the large screw I had prised from under the frame of my bed, a real thick wedge that I had spent weeks sharpening.

I pulled my arm back and whipped it forward with as much force as I could, plundering it into the old man's neck. With a kick to the chest, he fell to the floor, and I stuffed my pillow over his face to cut out any moans and groans that came from his disgusting mouth.

His blood spit across the rough, tatty, and colourless bedroom carpet. I smiled as it pooled and listened to his pitiful whimpers and gags and held his body down as he struggled for life.

Once he was still, I rooted for his keys, gathered the pre-packed rucksack from under the bed, and left as quietly as I could.

This time I couldn't afford to get caught.

There was no going back.

My meticulous plan was finally underway, the result of every spare moment I'd seized in the past month. It was clear to me early on that I couldn't settle for just a few miles' distance from the orphanage. I needed a clean break, a considerable gap between myself and any chance of being traced.

Initially, I'd thought about heading straight for the south coast. Portsmouth perhaps. Maybe Brighton, Southampton, or even Devon. They all flickered through my mind. In the end, I decided even that wasn't far enough. I needed to leave the country, start afresh in a place no one knew me and there was no chance of being found.

After a bit of deliberation, I settled on Ireland. More specifically, Rosslare — a secluded, tiny village resort on the country's east coast.

Getting there wouldn't be an issue. I had money. I'd never been a big spender and had spent years stuffing away notes that I accumulated from two years working a paper round my social worker thought would be good for me. She was right. Not just in the way she meant. Alongside the envelope of cash, I also knew I'd need to travel light. My bag only carried the bare essentials.

I'd figure the rest out once I set foot in Rosslare.

I had planned that I'd need two days to disappear. And providing everything went to plan, no one at Aston would realise I was gone until mid-morning — more than 12 hours after I'd left — when they'd open up my room and inevitably find the corpse, Alfred's corpse, that I'd left behind as a parting gift to those fuckers.

My first step was to get over to the train station.

Under the veil of the late winter darkness, I slipped out of the orphanage's front door. I scaled its surrounding wall and jogged to catch the last train to Oxford. There, I spent the night in a Travel Inn, which was cheap and beaten down. But luxury wasn't a concern for a fugitive like me. I needed safety and a few hours' reprieve, far enough from Aston to lie low and attempt some semblance of sleep.

Inevitably, I didn't catch a single wink that night.

With bleary eyes, I ventured back to the train station a little past 7:30, trying to maintain the illusion that everything was normal. Despite my attempts to reassure myself, a persistent unease remained, causing me to check over my shoulder constantly for any signs that I was being pursued.

What if news of my departure had leaked sooner than expected? The fear of being recognised haunted me and kept me on edge. Failure was not an option. For that reason, I had to stay vigilant.

I bought my ticket to Fishguard Harbour.

It was fucking cold that morning. Wind that was fierce and unforgiving lashed rain across my face as I impatiently waited for my train, silently pleading for it to arrive on time.

The weekend quietude cloaked the platform, devoid of its usual bustling commuters. The few people that did mill around kept themselves to themselves, drinking from their flasks, reading their morning paper, hopping on the spot to keep warm.

My train arrived on time. I bounded on and found a seat in one of the unreserved carriages. Out of sight, out of mind was what I was going for. I flashed my ticket quickly, and no one bothered me.

The ease of it all seemed almost surreal, the seamless progression unnervingly smooth. Yet, with every passing second, minute, and hour aboard that train, I drew nearer to vanishing without a trace.

The train rolled into Fishguard Harbour just after 12:30.

In my mind, I was picturing the orphanage in a state of chaos after discovering Alfred's stiff corpse atop a pool of blood in my old room. I took solace from being over 130 miles away, southwest.

Perched on the edge of Wales, I gazed out to the vast sea. Gulls squawked above my head, keeping a lookout for their next meal.

My freedom was the width of the choppy and murky Irish sea away. Rosslare might have been only a mere two hours away, but it remained invisible to the naked eye.

My next stop was to catch the ferry, which was just a short walk from the station. Even in the dreary late winter, this place possessed a beauty unlike any other. Verdant hills hugged houses built into their rocky embrace, while boats bobbed gently on the water.

I'd never been on a boat before. You didn't get to experience a lot in the system. Amid my escape, I pondered whether every day would be like this, a day of firsts.

I was one of the last to board. Our vessel donned blocks of white and navy stripes, very unremarkable and unassuming. I made my way to the deck and blended in with the other travellers — the men, women, and children waving goodbye to the loved ones they were leaving behind, faces a mixture of smiles and tears.

My overriding emotion was relief. I was saying goodbye as well. Not to anyone in particular, but to my past. In my head, I was giving the biggest and most defiant middle finger I could. To all that betrayal, loss, despair, hatred, and fear I had experienced from the moment my mother died.

To complete my disappearance, I needed a new name.

I'd mulled a few over and tossed many more aside during the journey up to that point. Yet, it struck me as the boat pulled away that the name I wanted — felt compelled — to adopt had been under my nose the whole time.

From this moment, my name would be Jessica Thomas.

ELIZABETH

Despite everything they went through as kids, Elizabeth and Esme were not a lot alike and their lives followed strikingly different paths after their shared childhood struggles.

All Elizabeth had ever wanted was a simple life.

Her aspirations revolved around the ordinary — the desire to be a mother and wife, to own a modest home close to family, friends, the local schools and the town. She'd wanted the simple job that she enjoyed and would allow her to look after her children and help Jonny pay the bills. Until a few months ago, she worked as a bookseller at the local Waterstones. She liked her to-do lists and organisation. Everything had a home. Everything had its place. In her spare time, the little time she had to herself, she read and wrote and listened to crime podcasts and went for coffees and brunches and met up with her monthly book club gal pals.

By contrast, Esme was an adventurer craving the next experience.

When her sister left for Newcastle University, Elizabeth had been happy for her, of course, but her absence created a noticeable void in their shared room. She was there on moving day, swelling with pride, as Ma and Pa helped unload the last of Esme's stuff in her room at Castle Leazes (an overly fancy name for student accommodation, if you ask Elizabeth). Like, wow, she was the first Stallard to go to Uni. But it had taken Elizabeth a while to get over the empty feeling Esme's absence left behind in the room they had shared after leaving the orphanage behind.

Esme wasn't like some of those Uni students who returned home every other week to cure a bout of homesickness. No, she was the one that only came home during holiday seasons, a suitcase full of washing in tow. Esme loved the city. It gave her a taste for a different life than what she had been used to growing up in a quiet suburban town. They were two ends of a spectrum.

From her final years at school, Esme had big plans and even bigger dreams that Elizabeth couldn't relate to.

After finishing her degree in Journalism, Media and Culture, she worked the bars for a year, saving money to go travelling and working, first across South America and then Asia a few years later. There were times when Elizabeth wondered whether her sister would come back at all.

Her spirit was boundless. Esme had been born to throw herself off mountain edges, ride elephants, traverse jungles, and camp under the stars. She wasn't interested in the simplicity that came with pen pushing, admin, and the standard nine to five safe job.

Much to Elizabeth's surprise, Esme did come back from Asia. Perhaps she got tired of living out of a suitcase and cramped shared hostels — Elizabeth couldn't think of anything worse — but with the travelling bug out of her system, Esme went full throttle into her career.

She moved to the Big Smoke. She climbed the career ladder, hopping between jobs every couple of years, chasing the next promotion and pay rise. She spent her weekends in bars and clubs and parties, living in her overdraft and off her monthly pay cheque to afford that lifestyle and the scrummy flat she shared with three other girls in Highgate Hill.

There was no boy on the scene, never had been for more than a couple of months at a time. That was if they were lucky, as Esme would say.

Busy, busy, busy was Esme.

But no matter how busy she was, Elizabeth's little sister always tried to come back up for a long weekend every couple of months to catch up with those she left behind. During those four days, typically Friday to Monday, she'd go back to living out of a suitcase and crash in her and Elizabeth's old shared room at Ma and Pa's. That would be the case until she caught the train back down to London late on Monday with a full belly and a suitcase packed full of washed clothes that had gone through the tumble dryer.

When Esme was around, the girls made a point of getting together. The four of them — Eevie being the newest member of this girl's only club — huddled around a table at an indie coffee shop having a gossip and a laugh as they picked their way through frappuccinos and lattes, cinnamon swirls, and blueberry muffins.

Esme usually did most of the talking. She had the most to share.

But something felt off to Elizabeth this time. Elizabeth noticed an uncharacteristic reticence in her sister's demeanour, a stark contrast to her usual engaging presence. When Elizabeth asked her questions, she'd only get a word or two back rather than the monologue answer.

As though Esme was fobbing her off.

And rather than a look of engagement, pulling herself forward on her elbows, smiling, and waiting to burst out laughing, her little sister's eyes were stern, her face severe when Elizabeth spoke. Then it disappeared when Ma was talking.

Esme was never very good at hiding her feelings. It was always clear as day if she had a problem.

And Elizabeth sensed she, herself, was the problem. She just didn't know why, or what she possibly could have done to upset her sister. She'd been mulling that question over when she felt her phone buzzing away.

St Andrews Academy flashed up.

On the other end of the line was a woman called Patty. Elizabeth didn't catch her last name, or why she was calling, over the surrounding chatter and the roar of milk being heated and frothed in the background by baristas.

"Sorry, can you give me a moment?"

Elizabeth stepped away from the table and out into the November breeze.

"Sorry. That's better. Can you say that again?"

Patty didn't beat around the bush and minutes later, Elizabeth was in her car.

Patty — something or other — was waiting at the reception entrance.

Elizabeth had arrived at St Andrews flustered and out of sorts after rushing across town. She'd been in such a rush that she jumped out of the car and nearly forgot to lock it. A rare curse slipped under her breath as she thumbed the lock button two, three, four times to make up for the fact as she trotted across the car park.

The wind had whipped up again and the sky above had turned far greyer, far darker, carrying clouds that had taken on the form of mucky sheep's wool that swelled with inevitable rain.

Despite wearing fat wedge heels, Patty was a short woman in her olive dress. She was holding one of the big red doors open for a sorry-looking kid and a burly man who Elizabeth assumed was the father. Patty glimpsed Elizabeth and strained to hold the heavy door open just a crack as she approached.

Elizabeth immediately spotted Rhys' mop through another set of doors and brushed past Patty, who was all smiles and pleasantries. Her overpowering perfume hit Elizabeth with a slap.

There was no time for that. She needed to see her boy.

"Mr Williams will be with you soon. Can I get you a drink or anything while you wait?" Patty offered.

"No, no, we're ok. Thanks." Elizabeth spat the words out, waving Patty off like a fly that paid her far too much attention.

She knelt in front of Rhys and lifted his sunken chin. Aside from the skin around his eyebrow now being a diluted purple, there were no other marks, lumps, or bumps — nothing to suggest that he'd been in a fight, as Patty had explained on the phone.

But Elizabeth realised that it wasn't a mark she should have been looking for.

What hit her harder was Rhys' spark. Or rather, the lack of it. He looked burdened. As if he was carrying the weight of the world on his shoulders.

"Talk to me, honey. What's happened?"

There wasn't time to get an answer.

The headteacher's door opened behind her. "Mrs McIntyre?"

Elizabeth recognised the voice from the tour of the academy she, Jonny, and Rhys attended a year ago.

Mr Williams, a broad-shouldered man with thinning grey hair, a stubby nose above a thick moustache, and a sharp jawline, greeted her with a handshake that swallowed her hand.

"It's good to see you again," he said. The feeling wasn't mutual.

"Shall we get right to it?" he asked, motioning her towards his office.

"Yeah, I guess," Elizabeth said before turning to Rhys. "Come on, hon."

Rhys shuffled past her and Mr Williams. Elizabeth followed closely behind.

RHYS

"I ain't seeing no fuckin' therapist!" Rhys blurted out.

He regretted the choice of words as soon as they left his mouth. The only saving grace was that at least he'd saved his pent-up frustrations for the car, rather than unleashing it in the head-teacher's office.

"Want to try that again, hon?" His mum's voice cut through, her eyes reflecting a rare fury in the rearview mirror. Rhys never swore in front of her — never. He turned his gaze to the rain-splattered window, the drops racing each other from the top to the bottom, tracking different paths as they did so.

His anger simmered. He needed to let it settle. His dad's words echoed in his mind — nothing good comes from acting in the heat of the moment.

Don't poke the bear.

He kept quiet.

"What'd do you expect us to do, Rhys? I knew nothing, absolutely nothing, about what was going on."

Silence.

"Rhys... come on. Why haven't you told me any of this?"

Silence.

"Rhys!" His mum's voice was sharp and irritated.

Silence.

"I can't help if you won't talk to me."

Silence. Until...

"What's the point? There's nothing you can do to help, anyway."

He threw his headphones on and began to scroll through his iPod, leaving his words lingering like a dense fog hovering within the Crossland.

JONNY

Jonny had been thinking a lot lately about a phrase his father used to swear by.

If you 'ave shit to sort, dig at the root rather than hack at the damn leaves.

It struck him as ironic, given his father's way of coping after Jonny's mum left was to drink himself into oblivion until the day he died. It wasn't exactly digging at the roots.

Like his father, though, Jonny realised he was dodging his problems, but instead of turning to alcohol, he escaped into video games — the one thing that always made him feel safe.

Growing up with an absent, alcoholic father in a rough estate, Jonny had poured hours into his SNES, Nintendo 64, and every other console he could get his hands on. His man cave at the bottom of the garden, filled with gaming consoles and collectibles, was now a shrine to that comfort.

Jonny needed those virtual worlds now more than ever. As he worked through his backlog of Final Fantasy games, he couldn't ignore how much he resented his father for promising to quit drinking but never following through.

His father's avoidance had led to an early grave, and Jonny realised he was doing the same thing, just on a different scale.

He was hacking at the leaves and not digging at the roots of his issues.

His phone buzzed, interrupting his thoughts. Liz's name flashed on the screen, and her text was sharp.

Come up. Ned u.

No kiss. Jonny swallowed hard, the acrid taste of the energy drink he'd just finished lingering as he gulped down the last swig. And just like that taste, the anxiety he felt remained. He paused his game and headed up the garden path, slipping into the cold, neglected house through the backdoor.

Inside, Liz was calling after Rhys from the foot of the stairs, Eevie hooked to her hip. Jonny's heart sank at the sound of a door slamming upstairs. Liz looked frustrated, pinching the bridge of her nose as she always did when stressed.

"What's happening?" Jonny asked hesitantly, his gaze avoiding her. Liz didn't answer. Instead, she pushed past him to fiddle with the thermostat in the cluttered kitchen. Then he saw it — her tick sheet on the table, the one with instructions for the beef joint that was supposed to go in the slow cooker hours ago.

"Jonny, where's the joint? Didn't you see my note?" Liz asked, her voice trembling with frustration. He tried to find a response, but guilt choked him.

"Have you been down in that shed all day?" she demanded, pointing toward the garden. Jonny had no excuse. He could only scratch the back of his neck nervously.

"I've just had the silent treatment from Rhys. My God, I don't need it from you, too," Liz snapped.

"I'm sorry," Jonny mumbled.

"Sorry? I don't want a sorry, Jon," Liz shot back, her voice rising before she took a calming breath, trying to keep her composure in front of Eevie. "I know you're struggling right now — I really do — but I can't do this on my own. I need you here, not out there while I take care of everything. We're supposed to be a team."

"We are," Jonny tried to argue, but Liz cut him off.

"Not from where I'm standing." Her words hit Jonny hard, echoing his father's advice about digging at the root rather than hacking at the leaves. He felt a knot of remorse tightening inside him.

"I'll fix it," he whispered, more to himself than to her.

"Jon, you can't even look at me when you say that," Liz said, her voice softening as she turned away.

"I need to sort Eevie out. We'll talk later," she added, heading upstairs, leaving Jonny standing in the kitchen, her words echoing in his mind as he realised how much he had been avoiding his problems.

RHYS

A glass of lemonade sat by Rhys' side, colourless and fizzing.

An unopened Angel Slice rested next to it. Rhys was idly scrolling online, a blues playlist looping through his headphones, his head resting on his palm in a relaxed posture. The anger that had simmered on the ride home had faded, scrubbed away by a couple of hours spent hunched over his sketchpad and playing on the Nintendo Switch.

In its place, the familiar feeling of guilt had settled in.

An hour ago, he had joined his mum at the kitchen table for dinner, eating a plate of chili con carne, fully expecting her to confront him about his outburst in the car. He imagined she'd want the truth, her arms folded and her face wearing an expression that clearly said, *well, let's have it then.*

But that conversation never came. Instead, after dinner, when Rhys took his empty plate to the sink and was heading back down the hallway, his mum called out for him to wait.

Instead of the harshness he expected, there was only gentleness as she caught up to him, padding softly in the pink fluffy alpaca socks Rhys had given her last Christmas. She hugged him and apologised, promising not to push him to talk about anything he wasn't ready for. Assured him that she would be there to listen whenever he was ready to open up.

She ruffled his hair, the way she always did, and kissed his head.

What is it about the nicey-nicey approach that leaves us feeling like a sucker?

His stubbornness — a trait he'd often been told he'd inherited from his mum — kept him rooted in place. He silently wished he had stopped her as she walked back to the kitchen, that he'd sat down next to her and let it all out.

Well, not everything. Not yet. But enough to let her in, even just a fraction.

But that window of opportunity slammed shut as his mum picked a small yoghurt pot from the fridge and began to feed Eevie.

Enough time to let the old devil on the shoulder convince Rhys that he shouldn't burden his mum anymore.

After all, it was his fault that she was dealing with so much.

It was his fault that his dad was the way he was now, a shattered image of the father he'd always known.

It was his fault that his little sister, Eevie, would never be the same again, too.

Those were his problem to bear.

He'd tried to take his mind off things and block out the 'moment' he could hear Eevie having downstairs.

He whacked the volume up on his headphones.

From Twitch to YouTube, he found himself on the homepage for Dungeons and Dragons, thought of the kids playing it in the academy library on lunch break.

Rhys had never played D&D before. He's watched *a lot* of Big Bang Theory and Stranger Things and thought it was just something the kids (the nerds) played out in America.

But seeing the other kids huddled together around a table in the library at St Andrews talking sorcery, beasts, treasure, and quests has got him intrigued.

There was loads of information. Too much to go through.

But after a few clicks, he found himself on Amazon looking at the starter kit. It was available for just under 20 quid.

He saved it to his mum's wish list, but there's a question burning in Rhys' mind.

He opened Google and with a sigh, he began to tap...

'Can you play D&D on your own?'

A notification pinged in the corner of the laptop as Rhys returned to scour through Quora threads, reading conspiracies and stories of people who had encountered those eyes.

You Have 1 New ChatterBox Request.

Rhys tapped it. These notifications — 9.9 times out of 10 — were usually just to tell Rhys that so-and-so was now online and that he should check in and say, hey.

No thanks.

Rather than saying hey, Rhys would click through just to clear the notification and return to whatever he was up to.

This was a 0.1 out of 10 notification.

Annie2152215221736121 would like to chat

Rhys paused, cursor hovering over the name, making sure he was seeing it right. Annie2152215221736121.

It had to be her, surely?

Rhys thought of the girl back at the library. How she'd appeared out of nowhere like a hail storm during Spring. And now the storm had swept back in.

Rhys brought up Spotify and killed the music — *Giant* by Rag'n'Bone Man had been playing. The saxophone beat had been about to kick in. The headphones dropped to rest on his neck.

Rhys observed her icon. Where you'd expect to see a filtered selfie — where a picture of Annie should sit — was vacant and grey. The only colour coming from the icon is the bright green ring that told the world she was online.

Rhys' own icon reflected the same preference for anonymity, devoid of any personal picture. A speech bubble hopped in the bottom corner of his screen, begging for his attention.

The thump thump thump of his heart matched its pace. He felt nervous. Couldn't fathom why.

The last words she'd said — the ones that had hit him harder than any of the punches Conor planted on him on that grotty gym floor that afternoon — came rushing back.

See you around, Rhy-Rhy.

Words had deserted him then. Lost in the mix of questions running through his head as she practically skipped out of the library after her mic drop moment.

Only one person called him Rhy-Rhy. Used to call him Rhy-Rhy.

And Annie had walked away like what she'd said was as normal as 'catch ya later, alligator.'

Now here she was again. Out of the blue.

A hail storm during Spring.

If... if it was her at all.

Rhys cautiously tapped the notification, taking him to an empty chat screen filled with colourful emojis and memes.

He hadn't seen this screen in what felt like forever. ChatterBox told him regularly that his last conversation on here was with Danny Waldron more than two months ago.

He sipped lemonade while he worked out what to say. How to get started.

But she beat him to the punch.

Annie2152215221736121 (7 Nov – 19:02)

Took your sweet time

ArMaccy08 (7 Nov – 19:03)

It really u???

Annie2152215221736121 (7 Nov – 19:03)

You won't find any answers on there

ArMaccy08 (7 Nov – 19:04)

What?

Annie2152215221736121 (7 Nov – 19:04)

You won't find them on those Quora threads you keep going on

ArMaccy08 (7 Nov – 19:06)

How do u even no that

Annie2152215221736121 (7 Nov – 19:06)

I heard about what happened with Conor in PE

ArMaccy08 (7 Nov – 19:07)

Way to avoid a question

Annie2152215221736121 (7 Nov – 19:07)

You ask too many questions Rhys McIntyre

ArMaccy08 (7 Nov – 19:08)

I dont even no what to say to that

Annie2152215221736121 (7 Nov – 19:08)

At least it's not another question

Rhys' fingers hovered over the keys. He typed a couple of responses but deleted them just as quickly, realising he, indeed, was asking yet another question.

He felt stumped and relieved when he saw the magenta speech bubble pop up again at the bottom of the chat. Annie must've got sick of waiting.

Annie2152215221736121 (7 Nov – 19:11)

I'm not going to tell you the answer. But I'll show you.

ArMaccy08 (7 Nov – 19:12)

Now?

Annie2152215221736121 (7 Nov – 19:12)

No. Saturday.

ArMaccy08 (7 Nov – 19:13)

Why then?

Annie2152215221736121 (7 Nov – 19:13)

Questions. I'll call for you. That's what kids do, right?

ArMaccy08 (7 Nov – 19:14)

Isn't that a question?

Annie2152215221736121 (7 Nov – 19:14)

You're funny...

You don't remember me, do you?

ArMaccy08 (7 Nov – 19:15)

???

Annie2152215221736121 (7 Nov – 19:15)

From that day. On the beach. I was there.

What you're going through. That's when everything started.

Rhys began to tap another message, but before he could finish, another notification popped up.

Annie2152215221736121 is now offline

And just like that, more unanswered questions remained for Rhys.

He stared at Annie's last message while his brain worked back to the day that changed *everything*.

FOUR MONTHS AGO...

DAY 1

That first day had started like any other.

With Rhys 'farting about' and his mum herding everyone into action.

"Rhys! Come on! I'm not going to tell you again!"

Her voice thundered up the stairs, threatened to blow his door down. A big bad wolf, not hungry for little piggies but for timely co-operation.

Mum was a holiday dictator with a folder stuffed with papers, booking forms, and trip information close to hand. The closer the holiday got, the more stressed she became, huffin' and puffin' as she worked through her checklist and made sure everyone stayed in line.

There were always some things you couldn't account for, though. Traffic was a good example.

The car ride down to Land's End for the annual all-family holiday should be a smooth four-and-a-half-hour drive. If everything went off without a hitch, that was.

But during the unsettled summer of 2017, that drive had been a total nightmare. And Rhys' mum hadn't let it go. It was a core memory that had tarnished every trip since, despite having no affiliation to lick. That event two years ago was a crash on the M5 near Cheltenham, which had turned that four and a half hours into more than seven.

Rather than see it for what it was — an unfortunate, unforeseen accident — Rhys' mum played the blame game. Made it clear that there had been too much 'farting around'. That it was their fault they'd found themselves in mile-long queues.

She was flustered, angry, seething within, barely speaking a word after their arrival past 8 in the evening.

That saying his dad told him — *don't poke the bear*. Rhys remembers that day being the day it originated from.

Two years on, those words incessantly buzzed around again.

Rhys crammed in the last few holiday essentials — a packet of sour Haribo sweets and his Nintendo Switch into his bag, which looked set to burst, with the essentials stuffed in like a crap game of Tetris.

Rhys galloped down the stairs, unwilling to have another telling off, and joined his dad and Eevie, who were already in the car, the engine ticking over. Mum locked up behind her, double-checked the handle as she always did, and climbed into the front passenger seat with a sigh of relief.

"Ready?" Dad asked.

"Ready." Mum returned.

There were fewer bigger problems during a long ass car ride than boredom setting in.

Especially with a restless three-year-old sister in tow. And when Eevie was bored, everyone knew full well about it.

Rhys wasn't sure how long they'd been on the road before she'd started getting restless.

It usually began with her calling his name, albeit not quite as expected. "Rhy-Rhy" came out more like "Wee-Wee." It was a running joke that never lost its charm, a joke Rhys had never truly appreciated until it was gone.

When the name-calling failed, Eevie poked, prodded, groaned, and moaned with clear disdain. And when all else failed, she unleashed the ultimate weapon — a real high-pitched, ear-busting squeal that would get dad's back right up.

Mum would always turn around and tickle her feet and give Rhys *the look.*

Keep her quiet.

And so he played the dutiful big brother (bwuva, if you're Eevie). At home, he was used to indulging her obsessions like hide and seek. He let her win at the board games, let her tarnish colouring book after colouring book, sprawled the Lego out and built the most weird and wonderful things, and took her down to the park a little way down the estate.

There wasn't any of that to turn to in the stuffy Crossland.

So he turned to the classics. Eye spy, spot the yellow car, guess the Disney-themed tune. Doing that for 30 minutes felt like a lifetime. It was ironic how bored he was after she fell asleep a short while after a pit stop at Sedgemoor Services. Her eyes had drooped, her head had lolled, and she was out like a light, mouth locked open ready to catch the flies.

Rhys peered ahead, checking the time on the dashboard.

He couldn't help himself.

"How much longer till we get there?" he asked.

The car pulled off the beaten track and into Highfield Barn just after 5.

The gates, just off a country road, were already open. Grandpa Ron's Toyota had stolen a place up on the drive. Esme had hitched a ride with him and nana Nellie from one of the train stations along the way.

This was the entirety of Rhys' family — that he knew of, anyway. Squeezed into two cars.

He had always known about his mum and Esme's adoption. He'd never known his other grandparents, or any other aunties, uncles, or cousins. Nor had he ever met anyone on his dad's side. He'd never known what it was like to have a big, tight-knit family. Not like his best pal, Danny Waldron. Rhys had tagged along to a couple of those overwhelming big family get-togethers — the Waldron house packed with relatives that would easily rack up into the 30s.

It was a bizarre thing for Rhys to think he could count all his relatives on two hands.

But it was enough. More than enough. The McIntyres and Woodleys were tight and, for as long as Rhys had known, had gone on holiday together.

And Land's End always was the destination.

This time around, it was the same barn they were staying in, too.

Highfield Barn was a stunning conversion. Its weathered bricks gleamed in the southern sun, nestled within a garden boasting benches encircling a firepit, flanked by endless seas on one side and untamed hills and wooded valleys on the other.

The inside was pretty neat, too. Spacious in every sense of the word, bright and immaculate across all three floors. Seriously, the place even had a freaking games room made up of an old Pac-Man arcade machine that Rhys still held the high score on. There were also pool and ping-pong tables.

"Last again," aunt Esme had said, a glass of wine already in hand, as the McIntyres hauled their bags through the door into the living room.

After unpacking and settling back in, the seven of them headed out. The sun, like a dusty orange disc in an unblemished blue sky, was just starting to set. The cool breeze sweeping off the coast soothed the skin against the still-warm temperature.

They walked to the nearby village and stopped at The Three Horseshoes on the corner of Fitz Street. Dad loved classic country pubs, especially ones that had fancy ales with weird names and a nice menu to boot.

They collected around a table in the busy beer garden to savour the waning light and warmth. They ate good food, laughed like it was in fashion, and planned the trip to Lizard Point the next morning.

"Don't you be up late," Esme said, jabbing a finger at Rhys, her eyebrows raised. "We all know what you're like!"

"Silly Wee-Wee," Eevie shouted, grinning like The Cheshire Cat.

They all laughed.

Rhys did, too.

DAY 2

The trip to Lizard Point was a blast.

The sun, fully rested and revitalised, hung high on a freshly changed blanket of blue sky. It was a lot breezier up in the hills, but Rhys didn't mind that. It made the baking temperature bearable for a lad who cursed his pale skin for not getting on with the sun.

As a result, and for as long as he could remember, his mum would always cake him in factor 50 sun cream before they even stepped out of the door, never willing to take any chances.

The seven of them had climbed into the two cars after breakfast and set out for a day of hiking. By midday, they'd spread their picnic blankets at the familiar hilltop spot, commanding a breathtaking view of Lizard Lighthouse, set against a backdrop of lush hills and winding trails.

Rhys had his camera and snapped away, capturing the lighthouse standing tall amidst grazing cows. He'd meant to have a crack at drawing it when he got back home.

The seven of them took a detour through the woods on the way back.

They stopped by the ponds so Eevie could see the 'fishies and duckies' and crossed into a park where a food and ale festival was being held. They got ice cream and parked themselves on bales of straw, listening and bobbing along to the bands playing under a gazebo. Eevie had stood at Rhys' feet, swaying lightly from side to side, mesmerised.

Rhys was whacked by the time they traipsed back in at Highfield Barn. His legs and feet ached. He napped for an hour, rising again just as three plates of pizza got served on a huge dining room table. The family ate in the living room, eyes glued to Eevie's choice of film: *How To Train Your Dragon*.

She lasted barely 20 minutes before she'd nodded off to sleep, her tiny hand clutching the end of a half-eaten slice of four-cheese.

Dad scooped her up to bed and Rhys followed suit shortly after the film ended, bidding everyone goodnight before slipping into his bedtime routine.

He settled into bed, intending to unwind with his Switch. He didn't even get around to getting the console out of the bedside drawer.

DAY 3

This was the day that changed everything for Rhys.

For dad. For mum. For Eevie.

Nothing had been the same since, but the morning had started like any other. Rhys' legs still ached like hell from the day before and protested against him even as he got up for breakfast. He remembered whinging about his sore muscles over his Coco Pops. Remembered how Esme had ribbed him, saying he sounded like nana whenever she climbed out of her chair.

They'd all had a lazy start to the morning before heading to Porthcurno Beach after lunch.

But a day at the beach didn't appeal to everyone in the barn.

"Ain't wasting a day lying around," grandpa Ron had declared over a bowl full of granola and a milky tea. He and nana Nellie decided to head out to Minack Theatre instead.

After breakfast, the two cars went separate ways.

When they met back up, nothing would be the same again.

Porthcurno Beach, nestled between rocky hillsides, seemed a gateway to an unreal paradise, a stark contrast to the world Rhys called home.

Towels and umbrellas and families speckled the length of the sand. The sun hung, isolated again, doing a kick-ass job of shining its rays on the pale masses who craved colour. Pungent sun cream rode the coastal breeze.

The McIntyres paused on arrival. Eevie was up on dad's chest, one arm clinging around his neck.

Rhys marvelled at the small waves of pristine turquoise water clambering onto the shore before retreating. The laughter. The half-built sand castles. The dogs. Logan Rock in the distance. The surrounding knobby cliffs that were covered with different shades of reds and yellows and pinks.

Dad's hand rested on Rhys' shoulder as he absorbed the beauty, a sight unparalleled. He couldn't envision a place more stunning, a hidden gem nestled amidst England's hills — a diamond in the rough.

While he took in his surroundings, Eevie was looking elsewhere. With her spare hand shielding her eyes, she was trying to be helpful and find a spot for them all to pitch up for the day.

"Daddy... daddy... there! Look," she practically burst with zeal, pointing where she wanted them all to go.

They marked their spot for the day with five towels, three umbrellas, and a red ice box full of water.

Rhys took his top off and lathered himself up with his first thick dose of sun cream for the day.

Rhys remembered throwing himself under an umbrella, locking his headphones on, and listening to his music. He remembered the sweat pouring off him within half an hour.

In front of him, he'd watched mum, dad, and Eevie build a sandcastle. Aunt Esme lay out in the sun, a raging ball of fire that singed the surplus oil trickling down her arms as she lost herself in a novel called The Silent Patient.

Two hours disappeared like footsteps in the dry white sand he lay on. That morning tenderness in Rhys' muscles waned. He climbed out of the shade with renewed vigour, ready to build trenches and sandcastles.

He remembered holding his sister's hand, stumbling as they ran towards and away from the waves that chased them onto the shore. He remembered pretending to get swept up, falling to the floor, pretending the waves were dragging him by his feet out to the miles of sea. Her laughter echoed through the shore, a sound etched in Rhys' memory,

It was the last time Rhys heard his sister laugh like that.

It was just after 3pm.

The sun was still searing the sand below, so hot that Rhys had to tip-toe back to the brollies like he was navigating coal straight out of a fire.

Mum had taken the car back into the village to pick up some supplies. Esme was up at the coffee shack that was hidden under a blanket of shade, protected by a jagged cliff dressed with a curtain of moss. She was drinking one of those cold coffees she liked.

Rhys wrapped himself in a towel. His shoulders felt cooked and raw and overexposed. His dad loomed over him as he wiped the last fiddly grains of sand from his feet, blocking out the sun momentarily.

"I'm going over to the shack to get an ice cream. What's your order?"

He'd pondered his options for a moment. "I'll have a magnum, please! One of those white chocolate raspberry ones."

"Cough up your dollar then," dad had joked, hand outstretched.

Rhys slapped him a high five, hoping it would cover the debt. It usually did the trick.

Eevie's choice was always predictable. She'd feign pondering, finger to her mouth, eyes drifting to the sky. But she'd *always* go for a Twister. Every single time.

She occupied one brolly and commandeered two of the towels. One of them draped over her head, a look that reminded Rhys of the Emperor from Star Wars. While she'd laid out the other to spread out and arrange the seashells that she'd collected.

Dad had asked her to stay under the umbrellas with Rhys. She nodded without paying attention, the words going in one ear and out the other, as she prepped her shells like they were going on display.

With a tousle of Rhys' hair, dad headed toward Esme at the shack.

That had been the last time Rhys remembered things being normal between them.

Because it was at that point, Rhys made the biggest mistake of his life as he succumbed to the fresh fatigue settling into his eyes, a weight as heavy as the weariness in his arms and legs from that morning. He closed his eyes.

At first, it hadn't sounded quite real.

Like he was in a visionless dream.

But then the voice became sharper, firmer. It brought Rhys back to reality with a bump.

"Rhys... Rhys! Come on, wake up! Where's your sister, buddy?"

The blinding sunlight forced Rhys to squint as he gazed at his father, holding a beer and the ice cream orders, concern etched on his face.

It had been there straight away.

In his voice.

In his alarmed expression.

Worry.

Panic.

Tightening on his features.

The umbrella beside Rhys stood empty, and the shells that were once neatly arranged were now scattered haphazardly.

Specks of sand remained where Eevie had been sitting cross-legged.

Dad had scanned the length of the shoreline from where they stood at the towels.

Once. Twice. Three times.

Rhys did, too. But it spread for miles and, given it was peak afternoon, crammed full of people.

He'd looked towards the spot where Eevie had been gathering shells and over at where they'd built their castle.

She was nowhere to be seen.

The first seeds of dread took root in his chest, and with each face that wasn't his sister's, the first shoots grew.

Dad had marched off, dumping everything in his hands into the ice cooler. He'd started shouting Eevie's name, one hand cupped over his mouth, acting as a projector. He spun one way and then the other to cover as much ground as possible with his eyes. He approached strangers, and Rhys could only watch on as they shook their heads.

Again and again and again.

Each time festered a little more despair and planted more seeds in his chest.

His unease turned to anxiety. Anxiety turned to desperation.

Rhys had started mimicking his dad.

His shout was more of a high-pitched wail. Tears streamed down his cheeks as he navigated through the throngs of people, every unfamiliar face a cruel reminder that none belonged to Eevie.

Behind him, he saw mum and Esme making their way back to the brollies, oblivious to the unfolding chaos they were returning to. Arm in arm. Laughing.

Dad had seen them too and ran toward them awkwardly, each step sinking into the soft ground. Rhys could only watch as the same feelings of dread and despair he felt seemed to spread to them like a virus.

Minutes dragged by, each one heavier than the last, as the family desperately scoured the beach. Rhys remembered those first waves of sickness that lapped him just the same as the tides that rose and encroached on Porthcurno's shoreline.

The difference was those waves retreated.

The search had turned frantic. Dad, mum, and Esme shot off in different directions. Shouting.

Then a yell pierced the chaos.

A woman and a young boy, near the shoreline, wildly gestured and pointed out to sea, clamouring for anyone's attention they could grab hold of.

Rhys sprinted toward the cries, his bare feet pounding on the hot, soft sand.

The urgency spread to those around him, fuelled by curiosity to see what all the commotion was.

Ahead, Rhys spotted his mum, dad, and Esme running toward the woman and small boy.

As he closed the distance, it became apparent what they were trying to alert everyone around them to. Three more people waded into the safety of the wet sand, their legs fighting against the low tide. One man, moving quicker than the rest, stumbled ashore. There was something cradled in his arm.

A body.

Still.

Lifeless.

The first thing Rhys noticed was the hair.

Fair. Long, but not excessively so. Clumped and tangled.

A sinking feeling settled in Rhys' gut

Time lost its meaning.

It had become an elusive concept, slipping away like grains of sand in the turmoil.

Every detail became painfully vivid.

Eevie lay still, nestled in her mum's arms, propped up by her leg. Strands of damp and twisted hair brushed aside, revealing a face that had lost its spark to the sea.

She whispered pleas for her to wake, mingling them in between sobs.

Dad's desperate calls over the phone echoed through the air, cutting through the distressing quiet.

People around them watched on in a haunted daze — crying, hands clasped behind their heads.

Parents hugged their children just that bit tighter than they'd ever before.

Sometime later, an ambulance crew rushed over to the scene.

Some gathered their things together, unable to watch the unfolding nightmare.

This was the sort of thing that you saw on the evening news, or a film, or a movie — something you never expected to touch your life.

Normal families on a day out at the beach during the school holidays didn't face such horrors.

Porthcurno Beach was no longer a paradise, nor a diamond in the rough.

It was the worst place on Earth.

The family split between the ambulance and the car as they rushed Eevie to the Royal Cornwall Hospital.

Mum stayed with Eevie. Esme remained behind at the beach with all the belongings to wait for nana and grandpa. Dad took the car and Rhys hopped in the backseat.

He couldn't bring himself to call shotgun and ride up front.

Not after this.

Rhys had braced himself for the angry reprimands.

What were you thinking?

How could you be so irresponsible?

But it never came.

Growing up, Rhys had always known when he'd done something bad. Like when he tested boundaries, been a pain in the ass, broke things, back-chatted mum, acted up, or stole a couple of quid out of his mum's purse for sweets. Because it was *always* his dad who dealt with it. And when he dealt with it, it didn't happen again.

And so Rhys sat in the back of the car waiting for the scolding that never came.

Instead, his dad had asked Rhys if he was ok. Rhys remembered looking up and peering into puffy red and disarming eyes through the rearview mirror. It was a look he'd never seen before.

Rhys didn't say anything. The guilt he was feeling was swallowing him up and wouldn't allow him to answer.

He just nodded.

They drove in silence for a while.

Rhys had constantly glanced up front at the TomTom sat-nav,

watching as the arrow inched closer to its destination, the time until arrival slowly getting shorter and shorter.

With around 10 minutes to go, his dad had caught him. Their eyes met again in the rearview mirror. Rhys looked away, embarrassed.

He finally broke the silence.

"Rhys."

Their eyes met again.

"Everything's goin' to be ok," he whispered.

Rhys just couldn't take it anymore.

This sadness *he'd* caused.

It was overwhelming, watching from an isolated corner as his mum had sobbed into nana's shoulder.

By her side, his dad's frustration had grown with every passing minute. His heel beat against the floor, getting louder and quicker as they waited and begged for an update each time a doctor, a nurse, or anyone looking slightly official passed them.

But each time none was forthcoming, the pool of concern deepened and swept them up.

Rhys replayed how his mum had explained to him when he and his dad had arrived, how they rushed Eevie on a bed straight through to the Intensive Care Unit, how they strapped an oxygen mask to her tiny head, and how the nurses spoke to each other.

Quick.

Demanding.

The way they do when the situation is serious.

We need this test. We need this scan. We need it *now*.

Rhys could picture it all, and the shame he felt was suffocating. A shame that was just as prevalent as the oxygen in his blood cells pumping around his body.

He glanced at the clock: 8:16. The seven of them had been at the Royal Cornwall Hospital for over four hours now.

"Rhys."

He looked up at grandpa who was beckoning him over while he fished around in his belt bag.

"Be a good lad, will ya," his voice sounded hoarser than usual. The smell of stale cigarette smoke lingered. "Take this and get a couple of bits out of the vending machines we passed by."

Rhys took the wad of coins and looked across to his mum, still leaning into nana's shoulder, her face full of sadness. But the corners of her lips fought it, curling into the weakest of smiles.

He inserted coins into the vending machines, each clink echoing in the sterile hallway.

The machines, sluggish and creaky, eventually surrendered sandwiches, crisps, chocolate bars, and drinks, dropping them one by one with a solid thud. He collected them, tucking them carefully into the wrinkly bag nana had handed him.

This was Rhys' first-ever visit to a hospital, and he knew he never wanted to come back to one.

Never ever.

Everywhere he looked felt bleak, contrasted by the bright LED lights overhead. Sickness and pain: people in chairs asleep, others throwing up into disposable sick pots, some groaning and writhing in discomfort. A little deeper into the waiting area, a couple nursed nasty cuts to their head. Beside them, two police officers watched over a man. His hands were bound, and he lolled from side to side like a pendulum, as drunk as a skunk.

The hospital had a unique smell — a mix of bleach, sanitiser, and sickness. A combination he knew he wouldn't ever forget.

Rhys thought about Eevie. How his innocent little sister needed help, just like all the sick strangers surrounding him.

Because of him.

The three words he just couldn't shake.

With the machine finally done, he bagged everything up and traced his steps back to the ICU.

As Rhys wrapped around the corner, he froze. His mum and dad leaned in close to a doctor — a middle-aged, portly man whose presence ignited a faint glimmer of hope within Rhys. His heart began to thump and race a little harder again.

He remembered the eagerness he felt to find out what was happening.

To hear the words that Eevie was going to be ok.

He had barely taken five steps when he stopped again, his fragile hope snuffed out in a puff of smoke. His mum collapsed to her knees, letting out a broken wail that chilled his blood as his dad rushed to catch her.

Desolation cut into both nana and Esme's expressions, hidden only partly by their hands, their bodies trembling with grief. Even grandpa, a man Rhys always saw as unbreakable, removed his glasses to wipe away tears.

The moment imprinted into Rhys' mind, etched as indelibly as the memory of Eevie being pulled from the sea.

THREE WEEKS LATER

That day at the beach became an unrelenting vision projected to the forefront of Rhys' mind.

After the events at the hospital, the McIntyres and Woodleys had packed their things up at Highfield Barn and gone their separate ways. Rhys had moved in with his grandparents on Clopton Road. Mum and dad had stopped down south and lived out of hotel rooms and an Airbnb — cheap roofs over their head while they visited Eevie every day at the Royal Cornwall Hospital. Esme returned to London, her life seemingly the only one returning to some semblance of normalcy.

The rest of the school holidays saw Rhys sequestered in the bedroom where his mum and Esme had spent their teenage years — a room suspended in time, a relic of their past. The walls, a faded plum hue, bore cracks of age. Antique cabinets and bedside tables clashed with the modern furniture Rhys was used to back home. The beds, a mere arm's length apart, shared the same grey sheets adorned with stars of varying sizes.

Underneath the beds lay boxes filled with his mum and aunt's accumulated possessions: books, pop vinyl collections, old cassette tapes, a treasure trove of VHS tapes (Rom-Coms in abundance), framed photographs, and vintage posters — a treasure trove of memories left untouched, perhaps intentionally preserved by nana and grandpa.

Despite nana's efforts to coax Rhys out of the room with day trips, clubs, movie nights, or helping grandpa at the allotment, Rhys had no desire or stomach for any of it. His sole focus lay in one daily occurrence — the evening phone call.

Mum had made a point of phoning every day at the same time just before dinner at 6. Rhys had got into a habit of hiding himself at the top of the stairs, most of the time minutes before, gripped with anticipation. Waiting for the cordless home phone in the living room to do its thing.

Rhys would clatter down the stairs on that first ring.

He was always within earshot, though. Rhys was 11-years-old, but he wasn't dumb. He'd watched enough TV to know that parents hid the truth from their children, that children got shielded and spared from it.

But the gravity of those conversations lingered ominously in the air.

And so he'd eavesdropped on his grandparents' chats with his mum as well, firmly believing that whatever was unravelling down in Cornwall was nothing good.

Rhys wasn't a stranger to weird dreams.

The type that worked him up into a bit of a sweat.

Even now, he still remembers one in particular. One where he took the form of a rat (at least he thinks it was a rat) and got chased through tight, suffocating pipes across a train graveyard in the dead of night.

He had no idea where it'd come from. Or why it had stayed with him after, an enigmatic survivor among the many that slipped into the abyss of forgetfulness.

And Rhys knew from the first time he awoke in a panic from his latest nightmare that it would take the same path.

He'd woken up in his mum's old musty room, atop the bed dressed in a fine black suit, shoes shining, tie wrapped in a perfect knot. The same suit he'd been wearing for his other grandad's funeral.

There'd been sniffles and crying out on the landing (unlike grandad's funeral, where only a handful of people gathered in a small room).

Rhys had gone to investigate the sound of the distress but had swung open the bedroom door into an empty crematorium.

Mourning filled the air of an illuminated room. At the far end, a small oak coffin, its top off, stood raised, highlighted by a lonely baroque candle holder that held three lit wax candles. Vines wrapped around the stems. Petals cloaked the base. It rested on a bier, atop two small steps, and as he reached the base of the wooden frame, he pushed onto his tiptoes to peer inside.

Eevie.

His sister lay still, wearing her favourite 'pwiddy' sage green dress. A lotus, similar to the one he'd taken photos of at the garden centre, in preparation for her birthday picture, was nestled loosely between her thumbs. She just looked like she was asleep, peacefully away in the land of nod.

Then the sniffling and the crying had halted.

Rhys had craned his neck to survey the room. He was alone.

His only companion left was the sound of candle wax dripping just beyond the polished oak coffin that held his sister.

He turned back to the coffin.

Eevie. She'd... she'd... looked different.

Soaked to the bone. Hair tangled. Colourless. Her sage green dress was much darker under the clear water that now filled the bottom of the coffin, lapping and receding over her, clinging tightly to her skin.

Rhys had lurched backwards, forgetting about the two steps behind him. The hard floor caught him with a bump. Shock swept away the pain he should have felt in his backside. He used his arms to put more distance between himself and the horror. He didn't get much further before he'd bumped into something.

A pair of legs. Woman's legs. Easily distinguishable by the long black skirt that draped over them.

Rhys had recognised that skirt. Again, from his grandad's funeral.

It was his mum's skirt. The one she'd bought specially.

He looked up and her face stared back at his, void of any sort of emotion. In looking up, Rhys had also seen that the benches were full of people, all staring right at him as he cowered on the floor.

The sniffles started. The cries came with it, swelling and pushing against his eardrums, seemingly getting louder and louder and louder.

Until he woke up.

Back in his mum's old bed. In his pyjamas — no suit, shoes, or tie in sight.

It was probably for the best. . . given the puddle of sweat he lay in.

"You must be excited about finally going home, laddy," his nana said as they turned out of Clopton Road.

It was a week or so after that nightmare, and Rhys couldn't make any tale of how he was feeling. Ever since he'd found out his mum, dad, and Eevie were coming home, he'd had a belly full of nausea.

Would things ever return to how they were before all of this?

The question had weighed heavily earlier that morning as he lay in his mum's old bed, staring up at the pale ceiling. All the while, his grandparents had a spring in their step.

Later, Rhys was midway through a bowl of chicken soup when his grandpa burst through the backdoor, calling for Nellie at the top of his scratchy voice. He hauled a filthy cardboard box in two hands, crammed full of cucumbers, tomatoes, and carrots.

The box landed on the table with a satisfying thud, leaving speckles of dirt on the table runner that nana wasn't too pleased about having to chuck into the washer.

But undeterred, grandpa had pulled out several carrots and marvelled at their size with a huge grin.

"Look at the size of 'em," he exclaimed, radiating the joy of a child on Christmas morning. That box of veg had been the first thing he'd grown since taking up space down at the allotment in the spring.

The joy in his grandpa's eyes made Rhys think of simpler, happier days.

Now, as he settled into the backseat of his grandparents' car, there was no joy. Only nerves. Sprouting faster than any of those vegetables ever could, growing further as they drove through familiar streets — past the supermarket, the cinema, and the estates.

While Rhys tapped his heels in the footwell, lost in thought. Up front, his grandparents hummed along to country tunes that Rhys had never heard before. Jim Reeves, Kenny Rogers, and the like.

"They don't make it like this anymore, laddo," grandpa had insisted.

Rhys' nerves started to ripen as the car took a sharp left onto the Green Meadows Estate and onto Moorcroft Drive — a thick tree trunk of a road that connected the whole estate and branched off into all the little streets, avenues, courts, and cul-de-sacs that made it up.

They passed the lone chestnut tree that stood watch at the base of Green Meadows. It stood tall and full of life, lapping up the sun's love. Memories he hadn't previously thought long or hard about flooded back, painting a collage of happier days that Rhys had taken for granted. Like last year's brisk autumn when he'd taken Eevie down to that tree to gather the biggest conkers they could get their hands on. A little further on was the kids' play area. It was nothing special. Rhys had always thought of it as pretty basic and unspectacular. Now, though, he could only think about how much his sister loved that park.

As they drove on steadily by, the park was full of dog walkers and kids and families he recognised. He spotted the Taylors (Ruby, George, their son Dawson, and their chihuahua, Ginger) that lived across the road — here, now, all having the time of their lives chucking a frisbee around that tiny Ginger chased without a prayer of catching.

The Taylors and the park were replaced by more new builds and more connecting streets that were still stained with dirt and truck tracks left behind from years of development.

And there was Sandon Mount.

About halfway up. Just off to the left.

Rhys swallowed hard, feeding the nerves that grew a little more in his stomach.

The door to number 25 opened before grandpa's hand had even found the handbrake.

That moment Rhys saw his mum again for the first time in three weeks, all of those nerves disappeared.

The car hadn't fully ground to a stop before he'd bolted out, tears streaming as he stumbled across the gravel driveway and into his mum's open arms. His mum had always been a hugger, and this was three weeks of absent embraces rolled into one. Her fingers sunk into his thick curly hair, replacing any residual feelings of nerve with a warmth that no person on this Earth could replicate.

She pulled away to observe his face. Rhys noticed her reddened, sun-kissed cheeks and the first drops of tears slid from the corners of her damp eyes. Mum was a crier, too.

"I've missed you so much, hon," she said.

Rhys couldn't find any words. He just grabbed her tight. Tighter than he'd possibly done before. She kissed the top of his head and they hugged the last three weeks out a little while longer.

Behind him, the gravel crunched under nana and grandpa's feet as their shadows gradually materialised, cutting figures that Rhys made out in between the strands of mum's hair that tickled his face in the warm breeze.

"He's been good as gold, he has," nana said with a rough voice. "Good as gold."

Reluctantly, the embrace came to an end. Bags needed to be retrieved from the car. As Rhys trudged back, he glanced over his shoulder, half expecting to find himself waking up back in his mum's old room, caught in a hazy dream where time blurred seamlessly.

But all he saw was his mum, nana, and grandpa.

All getting their own share of hugs and kisses.

Everything was going to be ok, Rhys whispered to himself.

Everything's going to be ok.

He cautiously stepped into the house he'd not seen the inside of for several weeks.

Rhys propped up his backpack and suitcase in the hallway, turned to say goodbye and thank his grandparents with hugs and high fives.

There was no sign of dad or Eevie.

He sat down on the sofa in the living room and scanned the familiar space while his mum finished up. But for the obscene amount of mail lopsidedly piled up on dad's chair-side table, everything was how he remembered.

Dare he say it, everything appeared normal.

The front door shut. Mum joined him in the living room, prioritising fixing up the wrinkle at the corner of the sofa throw before she sat beside him.

“Where’s dad and Eevie?” Rhys asked.

“They’re upstairs, hon. They’ll be down soon,” mum had said with a slightly off tone and a fleeting smile faltered, hinting at an underlying unease that settled into Rhys’s gut, sending up a fresh shoot of anxiety from his stomach.

Maybe she could read how Rhys was feeling and sensed his growing concern. She picked up where she left off. Her words came out slow and with struggle, broken up by large pauses and intakes of breath.

Each syllable had been hard to spit out and painted a painful picture.

She was doing everything she could to hold it together.

Rhys only listened as she relayed the last three weeks.

What Eevie went through.

Certain bits stuck in his head as others passed him by.

The fact his sister had been in an induced coma for five days.

The fact she’d suffered a cardiac arrest.

Rhys had known none of this, and the same guilt that had haunted him since that day on the beach returned with a vengeance, its weight growing heavier with each detail.

You caused this. This is your fault. There was no room for any other thoughts or feelings.

“Do you want me to explain any of this properly to you?” His mum had asked.

Rhys was old enough that he didn’t need any of this explaining. He knew exactly what it all meant. What he’d done. But he *needed* to know everything.

Mum went on.

"Well, the doctors, they said that her brain was without oxygen for a long time. How do I put this? Our brain, it needs that oxygen. Just like you or I need food. But... but without that oxygen, the brain can become hungry and starved. That's what's happened to Eevie."

"But I thought you said on the phone that she was much better?"

"I did, and she is. She's here, with us at home. Where she should be. But... I just need you to know that she. . . she's still very poorly. We all need to be patient with her."

Each word mum had used had been carefully picked, forming sentences that had been intricately pulled together with the impossible task of taking the sting out of this conversation.

The truth was, though, that there was nothing that mum could say that could take that pain or guilt away from Rhys.

He pictured his little sister on the beach. His little sister with a smile on her face as she padded along the hot sand collecting seashells in her bucket. The little sister he took to gather conkers last year. The little sister with whom he played hide and seek and coloured and played with through an endless stream of board games.

The little sister who was his plus one for pretty much everything in his life.

Would she ever be like that again?

Rhys asked the question. He needed to know.

Mum paused, unable to find the right words. The way she looked away from him was as incisive an answer as any words possibly could be.

A hot tear cut down Rhys' cheek but he held the rest back. This was about Eevie. Not him.

"Would you like to see her?" Mum had a tear in her eye, too.

Rhys nodded. He felt a soft squeeze on his shoulder.

Over by the landing, mum had called for dad. Not like she used to. The whole house used to hear her when she shouted from the bottom of the stairs.

No, this was softer. Projected in a way like it had been expected.

There was a shuffle above Rhys' head. A moan from the floorboards that would be Eevie's bedroom.

Rhys stood in the middle of the living room, listening as his dad took the stairs a step at a time.

Dad, carefully cradling Eevie against his chest, didn't look like himself. His eyes drooped and the hollows under them hung lower and darker. His stubble, clipped the night before the drive down south, was wiry and patchy and was as long as Rhys had ever seen it.

"Hey, bud."

"Hey."

There was a moment of silence like no one knew what to say or do next.

"I missed you," dad said to Rhys. His face didn't match the words.

"Missed you, too," Rhys responded. But he was only looking at Eevie.

Dad rested his chin lightly in Eevie's hair and began whispering down to her. "Look who we've got here to see you, sweetie."

Rhys stepped towards them. He took his sister's floppy hand.

The ends of her fingers twitched.

She peered into his eyes, mouth ajar, seemingly locked in its place.

There was no 'Wee-Wee'. No fiddling. No prodding. No giggling.

There was just nothing.

Like it was the first time they'd met.

Like he was a total stranger to her.

PART 2

A GIRL CALLED KARMA

ELISA

2000-2007

I was *finally* free.

Not just of Aston Orphanage, but of everything I associated with my old life.

I felt cleansed. Like I was washing away ingrained dirt from a soft fabric.

I was leaving all that shit behind, consigning it to the depths of my brain and locking it away. Never for it to be revisited.

How naïve I was back then, thinking that'd be the case.

For a long time, Ireland was good for me. For a long time, my new life across the Irish Sea had been enough.

But ingrained dirt on soft fabric is a bitch to get out.

No matter how much you scrub.

There's always a bit left behind.

This is the story of how my time in Rosslare unfolded.

The thought of starting from scratch can be enough to petrify some people.

I had no long-term plan. Nothing that went beyond escaping that god-forsaken pit of hell and boarding the ferry at Fishguard Harbour.

I had no friends. No family. No safety net or place to turn.

And yet this unknown was still better — so much better.

Under my new alias, Jessica Thomas, I set about trying to work out what to do next. From the moment I stepped out onto Rosslare Harbour, I was winging it. Shooting in the dark from the hip.

My priority was to get a roof over my head, somewhere I could spend a couple of nights while I worked out what to do.

It turned out I didn't have to look very far.

A stone's throw from the coast, off down a narrow street that cut off the main road, was the Bay View Inn. It was a cosy — if a little neglected — B&B sandwiched between two apartment blocks that were up for rent.

What I had thought would be a place to get my head down for a couple of nights, though, turned out to be my home for over seven years.

Behind the counter on that day was a woman with shoulder-length slate-coloured hair. Attitude as broad as her thick physique — the no-shits-given kind that didn't belong anywhere near serving customers.

But here she was, taking the 40 Euro I'd exchanged at a dingy booth back on the port. The exchange was brief, but still long enough for me to get a feel for that thick native Irish accent of hers. She didn't ask questions. She didn't ask to see any ID (thank God). She couldn't get rid of me fast enough. I was a nuisance, getting in the way of whatever it was she was up to at that very moment.

But that woman turned out to be my first genuine friend in this world.

Her name was Tina Ayling.

And she was Rosslare through and through. Not that it was supposed to have been like that.

Life bogged her down, you see. Just like it bogs so many of us down.

Tina never went into a great deal about her life. Like everyone else, I didn't want to pry too much for fear of getting on her bad side.

Still, behind closed doors and over a few too many Irish slammers, fragments emerged — enough to sketch a portrait of the Tina I'd come to know.

The Bay View Inn had always been part of her life — quite literally. She was born in the middle of the bar's floor, tables and chairs scattered all around her.

Those damn contractions hit her mother like a bitch.

Aside from that, the Bay View Inn was also owned by her two Catholic devout parents. But Tina strayed from that script, away from the Inn's legacy.

In her own words, she believed she was destined for more. She wanted more.

Tina had enjoyed school and developed a fascination for psychology. She'd planned to study it at the local college in Wexford and from there would leave Rosslare behind to pursue her University degree in Dublin. She was an outlier in a village where ambitions seldom sailed beyond the horizon.

But fate had its own designs for her. For Tina, life veered off-course in the cruellest ways.

She was halfway through secondary school when her mum, after a long and desperate wait, got diagnosed with motor neurone disease. If it wasn't hard enough that this god-awful disease took a greater, stronger grip on her mum's life over the ensuing couple of years, her dad then bolted, leaving nothing but a note that said he was sorry. That it had all become too much.

Fuckin' coward.

I remember saying that to Tina and she glared at me. A *don't you fuckin' go there kid* kind of glare. I got the feeling that she didn't at all blame her father.

Regardless, Tina had to shoulder the wreckage just months before starting her college education. But to look after her mother, help her run the Bay View Inn, which she refused to get rid of to fund her care, and take on full-time college — to keep all the plates spinning — was going to be impossible.

Something had to give.

Her mind was clear, and she'd known what she needed to do. Tina didn't complete another day at school after the day her dad left them high and dry. Her college dreams faded like mist, overcome by the weight of responsibility.

She followed the path that was laid out before her and didn't deviate from it. She stayed by her mum's side until the day she passed away (right there at the Inn) in 1972. Tina inherited the Bay View Inn — the only thing her mum had to her name bar a small savings pot — but it certainly wasn't received like a reward for staying by her side.

Sure, she could have sold up and moved on. The Irish were moving in their droves to America and she thought long and hard in those early days of joining the ride.

But she always came to the same conclusion. What would she do? Where would she go? Who would she be?

While the thought of starting over again hadn't bothered me, it had terrified Tina.

That fear became her shackles, chaining her to the Inn's ceaseless routine of checking guests in, tidying rooms, pouring pints and serving breakfasts.

It was a life steeped in simmering resentment and disillusionment.

That next morning, after I'd checked in at the Bay View Inn, I bumped into Tina again. She was taping a sheet on the front door, unaware of my presence.

I was going to spend the day exploring Rosslare, wrapped in the warmest clothes I had, while I got my bearings.

I'd said excuse me. Tina had let me by with a puff of annoyance. As she begrudgingly let me step out onto the quiet backstreet, curiosity snagged my attention, and I turned back to look at the sheet hanging in the window.

Kitchen and bar staff needed, it had messily scribbled on it.

I pushed the door straight back open.

Tina initially put me to work with pot washing and bar maintenance. Instead of a wage, I suggested retaining my room as payment while I worked for her. She agreed, making it clear it was solely because of the quiet off-season.

Once the place filled up, I'd have to go.

There were also a few other conditions I had to agree to as well. The most important of those being that I kept on top of cleaning the room (fine, my few belongings wouldn't make that job difficult), didn't play loud music (I had nothing to listen to music on), didn't bring guests back (no problems there), and, most importantly, was available *whenever* she needed me.

Well, who could say no to that?

It was a temporary fix that had landed on my lap. It was a means to an end while I worked things out. And while Tina could be downright patronising and obnoxious and moody back then, this was still a significant upgrade on life before Rosslare.

So, yes, I'd started in the kitchen, but as the weeks elapsed, something clicked. There was a change in the Bay View Inn atmosphere. Like a shift in the wind.

Tina became more cordial with me. She still had no time for small talk, but she was softer. She began to trust me with all matters of things around the Inn. Winter turned to spring and then, when summer came knocking, peak season came knocking right with it.

The tourists swept into Rosslare. The rooms started to fill. I remember counting them down, those final few vacant spaces like a sand timer on my room that I would have to give up for a paying customer.

It was me that checked the last available room out to a couple of old regulars from Kilkenny. I remember Tina standing in the main entrance, watching the pair take their key from me and climb the steps to go and settle in.

A young woman, not much older than me, came in later that day, asking if there were any vacant rooms.

Tina had looked at me. I'd looked at her, knowing full well my time was up and it was time for me to find somewhere new.

But Tina had turned to the woman and said they'd just filled the last room. After the woman had left, Tina walked to the front door and turned the sign around, the sign that made it clear that there were no vacancies left at the Inn.

I cried that night when I'd finished my shift, not because I'd not had to leave, but because this was the first real kindness I'd ever experienced since my mother had died.

It left an indelible mark on me, one I've never forgotten.

My fondest memories reside in Rosslare, a tapestry woven with moments that brightened my life.

There were the locked-in nights at the bar Tina hosted, celebrating my 18th and 21st birthdays. I relished Christmas again, similar to how I had felt as a little girl. It was in that village that I learned to drive with one of the regulars, and after passing, Tina surprised me by handing a spare key to her beat-up dark green Vauxhall Nova she had called Casa (yes, questionable choice, I know). It may have looked rough, but I adored that little run around.

Yet, it wasn't just these significant events that enamoured me with Rosslare.

It was the smaller delights — the sun-soaked summers spent on the beach, attending plays at the National Opera House, strolling through local heritage parks regardless of the season, embracing the spirit of festivals and community gatherings, and meeting tourists with their fascinating stories.

I got my first boyfriend, Adrian Hawkins, his name was. A local heartthrob with windswept brown hair, sharp cheekbones, and the physique of an '80s Liam Gallagher. It turns out looks weren't everything, as Adrian was a certified Grade-A Asshole beneath that facade. I lingered far too long in that relationship, later realising the superficiality of subsequent relationships that lasted only a few fleeting months at a time.

But beyond all these experiences, a common thread tied them together: Independence.

Rosslare gifted me a sense of autonomy, freedom absent from my past. It made me happy. It made me content. Unlike many of the locals, I was happy to call this place home.

But that all changed in 2006.

During an uncharacteristically muggy autumn, Tina died.

Right there in the place she'd been born in the Bay View Inn bar.

She'd closed up that night on her own, finished as she always did with an Irish Slammer to mark the end of another shift.

I found her the next morning, slumped in her chair, Irish Slammer untouched, her skin cold as ice and the colour sucked from it.

I felt blindsided.

In Tina's room, on the bedside table, I discovered a drawer crammed with unopened medication: inhibitors, beta-blockers, diuretics. Her heart had been faltering for who knows how long, and she had chosen to ignore it.

At first, I was furious. How could she keep this hidden from everyone, including me? It was more than just neglecting medicine; it was a choice between life and death.

It was only during her funeral at St Brigid's Church that it hit me.

Tina was a Rosslare woman through and through. Someone loved by the community she'd lived in all her life.

Those words were undoubtedly said with affection, but Tina would have despised them more than any other — a sickening reminder of the life that was robbed from her, that she didn't do anything about.

I concluded that she couldn't bear it any longer, and she felt that her life had become one big regret, a life she no longer wanted to be chained to.

It was Tina's passing that made me realise that I, too, remained tethered to my past. It was time for me to break free, to stop being a prisoner to history. Tina's departure served as a poignant awakening — a catalyst for me to move forward.

It turned out that there was one last surprise Tina had for me — the Bay View Inn itself.

She had left it to me in her will, posing me a predicament of the ID variety. Although I'd taken on Jessica Thomas' name, I lacked formal documentation to back it up and, up to that point, had never needed it. Inheriting the Inn was risking a heap of questions that I would have had a hard time answering.

So I called in a favour.

Declan O'Malley was someone who drank at the Bay View Inn from time to time. He was a good guy who knew his tech inside out, not that you'd know that from looking at him. At first glance, all you saw was a big burly guy who was more likely to be seen on a rugby pitch than sitting behind a computer.

Looks really could be deceiving.

Anyway, Declan was also a bit of a scrapper and in '03, he'd got caught up in a bar brawl out in Wexford. He'd needed an alibi and having got close with him since moving to Rosslare, I was all too happy to offer him one, on one condition: did the other guy deserve it?

"I only wished I'd hit him harder," Declan had said with a wry smile.

With my favour cashed in, Declan provided the necessary get-out-of-jail cards that not only cleared my inheritance of the Inn, but also aligned with my future plans. But to put those plans into motion, I needed funds.

Hence, the Bay View Inn hit the market as soon as it officially became mine.

The sale process dragged on painfully, each passing month intensifying my impatience. The Inn tethered my physical presence to Rosslare, but my mind was elsewhere — fixated on my two sisters. Esme, young and led astray by deceitful tales. Elizabeth, who abandoned me. They consumed my thoughts.

It was around this time that I started to spend more and more time on social media, following their lives from afar. The photos

I scrolled back through on an almost daily basis. Pictures of family holidays, camping trips, meals out, birthday parties, and Christmas' surrounded by presents and torn paper only fuelled my desire to act.

It turned out that Elizabeth had a boyfriend.

Jonny McIntyre.

It turned out he liked to post on Facebook a lot, too.

The sale of the Bay View Inn finally went through in April 2007. Not long after, it turned out that renovation work started on it and it had been turned into rental apartments.

I visited Tina's plot one last time to share the news with her. To say thank you for everything she'd done for me.

For being my friend.

I poured us both one last Irish Slammer, necked mine, raised the empty glass in the air, and plonked it beside her full one.

I had a ferry to catch.

SATURDAY 9TH NOVEMBER 2019

RHYS

He was doing his best to occupy himself.

Headphones on, music blaring a touch too loud, but just how Rhys liked it. The pencil he held carefully worked away on the second version of Eevie's birthday picture, carefully outlining the lotus that sat in front of a cascading waterfall.

His weary gaze shifted between the current drawing and the original, patched together by strips of crumpled sticky tape and Blu Tack hanging on his bedside wall.

But he couldn't keep focused. His concentration kept slipping and wandering. Normally, once Rhys entered his creative cocoon, he remained there, insulated from distractions.

Except one had sneakily found its way inside — Annie.

His laptop had sat on his bed, right below that torn picture. ChatterBox had hijacked its screen for the last 18 hours. But Annie hadn't been online since they spoke that Thursday night.

She'd been absent from the academy on the Friday as well. There'd been nothing. Not a single peep.

Each glance he took at the ripped drawing, to extract a detail for the latest version, led Rhys' eyes to Annie's dormant grey avatar on the screen.

He just couldn't help it.

Frustration brewed each time he noticed her continued absence, aggravated by his powerlessness.

The trail of their Thursday night chat lingered like a foul smell. His open box sat blinking at him, crying out for him to type something — anything — into it and make it feel useful.

The butt of his frustration lay with three particular lines.

Annie2152215221736121 (7 Nov – 19:11)

I'm not going to tell you the answer. But I'll show you.

ArMaccy08 (7 Nov – 19:12)

Now?

Annie2152215221736121 (7 Nov – 19:12)

No. Saturday.

He wasn't sure what he was meant to be waiting for.

But there was nothing he could do but wait to find out.

A couple of wrens caught his eye out the window a little later that morning.

They danced together mid-flight before settling side by side on the rim of next door's gutter. Their plump dark forms a vivid contrast against the clear mid-morning sky. Their unified chirps were in a three-way battle with the distant flurry of car engines that sounded off Moorcroft Drive and the barks from Coco, Mr Banks' chocolate Labrador, across the road.

Drawn in by the distraction, Rhys reached into his desk drawer for his camera. He touched his window out to not startle the two birds perched together a few feet away. Bathed in the late morning sunlight that was gradually being dimmed by encroaching clouds, the birds preened contentedly.

Despite the serene blue sky, left behind by the distant summer, the air was chill, a reminder of the late autumn bite. That breeze, strong enough to push around the bushes and tops of trees that decorated the fronts of the houses spanning Sandon Mount, tickled Rhys' bare arms as he began to snap away with his camera.

Up close shots. Long shots. A few different angles with the limited space he had as he leaned over his desk, as much as he could get before his subjects disappeared.

As the wrens eventually took flight, Rhys scrolled through his shots. His breath hitched from the first photo, stolen by a gust of disbelief.

The birds appeared to lock eyes with him through the lens, a glimmer shining in their gaze in every shot. His neighbour's house... was... it differed from what he saw with his own eyes.

The slate tiles, the sand-lime bricks, the mortar that bound them, and the ivy that clung against the side of the house. On the camera, it was all covered with lotus flowers of varying sizes.

Like it had been put through Photoshop. A blurring of realities.

With each flick of his finger, the lotus flowers bloomed and only grew bigger and bigger.

Impossible.

But Rhys didn't have time to process it.

There was a knock on his door.

ELIZABETH

For the last two months, Eevie had been Elizabeth's alarm clock.

That morning, her little girl had nudged her into consciousness just after half-five. The dusty purple of the dying night was slowly being replaced by what would become an unblemished royal blue.

She rolled over to where Jonny should have been, but as expected, his side of the bed lay vacant and cold. She was in no doubt that she would head downstairs and into the kitchen to find her husband down in the shed, a lonely hunched silhouette figure cutting through its frosted glass.

Before Elizabeth even set foot downstairs for her first coffee of the day, there was a meticulous routine to work through, one that, after months of muddling through, now ran like clockwork.

Sorting Eevie's medication for the day was first up — a cocktail of anticonvulsants, muscle relaxants, diuretics, and stimulants that Eevie would take throughout the day. Then there was bath time, getting her dressed, stimulation time with low lighting, and her favourite Disney music. Breakfast would then follow. All before finally attempting to brush her teeth.

All that combined took at least two hours, providing Eevie had none of her unpredictable moments.

On weekdays, these two hours would trickle away swiftly, like water swirling down a plughole.

There was also Rhys to sort — a nigh-on teenage boy who had no get-up-and-go in him, especially for school. He, too, was a constant task on her mental checklist that needed to be kept on top of.

In truth, it would be a remarkable day if Elizabeth found a moment to brush her hair or apply a touch of makeup, so she didn't have to be conscious of how pale her skin had got recently.

But weekends... weekends offered a reprieve, a respite from the relentless race against the clock and the burdensome juggling act of tending to Eevie and ensuring Rhys was ready for the day.

And so Elizabeth got through the routine that morning and had the pleasure of standing with a mug of coffee warming her palms while she looked out into the garden, watching as the sunlight touched the shrubs that had overgrown and a garden that was long and unkempt. Eevie sat behind in her highchair, calm, playing with a soft toy. Simple pleasures like this were the exception rather than the rule now.

Jonny had come through into the kitchen a little before 10 and Elizabeth decided she wasn't going to let him get away with another day of hiding in his shed. She was still so annoyed about how he'd wasted the day down there and done nothing to help her out from two days ago.

And so, she ordered him to go and take Eevie for a walk. A proper one as well. Not a 10-minute jaunt around the block. She insisted it'd do them both good. Well, it'd do all three of them good, but she wasn't going to share her ulterior motive.

Jonny had relented after a bit of convincing (why he was being so difficult, she wasn't sure) and as the door closed behind them after 11, the house descended into a rare tranquillity.

The feeling of unoccupied time was surreal for Elizabeth — space, quietude, an absence of perpetual vigilance. She crashed on the sofa with a freshly poured mug of coffee and settled with a book — an advanced reader copy of Blood Orange she'd been lent by her old store manager at Waterstones in town. Before opening it, Elizabeth doom-scrolled social media and then cleared her emails, looking in particular for anything from Walter Demick.

There was nothing.

Should she call him? She hadn't heard anything since they spoke early that week at Halton Haig Library. No. It was still early days. He wouldn't appreciate being pestered while on the job. Especially not at the weekend. He'd said he'd get in touch as soon as he had an update.

Elizabeth obeyed herself. She locked her phone and, *finally*, flicked through the pages of the paperback, stopping at her folded corner. She'd only got a quarter of the way through the book over the past month. A once vociferous reader who could easily devour three books a week, she now needed recaps just to jog her memory on where she was up to.

And then Elizabeth began to think of Rhys.

How little she'd spent time with him recently and who, like his father, would idle away his whole weekend in one place if she didn't do something about it.

She closed the book without finishing a single page.

Elizabeth cranked his bedroom door open an inch after a brisk knock.

"You going to come down and join me for some lunch, hon?"

The two of them rarely did this, but that was just the problem. When Elizabeth thought about it, she couldn't remember the last time she'd sat down and just eaten lunch with her boy.

The only time they spent together, really, was to and from school during the week. But even then, calling it quality time felt like a stretch. As Rhys had got older and become more independent, he'd just needed her far less.

Apparently, he did still need her to remind him to clean his room. She could barely see the floor through the clothes and rubbish as she entered.

"Earth to Rhys," she interjected, her tone laced with a hint of playful sarcasm after he'd not heard her the first time.

Startled, Rhys swivelled around, hiding whatever it was he was doing. "Sorry... what's up?"

"You going to come down and join me for some lunch?"

"Can't I have it up here?"

"No. You spend more than enough time in this pit. Come and experience a change of scenery for once. You wouldn't believe it, but there's more to this house than your room."

"Funny," Rhys retorted dryly.

"I know, right? And while you're down, we need to have a serious chat about the state of this room."

She watched as he dragged his feet into the kitchen, a visible sulk stitched on his face — a face that appeared as if someone had slapped it with the news that there was an afternoon of chores to get done instead of an invitation for lunch.

But at least the headphones were around his neck rather than over his tabs.

Elizabeth was already tucking into her fish finger sandwich at the dining room table, a long oak bench with green stubby legs. That table, more than anything, was a reminder of what the McIntyres hadn't been able to buy before moving to Sandon Mount.

For Elizabeth, it'd been love at first sight when she'd spotted it at IKEA and bought it just after they'd moved in on the new estate.

Before Sandon Mount, meals got eaten off trays in a cramped living room because of the box kitchen's limited space that only allowed one person at a time. Elizabeth had grown tired of feeling suffocated by the tiny house on Wayborough Falls and had started hunting for her dream house 18 months ago.

Green Meadows was the first new build site she'd visited when she'd brought up the prospect of moving a few months after Jonny's dad had died. The marketing brochure enticed Elizabeth, naively hooking her with the showroom designed for that purpose, but it was the kitchen big enough to house a dreamy table that the whole family (and guests if necessary) could gather around that sealed the deal.

And enveloped in that excitement of something new, the McIntyres had started with good intentions. They'd eaten together in the evenings when Jonny got off work, living the age-old cliché of talking about their days. Cliché or not, it was all

Elizabeth had ever wanted: all sat together eating breakfast at the weekends, having space for having family and friends over for dinner and parties, picking at spreads that Elizabeth took great pleasure in spending hours putting together.

Recently, though, half of that table had become a dumping ground for mail, school documents, and Eevie's medical notes. Sheet after sheet after sheet of it. All of it scattered around. The fruit bowl in the middle, once upon a time crammed with bananas and apples and grapes and oranges, was naked. It had been for some time.

Rhys walked in and took the seat across from her without saying a word — no surprise there. He skipped over the tartar sauce — also not a surprise — and shot a dollop of tomato sauce that lands on his plate with a messy splotch.

Rhys seemed distracted, his attention drawn to an unremarkable corner of the table as he chewed off the first corner of his sandwich.

She could hear a whisper of music escaping his headphones.

"Come on, Rhys. Let's have the headphones off while we eat."

He did as he was told.

"You look distracted. Want to talk about what's going off in that mind of yours?"

He answered with a shake of the head. She didn't want to press and risk him closing up further. Rhys had clammed right up again yesterday on the way to school and when she'd spoken to Ma about it, she advised her just to give her son some space.

"He's growing up. Soon'll be a teenager," she'd told her. "My life, I couldn't get anything out of you when you were his age."

They sat in silence for a while, picking at their sandwiches. Rhys' eyes were lost in the table top's random patterns.

Elizabeth's were lost on him, thinking first about how her little boy had grown over the last year. But she'd grown more conscious with every bite he took of that sandwich that he would disappear back upstairs in a shot without saying another word if she didn't say anything.

It never used to be this hard.

"So, tell me, what big plans you got on this afternoon?"

"Nothing really," Rhys replied, with a lazy shrug of the shoulders. "Maybe a bit of drawing. Bit of Switch. Bit of TV. I've got some history homework to do, too."

"Still redoing that picture for Eevie, yeah?"

He nodded.

"I'm sorry about what happened. I know how hard you worked on it."

"It's ok."

She tried talking to him about what he was playing on the Switch and didn't understand a word he said but she nodded along, trying to keep the embers of the conversation burning. TV was a little easier. He talked about the new series of The Dark Crystal he was starting and when Elizabeth had asked what it was about he explained in more than a couple of words.

The sandwich in his hands, though, was quickly disappearing.

"How about we do something this afternoon?" she asked, with a flash of inspiration.

The words made him prick his head up and gaze at her, a hint of surprise on his expression.

But why shouldn't they go out, just the two of them? Her life had been dominated by Eevie since the day she came home. The last time it was just her and Rhys... wasn't it a few months back when they'd gone to the garden centre so he could take photos of flowers for Eevie's drawing? You could hardly class that as a day out for an 11-year-old son, could you?

"We can go to the cinema, or head into town for a bit, or what about bowling? Yeah. We haven't done that in a while."

"What about Eevie?" he asked. The words stung. A reminder of just how much time she'd needed to take from her son's pot to put it into her daughter's.

How independent he'd needed to become.

"I'm sure your dad can handle her for a few hours."

Was that a hint of a smile she saw? She was sure of it.

"Yeah... yeah, alright then."

"That's it then! I'll get washed up here while you give your room a bit of a tidy-up. Once your dad is back we'll get going. Sound like a plan?"

He nodded. That smile re-emerged before vanishing again.

RHYS

Rhys bounded into his room, a buzz of excitement in his step. From under his bed, he dug out his pair of Nikes and laced them up, ready to head out.

As he did, he surveyed his room.

It's not *that* bad.

Sure, there were big piles of clothes that commandeered large spaces on the floor. The drawers were overflowing with clothes spilling out over the edges. Crumpled paper and empty sweet wrappers had gathered by one corner of his desk as if they were waiting outside a party they didn't have an invitation to. His bed sheets draped lazily, but what's the point in making a bed you're just getting back into later?

It's not *that* bad, he reassured himself again.

Nevertheless, Rhys had every intention of doing as he was told and giving it a quick spruce up. Just not right now.

Before returning downstairs, he revisited his desk and rummaged in the top drawer for the camera he'd quickly hidden away when his mum had knocked on his door. He turned it on, urging it to load faster. Finally, the reel opened.

Rhys couldn't believe what he saw.

The pictures. They'd changed again. The lotus flowers, which had eerily adorned number 23's side, getting larger with every picture, had vanished. The pictures, all of them, were impossibly normal.

As they should have been originally.

There's no way I imagined it. No way.

While he contemplated his sanity, the laptop on the bed, with its fan humming away, in need of a break after so long on the job, pinged to get his attention.

He had a new ChatterBox notification.

Annie2152215221736121 (9 Nov – 12:01)
Knock, knock! Can Rhys come out to play?

His heart picked up a beat.

What was it about Annie?

Only a couple of days ago, he'd only known her as another face among the many at St Andrews. A fellow loner, watching from the side. That was before she'd crashed into his life like a storm. And now, just as her ChatterBox notification lit up again, the same feeling bubbled within him as when she'd first messaged a couple of days back.

Annie2152215221736121 (9 Nov – 12:02)
Don't just stand there. Look outside!

He creased his face, puzzled, but obeyed the command displayed on the screen.

And there she was.

Annie.

Out at the edge of the drive, dressed in her usual all-black. Hair pulled back. One hand tucked in a pocket, the other waving at him in a way that reminded Rhys of how Kevin McCallister waved at the Wet Bandits when they're nabbed by the cops at the end of Home Alone 1, positively oozing derision.

Yet, something was off. Something unsettled Rhys.

The quiet. It was so quiet that it was loud and obvious. It was deafening. No birds sang, no distant car engines hummed, no sign of Coco's barks. Not even a rustle from the breeze.

It felt like someone hit a mute button somewhere, leaving Rhys with only the sound of his nose whistling.

"What are you doing here?" He said in a low voice after quietly nudging his window open further.

She cupped a hand to the ear, teasing. Daring Rhys to shout a little louder.

She dropped her hand and smiled. Just as she did, another message popped up on his laptop.

Annie2152215221736121 (9 Nov – 12:03)

You want answers, don't you?

Rhys leaned over the laptop in disbelief. There was no phone in her hands. There was no way she could have sent the message.

Was there?

When he returned to his window, Annie was no longer out by the front of the house. He looked right. Just a glance, but she was nowhere to be seen. He looked left. And there she was. Up by the entrance of the ginnel.

Another ping from the laptop.

Annie2152215221736121 (9 Nov – 12:03)

You coming or what?

Rhys wasn't naïve. This... whatever this was, it wasn't normal.

But, as it so often did, teenage curiosity got the better of him.

JONNY

Jonny kicked up the brake on Eevie's pushchair, stopping across the bridge at Hanburn Park.

Below them, ducks tracked aimlessly around the pond. One swan, off in the distance, arched its neck in their direction and fluttered its wings before returning to preen its muddied feathers. It reminded Jonny of how the regulars were down at the local pub when they took a break from their pint of cheap lager to give him a nod. Nothing more, nothing less. Just a shared dip of the chin as the sole sign of acknowledgement.

Who knows if the swan recognised them as they hitched up? The four of them — he, Eevie, Liz, and Rhys — used to come to this spot all the time when they had a quiet weekend, Eevie cradling a bag full of bread just as she would her favourite toy.

Used to. . .

The phrase that seemed to be the preface to every conversation and thought over the last few months.

While the McIntyres used to come here for a day out together, Hanburn Park was merely a convenient destination for Jonny that morning. It was the first place that came to mind where he felt might be safe.

It was late morning. The town would surely be rammed. Not just with weekend shoppers, but with football fans getting their first couple of pints in before heading to the ground. Jonny knew that routine well. Before kids were on the scene, he used to be one of them.

But the town meant more people. More people meant more eyes. Anywhere with more eyes was to be avoided.

Everything seemed to have become more intense over the last two days, Jonny thought. The things — impossible things — that had previously only lived in his mind and nightmares were now bleeding into his reality more often. At first, it had been difficult to comprehend for him. It couldn't be real. Surely not. Now, he was having a harder time saying otherwise.

Last night, he'd woken up past 11, alerted by a creaking floorboard and faint footsteps on the stairs and landing.

He'd lay there listening. Next to him, Liz lay undisturbed.

As the footsteps ceased, the door had begun to inch open. The soft and slow brush against the carpet told him so.

Jonny had turned to face it, watching, his body stiff and too damn scared to move, his breathing broken. The feeling he used to get when he was alone in the house as a kid while his dad was pulling another all-night bender.

The feeling a kid gets when they believe there is a monster hiding in the closet. Turns out as you got older, those monsters decided to leave the closet.

The door brushed to a stop, leaving just enough of a gap for Jonny to see a black figure — a human figure, Jonny was sure — standing out on the landing.

It had disappeared in the blink of an eye and against his better judgement, Jonny decided he needed to search for it. He scoured the house from top to bottom as quietly as he could, the kitchen knife he had been taking to bed with him gripped in his right hand and ready to swing.

But, just like every other time, there was never anyone — or anything — there.

After that, Jonny couldn't go back to bed. Jonny knew he'd not be able to go back to sleep and didn't want to run the risk of waking Liz. So, he'd taken watch over the house from his recliner, armed, listening, waiting, before he disappeared down to the shed close to 5 in the morning, once he heard Eevie rouse.

Jonny was able to nod off in small blocks but his body refused him a decent kip. He'd gotten used to watching the night get filtered out by the new morning light. And this morning, fuelled with a can of Monster and some painkillers, he'd walked up to the kitchen just after 10.

"Another rough night?" Liz had asked as Jonny held himself up by the cabinet, his nose sucking in the pungent fumes of black coffee.

"Yeah... sorry."

"No offence but you look like crap."

It was then she'd hit him with it. "You've spent enough time down in that shed this week. Go and take Eevie for a walk. Not just around the estate either. I mean a proper walk, like those we used to (*there it was again*). It'd do you both good."

Even as every instinct in his body screamed at him to say no, to make up an excuse, he couldn't.

How could he?

And so, here he was, out at Hanburn Park on the cusp of winter, its paths empty but for a few dog walkers, its murky pond sprinkled with fallen leaves, reflecting the faint morning light.

Jonny lifted Eevie out of her seat and held her tightly.

At first, he whispered in her ear and pointed with his other hand out to a group of ducks that swam around peacefully, paddling along without a care in the world.

She didn't react. Not like she used to.

Used to...

He held her tighter, gently holding her head into the fabric of his hoodie. Warm tears began to trickle down his face.

RHYS

From Sandon Mount, they'd walked the outskirts of town and across a field.

Farmland made up of dense uncut grass that brushed at Rhys' ankles like soft bristles. The smell of cow crap gave no space to the crisp pre-winter air on this land.

Rhys halted. His trainers sank into the soft ground in protest. He'd regretted wearing his nice Nikes the moment he'd landed his jump into the fields off of the fence.

"Come on, you promised answers," Rhys pressed.

But Annie forged ahead without a backward glance. She was in total control.

She knew it.

Rhys knew it.

He conceded defeat and continued to trudge through the grass, trying to keep up with Annie, who glided out in front.

At the end of the field, Rhys clambered over another fence, landing on a pathway running alongside an old stone wall.

Rhys knew exactly where he was, where they were going.

A place that was practically on his doorstep but lived out of sight and out of mind for good reason.

Annie stood at the entrance to Furarche Woods, waiting for him to catch up.

There were two types of people that Furarche Woods attracted, according to Rhys' dad.

By day, it brought your dog walkers and local strollers. By Friday night, though, it was where kids on the cusp of adulthood — those at the strange age where they don't quite pass for 18 — drank themselves silly and experimented with pills and powders and joints. Out of sight, out of mind.

For the latter, it was easy to see why Furarche Woods appealed. Even from Rhys' position at the entrance, the woodlands sprawled with thick, towering trees that cast a perpetual blanket of shade over the footpaths, even on the lightest of days.

"What we doing here?" Rhys asked, testing the waters. Annie only offered a look of derision.

"Gotcha. We'll see, right?" he responded.

On they went.

Overhead, leaves rustled a prayer in the breeze, mourning the fallen ones that littered the trails below them. Tiny twigs snapped underfoot. Pebbles shifted. Rhys' eyes multi-tasked between looking where he was going and making sure he didn't add a layer of dog crap to the mud on his trainers.

The deeper they entered, the gloomier the woods got. Strangely, the more at peace the woods felt.

"This way," Annie said, breaking off the path sharply into a pack of slender trees.

Rhys followed submissively, manoeuvring around the trunks, pushing away hanging branches that hooked at the fabric of his hoodie. Keeping track of Annie up ahead.

It was pretty clear from the array of crushed beer cans, flattened cardboard crates, and empty bottles of WKD and cheap cider (as well as other things that won't be spoken of) that this wasn't where the dog walkers meandered through.

Eventually, they emerged out into a clearing enveloping a single tree, one that didn't stand as tall as its other brothers and sisters, but was thicker at the trunk base that split off in two directions, forcing the body to slope. The Leaning Tower of Pisa sprang to Rhys' mind.

The black sheep of the Furarche Woods family.

The surrounding space bathed in beams of sunlight. Rhys stood in awe, imagining the type of photos he would get in that light.

Up ahead, Annie, cloaked in a shadow projected from the tree behind, probably anticipated Rhys was about to say something.

"Don't. . . Just watch."

The wind hushed, swallowing every sound in a curtain of silence.

Annie's arms lifted in unison, fingers meeting above her head to create a pyramid point.

Rhys half-expected her to launch into a ballet performance. She maintained that illusion as she stepped forward, her arms maintaining a precise right angle. Annie began to take slow, careful steps forward, like she was balancing a tightrope.

And then Rhys saw it.

The trail her spotless white trainers were leaving behind.

Clean and vivid purple and pink flowers — just like the lotus Rhys had drawn Eevie for her fourth birthday, just like the ones that had climbed his neighbour's house earlier that morning — sprouted from the Earth wherever her feet touched, forming a trail of inexplicable and impossible beauty.

Rhys stood rooted to the spot, flummoxed. His mouth hung half open. His eyes disbelieved what was happening right in front of him.

Annie spun gracefully, shedding her usual icy demeanour for a moment of warmth, her lips softening into an uncommon genuine smile as she stepped into the illuminated space outside the tree's shadow.

The rustle of branches above stole Rhys' attention. Birds, flocks of them, dropped in for Annie's show, resting on the branches and watching in wonder.

As Annie continued, Rhys knelt, letting his fingers caress the lotus head closest to him. Convinced it wouldn't be real. That his mind was playing a trick on his eyes. That all Annie was doing was pulling off an insanely good magic trick.

Yet, the flower felt as real as the soil it rested on.

Annie's feet came into his eyeline, the tips of her trainers tickling a petal of the lotus.

Rhys looked from the lotus up to Annie's face. He fell on his backside as her natural brown eyes turned black.

"You see me, don't you, Rhys? The real me."

Rhys traced a finger across the initials etched into the trunk of the tree.

JM + ES

The carvings within the heart were uneven and raw, with the letters embedded deeply and ingrained into the wood.

Those initials weren't alone either. Many inscriptions decorated the stout trunk of this odd tree, a wallpaper of lives cut into it.

Rhys' thoughts tangled. Could it be? Maybe, he told himself.

He thought of the old Swiss army knife his dad used for carving. The one Rhys' grandad — the one he never met — had passed down to his dad when he turned 16. Inevitably, it would end up in Rhys' hands when he was older, too. He'd been obsessed with that knife when he was younger.

It had held a magnetic allure for him as a child, a polished wooden handle in an aged yet pristine condition. His dad would let him hold the knife sometimes, even though it always had to be closed.

That knife made Rhys feel like a grown-up, like he was part of what his dad was doing.

"You know the rules. Be careful and... Don't. Tell. Mum."

Together, they'd whisper those words in sync.

One of many little things the two of them used to share.

Rhys looked back at the initials engraved into the tree. He wondered whether his dad had carved them. Maybe. But, damn, there had got to be a so many other *JMs* and *ESs* that lived around in the area. It was a big town, after all.

"Rhys?"

Annie's voice disrupted his thoughts. He craved answers, but never anticipated this. There was too much to process, much of it seeming implausible, the type of stuff that languished on the

Quora and Reddit conspiracy forums Rhys had been finding himself on more and more recently.

This was no conspiracy, though. How could it be? He'd seen it with his own eyes. The impossible becoming a tangible reality.

Yet still, he needed to make sense of it.

He kept his eyes fixed on the trunk, unable to look at the girl who stood behind him. He took a hard gulp, gathering the courage to speak.

"Ok, so... you are kind of like a ghost?"

"No. But if that helps you make sense of this, let's go with it."

"And... what? You say you're a version of...?"

"Karma. Close enough."

A girl called Karma.

"And I can see you because..."

"You're special," she said dryly. As though he should have known the answer.

"Come on."

"Ok. Because you became 'susceptible' to Us."

"Us? There's more than just you?"

"Am I *really* going to have to keep repeating myself? Yes. And that's because..." She was starting to sound like one of the inpatient teachers at St Andrews waiting for someone — anyone — to show they were paying attention and pipe up with an answer.

"Because all of us have a...?" Rhys choked on the last word of his sentence.

"Karma. Right."

"Eff off. This is bonkers."

"A load of scheisse, right?"

Rhys turned from the tree to face her again, finding a wood thrush perched on the end of Annie's finger, observing him curiously. Its head jerked one way and then the other in stunted photographic motion.

Annie fiddled with its tail before it flew back off to join its friends that were still hanging around the surrounding treetops, waiting in anticipation for whatever was to come next.

"So, there are others? Like me? That can see..." his hands moved back and forth, the words were still clogged in his throat.

"Karma. You can say it."

"And when I see someone's eyes turn black like yours did, I'm actually seeing someone's... Karma... what? Inside them?"

"Check you out, clever clogs."

"Come on, you don't need to be like that." The words came out in a sulk.

"Sorry." A quick roll of the eyes and a raise of the eyebrows was enough to tell Rhys that Annie wasn't sorry at all.

A brief interlude passed, caught in the cool breeze that had re-joined them in the clearing.

"Ok, so... are you my Karma."

"Bingo bongo."

Another question simmered, one that he was afraid to ask but needed — wanted — to know the answer to.

"Are you... are you here to punish me then?"

"Punish?" For the first time, Annie looked confused, like she'd been caught off guard.

"You know... like the saying goes... Karma's a bitch. I don't know..." he gave a swift shrug of the shoulders. "Like nature's way of payback or revenge or something for the things I've done."

"Gotta be honest, Rhys, I expected better from you. You don't *really* think that, do you? That Karma is like some sort of sidekick to the Grim Reaper? A bad-ass that goes around punishing bad people?"

"I dunno. Maybe."

Annie shook her head, disappointed. She stepped back and her body began to levitate, rising as slowly as a balloon. She sat herself down on the thick branch hanging above them. Rhys accepted what happened as though it was perfectly normal.

Annie planted her arms beside her slight frame and began kicking her legs, back and forth, back and forth, just like any other kid would do. Rhys followed suit. Annie's eye colour shifted back to that intense black, locking onto him.

"You think you deserve to be punished?"

He can't say the words. He just bites his top lip and shrugs again.

"For what? For what happened to your sister? You think I'm here to punish you for that."

The words, the confirmation, the finality of them, made Rhys feel sick and heavy, the way he did during those first few days.

After.

"Look at me... I'm not here to teach you some sort of lesson. You're doing a pretty neat job of trying to do that to yourself."

"Then why're you here? Why now?"

"Karma, or me in this case, we're not a bad-ass sidekick that goes around beating on people who make mistakes or bad decisions. Not like you think, anyway. Everyone has a Karma. Most of the time, we stay within and act a bit like a moral compass. You've heard of gut feeling, right? Doesn't exist. Not really. That feeling you get comes from us. But during every life, a person makes good decisions and they also make bad decisions and indifferent decisions. There's no black and white. And it's a mix of those decisions that will guide a person down a certain path. But, sometimes, and this is where We come in, there needs to be an intervention. Times when we need to step in and try and correct a path. That's why I'm here, why you can see me. Your trauma, what happened to your sister on that beach, has taken you down a path that you need guiding away from before..."

"Before what?"

"Before it's too late."

The words made Rhys shuffle uncomfortably against the tree's arm.

"You might not think it or see it but you're stuck, Rhys. You're stuck on an endless path of grief and blame. You blame yourself. You're grieving for what happened to your sister. For most people, that's natural, but you, you're on a closed loop you can't break out of. You've built up all this negative energy and if you don't break away from it, if you don't break away from this path, it will eat you up. That's why I'm here. To show you that you can forgive. That you can move on. That you are a good person. That there's still so much good you can bring."

"You make it sound easy. Like you can fix me with a snap of your fingers." Rhys' response was petulant. A tear gripped to the corner of his eye, threatening to spill.

"Well, let me ask you this... do you want to be on the path you're currently on? You want to keep feeling like this and letting assholes like Conor keep beating on you because you believe you deserve it for what happened to Eevie?"

He shook his head.

"Good, then let's try and get you off it. Trust me, you don't want the alternative."

"What's that?"

"That it takes over you completely. To the point that it's the only thing that you think about. I've seen it Rhys... it takes people to the grave."

"Maybe that's what I deserve."

"Talk like that again and I will turn into a bad-ass sidekick and give you another black eye to go with the one that you've got?"

The words coax a smirk from Rhys. "Well, at least I'd deserve that one then."

"Wise-ass."

Annie's eyes flick again, the black hue that covered them returned to a more appealing natural brown. She launched herself off the tree and landed with the grace of a gymnast.

"It'll be dark soon. You should get back. You've got one pissed-off mother waiting for you. She was looking forward to that afternoon out with you."

She turned away, back in the direction they came.

The two of them made their way back to the entrance of Furarche Woods.

In the distance, back towards town, the moon, previously hidden by an army of trees, was now visible, swelling towards fullness, hanging low in between dark wispy clouds, ready to take over the night shift from the fading sun.

Rhys scaled the fence he'd hopped over a few hours back, pausing midway when he noticed Annie wasn't following.

"You not coming?" he shouted.

"Nah, you're on your own from here."

"Ok. When will I see you next?"

"Soon."

"How soon?"

"Real soon. Now be off with you. There's a storm brewing."

As if by coincidence, a breeze blew across Rhys' face and nipped at his ears. Even through his thick hoodie, he was starting to feel the early evening chill.

He nodded at Annie and smiled timidly. She stood firm on the path, hands tucked away into the pockets of her plain black hoodie. She looked just like any other girl. One that has spent the day with her friends, enjoying the last remnants of a Saturday, about to head back home for dinner with her family and to settle in to watch a cookie-cutter movie.

However, looks can be deceiving — Annie was unlike any other girl Rhys had ever known.

He hopped over the other side and back into the farmland. His hands clung to the wood panels, almost refusing to let go. If he hung back long enough, maybe Annie would change her mind.

"Goodbye for now, Rhys McIntyre."

"Sure," his hands relinquished their grip. He accepted he was making the trek back home on his own.

He only took a few steps when Annie's voice called back out.

"Oh, and Rhys, word to the wise. Give Ralph a chance, yeah?"

"Ralph? As in Ralph Steadman? At school?"

"The very same."

Rhys pictured Ralph. The kid who was even smaller than he was. Head bowed, hidden under a hood, absorbed in his Nintendo Switch. The kid that, just like Rhys, hid away during lunchtime in the library. Sat on the same corner, lunchbox sat by him where a friend should be.

"Sure thing."

"He'll be good for you. You've got more in common than you think."

JONNY

It was late. Jonny didn't need a clock to know that.

As normal, he'd gone to bed a little after Liz had called it a night. He climbed under the sheets and closed his eyes. He'd given up hope of drifting off. The slightest of noises disrupted him. Had him on edge. Thinking about where it was coming from and what was causing it.

Then came the creak from the stairs that permeated the stillness of the night.

Jonny's back was to the bedroom door. His arm wrapped over Liz, her body rising slowly up and down with her deep breathing and light snoring. The tiny green light on the baby monitor on her bedside table, awoken from its two-year slumber earlier this summer when he'd dug it out of one of Eevie's old boxes and brought it down from the loft, blinked away behind a glass of water.

The alarm clock showed 11:03.

Another groan, closer this time. It reverberated through the floorboard outside their bedroom.

He slid his arm away from Liz slowly and rolled onto his other side, bracing himself for what he'd see through the small wedge left by the semi-open door.

Sure enough, there it was.

The black, ominous figure. An echo of the previous night.

Jonny remained still, refusing to let his tired eyes blink. He slid a hand under his top pillow and felt for the handle of the chef's knife that remained by his side.

The figure, the shadow — this thing that had been living in his nightmares — casually retreated back towards the top of the stairs.

Jonny wasn't going to let it slip away.

Not this time.

He swung his legs out of bed, barefoot and clad only in his boxers. His rough hand gripped the knife.

By the time he'd reached the top of the stairs, The Thing was at the bottom, turning sharply towards the kitchen. It moved with quick and silent steps. There and then gone in the blink of an eye.

Jonny sacrificed pace for caution, taking the steps one at a time. He used the stair spindles he'd installed himself to peek down the hallway. His butt hugged the wall under the array of family photos that had grown over the years.

His knife hand was up, ready to swing if needed.

The wind howled against the front door, rain peppering its surface. At the foot of the stairwell, spits of light from the street lamps cut through the front door window, intersecting with another stream that came through from the living room into the hallway. The smell of lavender air freshener still lingered. The cold always settled harsher in that part of the house and it bit at Jonny's bare skin.

With controlled slow breaths, Jonny held the knife up at chest level and readjusted his grip with a clammy hand. The muscles in his arm tensed. Even with that knife, he was scared as hell.

His eyes were locked on the kitchen. His limited visibility was only aided by three blocks of moonlight that rested at an angle on the floor below the sink.

It was only when he'd reached the kitchen that he spotted the figure again.

It wasn't in the house, though.

No. It stood motionless out in the back garden, caught under the moon's spotlight.

Jonny approached the worktop. He stared at It. He, in turn, assumed It was staring right back at him. A wordless exchange crackled between them.

He ran to the back door and yanked the handle. If it was an intruder it had to be unlocked. He couldn't explain it but he wasn't surprised when it wasn't. He glanced a look over his shoulder to make sure It was still out there in the garden as he fumbled around aimlessly for the key on the window sill.

Once he'd found it, he wrenched the door open and ran into the rain.

RHYS

He'd heard the movement out on the landing over the low hum of music from his headphones.

Sleep had been evasive. Rhys had tossed and turned. He'd forced his eyelids to close and clenched them, willing himself to drop off as he listened to the brewing storm outside and the ticking of his bedside clock.

After about an hour, he finally admitted that thoughts of Annie and the afternoon at Furarche Woods still had him totally wired. After an hour of futile attempts, Rhys finally gave in and turned on his Nintendo Switch to play a remake of *Ichigo: A Child of the Sea* — a game his dad adored back in the '90s.

Rhys had been playing for a good hour when he'd heard hurried steps from his parents' bedroom. That itself wasn't unusual. His dad often wandered downstairs at odd hours, never to return. But this time, it wasn't just the footsteps. The kitchen door slammed shut abruptly a few moments later, cutting off a wail of wind as quickly as it came.

Rhys paused the game, dropped the Switch on his bed, and headed downstairs.

The cold that lurked at the bottom half of the house pinched through his pyjamas.

"Dad," he whispered.

Once. Twice. Three times.

But the house was silent.

He peeked into the living room before focusing on the kitchen.

And there he was.

Rhys saw his dad outside, standing beyond the erratic bursts of rain that battered the window, his eyes wide with fear. His dad glanced around frantically, scanning the yard as if searching for something — or someone. Whatever it was that had him so agitated.

Only stopping when he noticed Rhys watching him from inside.

After a few tense moments, he gave up and hurried back inside, soaked to the bone. Rain dripped from the ends of his tousled hair. His skin, speckled with raindrops, was turning blotchy, his usual pale turning pink and red.

"What're you doing up?" his dad asked, holding back his chattering teeth.

His hands trembled as he faced Rhys, who noticed a knife clenched in his dad's grip.

JONNY

"Don't worry about that. I thought I saw something out in the garden."

Jonny stowed the knife on the kitchen worktop, out of sight. His shivering limbs betrayed the cold that had pierced through him. Drops of rain ran off his hair and face. He grabbed the nearest tea towel and patted himself down.

"Saw what?" Rhys inquired.

"Nothing. It doesn't matter," Jonny deflected evasively, keeping the towel covered over his eyes. Just in case.

Rhys' eyes had been as they should when he first came into the kitchen. His hereditary hazel lit up in the moon's rays. Still, there was no telling when or if they would change.

"Come on, it's way past your bedtime, bud. Get yourself back up. I'll get cleaned up here and be right behind you."

A blatant lie.

"You sure everything's ok?"

"Positive. Now, go on."

And with that, Rhys departed.

His son had glanced back at him at the foot of the stairwell, the darkness cloaking him as a silhouette. Jonny gave him a final comforting *everything's ok* nod. Jonny waited, ears trained for the fading steps along the landing, before he pulled the towel away from his face.

But everything was far from ok.

He kept listening out. First for the creaks of floorboards and then finally for the brush of carpet that would inevitably come as Rhys closed his bedroom door.

The dam burst.

Tears broke down Jonny's soaked face as he hunched over the kitchen sink.

"What do you want? What do you want? What do you want?"

The words came out in quiet chokes.

As he looked back out to the night and the rain and the wind that consumed the outside world, he was sure he saw It again.

Fleetingly.

There one second and gone again, absorbed by the shadows.

ELISA

2007

It's a strange feeling, returning to a place you never thought you'd step foot in again.

After my train chugged into the station, a tiny set-up with two open platforms outside of town, I caught a taxi. It navigated the familiar streets, buildings, and people I'd left behind. Everything looked the same as I left it — aside from the odd crane here and a renovation taking place there. Its high streets would look different again just over a year later when the Great Recession set in.

The security shutters, once drawn only at night, now remained a permanent feature for some emptied high street businesses and shops. The locals and indies didn't stand a chance against the tidal wave of chains and online boom.

I didn't find myself suddenly overwhelmed by a hidden flood of emotion or sentiment at being back — only resurfacing disdain.

That didn't surprise me. What I hadn't anticipated, though, was the nagging uncertainty that crept in during those first initial days and nights, as I'd settled into my new shared house, wondering whether I'd made the right call coming back.

Self-doubt isn't my forte. Contemplating opening up old wounds is one thing, but the actual act of prying them open is an entirely different ordeal.

But any hesitation I felt dissolved the moment I laid eyes on *her* for the first in over a decade.

You can glean a lot from a quick poke around social websites like Facebook and Bebo.

Everyone's so public on there, sharing mundane updates no one cares about in the hope of attracting digital validation.

I find it all so sad.

With my sister, though, both Facebook and Bebo were my friends.

During the months I waited for the sale of The Bay View Inn to clear, I'd spent time learning who Elizabeth's friends were. Where they hung out, the things she liked to do, what was on her mind, what she and her boyfriend Jonny got up to, and also where she worked.

It was that last point that gave me my way in.

Three days after leaving Ireland, I called up the Waterstones she worked at as a bookseller, according to my new friend, Facebook. I left it until the middle of the morning to find out if she was in that day. The voice that answered wasn't hers but that of her purported 'work wife' Torey.

I'd seen plenty of her across Elizabeth's Facebook. A hip gal with her hair faded at the sides below a short messy mop of blonde hair that was stained with pink highlights. She flaunted flashy fake nails, wore colourful and bold makeup, and often chose cocktail dresses that left little to the imagination.

As I always did, I introduced myself as Jessica Thomas and placed an order for a paperback copy of *If I Stay*. Just for the record here, I did want the book. It was a convenient excuse for my call.

And before letting Torey go, who layered her phone voice on thicker than clotted cream, I said I had discussed a separate order with an Elizabeth Stallard (I think that was her name, I added for extra measure) a couple of days before and asked whether she was in that day. I spun a tale that she'd been ever so helpful and I wanted to come by the store to thank her in person.

"Awww, babe, that's sooooo sweet. Liz will love that," Torey said the words with sickening sweetness. Too much of it was enough to give you a tummy ache.

Torey told me my sister wasn't in that day but that she would be back in first thing tomorrow and I could call back then.

I thanked Torey for her help and hung up. I had no intention of calling back.

The following morning, I secured a prime spot near the front window of a café named Blue Jays, conveniently positioned directly across from the Waterstones.

I'd got there in plenty of time and sorted myself out with a flat white, a granola and yoghurt pot, and a brownie (we all deserve a treat from time to time).

I kept watch of the entrance in between sporadic spoonfuls of granola, just in case Elizabeth was an early riser. The coffee machines were whirring away in the background as cups got filled and more orders got taken.

It's hard for me to say now whether I'd got caught up in the moment, had a lapse in judgment, or was just downright stupid, but what I hadn't accounted for was that Elizabeth could actually come into Blue Jays herself.

And yep, you've guessed it, that's exactly what happened.

She practically passed right by me, almost shattering my plan before it had even begun. Jonny, decked in his construction hi-vis gear, opened the door for her and she bounded in, inches separating us, with a spring in her step.

I watched as they joined the queue and ordered their coffees to go. My mug took on the role of a shield for the bottom half of my face as I surveyed them and got a feel for the woman she'd become.

Nothing much had changed at all. She'd had the obvious growth spurt and developed a cluster of acne on her cheeks. But she was still as plain and unassuming as I remembered her.

Just happier.

Her eyes and smile glowed with love whenever she looked at Jonny. I sat there knowing I could wipe her beaming grin right from her face with a simple tap on the shoulder and a '*hello there. How have you been, little sister?*'

I thought about it. How satisfying it would be.

But that wasn't the plan. I hadn't come back to shoot my shot in one go.

Instead, my focus was on the guy paying for their takeout coffee.

It was about a week later when I saw Jonny again, this time far more intentionally.

He was across from me at the lager-stained bar of The Brown Spaniel. I'd used Facebook to stake him out as well, you see. It had been easy to work out that the Spaniel was his local boozer. He had a stream of photos and posts tagging him at this pub, mostly from Friday nights.

And true to form, there he was. Out with the boys at the starting line for a night that would inevitably end at one of the beat-up nightclubs in the town centre and a dirty kebab and cheesy chips to finish with.

The only prize on offer for making it to that point would be a vicious hangover the next morning.

I have to be honest. I could see the appeal with Jonny. He was far better looking in the flesh than when I'd first gazed upon him on social media.

But there was always something that inevitably let a man down. Jonny's flaw was his taste in clothes. He stood a few feet from me. Long sleeve top, baggy jeans that looked like they'd had the colour sucked out of them, scuffed trainers tied together by laces that flopped around like bunny ears. He embraced minimal effort. A look that said that, unlike some of his mates, Jonny wasn't out to impress.

I listened closely as he got in a round of shots. Sambuca. The devil's drink. His pals were lairy over in the corner, shouting profanities and breaking out into fits of belly laughter, as young men often do that don't have a care in the world. I watched Jonny join in from his spot at the grotty bar as the bartender filled a tray of shot glasses with his order of liquid death.

All I needed was a passing glance.

Sure enough, it came. Jonny had handed over a couple of notes to the girl behind the bar. Our eyes met briefly as he received his change from the bartender, my carefully applied red lipstick drawing his eyes in. It was a fleeting connection, but it was enough.

I sat back and sipped at my wine, satisfied as he retreated to his chums in the corner. I watched them as they clinked the tips of the tiny glasses and necked the sambucas in unison. The glasses banged against the table. They scrunched their faces up and sipped their pints to strip away the aftertaste.

I got another glance from Jonny. This time it came hand-in-hand with a smile.

Jonny was back up at the bar half an hour later in need of another pint of cider. I downed the last tiny pool of my wine and closed the gap between us, resting on my elbows. A matter of inches separated our waists. I hoped the freshly applied splash of Daisy perfume would overpower that scent of rank beer.

Breaking the ice was easy.

"Looks like a big night's on the cards," I remarked softly, knowing the jukebox and the raucous chatter swirling around us would swallow my words.

He hadn't heard me. Of course he hadn't. And so he leaned in close, placing a hand on my bare shoulder. I remember the cheap Paul Smith aftershave he wore that night. I tilted my head back, my lips inches from his lobe, and repeated myself.

That's how it started.

We chatted a little as he made quick work of his latest pint. He was tipsy at that point and would undoubtedly be as drunk as a skunk later on. His friends winked and teased him as they passed by us on their way to the gents, their seals broken. One of them — his name escapes me — said they'd be leaving in five minutes for the next bar on the night's hit list.

Soon after, they rolled out the door one by one, hands clasped around each other's shoulders like a wild version of the conga. They beckoned him to join the back of the line.

"It's been good chatting. Maybe I'll see you around," he'd said.

"Maybe," I replied.

After that first night at The Brown Spaniel, I'd made a habit of showing my face on a Friday night. Most of the time, he would show. I said something like 'hey stranger.' He'd smile. I'd smile. He'd go about his night. I'd go about mine.

But the pace felt too slow for my taste. I'm used to guys taking the lead, but Jonny showed no inclination to make that move — even when one of his buddies tried his luck.

It was the middle of spring when I decided to give Jonny a nudge in the right direction. I left him the number of a burner phone I'd bought when I'd moved back from Ireland, slipping it, old school, over to him on a paper napkin while he got in a tray of shots — yes, a lot more sambuca.

Control is crucial to me. So, you can imagine my frustration when the next phase of my plan rested entirely on Jonny and whether he'd grow some balls and get in touch.

There was no text or call for nearly a week.

That irritated me.

A lot.

I could feel my window of opportunity closing and by that following Wednesday, my nights had become consumed by thinking about what I was going to do next.

But then the tables turned. It was a Thursday night. I was in my room with a glass of cheap wine, watching whatever was playing on my second-hand TV, when my phone vibrated on the bed next to me. I didn't need to recognise the number.

There was only one person who had the number for this phone.

"Hey, u goin 2 be at the Spaniel tomorrow?"

Remember what I said earlier? About getting caught up in the moment, making a foolish mistake at Blue Jays? Well, with Jonny, I was, unequivocally, foolish.

For the first time in my life, I'd fallen in love. Head over heels, stupid, silly, in love.

To be clear, this *wasn't* the plan. I merely wanted to get under his skin and drive a big old wedge between him and my sister and help him see her for what she really was. She doted on him, just as I'd doted on my two sisters back at Aston Orphanage. I wanted to take that away from her, just as she had done to me all those years ago.

Maybe it was Karma's doing. My punishment for what some would call meddling. I ended up having a stake in the game, becoming entangled in something I never intended to. I fell for a man who was only supposed to be a pawn in my plan.

We'd been seeing each other in secret for around six months when Jonny decided to break things off. Coincidentally, it had also been the last time he and I had spoken.

We were back at the Spaniel (where else). It was a few weeks before Christmas. Jonny, still in his work overalls, had snagged a quiet booth. His scent of hard labour enveloped him as much as the overalls. I love that smell of a man, that musty odour. Far more than any spray of Joop, Paco Rabanne, or Klein. I didn't mind it stealing my nose's attention from the initial waft of evening meals; turkey, beef, chicken, roasted potatoes, gravy, and mint sauce that filled the room when I'd rushed in to escape the rain that was coming down by the bucket load outside.

Jonny had got in my usual large white wine order waiting for me, fizzing away. But I had no intention of touching it. You see, I'd come to the Spaniel with my own news to share that night. An early Christmas present, if you will.

I'd sat across from Jonny and probably made some pathetic clichéd comment about how shit the weather was, building up the courage to drop the grand reveal. I had no inkling about what was going to happen next. It was only when I reached out to take his hand and lose my fingers in his that I realised something wasn't right.

Jonny slid his hand out of my reach. His face was a picture of agony.

"I can't do this no more," he'd said.

I feigned ignorance, asking him what he meant, though I knew exactly what he meant.

It's ironic, isn't it, that my initial plan had been to get under his skin and drive a wedge between him and my sister? Yet, here I was, in this tiny corner booth, a total bystander, watching on as a chasm opened between me and Jonny before my very eyes, and could do nothing to stop it.

"This about Liz, yeah?" I asked, holding back a tear, my anger seething beneath the surface.

His silence was the only confirmation I needed.

A glass smashed in the background. The pub erupted around us, mocking the poor sod that had dropped his pint en route to the bar. They could quite easily have been mocking me as well, the woman in the corner booth who was being dumped by the guy she unexpectedly fell hard for just before Christmas.

She got what she deserved, some would say.

"How'd she find out?" I asked.

"Does it matter?"

"Tell me."

"Torey."

"Torey?"

"She caught us last weekend at Geppettos."

Geppettos. It was a café we met at during his lunch breaks sometimes. Out of town. Far enough away to comfortably feel like we wouldn't bump into anyone who might recognise us and start asking questions.

And that was that. Jonny, spineless as he was, said he was sorry. He necked the remainder of his cider and climbed to his feet. I didn't look at his face. I couldn't. But he stopped, for the briefest of moments, by my side.

"I... I'm sorry."

They were the last words he said to me before he trudged towards the exit.

That rogue tear made its escape as everyone around me continued to have a good time.

Fuck it.

I grabbed the glass of wine and necked it.

That night might have been the last time I talked to Jonny, but it wasn't because I didn't try.

Texts went unanswered, calls went to voicemail. His voicemail was the only trace of his voice I had left. It felt like he'd erased me from his life completely. Like I meant nothing.

It's unbelievable what you can do with digital photographs these days. With software like Photoshop, you can alter, tweak, and cut them to create a whole new narrative. That's how I saw what happened between Jonny and me. It was as though he took all our shared moments, our memories, and edited me out.

We were happy. We really were. We'd talked about a future together, a future where he left Elizabeth. A future where we started a new life together somewhere else.

I should have known better.

Anyway, after a couple of days of being ignored, I had to see him. I couldn't help myself. I knew they had a house together out on Wayborough Falls. I'd dropped Jonny off at the bottom of the street a few times when we'd seen each other and so I'd jumped in the old Corsa I'd bought after moving back from Ireland and drove over there.

Wayborough Falls was bleak, a neglected road flanked by worn-out Council houses — not an inch between them. The sky hung heavy, a thick, dark grey blanket.

It was a Sunday, and I'd pulled up on the street around mid-morning. I was being driven totally by impulse and had not thought about what I'd do once I'd pulled my handbrake up and killed the ignition. I know there's more to it, but all I could think about was that he'd chosen *this*. He'd chosen *this* over me.

While I was busy psyching myself up, their front door opened. Jonny appeared first, bundled up in a thick, yellow winter coat. He stood off to the side, and that's when *she* appeared. Elizabeth, too, wore a coat over a cotton jumper and it was then that I saw it, the small, but undeniable bump of her belly.

I felt a storm raging inside me. Anger drowned out any other emotion I might have had. Jonny stepped aside, offering a hand to Elizabeth. She ignored it, walking past him. Her demeanour was far from the merry girl I'd seen at Blue Jays six months earlier.

She headed straight to their car's passenger side, leaving Jonny behind to lock up the house.

I followed as they drove out to a car park on the edge of town.

We were outside Furarche Woods.

I hung back and parked up across from them, watching as they climbed out and pulled on walking shoes from the boot. I watched again as Jonny offered to help Elizabeth out, so she didn't have to bend down and put pressure on that *precious* bump of hers. But just as she did back at the house, she shrugged him away — this time with a brisk waft of a stubborn arm.

They walked on into the woods, an invisible barrier keeping a gap between them. I made my move, burying my head under a thick hood while I grabbed the large kitchen knife I'd brought with me from the footwell and tucked it inside my coat.

The scent of damp earth and rain filled the air. In those woods, my footwear choice backfired; my flats got caked in mud, and the cold seeped into my feet.

I kept a safe distance from Jonny and Elizabeth, making sure I had enough cover between me and them that they'd mistake me for just another person out for a Sunday stroll.

There was only one other person insane enough to be out here today, a lonely man with a springer spaniel that raced away ahead of him, full of beans. It'd had a good sniff around my feet before returning to its owner.

On we go.

After about 10 or so minutes, Jonny and Elizabeth had travelled deep into the woods. There was no one else around us and I pulled the knife out from inside my coat and stuffed it into my pocket. My impulses were kicking in again and I only had one thought running around in my mind, chugging away like a runaway train.

I was going to kill them both.

But then they peeled away from the path and into a pack of trees. I thought they might have spotted me and were trying to get away. For a moment, they had escaped my eyeline. I panicked and ran to where I'd last seen them.

They came back into view and I hung back behind a large trunk, watching as Jonny led Elizabeth around clusters of trees and through into a clearing. I followed, keeping myself covered where I could until they stopped next to a single tree that looked disfigured in its centre.

They were staring at the thick trunk, talking. I couldn't make any of what they said out. All I kept thinking at that moment was how perfect this was. We were away from the path, totally out of sight. It could be days before anyone would find them here.

I grasped the knife and went to make my move.

That was when I felt it. The unrelenting knot in my stomach.

It was a pain like no other I had ever experienced.

One that took me down.

I tore the back of my coat as I slid against a tree and collapsed onto the ground. I'd had cramping before, but nothing like this.

This time, it hit me like a truck, out of nowhere, and I was doing everything I could to conceal the agony burning from my stomach, desperate not to alert Jonny and Elizabeth to my presence. I covered a chilly hand over my mouth and squeezed hard.

Pinned by the pain at the base of that tree, I struggled in the mud, an invisible force restraining me from fulfilling my purpose. There was no chance of retreating to the car either. I had no choice but to endure it, to wait it out.

I'm not sure how long it took before Jonny and Elizabeth started walking back towards me. The rain still spattered as they headed my way. If I stayed put, they would definitely spot me. I curled up for cover and bit down hard on my hand to stifle any sounds.

I could only watch as they made their way back to the path.

Until recently, that had been one of the last times I'd seen Jonny and Elizabeth.

It was also the day that I lost my daughter.

I talked about losing her in a support group meeting a few years later. I was so early — only 9 weeks in — and I remember being asked by another member how I was sure it was a girl.

I told her it had been mother's instinct.

I *knew* I was going to have a girl. And I'd already picked out the name and had pictured my future with her.

Annie.

MONDAY 11TH NOVEMBER 2019

RHYS AND JONNY

Tick... tick... tick... tick... tick...

Rhys sat slouched in a worn plastic chair, arms dangling by each side like an idle puppet. He was in a pokey office just outside of upper school, mesmerised by the broken minute hand of Mr Roberts' clock.

The room was bland and tasteless. Had to be smaller than his dad's shed at the bottom of the garden, Rhys thought. He considered standing and stretching his arms outwards to test that theory, but didn't want to look foolish should anyone walk in and wonder what the hell he was up to.

The room barely accommodated a corner desk that almost kissed the far wall. Above that were a couple of shelves with a handful of thick paperback books that could double up as doorstoppers, spines wrinkled and ripped. There was also a standard filing cabinet that was crammed in between the wall and doorframe.

That was pretty much it.

Only bits of splitting plaster decorated the box room's bare walls. There were no calendars or pictures or certificates — just that clock that had forgotten how to function properly.

It read 11:27. But Rhys didn't need that clock to know that it was just after 9. His thoughts, much like the erratic minute hand, had been looping around one subject all weekend — Annie, Karma... where to even begin with all of that?

A bang on the door sharply brought him out of his trance. It was stuck against the floor and, after a bit of a struggle, swung and banged against the cabinet. Mr Roberts barrelled in, a mug of something hot in one hand, and a brown leather satchel that rolled against the back of Rhys' chair in the other.

Mr Roberts looked out of place at St Andrews. He wasn't like the rest of the teachers or staff. He was much younger, probably in his late teens or early 20s. Acne scars dotted his face, under a cow lick comb-over, and he didn't have a scratch of facial hair. Rhys reckoned that if the school counsellor swapped his formal pink shirt and dark jeans for a St Andrews uniform, he wouldn't look out of place among the kids in their final year.

"So, how was your weekend?" he asked, after settling into his chair and apologising for being late.

They say first impressions matter, right? And this first question irritated Rhys. A pointless pleasantry. Is this really what he was here for?

"Not bad, I guess," Rhys replied curtly.

There was more, too. Like Mr Roberts was carving out time as he organised himself. This went on for about five minutes — maybe even longer. It was impossible to tell by the stuck clock above. Unlike Rhys, Mr Roberts liked small talk. He spoke about the dismal weather, some 'trashy' film he watched over the weekend on Netflix. Finally, he asked Rhys if he was excited about the school trip later that week.

But, finally, there was a gear shift. From a drawer, Mr Roberts pulled out a couple of sheets of paper and attached them to a clipboard that sat neatly on atop his crossed legs.

From the guy that first came in — a guy that looked barely out of school himself — he now looked in his element, ready for what was about to come.

Rhys wasn't sure he was. He began fidgeting with a loose thread on the cuff of his jumper.

"So, shall we get started," Mr Roberts said.

Dr Nielson leaned forward from his casual pose, elbows resting on his thighs, fingers interlaced.

Jonny could sense the frustration radiating from him.

"Come on, Jonny," he urged. "You haven't come all this way just to look out the window, have you?"

Taking a deep swig of water, Jonny scratched his burning neck. The thought of sitting here and airing his issues left him feeling uncomfortable. He already knew therapy wasn't going to be his thing. He didn't believe talking could resolve his problems, strip them away like old wallpaper. Jonny never thought he'd be 'that guy'.

The whole thing made him feel weaker, incapable of dealing with *this* on his own.

But a promise was a promise. Liz had made him swear that he would give Dr Nielson a chance after he'd admitted to abandoning the first session last week. After all, Dr Nielson had come so highly recommended by one of her gal pals, who also swore that this guy 'worked wonders' on her fella.

From that moment, Jonny had mockingly referred to the man sat across from him, hunched on his elbows, as Worked Wonders

Nielson. A name that, over time, had started to piss Liz off. She'd wanted Jonny to take it seriously, no matter how he felt about it.

So, here he was. Only out of obligation.

Nielson probed again, shifting slightly into Jonny's line of sight. The guy was old. He'd been around the block and back again, but was, seemingly, now enjoying the best that life had to offer. He was well-groomed and well-trimmed. Trendy with a thick cardigan with chinos. A plush and large office to match. Jonny couldn't help but wonder... how could someone like Nielson possibly give a shit about someone like him?

"Shall we?" Nielson asked, his face a picture of steel.

"If we have to," Jonny replied reluctantly.

Mr Roberts scanned over his clipboard notes and played them back to Rhys.

"Looking here, it looks like there have been a few issues with another boy in your class. Conor, right? Shall we start with that?"

Rhys remained silent, his fingers still tugging at that loose thread on his jumper, eyes searching the floor for a response. He was thankful he didn't get a chance to answer.

"Rhys," Mr Roberts softened his tone, setting aside his notes. "I understand it's been tough."

He scooted his chair forward, closing the gap between them.

"Whatever we discuss within these — albeit small — four walls stays here with me. I mean it. Moving to a new school is a big deal. I'm here to listen, and who knows, maybe help make everything a bit easier. Would it help if I shared a bit about myself first? It must be weird pouring everything out to someone you've never spoken to before today."

Rhys nodded, finding himself at least willing to listen.

Mr Roberts gave him a whistle-stop tour of how he came to be at St Andrews. It turns out this guy who looked barely old enough to be out of a school uniform had finished University in the summer just gone, graduating from Edinburgh where he had, unsurprisingly, studied psychology. He'd moved back to town for his mum, who was sick and was struggling to make ends meet. Not the original plan, but "you gotta do what you gotta do sometimes," he said.

He didn't go into what that plan was, but the original career he'd mapped out for himself — back when he was Rhys' age — was that he wanted to be Officer Roberts, rather than Shrink Roberts. Rhys couldn't picture him wearing a police uniform, chasing down the bad guys, baton raised high, screaming stop in the name of the law. It just didn't fit. Mr Roberts agreed.

After finishing, Mr Roberts settled back in his chair, fingers nestled in between one another, a relaxed smile on his face. "It happens a lot in life. Plans rarely turn out exactly as we imagine." How philosophical of him, Rhys thought. But he was anticipating that Mr Roberts was going somewhere with it.

"After going over your notes, I reckon I'd be right in saying that the last few months haven't exactly gone how you thought they would either, right?"

Nielson didn't waste time getting to the point.

"Can you talk me through what happened with your daughter?"

The heaviness of Nielson's question seemed to contract the expansive space around them. The directness of it was uncommon. Most people tiptoed around the subject, afraid to offend or stir up pain.

But that's what they paid Nielson for, right? To navigate the difficult topics everyone else avoided? To tackle what others couldn't? Maybe he was looking for a reaction?

Jonny, however, didn't want to dive into that abyss.

"No? Then where would you like to begin, Jonny?" Nielson said firmly.

Jonny's gaze remained fixed on the world beyond the window, the scenes outside mere flickers against the reflective glass. His gut twisted with tension as he shifted in his seat.

"No one said this would be a walk in the park," Nielson continued. "But I can't begin to help you if you don't talk to me."

"What do you want me to say?"

"How about we start with how you're feeling today?"

"I don't know. Tired," Jonny murmured.

"Tired of what?"

Jonny shook again gently. How could he possibly talk about any of it without sounding weak or off his rocker? His refusal only served to irk Nielson.

"Why are you here, Jonny?" Nielson asked, voice laced with obvious annoyance.

"I'm not sure."

"You see this as a waste of time, don't you?"

Jonny didn't need to speak to give Nielson his answer.

Nielson leaned forward, his demeanour shifting to a more comforting tone. "Jonny, I'm not here to force you into anything. These sessions only work if you're present and are engaged. Tell you what... indulge me this one session. If it's not for you, we leave it there and we can work something else out. How does that sound?"

Jonny took a deep breath, nodded reluctantly, recalling his agreement with Liz. A promise is a promise, after all.

"Let's go back to what you said. Tired. What are you tired of, Jonny?"

"Of... of this feeling. After what happened..." Jonny struggled to articulate it. "It's... it's hard to talk about."

"Trauma often is."

Jonny's lips pressed into a thin line. He nearly smiled. He couldn't accept that premise. "What happened to my daughter was trauma. This, this is nothing in comparison."

"Trauma isn't a one-size-fits-all boot, Jonny. It's not a template. I read about what happened out on that beach and can only imagine how hard it has been for you and your family."

Jonny drained the last of his water, took a long deep gulp, stared at the floor a little harder. If only he could drain away this feeling as easily.

"How about we start at a comfortable point for you?"

"I don't know where."

"Well, beginnings often help," Nielson prompted.

So that's what Jonny did.

He began with the context. He spoke about growing up, glossing over what life had been like with his dad. He talked about Liz and how they met when they were in school. He spoke about having kids, how tough it was at the beginning. He spoke about the life-changing move out of the pokey house on Wayborough Falls and into the spacious new build at Sandon Mount. He'd never really talked to anyone about this before. Not like this. On reflection, it all sounded so perfect.

"We *were* so tight. I know every mother or father — family — probably tell you the same thing, but we *were*, y'know," he said.

But Nielson had a way of grasping for and holding on to the things that mattered.

"Were?" he inquired.

The single word left Jonny sinking in the familiar sludge of guilt. He backtracked, unwilling to go down that rabbit hole just yet. For as long as he possibly could, Jonny focused on a happier time. He talked about Eevie. He talked about Rhys. He talked about his amazing wife.

But he was running out of road. There were still a lot of miles on the clock to work through in this session. The road led him to talk about those first two days they'd had together in Land's End. But he realised all he was doing was delaying the inevitable. The conversation had found a way of circling back.

"What happened, Jonny?"

Jonny sucked hard at his top lip. Took a deep breath, preparing himself to recount the day that haunted him most. After he'd finished, a heavy silence set in. It could have been for a matter of mere seconds but it felt so much longer. Nielson, composed and calm, finally spoke.

"Is there a part of you that blames your son for what happened?"

The words floored Jonny, stirring a mix of sadness and anger. His emotions surged like a boiling kettle, steam rising. He got to his feet, turned on his heel to head towards the exit. He was done. Didn't want to listen to any more.

"Jonny, I'm not here to make you feel better about yourself," Nielson said.

"Then what the fuck am I doing here?" Jonny snapped.

"Listen, it's my job to help you make sense of how you're feeling so that we can find a way forward together. If you're honest with me, we can do that. But that means asking and answering hard questions honestly."

The temperature valve was turned down. Jonny's anger simmered. He scratched his neck and looked back out at the cityscape beyond the window, out to the grey skies and cranes that worked within the bustling town centre. Seeing it made him think about his job, the job he loved and missed.

He'd do anything to go back to the days before again. But that was an impossibility. All he could do was tackle it head-on.

Dig at the root rather than hack at the damn leaves.

"No."

"No what, Jonny?"

"No. I don't blame Rhys," Jonny said, slowly returning to his chair. "What happened to Ee, that's on me."

He took a beat to finish what he wanted to say. "It was my fault. And I have to live with that."

This time, Jonny was too slow to catch the stray tears that cut a slick path down his cheek.

"If I'd just kept my eyes open. If I'd just waited for mum or dad to get back. If I'd just done that."

If... if... if...

And there it was again.

Mr Roberts wore that mask of pity Rhys had come to resent. He let out a croaky breath, wrestling with himself not to cry. He didn't deserve to cry.

"Everyone looks at me like that."

"What do you mean?" Mr Roberts looked taken aback.

"Like I'm the victim here," Rhys blurted, his frustration creeping out.

Mr Roberts inched himself closer. His chair emitted an unpleasant squeak as it scraped across the floor. "Rhys, have you spoken to anyone else about how you're feeling? Mum? Dad? That aunt you mentioned? Your grandparents when you were living with them?"

Rhys shook his head. The weight of silence hung between them.

"Do you think they know you're feeling the way you are?"

This time, there was just a solitary shrug of the shoulders.

"Rhys, you've gone through a lot as a family. I can't even imagine how much. And while I don't know your mum or dad, or have had a chance to speak to them for that matter, I know the last thing they would ever want is for you to be bottling this up and them not know about it."

"But that's just it, isn't it?" Rhys lifted his chin into Mr Roberts' sympathetic gaze, that appeared to be ingrained into his face. "They have enough on their plates because of what happened. Mum's got a lot with Eevie, Dad's not working because of what happened. Because of what I did. Why would I burden them with this, too?"

Voicing those thoughts felt like inflicting fresh wounds. What if Rhys was right? What if his mum and dad did blame him for what happened?

"I'm sure that's not true at all." Mr Roberts countered. "Rhys, what happened wasn't your fault. It was an accident — a horrible, horrible accident. But this... this is a lot to cope with, especially when you throw starting a new school into the mixing pot."

Rhys was unsure of what more there was to be said.

"Look, I meant what I said earlier. Everything you say here is private, never to be heard by another soul, but I'd hate to think that you feel you can't talk to anyone else. If that's not your mum or dad, what about a friend, perhaps? Is there anyone else?"

A wisp of air left through Rhys' nostrils. Maybe there was.

Nielson rose from his seat, taking the small empty glass from Jonny's hands. He suggested Jonny take a moment while he wandered to a cabinet near the window. Atop it was a couple of bottles of water, a fancy old kettle that he flicked on, an array of coffee sachets and tea bags of all different colours marking weird flavours. There were also cakes and biscuits.

"Can I get you anything?" Nielson asked.

"You got any whisky hidden away?" Jonny thought for a moment about his dad and the countless times as a child his old man had asked him to bring him the 'bottle of the good ol' brown stuff' and regretted the comment instantly.

It turned out that Nielson, who'd held a face like steel up to now, could smile. "There's nothing like that here, I'm afraid. Can I tempt you with a coffee?"

"Water will be just fine, thanks."

Returning with their drinks, Nielson resumed their conversation. "You say you feel at fault for what happened. Can you explain that to me?"

"Why? Seems simple to me. I left my kids alone when I shoulda waited. Isn't that enough?"

The words came out harsher than Jonny had intended, but stopped himself short of saying sorry.

Nielson took a sip of his coffee. Too hot. He pulled that face everyone instinctively pulls when their lips get burned. He rested the mug on a coaster and continued.

"What we have right now is the context. But context can only take us so far, Jonny. We've got to drill down to see what else is down there, what else there is to unearth and unpack."

It was the type of talk Jonny associated with people like Nielson. "Sounds like some philosophical bull, if you ask me."

Another smile. A hint of a snigger, too.

"Well, you've already agreed to give me a chance. So, let's test that theory."

"How?"

"I'll tell you what I think from everything I have observed so far."

"It'll make a pleasant change from you just asking questions."

Nielson smiled again as he emptied a couple of sugar sachets — the kind you get from a café — into his mug. He settled back and blew softly at the steam. His eyes worked on Jonny, uncovering him.

"Let's start where you did — with your father. You barely touched on it, almost as if it's a part of your past you avoid. No mention of a mother, so it was just the two of you. It wasn't a happy time in your life, was it? I imagine he was a hard man, maybe even a little cold, too. Someone who didn't talk about their own emotions."

"I—"

"Let me finish. I think when you became a parent yourself, you vowed not to be like him, that it'd be different for your kids. I also think, judging by how you scratch at your neck and the fact that I can count on one hand how many times you've looked me in the eye during this session, you're someone who struggles with their emotions generally. Don't like to give much away or show vulnerability. You're the reliable dad, right? The guy the family can depend on with their lives. The man who would do anything for his wife and children and would make sure they have everything they need to have the best life possible. Be the best dad possible, better than how your own father was. It's admirable."

He paused to take a sip of his coffee, doing so without flinching this time. His words hung in the air, pregnant with meaning.

"As a father wanting to be nothing but the best for his family, the guy they depend on, it must be difficult to comprehend working through what happened to your daughter. How that one thing has changed her life, your life, your family's life so dramatically. I don't *actually* think you blame yourself for what happened to your daughter. But rather I think you feel like you've failed her."

Jonny couldn't muster a response. Deep within, he felt a hammer hit a nail's head. There had been one thing Nielson had got wrong but he wasn't going to go into that.

Nielson continued. . .

"There is one question I have, though. Where does that want to be the best come from? It seems there might be something more than just your father's influence at play here."

"Like what?"

"Like you're making up for something else, perhaps."

Rhys found his thoughts inexplicably wandering to an episode of Family Guy.

It was the one where Lois Griffin drove Brian, the family dog, past the park. He'd gone nuts for it, climbing over the back seats, yapping away, refusing to let his favourite peeing spot go until it was out of sight.

People are just the same, aren't they? First his mum, then Mrs Johnson, now Mr Roberts. Not in the sense of obsessing over marking a territory — that'd be weird — but not letting things go that are in their line of sight. Drive past the park and the dog will go nuts for it. Give a school psychologist some interesting information and they cling to it, doing what they can to get more out of you.

"So, they're a friend outside of school then?"

Rhys had instantly regretted the mention of Annie. Mr Roberts had clung to it just as Brian had clung to that hope of going to the park. Yet, discussing Annie openly was out of the question. Rhys knew how it might get perceived. It'd just invite more questions and more sessions. Everyone would think he'd lost the plot — the 11-year-old kid so messed up that he had an imaginary friend.

Rhys wasn't kidding himself, though. He, too, had wondered himself whether it had been some elaborate dream. That Annie — Karma (whatever) — was something his mind had conjured as a way of making sense of things.

But he'd dismissed that as quickly as he thought it. This — Annie — it was as real as anything else and so he kept his answers brief, hoping Mr Roberts would move on.

"Yeah, someone that lives on the same estate."

"That's good, really good. We all need someone to talk to." Mr Roberts said, waiting expectantly for more, hoping for another tidbit to grab onto. But when none came, he shifted gears. "For what it's worth, I still think your mum and dad would understand."

"Maybe."

"I think so. Look, we haven't got long left and so I want you to know that you don't have to deal with this on your own. I know you've got your friend, but my door is always open. I know Mrs Johnson thinks a lot of you and also wants to help, too."

Rhys had no intention of taking Mr Roberts up on dropping by uninvited. The reality was that he wouldn't have been here at all if it hadn't been forced on him. But, admittedly, he felt surprised. He couldn't deny that the session hadn't been as dreadful as expected.

Mr Roberts leaned back in his chair, taking his foot off the gas, slowing down the session to a roll. "And look, it wouldn't be a session with me without a little homework."

The H-word. Rhys recoiled at the mention of it. He still had the IT assignment that he'd forgotten to look at over the weekend. It had taken a back seat to everything else that had happened, including a trip to the woods with a girl called Karma.

"No, no, come on," Mr Robert blurted out, hands out in assurance. "I promise it's nothing much. I want you to leave here today and do three things for me. Just three. First," Mr Roberts holds out his hand and pulls on his index finger. "I want you to cut yourself some slack. Yeah? You might not be ready to believe that what happened this summer wasn't your fault yet, but that'll come with time. Ok? Second," the middle finger unfolds. "I'd like for you to try and talk to either your mum or dad."

Rhys let his head droop backwards with despair.

"I know, I know. You've had enough of me going on about it but hear me out. They only want what's best for you and telling them what you're thinking and feeling will help far more than me or Mrs Johnson or anyone else ever can. Right? Please give them a chance. Maybe they'll surprise you. Third and last," the finger next to his pinkie drew out. "I want you to take this."

Mr Roberts yanked out a spare piece of paper from his neglected clipboard and tore it in half. One crisp rip. One-half remained lonely on his desk. The other was scrunched up and tossed towards the bin. To no surprise, it bounced a good 30 centimetres, maybe more, from the intended target.

"That was so bad," the way Mr Roberts drew out his words made him sound boyish, belying his position. Back to the other half of the sheet, he frantically began scribbling something down before pressing the paper into Rhys' open palm.

Rhys took a peek. . .

> FORGIVING DOES NOT ERASE THE BITTER PAST. A HEALED MEMORY IS NOT A DELETED MEMORY. INSTEAD, FORGIVING WHAT WE CANNOT FORGET CREATES A NEW WAY TO REMEMBER.

"That, right there, is one of my favourite quotes, from a chap called Lewis B. Smedes — not important for you to remember. I won't be quizzing you on that," Mr Roberts had finished with a geeky chuckle, perhaps hoped Rhys would follow suit. But it was a lame comment — a bad punchline — and he moved on quickly.

"All I can say is that at points in my life, those words have helped me. Who knows, maybe you will find them useful, too."

Rhys looked at the words but struggled to digest them. Not in one hit anyway. He would need to go back and re-read them and decipher the shoddy handwriting. He folded the paper in half and crammed it deep into his coat pocket.

"Thanks, sir."

"Not too lame?"

"No," Rhys lied.

A distant bell clanged outside the walls of Mr Roberts' office.

"That's us then. Looks like you'd better be off for your second period. What you got next?"

"English... I think," a case of the brain fog had descended.

"Loved English when I was in your shoes. Thought of doing something more with that before going into this. Creative writing, perhaps. Anyway, I won't bore you with the details. I don't want to make you late."

Rhys jumped to his feet. The chair gave a wheeze of relief. His backpack slapped his back as he slung it over his shoulders and headed towards the door. He stopped short of opening it.

"How'd you feel about me talking to Mrs Johnson about sorting another session for us? Maybe for something in two weeks?" Mr Roberts called.

It was the question Rhys had dreaded.

Rhys rested his hand on the doorknob and turned back,

sucking his lip and rolling his head. He couldn't bring himself to say no and leave, knowing the last thing he'd seen in the pokey office was Mr Roberts' face, full of masked dejection. He wasn't ready to carry any more guilt on his shoulders.

"Ah, um, yeah... I guess."

Mr Roberts leapt to his feet, pleased as punch with himself at a job well done. "Great, I'll get something sorted for us."

His pink shirt rode up his back as he bent to pick the crushed paper off the floor that he'd failed miserably to lob into the bin. He hovered over the empty blue plastic tub and slam-dunked it in this time.

Before leaving, Rhys turned back one last time.

"Sir... just so you know, your clock's not working."

As the time ticked down on their first session together, Dr Nielson's questions had moved away from what happened at the beach and had become predictable.

They'd felt like a worn-out path, tracing back through old terrain that was way back in the rearview mirror — parents, childhood, relationships, work, and the like. The counselling clichés Jonny was aware of but had little patience for. He couldn't see the past's connection to what he deemed to be the actual root cause, nor why talking about it mattered.

But he indulged Nielson's questions. If anything, just to prove this whole thing was a waste of time.

Nielson loved his metaphors, too. He kept referring to this session as being like starting a new jigsaw puzzle straight out of the box. You need to start with the outside pieces to build inward to make your picture. The image made Jonny cringe.

For Nielson, the external pieces of Jonny's puzzle were the events at Porthcurno Beach. Having connected those fragments, Nielson probed further, returning to Jonny's father — given how quickly he'd skirted over it earlier.

Jonny acknowledged that Nielson had been right in his assessment to a certain degree. Indeed, he had grown up without a mother who abandoned him without so much as a goodbye when he was a young boy, leaving him with a dad who was hard as rusted nails and whose emotional capacity to be a doting father had been eroded.

But where Nielson had been wrong was his assumption that Jonny had loved his father.

His father, the reckless alcoholic. The man who'd brought woman after woman back to the apartment. The guy that, one day, nipped out for a cigarette and didn't come back until several days later. Jonny recalled one time calling the police when he was 8, shitting himself that his dad might be lying dead behind one of the local boozers in town. His dad had given him a real good hiding for that, and Jonny had never called the cops on his old man again.

Truth was Jonny had needed to grow up quickly. He needed to learn to fend for himself.

There was another thing that Nielson had been right about, that Jonny had never wanted to be like his father when he'd become a parent himself. His children were the best thing in his life. And they would only get the best from him.

Yet he had failed, hadn't he? He'd let them down, and it had come at an enormous cost.

Nielson sat back, inhaling the last of his milky coffee with a look of intrigue while he mentally picked up the jigsaw pieces and slotted them into place, seeing what fit where and what didn't.

That led Nielson to Liz next. A much easier conversation. Happier times. Those first memories of how they met at the local dusty youth club, Dynamic (aka Dyno), when he was 15 — she 14 — still brought on the same smile now that it did back then.

He'd first met her in late spring. It'd been hot for the time of year, the sort of weather where the boys rode around town on their bikes, topless, the lip of their boxes hanging out, looking like a bunch of assholes. In a place where most teenage girls wore tight clothing and dressed to stand out, Liz was different, the outlier. There she was, hiding behind a small group of girls in ripped baggy jeans and an oversized S Club 7 t-shirt. He can still picture it now, with her blonde hair held up by two bobbing pigtails.

It had taken Jonny a couple of weeks to pluck up the confidence to even speak to Liz. She was always with a little group of her friends and there was no way Jonny was going to start talking to her and get shot down in front of them.

But one afternoon, a little window of opportunity opened. Her little group had gone to the toilet and Liz sat alone on a stool looking out into the market street that was starting to shut up for the night.

His palms were sweaty. His heart had pounded. The warmth of his nerves reverberated. All that build-up. All that tension. He'd never felt like that before. The irony was that it wasn't Jonny who had spoken first.

"Are you going to just stand there? Take a seat," Liz had said. As direct then as she was today.

And that's how it had started. Jonny had fallen for her hard. That had brought some insecurities to roost, insecurities he'd never felt before. He'd constantly fretted she would find someone else, someone better. That she'd leave him. He got angry when he'd seen her talking with other boys or if someone looked at her inappropriately.

That was what love felt like to Jonny McIntyre. Messy. A bit of a head fuck. But he simply couldn't live without it. With a lot of effort, things did get better. Those insecurities subsided, only rearing their ugly head from time to time when he overdid it with the booze.

Fast forward and Jonny had proposed to Liz on her 18th birthday, during a long weekend in Northumberland that he'd spent months saving up for, working hard out on the yard. He'd popped the question right out by the coast, Alnwick Castle off in the distance, sun ducking behind a tower. She'd said yes immediately.

They'd always planned a long engagement. Jonny had scrimped and saved every penny for years so he could give Liz the wedding of her dreams.

But then she'd fallen pregnant, just after she'd turned 21.

Nielson had sensed Jonny's tone.

"How did you feel about becoming a father yourself after your experiences with your dad?" Nielson had asked.

It had come as a shock rather than a nice surprise. The sentiment he should have felt was consumed by a pool of worry that he — they — weren't ready to have a child when they were barely making ends meet with the rented house they had on Wayborough Falls. For Liz, there was no other option. But before little Rhys had even arrived, Jonny had gone off the rails, veered off course. Done something really stupid.

"What was it you did, Jonny?"

Jonny scratched his neck one last time as he prepared to share the last of his puzzle pieces.

ELIZABETH

"Did Esme seem... I don't know... a little off to you last week?"

Elizabeth had been stewing on the question for a good hour or so after arriving at Ma and Pa's for a catch-up and to drain time. She'd been waiting to get Ma on her own to find out an answer to that question that had gnawed at her over the weekend.

Elizabeth knew her sister. While their lives had taken different paths, and while they weren't what they once were, Elizabeth knew Esme better than anyone. She could sense when her younger sister was not her usual self when they'd met last week.

"No less than usual," Ma replied. She finished the last of her cherry bakewell she'd picked up from the morning market, wiped away the crumbs from her cable-knit cardigan. She hocked up a heavy cough.

"Every time we seem to see her, there's always something new happening," Ma continued.

"You think she's ok down there in London?"

"Oh, she's fine. New job, new place, and who knows what else she's got herself into. She's always been a whirlwind, moving a hundred miles an hour."

"Maybe," but Elizabeth knew there was more beneath the surface.

"And honestly, if something was up, we'd be the last people she'd tell.

"What'd you mean?"

"Well, the same goes for you, for that matter. I only ever found out if something was happening with you pair from school or someone else when you moved in with us."

"We never wanted you to worry about us."

"And how's that working out for you right now?"

Ma had a point.

Truth was, Ma knew very little about any of the troubles and scrapes Elizabeth had been in — as few as they were, anyway. Elizabeth had always hidden them, whether they were big or small. If she fought with Jonny, she would never rock up at theirs looking for a shoulder to cry on or her old bed to sleep in. When money was tight and paying rent was a struggle, she never went to them for money. She never wanted to bring any drama to Ma and Pa's door. Taking her and Esme away from the Aston Orphanage all those years ago was a debt she felt she could never repay, let alone with interest. She never wanted to let them down.

However, with Esme, things were different. No matter what happened, they could always confide in each other. Together, they'd work things out, making sure Ma and Pa never had to worry about them.

Elizabeth couldn't put her finger on this one. Something was off last week when they were together at the coffee shop.

Esme avoided her eyes as though they'd passed over something nasty. It was the subtleties that troubled Elizabeth. Her straight lips pulsed an unpleasantness Elizabeth didn't recognise. Esme always wore a smile.

But why?

That was a mystery that wasn't going to get solved right here, right now. Elizabeth snuck a look at the clock on the mantel. She needed to head off soon to collect Rhys from school. Ma and Pa also reserved Monday afternoons to help out at the community centre outside of town. There'd been an endless fight against the Council, who was talking about closing it down for good. Ma and Pa would be damned if they let it happen.

"Any more tea?" Pa shouted through from the kitchen.

Ma looked at Elizabeth, who just waved a hand in response.

"You can fill a flask for us, but Liz will be heading off soon."

"Righto," he shouted back through. A couple of chesty coughs chased after.

On the shaggy rug, Eevie was flat out asleep, angled in the peculiar way she used to when she was a baby, arms sprawled out, frog legs arching together. It was a shame Elizabeth would have to move her, end her peace. It had been the first bit of prolonged harmony Elizabeth had enjoyed today. She'd written out her weekly to-do list and stuck it to the fridge that morning. There was a lot she'd put off doing around the house recently, and she'd had every intention of getting stuck into it.

Alas, Eevie had had other ideas. She'd needed a little more attention than normal. On top of that, Esme, and the build-up of housework, there had been other things on her mind, too. Enough to make another list out of.

Her thoughts had darted around, unwilling to focus on any one thing.

She'd thought about Rhys.

And Jonny.

And Walter.

And Elisa.

Growing up, the motto Pa had always passed on was to control what you can control.

The problem was that Elizabeth was starting to feel like she had no control over anything.

Ma and Pa walked with her down to the Crossland.

Eevie had inevitably stirred and had woken from her catnap. It had been about 40 minutes but Elizabeth thought it would do her little girl the world of good.

She buckled Eevie into her toddler seat. Ma and Pa stepped forward and gave their granddaughter a bunch of sloppy kisses and told her to be good, just as they always did.

They closed the door, and each hugged Elizabeth, too. Over Pa's shoulder, Elizabeth couldn't help but notice Mr Dorset wasn't standing in his usual place in the window to see her off.

"No sign of Mr Dorset today? Something terrible must have happened."

"Finally giving the street a break," Pa remarked with a chuckle, craning his neck to check.

"We've never had any luck with neighbours," Ma added.

"You say that, but, you know, he's not all that bad," Pa said, holding back a cough before starting up again. "We getta chatting sometimes when I'm out at the allotment. Nice guy. Harmless. I don't think he's all there, though, if you know what I mean?" Pa tapped the side of his noggin to emphasise the point.

"I told you he knocked on ours the other day, didn't I?" Ma interjected, a hand nudging Pa's elbow.

His words chased the coughs this time.

"Rings a bell. Came over blathering about someone being on the street that shouldn't be or something, yeah?"

"Something like that. He said there'd been a car he didn't recognise pulling up across the street over the last few days. Same time in the afternoon. Said it was a Peugeot. One of the big ones. Driver wouldn't get out and then an hour or so later they'd be off again."

"Right... So..." Elizabeth said, bemused.

"Exactly. He wanted to know if we knew anything about it or had seen anything. Of course we hadn't. Apart from last Wednesday and Friday, we've been out most afternoons."

"And that was it?"

"And that was it. Told us to keep alert and that he was going to speak to Frank and Betty across the road. I told him to do just that and thanked him for letting us know. Anything to get him to move along."

"As I said, harmless... but I don't think he's all there," Pa said, again.

Elizabeth knew she had pushed Rhys too hard again.

That her eagerness to be supportive had grown overbearing.

She'd barely shifted the Crossland into third gear. St Andrews hadn't even disappeared in her wing mirror before she'd delved in.

"Soooo... how did it go?" Elizabeth asked Rhys, bypassing the usual pleasantries of how his day went and whether he'd got up to anything fun.

"What?"

"You know what... with Mr Roberts?"

"Oh. Yeah. It was fine."

"Did it help?"

"I don't know... I guess."

She was looking at Rhys through the rearview mirror as she spoke. "I just want you to know how proud..." but Elizabeth trailed off after seeing Rhys withdraw into his own world. He pulled out his iPod and locked his ears into the headset.

He'd shut her out again. Her frustration started to simmer away.

"Rhys, come on. Take your headphones off. I'm trying to talk to you."

Nothing.

"Rhys..."

Nothing.

"Rhys!"

Again, nothing. Rhys was looking out the passenger window into the throes of the town centre that was still bustling, her voice drowned out by a playlist. That or he was plainly ignoring her.

The after-school traffic had built up in town. The lights up ahead were on red. The Crossland slowed to a stop. Without thinking, she reached behind and snatched Rhys' iPod out of his lap. But his reaction was immediate, defensive. He clawed at her coat.

"Mum. What the fuck. Give it back."

Eevie's wail drowned his shout out. Through the mirror, Elizabeth could see her girl's arms thrashing, cheeks reddening, her legs stretching as she struggled against the seat straps.

Elizabeth immediately regretted what she'd done and let Rhys take his iPod back. The only thing she could do for Eevie from her position at the front was attempt to comfort her with her voice. She tried the usual soothing sounds and techniques — even the ones she'd seen on Instagram from the groups she followed — but everything only seemed to push Eevie closer to hysteria.

In *any* other situation, she'd drop everything to pick her daughter up and rock her, give her kisses on the neck. But she couldn't just stop. The traffic was beginning to shuffle forward again. A sharp toot of the horn behind her forced her to drop the Crossland's handbrake and follow the snaking line up to the traffic lights.

"Shhhh. Shhhh. Shhhh. Please, Eevie... please calm down, sweetie."

But just like Rhys, her daughter wasn't interested in her words.

Elizabeth felt a pang of panic. Her hands gripped the steering wheel. The traffic ahead wasn't moving nearly quickly enough for her liking. Her neck and cheeks began to burn. Her eyes, threatening tears, crossed from what was happening in front of her to what was happening behind, like they followed a fly that couldn't decide where it wanted to land.

And then she heard Rhys unbuckle his belt. He slid over next to his Eevie and began to use the techniques she'd taught him during that first week back from the Royal Cornwall Hospital.

Since then, she'd never seen him need to use them. She'd always been there.

Slowly, Eevie's wails subsided into moans. Her shoulders relaxed back into her chair. Her arms rested. Her eyes, glued to her brothers, began to droop and eventually, they closed.

"Rhys, I..."

Before Elizabeth could finish her sentence, Rhys had bolted straight out of the car, storming up the gravel path and into the house. He didn't turn back.

Not once.

Elizabeth slumped into her seat, eyes closed, exhaling a deep breath, heavy with regret. She massaged the weight building on her forehead. She could feel the slow headache coming on.

How had she let things escalate like that?

Glancing in the rearview mirror, she could see Eevie was still sound asleep. Elizabeth had anticipated a wide-eyed response from her after Rhys had slammed the door. But the unexpected peacefulness was a relief, offering a fleeting moment of calm before what was to come: the evening rush of preparing dinner, attending to Eevie's needs, tucking her in, and tidying up the chaos that was left behind.

Elizabeth fished her phone from her coat pocket. She'd felt it vibrate four, maybe even five times, after leaving Ma and Pa's.

It'll most likely be an email or a notification from either Facebook or Instagram. Less likely a WhatsApp from Esme. What

Elizabeth was hoping for — and had done each time her phone buzzed over the past week — was an update from Walter Demick.

Up to now, they'd only come fleetingly. Each time a text from Walter had come through, her hope had swelled. And then it would pop as she opened it to see a couple of follow-up questions or further details he'd wanted to check or clarify.

There'd be nothing groundbreaking. Nothing for her to hold on to.

It's still early days, she'd told herself again.

This time, there was nothing from Walter. Just a couple of Facebook notifications and the usual sales emails from Next, ASOS, and Wallis.

With a resigned sigh, Elizabeth stashed her phone back in her pocket.

Early days or not, it's that hope that left her disappointed.

She cautiously ascended the stairs.

A glass of warm milk sloshed around in the mug she carried.

Elizabeth did her best to avoid the creaky floorboards. Coaxing Eevie to sleep had taken an hour. It'd been easier when she was a baby. Eventually, though, after a bit of fighting and a few tears (and not just from Eevie), her eyelids had closed and her breathing became a rhythmic backdrop against the white noise that played through a portable machine throughout the night.

As she reached the landing, the familiar hum of the machine greeted her ears. She paused, ensuring her silent approach hadn't disturbed that rhythm. She wasn't quite prepared to switch back into 'mum mode' just yet. The past few hours had drained her. She hadn't learned from the earlier confrontation with Rhys in the car. Dinner had turned into a clash with Jonny, as she probed about his first session with Dr Nielson. Much like Rhys, Jonny had shut down and retreated to the shed, leaving his dinner untouched to grow cold on the table.

More amends to be made.

Content that Eevie hadn't stirred, Elizabeth tiptoed on down the landing and tapped on Rhys' room. The usual two and in.

"I come in peace."

Rhys sat hunched at his desk, scribbling away. Headphones over his ears. She thought — hoped — he just hadn't heard her. She closed the door gently and made her way over to him, taking note that the room was far tidier than it had been at the weekend. Clothes were no longer strewn on the floor, trash had found its way into the bin, the plates and bowls left over at the weekend had been brought down, washed, and were back in their rightful place.

Setting the glass of milk on a coaster, Elizabeth caught Rhys' attention, interrupting his drawing — the newest version of the picture he'd drawn for Eevie's birthday, the beautiful lotus in front of a waterfall. It almost took her breath away; how talented Rhys had become, how beautiful his pictures could be.

"Oh, hey," he said, lowering his headphones down to ride his neck.

"It's looking good again, hon."

"It's ok. Getting there."

"Ok? It's amazing."

The muted silence did not surprise her. Compliments never were his thing.

"I'm sorry, Rhys. For earlier. In the car."

"Me, too."

"No, no. You did nothing wrong."

"Sure?"

"Sure I'm sure."

He smiled. She smiled, too.

Elizabeth gave his hair the usual ruffle. "Friends?"

"Friends."

"Right. I'll leave you to it."

"Ok. Is it fine if I bring the glass down in the morning?"

"I'm sure I can let you off with that. Just this once."

She made her way back to the door. "Great job sorting your room out, by the way. We can expect it like this all the time now, yeah?"

"Sure..." the flick of his satirical eyebrows said it all.

Elizabeth left feeling like she at least got one thing right today.

ELISA

2008-2019

I moved to London during the New Year of '08.

I can almost feel your sigh and hear what you're thinking. Really? This again?

But after what unfolded in Furarche Woods, everything seemed to lose its significance. I lost my baby in the most undignified way, wriggling around in agony against a sodden tree in the mud, losing thick clots of blood that seemed to have no end. I had stifled the urge to let out cries that would carry my pain through the branches above me. Something within me changed. I had lost a part of myself and I was no longer motivated by anything else.

I had that clarity a few days after what happened. I was back in that coffee shop in the town centre. Blue Jays. I sat in the same seat that gave me a prime view of the Waterstones directly across the cobbled street, rain distorting the view.

I observed Elizabeth's arrival a few minutes before her New Year's Eve shift, her eyes fixed on the ground, umbrella up, a thick coat concealing the bump that I now recognised.

She wasn't smiling as she had been that first time she'd caught me off guard and walked right by me. That day, she'd exuded infectious joy. She'd been high on life. High on Jonny. A permanent smile stitched into a face that reminded me of our mother's.

Turns out that smile wasn't so permanent. This version of her was downtrodden — the colour washed away by the fine rain of a grey winter.

But it was nothing to do with the weather. I knew it was because of me.

Me and Jonny.

But the satisfaction I thought I'd feel was absent.

She wasn't just the sister who abandoned me to wither away at Aston. She was also a reminder of my loss, the life she was carrying that I would never see.

That, for me, was just too much.

I moved into a studio apartment on Roxley Road, in Lewisham, just over a week later after New Year.

There was no meticulous research or endless hunting for the perfect place. I simply wanted to secure somewhere as quickly as possible.

The apartment was fully furnished. Open plan. Neutral colours and plain wallpaper right through and top to bottom. Fairly modern. Within walking distance of the shops, market, and tube line. I'd got lucky with it and it was worth every penny alone for its promise of solitary.

Worth it or not, it wasn't cheap. I still had a sizeable chunk of money left over from The Bay View Inn sale to fall back on. But after more than eight months without work, my expenses were mounting, and that money wouldn't last indefinitely.

I returned to the only thing I knew. Bar work. I pick up shifts at two bars — The Anchor's Drop and The Blue Moon — working six-day weeks. Eventually, I phased out The Anchor's Drop to focus on The Blue Moon, a decision that would end up changing my life.

London is well renowned for its fancy bars, the glitzy clubs, the nightlife that makes you terrified of looking at your bank account the next morning.

You'd never find The Blue Moon in the same sentence as fancy or glitzy.

It reminded me of The Bay View Inn. Somehow, amidst its decay and neglect, I strangely found comfort at that bar that had long lost its colour. Stains covered the carpets everywhere you looked, and the windows were filthy. It had more tables on its last legs than not and the toilets stank, stale of cigarettes, piss, and shit — a breeding ground for clunks of mould and grime. A state that no amount of freshener could salvage.

If you have ever watched The Inbetweeners movie, one of the main characters, Will McKenzie, comes out with a line towards the end of the film that sums up the vibe of The Blue Moon.

'It's a shit hole, but it's our shit hole.'

It was owned and run by a guy called Rahul Varma and his daughter, Adya. Rahul was in each day, no matter what, always in a different variation of t-shirt adorning his favourite rock bands, Guns & Roses, Mötley Crüe, Foreigner, Tom Petty and the Heartbreakers, and Def Leppard, to name a few.

The plastered memorabilia and photos of them all caught the eye. Rock music from the juke set the rhythm.

And the local punters embraced it. They'd come in their droves on a Thursday, Friday, and Saturday night, funnelling in off the high street. If you were looking for a cheap and cheerful night in London, The Blue Moon was your place. Local bands played (rock, of course). The mic didn't get a rest during karaoke. And some claim (though it is unverified) that The Blue Moon also gave birth to extreme bar bingo.

It was where I spent the majority of my days and nights during that first year in Lewisham. However, 2008 remains a foggy period in my memory. If I wasn't pulling pints or filling shot glasses, I was drinking them. Large quantities that would leave me feeling nothing. During the times I wanted to feel something — something other than never-ending, unbearable thoughts and pain — I turned to men. An endless line of one-night stands that gave me a moment's relief and nothing else.

A temporary quench.

None were memorable. None provided anything more than a service that briefly papered over deep cracks.

That was until I met Gregor.

Let me tell you a bit about Gregor. The unlikeliest of men that would save my life.

He'd moved to London towards the end of 2008, a few blocks

from my apartment, working as a designer for commercial office spaces at a company called Scale Ltd.

Gregor was the type of guy that had never been in any sort of trouble in his — then — 26 and a bit years on Earth. He was a simple man with simple tastes, not adventurous in the slightest. He was rigorously, sometimes annoyingly, consistent. His life — Monday to Friday — was always the same.

He was a big guy when I first met him, 18 stone plus, I'd say. Just under 6 feet tall. I'd never seen him wearing any other than plaid shirts or turtlenecks, smart chinos of differing colours, and Dr Martens boots. He had dark blonde hair that was thin and fluffy and lay short and flat. I'd suspected he wasn't from here, and his faint Polish accent confirmed my theory.

He started coming into The Blue Moon after work on Friday with some of his colleagues. Same time, just shy of 5pm. Same drink — a small Sauvignon red wine. And if the booth was available, he claimed his spot at the far corner, right beside the grimy window overlooking Deptford High Street.

We talked when he was in. The usual shit: work, life, recession, weather.

At that time, he was just like any other punter. Just not as forward or flirty towards me and Adya.

As time passed, Gregor started coming in more regularly. He joined the darts and snooker teams, his one drink turning into several. He came in to watch the football at the weekend. Then he started coming to our extreme bingo nights.

Whatever the occasion, it always came with a Sauvignon red in his hand. I'd given up asking what he'd like.

"Usual?"

"Usual," he said.

It was one of those winter Saturday nights, late in the season. Usually, I'd be working at The Blue Moon for the extreme bingo nights, but Rahul hadn't scheduled me for this shift.

The thought of having nothing to do didn't sit well with me. Those were the times when the voices inside my head became the loudest. So, I decided to get dolled up and head straight to The Blue Moon. Instead of taking orders, I made them. Instead of calling out numbers on a crackly mic, I grabbed a card, hoping to complete a line and win a night of free drinks.

True to form, I got wasted. Totally and utterly word-slurring, body-swaying, stomach curdling, wasted. I left with some guy I hadn't seen in the bar before. He'd come over and bought me a few drinks during the last hour. I asked him to walk me home. It was pitch black outside, and my apartment was only a short 10-minute walk away.

We barely made it three minutes before I found myself down a side street, retching. The cool air was as unforgiving as the kamikaze shots from earlier.

That guy — whoever he was — stayed with me, patting my back as my latest binge made a swift exit onto the cold pavement. But then, I felt his hand wandering where it shouldn't have been. I pushed him away, stumbled as I did, and lost my footing.

Using the wall for support, I felt him closing in again. He spoke, but I couldn't make out his words in my drunken fog. I pushed him off once more, ending up on my knees.

That's when I heard another voice shouting behind us. Lost in a haze of arguing and close footsteps, I felt another hand on my forearm, helping me back to my feet.

When I looked around, the other man was gone, replaced by Gregor.

Gregor would become only the second man I ever loved.

He brought peace and calm to my impulsive spontaneity and, sometimes, illogical rashness — yeah, I don't mind saying it. Who are we if we don't accept our own flaws, right?

I have a lot to thank Gregor for. Far more than just that first night. He saved me, but in a way, I feel like I saved him, too. While I had been drinking my problems away, it turned out the odd small glass of Sauvignon red Gregor had started having here and there had become two glasses, then three, then every night. A casual drink became a habit and then a problem he had been increasingly blind to.

Even though it had been right under his nose, it took someone — me in this instance — to shine a light on it. When we started seeing each other, he was drinking his wine as though it was fruit juice. The first time he invited me to his studio apartment, his kitchen worktop displayed an endless line of empty bottles waiting to be re-homed in the recycling bin.

AA was his suggestion. It hadn't even crossed my mind. But that's Gregor all over. Once he sees a problem, he just had to fix it. He obsessed over it like one of his work projects. Gregor took it seriously. Far more than I did. While I kept my thoughts and stories to myself, Gregor was an open book. The group hung on to every word of his Polish tongue with intrigue. It turned out he wasn't just a support for me. Maybe he saved others in that group.

Gregor inspired me like no one had before, to aim higher, to dream beyond The Blue Moon. With his encouragement, I enrolled at the Open University, starting with a wide-ranging Access Module in People, Work, and Society, while I contemplated my path and what I wanted to do with myself.

I thought about my education. I knew firsthand what it was like to be neglected, marginalised, deemed unworthy because of circumstances beyond my control. I wanted to help kids like me, those shoved to the sidelines. Kids deemed to stand no chance in the real world for no other reason than their upbringing and the bad hands they got dealt. The world had enough teachers who read from textbooks, scribbled the classes they had planned on a blackboard, critiqued without a thought for development, and then clocked off once they'd done their bit. Not using their opportunity to influence at all.

But as kids like me knew all too well, sometimes we needed more. I began to believe I could offer more. And so I completed my degree in Primary School Education. I took a placement in 2014 at Prendergast Vale School and ended up taking a full-time position off the back of that. I knew from day one that it was what I was born to do. I had Gregor to thank for opening my eyes to that.

We got engaged later that year, under the sun setting on Puerto Morelos beach during a holiday in Cancun. We'd been together six years by that point. A year later, we married in Poland. Out at a beautiful historic church in Swiebodzin. St. Michael's, it was called. A place where generations of Gregor's family had been married and buried. The day was beautiful. Late spring. A slight breeze hung in the air. The sun blessed us with as much warmth as the majority of Gregor's family did. There was a mix of guests over from UK from his dad's side (which helped make me feel more at home) and Polish from his mother's.

The day was special to Gregor for more than me taking his surname and sharing the occasion with the family he now rarely saw. You see, Gregor set himself a goal — to shed four stone off his 18. To get back into the shape he'd been in before he left to pursue new dreams and possibilities in the Big Smoke. All before bad takeaways and excessive amounts of Sauvignon red took hold.

And Gregor being Gregor, he did it. Stuck to a plan rigorously with as much effort and passion as he did with everything. Living your life with someone, you don't see the big changes they make over time. It was only when I walked down the aisle and saw him in his wedding suit, a blue three-piece he'd concealed from me, that I noticed. The magnitude of the change. It fit his trimmed assets like two jigsaw pieces that were made each other. Like me and him.

There was only one issue with the day and it revolved around an inevitable question that tends to rear its unwanted head during the beauty of a wedding.

"So... you two must be thinking about kids now, right?"

I even specifically remember Gregor's beast of a mother, Ozella, asking "When are you going to make me a grandmother then?" Her Polish tongue was thicker and more obvious than his.

There was only one problem with that.

Gregor had no appetite for having kids.

For a time, I convinced myself that I hadn't wanted kids either. That I didn't want to risk going through what happened at Furarche Woods again.

But that dreaded, incessant question... "So, kids next?" Those words on my wedding day were akin to a key unlocking my personal Pandora's box, setting loose a flood of buried thoughts and emotions lurking in my subconscious.

The lid flung open, releasing a stream of suppressed sentiments, each bubble of emotion rising steadily, refusing to dissipate as they reached the surface.

They weren't just individual thoughts; they united and grew into an army, demanding recognition and attention until they were impossible to ignore.

I needed a future that had at least the prospect of children featuring in it.

In our houses and our homes, we have many doors.

Now picture each hinge creaking and squeaking with every push or pull, or the bottom edge scraping against a hard carpet from a poor fit.

It's maddening, isn't it?

I obsess over things like that. Just as I do when mould creeps between bathroom tiles or a stubborn stain finds its way onto a feature wall, glaringly obvious once noticed and demanding my attention until they're fixed.

After the wedding, I began to fixate on Gregor's insistence that he didn't want children.

I had known his stance long before, yet I held onto hope that time might shift his perspective. It didn't. As the days, weeks, months, and years went by, his decision loomed larger, growing more intense until it felt suffocating, like invisible hands tightening around my throat.

Refusing to let me breathe.

Things came to an unexpected conclusion in November 2018.

I'm not going to draw this out for the sake of creating drama. Gregor died. He was involved in a horrific car crash on the M25. In the end, that pileup had claimed 12 lives — men, women, children, gone in the blink of an eye — with many more injured, some life-changing, forever altered by the tragedy.

Google it. You'll know exactly which one I'm talking about.

They rolled Gregor into the Spire London East Hospital with broken bones and paralysis from the neck down. He'd never walk again. He struggled to control his breathing. The doctors and nurses saw no way to save him. The autopsy whispered one story, but the reality spoke another.

He'd live but he wouldn't.

I won't divulge every detail here. I'll save that, everything that happened over the four days that followed the crash, for another time. But you have to know that my intervention was the hardest thing I've ever had to do. By the end, I felt it was a necessity. I had toiled over what our lives would be like and made a decision that I was saving Gregor from a life not worth living.

I'll confess, there was a part of me that saw ending his suffering as an opportunity. He had denied me the one thing I wanted most in this world. I thought I could force upon myself a future which had just me and Gregor in it. That I didn't need to have children. That it would be enough.

But post-crash, that vision faded. There was no happiness, only a canvas splashed with resentment and confinement. No matter how much I adored Gregor — and I *really* did love Gregor — our existence would have been desolate.

If I'm deemed to be heartless for showing him mercy and freeing us both, I will take it like a slap in the face and move on. But ask yourself now, honestly, would you be able to stay with that person across from you on the sofa if you were in my shoes? Could you dedicate your life to being a carer at the peak of your life?

That night, after I had got back to our flat from the hospital, I went into the cupboard and poured myself a drop of Gregor's favourite Sauvignon red that he reserved for special occasions. I toasted to Gregor. The unlikely man who'd saved me from my lowest and gave me the chance to rise again.

That brings you to now. If you're still with me, I want you to know it's been cathartic, writing everything down like this. I don't attest to being the best writer but, whoever you are reading this, I hope you have some understanding of why I have done what I have.

However, this isn't the end.

An opportunity beckoned me back home, like a siren's call — irresistible and impossible to ignore.

TUESDAY 12TH NOVEMBER 2019

RHYS

The day's mood was dour as Rhys stood across the school gates earlier than normal.

The sun, only just climbing over the horizon, strained against a fresh wave of dense clouds. Rain was threatening. Rhys had felt a speck on his cheek as he climbed out of the front passenger seat of the Crossland.

A dingy white double-decker bus occupied the typically vacant spot in front of the academy. Engine idling. The driver absorbed by the morning's paper. A line of kids from his class queued to board.

Rhys scanned the road out of habit — left, right, and then left again. It was far quieter than normal. St Andrews had another hour in bed before its gates would open and the lollipop lady would appear and bring her shot of colour and energy to an otherwise drab street.

Rhys, hands wrapped around the straps of his pack, began to cross the road but was beckoned back to the driver's window by his mum.

She looked sad today, Rhys thought. Downcast. Tired. Perhaps a bit of both. She'd only asked a couple of questions during the drop-off, but didn't push him. There'd been no need for the headphones. Mum had flicked the radio on for a change, hummed away to the music on Heart Breakfast and played along to the morning quiz, berating the caller who got a basic question about Britney Spears horribly wrong.

The window rolled down as Rhys lined up beside it.

"Have a great time," she said.

"I will."

"Come here."

She gave him a big mum kiss on the cheek and messed with his hair. The way she always had.

"Go on. Be off with ya. I love you."

"Yeah, yeah. Love ya, too."

He didn't give her a kiss or a hug. The bus was only a few feet away. And who knows who could have been watching?

Rhys flicked his gaze around the bus, catching a mix of stares. Some eyes were normal. Some were that deep endless black — their inner Karma on full show.

On the top deck — window side, right at the back — Kyle glared at him through his own eyes, like an orc from the Lord Of The Rings. His piggy nose fogged the glass and Rhys shifted uncomfortably, scanning the empty road again.

Still quiet.

He trudged across to the other side, his wellies making that odd sound they do as they clobbered against the wet tarmac.

To the right, past the chicken fencing, in the school car park, Rhys saw someone climb out of a 05-plate dark grey Volkswagen Golf. He recognised the beaten brown satchel right away.

Mr Roberts also noticed Rhys after locking up the motor. His raised hand complemented a flash of a smile that disappeared in a blink. He stuffed his hand into the depths of a big trench coat pocket and turned on his heel. He was almost power-walking towards the looming academy buildings.

“Come on, Rhys! I reckon you’re the only one we’re waiting on,” said Mrs Johnson behind him. Chirpy as ever as she ushered him onto the bus.

After hopping on, he nodded to the old chap behind the wheel. His head of thinning grey hair looked up from his paper, eyes distant, as if staring past Rhys at Mrs Johnson.

“That it?”

“That’s it.”

The doors folded behind him. Rhys scanned the lower deck for a spot to park himself for the 30-minute trip to Hilltop Adventure Park. He hoped for a seat all to himself, but was fresh out of luck. Being last on meant it was slim pickings, but, as his mum would tell him, it was his own fault for draining every last minute he could again before leaving. Still, anything beat being forced to go upstairs.

And so he took the first vacant spot he could see halfway down the aisle on his right. Rhys took a pew. He glanced over to see who he’d sat next to. Their head was bowed, hood up, resting on a cap. A tuft of green sprouted out of black hair, covering eyes that were fastened to the Nintendo Switch in his hands.

Ralph Steadman.

Word to the wise. Give Ralph a chance, yeah? Annie’s words rewound and played in his ears.

Rhys stowed his pack by his feet and squashed it in with his legs, watching as Mrs Johnson approached.

"Ralph, can you put your game away and pull your hood down, please? I need everyone's attention while I go through some house rules."

"Sure. Sorry, Ms."

"Righto. Morning, guys! How're we all doing today?"

The bus fell silent in anticipation. Mrs Johnson ran through the day and what was to come. She talked through the safety rules — seat belts must be worn at all times, no standing up, no leaning into the aisle. Yadda, yadda.

"Any questions?"

Silence — aside from a couple of rogue coughs at the back.

"Great. If any of you need anything you've got me and the lovely Ms Inglethorpe up at the front."

Ms Inglethorpe opened a hand and closed it, smiling a toothy smile. Ms Inglethorpe was a stumpy old teaching assistant who showed up in classes from time to time. She always wore a cardigan. Always. And they always smelt funky, like an old woman. Some of the other kids called her Ms Mingerthorpe.

Mrs Johnson gave the same speech up the stairs and after she'd returned to her seat up at the front and gave the driver a thumbs up.

The bus had only started going down the hill when Rhys felt the softest of taps on his shoulder.

"Sorry. You want one?"

Ralph, hood pulled back up, held out a Twirl bar. It wasn't that chocolate bar that caught Rhys' attention, though. It was the eyeliner Ralph wore — a subtle flick at the corner of each eye. He later noticed the perfect curl of his eyelashes and the soft blush of foundation that covered his cheeks, which had a smattering of chocolate freckles and moles.

Rhys slipped his eyes away, not wanting to get caught staring the way everyone else at the academy did. He nodded and gratefully accepted it. He never said no to a chocolate bar.

It was strange that after three months, this had been their first real interaction. Up to this point, St Andrews had separated them — mainly on perceived intelligence. From day one, Rhys had been filtered into the top sets, Ralph in the bottom. Aside from the morning and end-of-the-day registration, their paths very rarely crossed.

What do you say to someone that you barely know and have never spoken to? What do you say to the kid who gets wolf-whistled and called a puff at every corner he turned?

Rhys had looked over a few times at Ralph as he played on the Switch. Turned out he was playing *Ichigo* as well, but was just a little further behind Rhys in the story. Ralph breathed heavily through his nose as he tried and failed to work out the puzzle he faced in the Cave of Inga.

"You gotta dig a hole in the wall back there," Rhys said.

"Huh?" Ralph responded, looking away from the screen.

"Sorry. There's a rope behind it that you can use to scale to the top."

Rhys watched as Ralph guided Ichigo to the back of the cave and chipped away at the rock face with a pickaxe. Lo-and-behold, a hole appeared and Ralph discovered the rope he needed tucked away in a box behind it.

"Thanks," Ralph said.

"No worries."

"You play, too?"

"Yeah. It was one of my dad's favourite games when he was younger and he told me I should play it when the remake came out."

"Mint, isn't it?"

"So good," Rhys said, smiled.

The bus pulled up at Hilltop Adventure Park just after 9.

Memories flooded back. Rhys had last visited during the summer, a month before the trip to Porthcurno Beach. The place buzzed with people that day, a real scorcher. The kind of day you didn't forget your sun cream and a hat.

There was no danger of that this time, though. The park was just waking up, seemingly reluctant to embrace the damp and chill of November, with far fewer people milling around to cater to and entertain. Still, Rhys found this place serene. Beautiful even. Off to the left was the little shopping complex that was offset by a peaceful lake that stretched for miles. The shutters of a souvenir and crafting store were just starting to lift, while two doors down a woman massaged the small of her back as she stretched out from scribbling on a blackboard outside the sweet shop – *Tuesday Special! 2 for 1 on Pick 'n' Mix!*

Despite the early hour, a few early risers had taken up residence in Cinnabon. Rhys could smell the coffee and cinnamon buns that were to die for out in the car park, lingering and tempting on the moist air, reminding him of the cakes, cookies, coffees, and juices he, mum, dad, and Eevie had devoured on one of the last great weekends the four of them had together.

Off to the right, there was a seating area and an assault course full of climbing frames of all different sizes that didn't have an inch to spare on that summer's day. Rhys also noted the sign for archery pointing off towards the woods and remembered him and his dad completing the course together. It had been his first time armed with a proper bow and arrow, and Rhys had loved it. He'd pretended he'd been Legolas, killing orcs that blocked his path. His dad had promised they'd come back sometime soon.

Sometime soon had yet to arrive.

There wouldn't be any bows and arrows involved today. Or assault courses, for that matter, either. Instead, Mrs Johnson would be leading her army of first year kids into the woods for a day of team activities.

"If you think you're here for a jolly day out, you can think again," she'd reminded them, her voice rising over the chatter and chunter as the kids filed out of the bus. "Yes, we're here to have fun, but we're also still here to learn!"

Ta very much for the reminder.

Rhys lined up against the bus with everyone else, making sure he was next to his new buddy, Ralph. Mrs Johnson, Ms Inglethorpe (Mingerthorpe), and two other people who wore matching, and frankly quite awful, outfits that looked like they had been recycled and stretched out from one of the local scouts' groups stood in front of them.

Rhys didn't catch the name of the man. He thought he heard the name Scout Russell. While he definitely caught the woman saying her name was Scout Abbott. They introduced themselves as the class's guides for the day.

From there, the class was split into two — classic Groups A and B — each was handed a map, a collection of activity sheets, and sent off in opposite directions.

It made a nice change that Rhys and Ralph were not being separated as they trudged the winding path together at the tail of Group A into the woods.

Once Scout Russell led Group A to their starting point midway up a muddy hill, another split ensued with two designated captains: Kyle, predictably, claimed one spot, and Charlene Osman, with her distinct brown curls that wound from root to tip, took the other.

Rhys and Ralph were engaged in a quiet conversation at the back when Kyle's voice pierced through, calling Rhys' name. At first, Rhys hesitated, rooted to the spot by surprise. "Come on, come on," urged Scout Russell, nudging him forward.

Rhys glanced around, hoping for someone, perhaps Mrs Johnson, to intervene, but no help came. Reluctantly, he fell in line behind Kyle, who towered over him and he'd gave Rhys' hair a rough ruffle as he trudged by.

The only consolation was that Ralph would also be on the same team.

Not that Kyle had a choice. Ralph had been the last to be picked — the kid neither captain wanted in their corner. Ralph plodded over and Rhys sniggered to himself as Kyle dropped his neck backwards and gazed into the treetops with despair.

Scout Russell led Kyle's team in one direction, while Charlene guided Mrs Johnson's team in the other. They dedicated the first hour to completing the unimaginatively named Hilltop Time Trail. Rhys and Ralph found themselves tailing at the back, ticking off their sheets and documenting the various trees and flowers along their path, using the trail markers.

The simple aim was to beat the other team to the finish line.

You'd think having Scout Russell by your side would be an advantage. That wasn't the case. He traipsed along up front with Kyle, offering little guidance.

While Mrs Johnson had preached team building and communication at the start of the day, there was no such thing with Kyle in charge. It was very much his way or the highway.

"Shut up, will you! I'm trying to concentrate. Fuck wit!" he'd shouted at Benji Cooper after he pointed out that they'd taken a wrong turn. Kyle gave Benji a shove on the shoulder for his troubles, and Benji didn't pipe up again. Scout Russell didn't have a lot to say. Maybe he didn't fancy his chances against Kyle, either.

So, yes, the big sucker messed up a few times and as a result, Group B was the winner. The endpoint was a tiny café called Roast & Toast. A canopy was erect outside it, shielding a cluster of wooden benches and tables from the unpredictable winter weather.

Everyone took 10. Ralph left Rhys' side and joined the growing queue for the toilet. Rhys heard someone remark about Ralph needing to join the ladies' line.

Rhys, elbows resting on the top of his knees as he took the weight off his feet, caught Kyle shamelessly eyeballing him again from across the canopy, just as he had done from the bus outside the academy.

If looks could kill, he thought. If looks could kill.

And even as Rhys turned away, he could still feel that hateful glare dreaming of beating him to a pulp.

He heard the crack and the fizz of a fresh can being opened before he saw Ralph thump down on the bench across from him.

Taking a sip, Ralph extended the cold can of Fanta to Rhys, who gratefully took a small swig before passing it back.

"Thanks." Rhys couldn't remember the last time he'd shared a drink with anyone.

The day's activities continued. Orienteering was next on the day's agenda. The two teams stayed as they were. The scouts handed out a fresh collection of maps and sheets, marking eight locations to find around the woods in 40 minutes before everyone met back at Roast & Toast for lunch.

"And remember, it's all about teamwork, guys. Find all eight markers and there will be a prize in it for you," Mrs Johnson had shouted, breaking through the chatter and intrigue among the group.

Unless the prize was an early bus ride home, Rhys didn't care.

A boy can dream, though, right?

He may well look a little silly, but Scout Russell oddly reminded Rhys of someone.

Mr Roberts.

They didn't look alike. Far from it. Under his neatly groomed buzz cut, Scout Russell sported a flourishing beard that Mr Roberts could only dream of. There were spits of grey in his hair and lines trailed his forehead. He looked like an adult rather than someone impersonating one.

Perhaps recognising how difficult Kyle had found the first activity, he came alive during orienteering, as if a different person had taken his place. This guy was in his element: helping make sense of the map, talking about the wildlife that circled them, navigating the paths hidden by a wet blanket of multi-coloured leaves.

It made Rhys think of Mr Roberts the previous day. His clip-board at the ready, one leg resting on the other, prepared to glean information, a story, and create the meaning behind it.

All Scout Russell wanted was for the kids to take a slice of his passion for the outdoors. Try as he did, though, no one wanted a piece of it. The other kids, they just took the mickey.

Perhaps he didn't give a monkey about that, though. Maybe he was even used to it. Regardless, his enthusiasm never dampened. But it made Rhys think. He, too, had made a judgement. He'd judged Scout Russell based on a silly uniform, just as he had with Mr Roberts for looking so young.

He looked over at Ralph. Head bowed, his quiff of green hair bobbing with every step. Another person everyone else had judged. Rhys knew what the other kids said about Ralph. All for how he looked. Rhys had also found it strange. A boy — the only boy at St Andrews — wearing makeup. But no one, including him, had taken the time to get to know the boy behind the makeup. The boy that breathed the same air, ate the same food, liked the same things, played the same games, like Ichigo.

He wanted to change that.

"Can I ask a question?" Rhys asked.

"Shoot."

"Why do you wear... y'know?"

"The makeup?"

"Yeah. why..."

"Do I wear it?" Ralph interjected.

Rhys nodded.

"It helps me feel like a better version of myself. I only use a small amount, but it makes the world of difference."

Rhys didn't know how to respond. How can he possibly understand? But that's just it, isn't it? He doesn't need to understand.

"Does it bother you?" Ralph asked.

"No."

"You sure? I'd get it, you know."

"Not one bit."

The first sign something was wrong was when Kyle joined Rhys and Ralph to make a team of three for a new challenge.

Scout Russell had called Group A to halt about halfway through the trail. With one foot atop a fallen tree trunk, he instructed everyone to split into threes for a timed exercise.

"On sheet 3, there are a set of clues and five symbols. Your challenge is simple: the first team to find all five in this area around us will win an extra prize when we return to Roast & Toast."

Rhys paired with Ralph. But without saying a thing, Kyle silently positioned himself beside them, a menacing grin plastered across his face.

"We all ready then?" Scout Russell said. Rhys didn't dare protest. "You've got 10 minutes. On your marks. Get set... Go!"

The groups hurried off in different directions. Kyle waited for Rhys and Ralph to make their move and followed behind, mimicking their slow steps. Until then, Rhys and Ralph had immersed themselves in chatter about video games and music. Kyle's presence made them both clam up. Together, the three of them strayed further from the others. It felt too late to change course.

Kyle spoke behind them. Said he thought he saw one of those symbols at the base of a tree trunk from the direction they'd just come from. Rhys and Ralph were still silent. Their shared history taught them it was best to keep schtum. But Kyle didn't decide to lead the way. He gave Rhys a nudge in the back, directed him towards a thick clump of trees.

That was the second sign something was wrong. Kyle was taking Rhys and Ralph back to where they'd come from, where the trees hugged together to make a thick wall.

Rhys' throat went dry with an overwhelming sense something bad was about to happen.

"Think it's behind that one, Maccie. Have a look, will ya?" Kyle pointed.

Rhys glanced at Ralph, pleading for help. But Ralph was just as scared as he was. He looked back towards the rest of the groups. No one was paying them any attention.

"Are you deaf?" Kyle snapped. He grabbed hold of Rhys' shoulders and pushed him closer to where he wanted him to look.

Where he wanted him to be.

"Ok, ok," Rhys stammered as he stumbled forward, adjusting his coat and bag, approaching the tree hesitantly.

The third sign something was wrong was when he heard the sound of leaves being crushed and brushed aside under heavy feet.

There was no time to react.

A hand — clammy, dirty, and foul — wrapped around his face, covering his mouth and nose. An arm, like a vice, clamped his head in position beneath his chin.

"Surprise, little fucker."

The words hissed with recognition.

Conor, who Rhys hadn't seen since he'd been excluded after the incident in the gym.

Rhys struggled to breathe. Broken whistles of air rose from his nose and tickled his eye through the gaps in Conor's hand. He glanced to the left. Ralph, too, struggled to break free, thrashing against Kyle's grip.

At that moment, Rhys' head got yanked back. He could see Conor's face. His right cheek bore a deep black and blue bruise. His eyes — the normal dark chocolate brown — pulsed with anger.

"We're going for a little walk, Maccie. That way."

Conor's forceful guidance left Rhys on wobbly legs. Powerless and consumed by genuine terror, Conor directed him away from the path, away from Scout Russell and the rest of the class.

Conor tugged and yanked Rhys viciously around trees and flailing branches that had hung in place peacefully.

And soon after, the four of them disappeared from view, leaving them unseen and isolated.

A sharp knee jabbed into Rhys' back, forcing him down to the cold and damp Earth.

The four of them were in a clearing by the side of Hilltop's murky lake, where tall grass and untamed weeds provided an eerie privacy.

Rhys attempted to lift himself back up, but Conor was on him again. His dirty hand pushed the side of his face, squashing it among the dead and moist leaves that clothed the mud beneath.

Try as he did, Conor's trailing knee obscured Ralph from view, but Rhys heard it all. Heard Ralph being tossed to the floor by Kyle, like an unwanted doll disposed of by a toddler. Kyle, as big and thick as a troll, towered over Ralph, smug in his smile. Rhys could only listen as a heavy thud drew a cry of pain.

"You want some more, puff? Yeah, you want some more!"

Another kick. Another yelp.

Rhys watched Ralph crawl into view, wet leaves sticking to the side of his face. His eyes stayed tightly shut, holding back the pain and tears. He shielded his stomach with his arms, bracing for more blows.

"Leave him alone," Rhys spluttered, his voice weak and fractured. Tears pooled in his eyes as Conor and Kyle mocked him.

"Yoh, check it out, Ky. Maccie's got a voice after all." Conor laughed. Kyle laughed with him, just as always. Rhys attempted to wriggle himself free, but Conor came down with more force on his face.

"You a puff as well, Maccie?"

"Just get off."

"Have it your way."

Conor leapt to his feet. His hands clasped around the collar of Rhys' coat, from which he dragged Rhys closer to the grass verge. Rhys dug the heel of his wellies into the ground. He slapped Conor's arms. He made things difficult, but not enough to stop his ass from being dragged over to the lake.

Rhys felt the ground slope. His head was hovering over the dirty water. He used every ounce of energy he could muster just to make sure it stayed that way.

But it was no use.

He felt weak. Powerless.

Conor's weight was pushing him closer, inch by inch. That or the water itself was pulling him in. Wanting him.

Eventually, it took him under its filthy and cold embrace.

Panic's grip was stronger than Conor's. Pure instinct kicked in. His body wriggled and struggled frantically, kicking up dirt that clouded his view of the world beyond. The sounds above were less clear. He screamed into a cloudy haze. Air bubbles danced across his eyes.

That was it.

He began to think that he was going to die.

Then a moment of reprieve.

Conor yanked him out of the water. Just for a second or two, and then he was back under again. Conor was teasing and playing with Rhys' life in the grip of his hands. Each time Rhys would return, choking and spluttering and fighting for precious breath. He begged and pleaded with Conor, under his bottom lip which pouted and was laced with the usual derision.

Conor nodded along, hearing Rhys' words but choosing to ignore them as he enjoyed the moment.

"I'm getting sick of hearing you bitch and whine, Maccie."

Rhys was submerged again, with no reprieve in sight this time. Unable to hold his breath any longer, his body weakened, and the fight drained away. Life seeped out, pulled by the freezing lake, and the dwindling light above began to fade.

But something changed.

There was a change in tone. Intense muffles above.

Conor's weight disappeared and Rhys managed to push himself free.

He flopped onto his back, gasping desperately for air, coughing and spluttering to rid his mouth of lingering dirt.

"The fuck you doing here," Rhys heard Conor spit.

Then Kyle said, "Con... who're you talking to, man?"

"What do you mean, dickwad? She's right there."

She.

A gust cut through the thick uncut grass and weeds and roused in the clearing. The leaves lifted and swirled. The water behind Rhys stirred, rippling away from the scene. The trees guarding the space rustled menacingly. Rhys wanted to put distance between him and the lake, but Conor stopped him.

"We ain't finished here, Maccie."

Rhys looked to see who had joined them.

Annie.

She etched towards them from the hidden entrance of the clearing. The hanging branches moved aside, paving a clear route for her. After a few strides, she stood dead still. Same bland black clothes over a scrawny body, hair up in its immaculate bun, undisturbed by the touch of the heavy wind that followed her in from the depths of the thicket of trees.

It looked like Annie, but not at the same. Not the one that came calling just three days ago. Her kind eyes. Her soft face. Her lips with a tiny lick of a curl in each corner. They were all gone, blown with the wind out to the lake behind them.

"You come to see Maccie take a little swim, have you?" Conor shouted, smug.

At the far end of the clearing, Kyle looked bemused by what was going on. He looked from Conor to the space where Annie stood, trying to work out what was happening. Like his mate had gone doolally.

"Con, seriously. Who the fuck are you talking to, man?"

Ralph still hugged the ground, but he was no longer cowering. He'd become a spectator to what was about to happen. Rhys could tell Ralph saw it, too: the thick branch that rose slowly into the air, out from the pits of a deep brush of weeds and swung in its place like a baton. The crack against the back of Kyle's head was sickening. His body went limp as he collapsed face-first with a soft thump. Lights out, as Rhys' dad would say. Lights out.

Ralph scrambled away from the body, tearing up the bed of frail leaves that attempted to stick to his wellies and trousers as he ran. He was too quick for Conor, who only took a single step toward Ralph before he gave him up as a lost cause.

"I'm not done with you either, you fuckin' puff," Conor shouted, his words swallowed by the trees as Ralph disappeared into the woods.

Annie ambled forward again until she was about 12 yards away from where Rhys lay. The wind settled. Birds, both small and big, congregated in the branches behind her.

"Do one. Or do you fancy going for a dunk as well?"

Annie looked utterly unfazed. The threat was meaningless to her. She angled her head to the side, sucking at her top lip.

"You should know how it feels, Conor."

"Fuck you talking about?"

"To feel helpless. Come on. You know what I'm talking about. Like when you're hiding under the bed. Hiding from your dad. Or when you sit at the top of the stairs, crying as you listen to him scream and beat your mum at night, wishing you could help. Wishing you could do something, but knowing you can't."

Any response Conor was trying to articulate got stuck behind a knot in his throat. Until finally...

"What the hell you talking about?"

"Really, Conor?" Annie replied, whimsically.

Rhys' eyes flicked between the two of them. He was a participant in a play, waiting for his cue.

"You don't know what you're talking about, bitch." Conor spat the words out slowly, each syllable carried by the sting of his anger.

Rhys looked back at Annie. His eyes implored her to meet his gaze. To tell him what to do.

But they weren't forthcoming. Her eyes stayed on Conor the whole time.

"Makes you feel like a coward, doesn't it? Knowing there's nothing you can do to help your mum."

Conor's hands balled into a fist.

"This is your last chance, Conor. You've been warned before about the path you're on. The danger that comes with it."

"And what're you going to do? You're going to start something here and now? Over this dweeb?"

"Don't do it, Conor."

For a moment, the two of them locked eyes in a standoff— two cowboys ready to duel, fingers tickling the butt of a gun. A shoot-out that would only leave one standing.

Conor drew first. "Fuck this. I've had enough."

With a big heave, Rhys got yanked up from the ground by his coat.

The same instincts kicked in.

"No, no, no. Please! No. Get off! Con... please don't."

Rhys slapped and scratched hard. But again, it was futile.

"Annie!"

His back was soon over the lip of the grass verge again. The freezing water rocked in and wrapped around his shoulders. Rhys continued to slap and pull at Conor's arms. All to no avail.

Water sprayed left and right.

He closed his eyes and held his breath, waiting for the inevitable.

But the inevitable never came.

“Fuckin’ bitch!”

Conor’s scream echoed through the clearing. Whatever had happened had forced him to release Rhys’ coat and stumble backwards. He clutched the back of his head. Blood, like a litter of tiny grass snakes emerging from a hole, streamed through the curls of his hair, winding down to his knuckles.

Conor looked over at Annie. She was unmoved. In front of the trees that whispered in the wind, a cluster of jagged stones and pebbles hovered by her shoulders. A dozen, perhaps, awaiting her command.

A single one flew past her at an astonishing speed. It stopped dead in front of Conor’s face, just a fingernail away from the bruise that stained Conor’s right cheek, forcing him to flinch and wince.

The disdain Conor carried when he grabbed Rhys on the trail had vanished, exposing only a shadow of the person Rhys had known. Conor was just like him — vulnerable, scared, maybe even broken.

“What... the fuck... is happening,” The words tripped in Conor’s mouth.

The pebble, no bigger than a button on a Nintendo Switch, teased in front of Conor’s eyes before whizzing over his shoulder and skittling across the water into another thicket on the other side of the lake.

Conor didn't heed the warning. From his pocket, he brandished a small knife, flicking the sharp of it up with a push of a button that got him excited again. Rhys weakly attempted to grab Conor's arm, to stop him from getting into a fight he knew he couldn't possibly win.

"Conor, don't. You don't know what she's-"

"Fuck off, Maccie," Conor slapped back, slashing the knife at him. "You want some of this as well, fuckface?"

Rhys slunk back to the ground.

"Didn't think so."

Conor started towards Annie, armed and ready to swing, but he didn't get a chance to take even five steps.

The soft ground shifted. Rhys felt the vibrations through his planted arms. A tree root snapped out of the ground, lifting Conor to the air where he stood, sending him sprawling onto his backside. The ends of the roots, like thick black tendrils that reminded Rhys of the vines from the Upside Down on *Stranger Things*, clamped Conor's feet in place.

Conor hacked at the roots with his knife, too distracted to notice Annie approaching. She paused at his feet, watching him flail and slash aimlessly.

"Get the fuck away from me, freak!"

Flushed, Conor's face contorted in frustration. More roots, more tendrils, climbed out of the ground, nestling in between and embracing one another, right around the base of his chin. They slowly began to squeeze and Conor dropped the knife. His fingers, coated in dirt, pawed at them as he fought for breath.

"Annie, come on... stop!" Rhys squealed.

She ignored him.

This was her show.

She was calling the shots.

And Rhys didn't know how far she was willing to go.

For a moment, Rhys thought he'd got through to Annie.

The roots around Conor's throat loosened, revealing a rough line of uneven scratches and smears of blood. He gasped for breath as he got to his unsteady feet. He attempted to run. But Annie hadn't finished with him.

Not yet.

Another tree root climbed out of the ground and pulled him back to the dirt with a whine. Annie was toying with him. It made Rhys think about all those times Conor had messed with him since September. Was he supposed to be enjoying this moment of what... sadistic justice? Revenge? Karma? Was he supposed to be revelling at the moment the one person he hated more than himself got his comeuppance? No, he felt no joy or satisfaction in watching Annie do this. Just pity. Sadness.

Annie, so slight in stature, towered over Conor, who cowered and pleaded in indistinguishable whispers.

"We warned you," Annie said.

"Annie," Rhys shouted, to no avail.

"Shall we find out how you like being repeatedly hit as you lie defenceless on the ground?"

The mud spat out more rocks. Some the size of a fist. The first pounded into Conor's arm that protected his face. Blow after blow followed, forcing Conor into a similar fetal position Rhys had occupied on the gym floor.

"Annie, stop! He's had enough!"

The stones dropped to her feet. Silence fell over the clearing for a brief, excruciating moment.

The ground rumbled again. As it had done before. The roots were moving. Rhys could feel it.

Two more roots climbed out from the underworld and grabbed Conor's ankles. His scream punctured the air as they yanked him past Rhys and towards the lake.

Conor's head dangled over the water. He snivelled as he fought against an invisible force to avoid submersion. The water lapped him up, leaving his limbs flailing in the grass. Almost a playback of the position Rhys had found himself in just five minutes earlier.

At that moment, he thought of Eevie. His sister going through the same experience he and now Conor had gone through. A brush with death that had gone as close as it could have. How must she have felt as the tides pulled her tiny body out, as she paddled with every ounce of energy to stay afloat? Helpless and hopeless.

Rhys couldn't change the past, but he could act now.

He finally climbed to his feet and lunged forward. He attempted to grab Annie's shoulders, but his hands went straight through her. Like he was grabbing at air. He'd forgotten that he wasn't dealing with anything human.

Rhys recollected himself and peered deep into a face absent of emotion.

"Annie. Please, just look at me. Please stop this. Please!" His voice carried Conor's desperation.

Finally, she responded. Hearing and filtering his plea. Annie looked away from Conor and gazed into Rhys. Her coal-black eyes disappeared like condensation, revealing the white and the brown of her iris.

She didn't say a thing. She didn't need to. Rhys knew it was over. From behind, he heard Conor releasing harsh coughs as he climbed back onto the lip of the verge. Rhys angled his neck until he could see Conor on all fours out of the corner of his eye. He took a moment to summon the courage he'd never had before in Conor's presence.

"Just go. Get out of here... ok. Go."

There was a pause. Trepidation. Maybe Conor was unsure whether it was done. A slow whistle of fear from his nose stole the silence.

"Go," Rhys repeated.

Conor scrambled to his feet and ran as fast as he could towards the trees and back towards the trail. His heavy footsteps, the crush of winter leaves, got quieter and quieter until they were no more.

That just left two. Well, three. Kyle was still sparked out by the side of the trees. Rhys jogged over and knelt beside him. There was a big splodge of blood above Kyle's right ear.

"Is he..."

It felt weird saying the D-word. Rhys didn't want to think about it.

But when he turned around to get some sort of confirmation from Annie, she was nowhere to be seen.

It's funny how things work out sometimes.

Rhys couldn't miss the irony of sitting on a fallen tree trunk, wrapped in Scout Russell's awful coat. Some might call that Karma, too.

Ralph sat beside him, clothes ditched as well. The green quiff of his hair was wet and matted, while his eyeliner had taken on a life of its own, running in various directions.

"You ok?" Ralph asked.

Rhys nodded. Ralph had only been the second person to ask that after Scout Russell.

It turned out that Ralph had hurried back to where they'd left the rest of the class. Scout Russell followed Ralph with the group in tow, back to the clearing. Russell, with a grave expression that said he hadn't dealt with many situations like this, attended to Rhys first before rushing over to Kyle, who was out for the count making a leaf and mud angel.

The gossip had started almost immediately. The looks and whispers among the different clusters of the class, all inevitably creating their tales that would spread virally across the rest of his year when they got back to St Andrews. Even the wildest imaginations would fall short of the reality.

Dirt clung to Rhys, his hair drenched to the roots. He had shivered until Russell pushed through the thicket and wrapped him in his coat. As awful as it looked, the thing kept him warm. Rhys watched the rising concern around Kyle, who sat up, groggy but clearly alive.

But what would happen next?

Rhys wondered whether he'd be in a world of trouble. An ambulance was on its way. Three kids (four, including Conor, who wasn't supposed to be there at all) had left the trail. One of them was unconscious, with a patch at the back of his thin blonde hair thick with blood and undoubtedly a thumping headache to match. Another two looked like they'd had a roll around in the mud and gone for a swim in the lake. Rhys wondered how he was going to explain this one.

"You can see them as well, then?" Ralph asked, breaking his thoughts.

The pair looked at each other with a shared silent recognition. Annie's words replayed in Rhys' head again. *You've got more in common than you think.*

A lady in hi-vis guided another group through the thicket into the clearing. At the head of it was Mrs Johnson. Ms Inglethorpe was in a few steps behind, with a second woman in hi-vis carrying a first aid kit by her hip.

Mrs Johnson skipped over to the tree trunk first. She knelt, bringing herself to Rhys and Ralph's eye level. She asked if they were ok in that sweet, sweet voice. There was no anger. Just concern. The inquest hadn't started. Not yet anyway.

But Rhys was taken aback as she brushed his cheek with a gloved hand, warming his damp and cold skin. Her perfume ran up his nostrils. She didn't say anything. Nor did he. He just watched as her eyes darted around his face.

Then he saw something. Something he'd never noticed about her before.

Her hair. It was-

"Ms Johnson, can we borrow you over here for a moment, please?" a voice interrupted.

She either didn't hear the call or decided to ignore it. Behind her, the Earth squelched and a shadow emerged over them. It was Scout Russell, looking a little shy and still stressed.

"Ms... sorry... can we borrow you for a moment?"

"I heard you the first time," she snapped, hushing him like he was one of her students. "Christ. Give me a second while I check on these two, will you!" Scout Russell skulked back towards the group that circled Kyle. Silence fell over them as well.

It was a side to Mrs Johnson that Rhys had never seen before, her soft exterior vanishing as if someone had flipped a switch. He couldn't help but look again at her hair as her usual smile returned.

Perhaps she had noticed Rhys was still looking at her hair. She stood briskly fiddling and readjusting the tangles above her forehead.

"I'll be right back. You, both of you, wait right here, ok?"

"Ok."

She smiled before turning on her heel and kicking through the leaves over to the two scouts and one of the ladies in hi-vis.

ELISA

I take the same route home from work each day.

Down past the walking trails, up around the corner past The White Bear and over the narrow bridge that connects to Wetherby Way. It takes me past the neatly cut conifers and shrubs that line the single row of four-bed fancy detached houses, their pristine driveways and multiple luxury cars.

This part of the village attracted your finer folk. It was the sort of place people like me didn't end up or belong.

But here I was, and that's possibly why anything out of the ordinary stands out, like a bulging stye beneath an eyelid.

You can't help but notice it.

The stye in question appeared a few days ago. It was a grey 12-plate Honda Alabaster that I had never seen before but had become a constant presence, lingering everywhere I turned.

It had parked in the same spot each time, just a few houses down from my own. I thought, perhaps, it belonged to some-one visiting a neighbour. Maybe the Bushell kid who I know had gone off to University in the summer. Maybe a grandson or daughter checking in on their grandparents. Or simply an old friend swinging by.

Those theories got chalked off when I drove back from work a couple of days ago and noticed someone skulking in the driver's seat. That itself wasn't the problem. The fact they were still there a few hours later set my paranoia off like a hornet's nest being poked.

I found myself keeping a lookout for that Alabaster. It was an itch in my brain that no amount of scratching would satisfy. Most evenings, I'd watched from behind the curtain of the guest bedroom window, tracking its movements. For the past two nights, it had driven off around 8, vanishing into the darkness.

And then it would return the following day. I can't be certain, but I am convinced I began to see that same Alabaster outside of work, too. Maybe it was all in my head. Maybe I was putting two and two together and getting five.

There isn't room for coincidences in my world. If you smell burning, it's because there is a fire.

And I smelt burning.

I knew I was being followed.

And I decided to do something about it.

As expected, the Alabaster was hogging its usual spot as I returned from work.

I parked up behind it and killed the ignition, but not the electrics. I needed to leave my beams on to see. This time of year, darkness didn't just creep up on you. It jumped out, like a Jack-in-the-box. You'd look outside at the day's sky one moment and look again in no time at all to be faced with a brooding night sky. And, as nice as this estate was, the street lighting spread thinly across it, leaving an ominous and lonely feeling during the late autumn and winter.

Tonight, the Alabaster was unattended. I lined up slowly beside the driver's side and could see the front passenger seat was littered with empty bottles of Pepsi Max and Diet Coke and crinkled crisp packets and torn-open sandwich boxes. The type you'd find in the chilled meal deal section of a supermarket.

The top of a flask gleamed in my car lights behind the handbrake. A web of darkness covered the back. A cluster of belongings cluttered the space, including a wrinkled shirt hanging on a hook across the back passenger side window. Left there after a hard day's work or just to hide the contents of the back of the car from prying eyes? It was hard to tell.

After checking my surroundings, I tested the handle. Locked. Of course, it was locked. But it's always worth a try. I ambled around to the boot, hoping for better luck.

But I got stopped in my tracks and nearly enough jumped out of my skin as I turned around.

A man stood in front of me.

No one I recognised. He was hard to make out at first. He wore a big slouched beanie hat and a thick scarf that cocooned his neck up to the butt of the chin. My car lights projected his silhouette over me. His frosty breath hung in the air.

"Can I help you, Miss?" he asked, not looking all that impressed that he'd caught me snooping. I could tell that much and put on my best disarming smile.

"Not at all. Your car I take it?"

"That's right. Something wrong?"

"No, no. I'd just seen that you'd been parked up here over the last few nights. I didn't recognise it and wanted to see if you were, I don't know, lost or needed something."

The man smiled. He cocked his boot open and threw a backpack in. From where I stood, I could see stacks of folders, a bag of groceries, and a yellow basket filled with car maintenance bits and bobs crammed into the far corner. He slammed the boot shut, sensing my eyes, and walked past me, pulling a set of keys from his coat pocket.

"No, not lost. It's real nice up here, isn't it? I'm looking into possibly moving into the area. You live in one of these, I take it," he said, waving a finger across the houses.

I decided to call him out on his bullshit. "I do. Just a few houses up that way. But I think you know that, don't you? Mr..."

The man gave his best shit you got me look.

"Demick. Walter Demick." He offered a hand that I didn't take. He quickly stuffed it back into the warmth of his pocket.

"What're you doing here, Mr Demick? What is it that brings you around this neck of the woods?"

"I told you, I'm looking at moving this way?"

"Come now. We don't have all night."

"Fine, you got me," Walter was being playful with it. "I'm looking for someone."

"Are you now?"

"Yeah. Actually, someone that went missing a long time ago. Someone presumed to be dead. But I found some stuff. Some really interesting stuff. And when you go digging, sometimes you just end up digging up things people don't want to be found."

"Sounds like you've got one hell of a job there."

"It never disappoints."

"And your digging has led you here? Of all places?"

"It has. I thought this one would be more difficult, to be honest, but it's amazing what you can find when you ask the right questions and look in the right places."

I covered my anger with another smile.

I thought this one would be more difficult.

I knew where this was going and felt as though this man was mocking me.

Walter swung the driver's door open and stuck the key in the ignition.

"I need to be getting off. But before I do, do you mind if I ask you a question, Miss?"

"Sure," my tone turned passive-aggressive. Trying to keep a mask on that was slowly being torn away.

"How long do you intend to hide out here for, Miss Stallard? Or is it Miss Thomas? Or is it—"

"I don't know what you're talking about."

"I'm sure you don't."

"Good evening, Mr Demick."

"And to you, too."

I got back in my car and watched as the Alabaster pulled off and drove slowly up the incline of the street.

My breathing, it was all over the place. I smashed my hands against the steering wall and pounded the side of my door with a fist until it hurt.

I couldn't let it end like that.

WALTER

The key card slipped from his grasp. A curse fell from his lips and chased after it.

Walter was just in time. He awkwardly wedged the door open with his elbow. Some would call it a lucky break. Walter knew some people thought he'd had a lifetime of those. Made a career out of them.

Not Walter, though. To him, there's no such thing as luck. It all boils down to hard work and graft. You have to make things happen in this life.

The past week encapsulated that. There'd been a lot of making things happen. His arms were proof of that. Folders on top of folders. Research on research. Notes and more notes.

Alongside his work. loaded grocery bags hung off his forearms — one was close to bursting. With a heave and a huff, Walter forced his way past the heavy hotel door and into his low-lit room.

The door slammed shut behind him as he deposited the contents of his arms onto the bed, creating a chaotic mess. Folders scattered over clean towels. Some of his groceries climbed out of their plastic bag, so too did a bag of chips he'd picked up from the local chip shop. Walter tossed his backpack against the pillows.

His muscles eased with the unburdening. The next stop was the pisser.

He took a long leak in the semi-dark and splashed his face with water. He briefly surveyed the mirror, contemplating the features time had etched over the past year — the lines, the wrinkles, the tinge of grey.

Time waits for no man.

Wise words his dad had passed on to him in the '60s growing up in Hackney when racism was casual and noses turned up as you walked by. Walter hadn't understood those words back then. When he had all the time in the world and not a care to give.

"You'll see," his dad used to respond. And now he did see it. Walter found himself passing on those same words to his son, Virgil. One day, he will understand too.

The key card.

Walter dipped back out into the hallway and collected his room key from the floor. A long way down the corridor, a couple was just checking themselves in for the night, luggage bags resting against the plain white wall. He can see that much. Without his glasses, he'd be hard-pressed to guess anything distinguishing about either one of them beyond that one was a man and the other a woman. Sight. Just another thing that was beginning to let him down.

Back inside, Walter felt the cool nip of what had been his temporary home. He padded over to the window and pulled it shut. He thought of his wife, Izzy, as he did so.

"You've gotta let the fresh air in," she always said.

Whether the temperatures peaked at furnace levels during a glorious summer's day or sunk below minus during the winter, she always had them open. Letting the fresh air in. Walter loved a lot of things about Izzy. A damn good woman, she was. But, hell, she was also a pain in the ass for leaving the windows open. It irritated him, just as someone picking at their nose or biting their nails would irritate most people. Lords knows all about that, too. For a lifetime, Izzy had clocked him around the back of the head whenever she'd caught him nibbling the ends of his fingers, deep in one thought or another.

Caught red-handed in the act.

However, the beauty of being out on the road meant he could get away with his bad habits in blissful peace and ignorance and could close a window without repercussions.

Walter went one step further and whacked up the temperature to fill the room with warmth. From the empty desk, he grabbed the remote and turned on the evening news before settling on to the edge of the bed and taking long swigs from his bottle of coke. His lukewarm chips were picked at, decent but not a patch on Whitby's fish and chips.

He pulled out his phone. He had two missed calls from Izzy. She *always* checked in with him around this time when he was away working and he made a mental note to call her back later. He'd be calling with good news, too. He'd be home the day after tomorrow, just in time for a quality weekend together. Walter planned to take her to El Romo, the nice Italian place she liked in town.

Before that, though, he needed to tie up a few loose ends.

Walter finished the last of his chips, disposed of the evidence of his latest takeout into the trash. He picked up the folders and files that layered one another, creating a domino-looking effect, and heaved everything over to the desk that had been his office for the week.

He wanted to stand. The back of his legs ached with mild cramps from all the sitting — not just this past few days but throughout his career. He leaned into his file, turning the pages made up of timelines, sheets of data, post-it notes, calls, and his research, all coming together to dot the I's and cross the T's. He was a stickler for the details. Always had been. It was the detail that made things happen.

Walter had everything that he needed. He was sure of it.

He sipped his Coke, satisfied with the narrative he built. For him, there was no greater buzz, whether it be as a journalist with the latest exclusive scoop or now as a private investigator finding someone who needed to be found.

He searched for Elizabeth McIntyre's number on his phone and hit call. It buzzed four or five times. No answer. Straight to voicemail. He decided to leave her a quick message rather than text.

"Hey, Elizabeth. It's Walter Demick calling. Can you give me a quick call back when you get a moment, please? I've got some news for you that you're going to want to hear."

Done.

Walter's excitement was suppressed. He was going to need to sit on it for just a while longer. After taking a long gulp of Coke and burping, his attention turned to the news. Israel had conducted airstrikes in Gaza. There had been a train collision in Bangladesh that had killed 16 people and injured dozens more. The Venice mayor declared a state of emergency after flood levels in the city reached their highest level in 50 years.

Walter shook his head. He often did when he watched the news. He liked to keep up with affairs around the world but it didn't half leave him feeling on a downer afterwards. World's gone to shit.

He was just about to head to the bathroom for a spruce-up when there was a knock on his door.

He casually swung it open, fully expecting it to be one of the hotel staff, but before he had time to react, something hard and blunt slammed against the top of his head.

Walter staggered backwards and fell to the ground. He was in a total daze and his head throbbed and pounded with agony.

With one arm, he dragged himself past the glass of Coke he dropped and towards the bed, clambering for his phone to call for help.

The door slammed behind him. Feet brushed against the carpet.

There was a voice. Another blow came down on the back of his head. Then another.

And Walter Demick's world went black.

JONNY

He was coming back in from the shed when he saw Elizabeth's fists pound against the dining table.

Old instincts took hold.

Without overthinking, he ran inside and wrapped Elizabeth in his arms, letting her raw, built-up emotion spill onto his jumper.

Rhys had come down from his room to find out what was going off. Jonny told Rhys his mum would be ok and asked him to take care of Eevie.

There was the crushed yoghurt pot on the table — a superficial detail. Jonny knew this wasn't about the pot or the surrounding mess. Nor was it about Eevie being difficult at the dinner table.

This was more. Much more.

This was everything: months of shit colliding together to form a wrecking ball that brought down a wall. The wall in question was the one Elizabeth had built and held together for months — all to maintain some sort of stability at home when everything and everyone around her seemed to be falling apart.

And what could he say about that?

This wasn't something a mere sorry could fix.

Because Jonny knew. He'd been part of that wrecking ball.

ELIZABETH

It all began down on the beach.

An overwhelming force building and consuming her.

The tension. Stretching. Expanding.

Over the last few months, that tension had been tensing under a weight it could no longer take and eventually, it snapped.

Elizabeth had been sitting trying to feed a yoghurt to Eevie at the kitchen table, one hand nursing the small of her aching back. Her little girl, an awkward feeder at the best of times anyway, tossed her head from side to side, dodging the spoon that tried to manoeuvre its way into her mouth.

As a toddler, she used to love it. She'd follow it around with her tiny eyes and lunge at it when it was close enough, peering thankfully into her mummy's eyes as she devoured every last drop from the edge of the spoon.

"Ee, come on. You love this," Elizabeth coaxed, but Eevie persistently slapped the spoon away, more tossing and turning.

"Ee, please."

More slapping. More tossing. More turning away.

"Ee! Just..."

With both hands, Eevie hit the spoon from Elizabeth's hand. It clattered against the tile flooring.

And with it, Elizabeth's thin wire of patience tensed beyond its limit.

"Just listen!" She slammed the pot on the table.

The table shuddered slightly under her hands and collected a thick pool of purple yoghurt that leapt into the air.

Eevie cried instantly, hysterically. She thrashed around in the chair and screamed. Elizabeth dug her fingers into the roots of her hair, angry at herself for slipping.

Losing control. Like this. At her daughter.

She didn't see Jonny come rushing through into the kitchen from outside. Elizabeth only felt herself being pulled into his tight embrace and it was there that the dam finally burst and every bit of emotion that had built up over the last five months came spilling out in her cries and tears.

EARLIER THAT DAY

Eevie had roused awake earlier than normal.

Before the sun had woken from its own slumber.

Elizabeth, on the other hand, had been tossing and turning even before that. Her mind had been restless and on the go. Refusing to relent on its many obsessions. Once the mental whirlwind began, there was no turning back, and she found herself grappling with thoughts until the morning light emerged.

Her eyes throbbed as she peeled herself from bed at just gone five. A mild headache loitered. The day's long routine awaited, starting with getting Eevie ready for the day. They needed to be out the door earlier than normal to drop Rhys off for his school trip.

By the time Elizabeth returned home, more than four hours had passed, and she was on her fourth cup of coffee. Eevie slapped away at her breakfast as Elizabeth looked around the house.

All she could see was a mess.

The dust that had accumulated, the stains, the grime, the droppings that littered the carpets and floors, the things that had found a home in the places they didn't belong. It all irritated and gnawed at her. The mess, though unchanged, seemed magnified.

Just another thing to think about.

How long had it been since she'd last had the time to clean? Weeks? Months?

Before the summer, she had tackled housework every week religiously — a Thursday task before the kids were back from school and nursery during her day off from Waterstones.

To her, there was no greater satisfaction than a clean and maintained house. Well, that and a good book, of course.

But time had slipped away, and as Elizabeth looked around, she knew she couldn't delay it any longer. This was one thing she didn't need to be obsessing over. So, she started as she always did: with a list. Noting down all the things that *would* get done today. There was:

Clean bathroom

Dust

Hoover

Deep clean kitchen

Mop

Change bedsheets

The fridge was also looking bare of the essentials. She didn't have the time to get out to the shops on top of everything else.

Jonny.

While she could have got Jonny to help her with the cleaning, he'd only have done a half-hearted job. If there was a cleaning job that needed doing around the house, it wasn't given to Jonny. But she could give him a list and send him, bags in hand, to the local convenience store. He could take Eevie with him while he was at it.

That he could do.

She scribbled another list out quickly and sent him on his way just after 9:30, with Eevie at his hip. Elizabeth chucked on some scruffs and tied her hair back in a careless bun. She meant business, and she got straight into it after making a fifth coffee.

Start with the bigger tasks you loathe most. That was Elizabeth's mantra. It'll only get easier after that. So Elizabeth dived straight into tackling the bathroom grime and mould, grimacing as she scrubbed and wiped, washed, and cleansed. Then it was the kitchen's turn. The hard floors after that.

~~Clean bathroom~~

Dust

Hoover

~~Deep clean kitchen~~

~~Mop~~

Change bedsheets

Each cross used to make her feel giddy and satisfied. This time it was strained relief.

The feather duster, polish, and hoover cried out to Elizabeth, feeling neglected and begging to get involved. There was still time for that, but she hit pause on the housework and took Eevie off Jonny's hands after he'd returned with the shopping.

He put the groceries away. Eevie exchanged hands again straight after so Elizabeth could scramble some eggs for dinner.

Her eyes clocked a large Galaxy bar hiding under a packet of lettuce in the bottom drawer. Sneaky bugger. She hadn't put that on the shopping list. She smiled to herself, thinking that it wouldn't be there come the end of the day.

A few minutes later, that smile got washed away.

Before she'd even got a chance to break off a square of the Galaxy bar.

Her phone started buzzing just before 12.

It was an unknown number that carried Patty Maxwell's voice. The St Andrews receptionist was chirpy and overbearing, as normal. A tone out of tune with the context of her call.

Elizabeth needed to get to Hilltop Adventure Park.

What on Earth's happened now?

When she arrived, there was an ambulance parked up, surrounded by a crowd of kids. Away from the group, Rhys was with a teacher who introduced herself as Ms Inglethorpe. Her boy, wrapped in a towel, stood covered in dirt from head to toe, his hair soaked to the roots.

"Rhys. Look at me. You can't keep pretending nothing's going on here."

The conversation waited until they were in the car, but Rhys remained unresponsive. Seated at the back of the Crossland, he avoided eye contact and deflected Elizabeth's questions. Absent were the usual headphones clamped around his ears; instead, he stared out the window, lost in profound contemplation, almost entranced.

He'd rushed to his room as soon as they got back home, leaving muddy footprints and chunks of dry mud in his wake. Elizabeth shouted up after him, ordering him to get out of his dirty clothes and straight in the shower.

Eevie was in the living room with Jonny, bawling her eyes out. Paw Patrol played on the TV, volume up way too high.

The morning's obsessions came rushing back to her. The unfinished list. The feather duster, the polish, and the hoover. The dinner dishes. The fresh mud in front of her.

Overwhelmed, Elizabeth closed her eyes.

Tension growing.

Tension straining.

Still so much to do.

On she went, ploughing through her list. One thing at a time.

At 5:30, Elizabeth found herself racing against the clock, the housework still unfinished.

An incomplete list lay on the table, a reminder that some tasks would spill over into the following day.

Dinner cooked away behind her, just a few breaded chicken slices from the Co-op sizzling under intense heat, pasta softening in a bubbling pot. She'd stir in a mix of Uncle Ben's carbonara sauce, sprinkle on a pinch of cheese before serving.

There was no time for anything else.

Eevie needed to be fed before the pasta needed to be drained.

Tension growing.

Tension straining.

Until it finally snapped.

Eevie threw her head back and forth as Elizabeth tried all the techniques in the book in vain. The things that had so often worked let her down. She pleaded with her little girl, but everything fell on deaf ears. A horrible clammy warmth built up under Elizabeth's knitted jumper as she willed every fibre within herself not to show her desperately crumbling patience.

But she couldn't help it.

Much like the queasiness that accompanies sickness, her anger and frustration churned in the pit of her stomach — a noxious blend of Eevie, Rhys, Jonny, Esme, Elisa, Walter, and unchecked to-do lists.

A recipe gone wrong.

Most of the time, she'd be able to take it down to a simmer.

This time, she finally boiled over.

As Jonny rushed in and held her tightly, Elizabeth felt, for the briefest moment, like she had her husband back. The one before Porthcurno Beach. Like someone had flicked a switch or rushed them back to a simpler time. A time when she didn't have to put on a brave face like a mask of make-up that never came off.

It took Elizabeth right back to when they were teenagers. When they started going out. Those arms, so comforting and safe. Arms that took all your troubles away.

She sobbed buckets for a little while, staining a patch of his favourite beige jumper. She heard him say something, not to her but to Rhys, who'd come down from his room to see what all the commotion was.

"She'll be ok. Just give her a moment," he said, pulling her in closer. Protecting her. Making sure their boy didn't see what she was going through. Rhys turned to soothing Eevie. Just as he had done in the car the day before. He always did have a way with his little sister.

Elizabeth felt Jonny's lips on her forehead, the roughness of his stubbly cool cheek above her ear.

From behind, Rhys wrapped his arms around her, too. Her two boys.

There for her when she needed them.

There they stood in an embrace until everything started to subside and feel ok again.

"I'm sorry, baby girl," Elizabeth murmured softly, twirling a strand of Eevie's hair around her finger. Her daughter nestled into Jonny's chest, red puffy eyes gazing at the LED ceiling lights. The calm had returned, yet even after the situation had de-escalated, Elizabeth found herself swimming in a sea of guilt.

"There's nothing to say sorry for," Jonny said reassuringly, giving Eevie a peck on the forehead. He sent Rhys back upstairs and took Eevie through to the living room, giving Elizabeth space to recollect herself and get straightened up.

She wiped her eyes and cleaned the mess up around her. The soggy pasta came off the hob and went straight into the bin. A new batch replaced it in a fresh pot of water that was left to bubble. The chicken slices came out of the oven a little overdone but acceptable.

Satisfied the hob was doing its thing, Elizabeth parked herself at the dining table, palms massaging her temples. Out of the corner of her eye, there was a brief flash of blue from her phone.

A new missed call.

Before she could check, Jonny returned to the kitchen with Eevie and settled her back in her high chair. Eevie remained quiet, a line of dribble escaping her mouth, fixated once again on the LEDs.

Jonny took the seat across from Elizabeth. His fingers twirled amongst hers as he gave her one of his reassuring *you've got this* and *you're ok* smiles.

A smile she hadn't seen for so long.

They ate in silence. Eevie couldn't decide whether to watch Peppa Pig on Jonny's phone or continue to inspect the kitchen lights. Only once they finished and Jonny took the dishes to the sink, Elizabeth spoke up.

"I'm sorry, Jonny," she said, holding back new tears and fresh self-loathing.

"What?" he responded, his face puzzled — a *what the hell you on about* look that time. His eyes were evasive.

"I'm sorry," Elizabeth repeated.

Jonny lay the dishes down by the sink and returned to the dining table. He shuffled a chair over to sit beside her, took her hand and enveloped it in both of his. His brows furrowed.

"Listen to me. There's nothing — *nothing* — for you to be sorry for."

He paused, taking his time, as though he was weighing things up. Elizabeth heard the cogs turning.

"You've dealt with *so* much. So much. It's me that should be sorry," his voice was soft. Softer than she'd heard for a long time. "You've kept *us* goin'. I know I've been a total mess. I've not done enough and I need to sort some stuff out. I'm trying, Liz. I want to be better." He began to tilt his head around. "Not just for you. But for Eevie. For Rhys. I... I've not done enough to help, but I promise it's going to change. I'm going to fix this."

One of Jonny's hands left hers to caress her cheek. His rough palm, weathered from years working on the yard, was clammy and warm. She fell deep into it, let it massage her cheek. A stray tear crept out and left a slick trail down to her chin.

Elizabeth pulled away. She took her husband's hand in hers this time. She believed him. Just as she had done 11 years earlier when he had last uttered those words.

I'm going to fix this.

Words that he might not think about anymore, but ones she would never forget. What happened 11 years ago, had been the hardest point of their relationship. It had been a rocky road. But he'd kept his promise back then and, together, they'd got through it when others had written them off.

Elizabeth knew he would be able to again.

"Love you," she said. Again, she couldn't recall the last time she'd told Jonny that. Everything that had happened over the last few months had just got in the way.

"Love you, too, Lizzy."

That nickname transported her back to the summer of 2002. She remembered those days as clear as a pure and untainted ocean. Days when they met at Greenway View on a Friday night. Nights when it was just the two of them, his arm draped across her shoulders pulling her in. Nights when many of their friends gathered at one of the local youth hotspots to listen to rubbish music, smoke weed, and neck cheap cans of cider.

They never felt like they were missing out, though. Back then they would watch the sunset on a perfect summer's day, that flawless blend of yale blue and burned orange in the cloudless sky.

"Hey, I forgot to tell you. I saw a flyer for a Breakfast with Santa over at Leppings. What'd you think?"

"What do you mean?" she asked.

"I mean, do you think we should go? The four of us?"

Again, when was the last time the four of them had done something — *anything* — together? Not since everything became so, what was the word? Fractured.

Breakfast with Santa, Something that was so basic but yet meant everything to Elizabeth.

"I can't think of anything better," Elizabeth replied.

Jonny arched across to Eevie, taking her attention away from the lights above.

"You want to go and see Santa, Ee?"

Who knows what she thought? She did acknowledge her dad, though, pressing her lips together and pushing out a puff of air and spit. That was good enough for Jonny who mimicked her — minus the spit and dribble — while Eevie's arms danced around above like they were being controlled by a puppet master.

Jonny got up, scraping his chair back on the hard floor. “Liz, leave the dishes. I’ll sort ‘em. I’m just gonna nip to the loo and check in on Rhys.”

As Jonny disappeared up the stairs, Elizabeth felt something she hadn’t felt for what seemed like an eternity.

Hopeful.

Then she reminded herself. One day at a time, Elizabeth, one day at a time.

JONNY

Think of a phobia, and how it can make a person feel.

Something like heights, or spiders, or tight and crowded spaces, or darkness, or failure, or even a certain clown peering at you through a roadside grate.

Whatever it is, that phobia has the power to induce an overwhelming and uncontrollable sensation, a sour cocktail of nausea and anxiety, topped up with hot sweats and a heart that doesn't just beat but pounds against your chest.

That's exactly how Jonny felt when Elizabeth asked him to *just* head out to the local convenience store and grab some essentials earlier that morning.

If the boot had been on another foot, Jonny would have told that person to get a grip on themselves. But the boot wasn't on another foot. It was on his foot, and he was downright terrified of that fact.

He had vehemently refused before Elizabeth could finish her request, his mouth operating on autopilot with its rejection.

"Oh, you've got other plans, have you?"

Jonny's silence was all the answer she needed.

"Well, you can help me out for a change, then."

And that was that.

He'd headed upstairs and took his time in the shower, washing away the weariness left behind by another sleepless night. Another night of that black shimmering silhouette stalking him, making its presence felt in his own home.

There was no hiding from it, no door he could slam to make it go away, no words he could shout that would get it to back the fuck off.

Jonny killed the flow of water and got out to another smiley face, thumb drawn into the steamed-up mirror. He'd not just looked for it, he'd expected it. He ran across and wiped it away immediately, leaving him looking at the broken, gaunt man he'd become through the re-emerging condensation.

That was how he was starting to feel. Broken. Fucked up.

Driving out of the estate, with Eevie strapped half asleep in the back, Jonny saw them everywhere. Those eyes constantly pulled his own away from the road ahead. Just off the Green Meadows Estate, he'd been locked in a staring contest with a young boy, sandwiched beside, Jonny presumed, his mum and dad. Jonny thought the boy could be no older than seven. But his eyes were black, his lips straight. Both made his innocent face terrifying as it followed Jonny's down until he was out of sight. Jonny had needed to slam on the brakes at the roundabout at the bottom to avoid ploughing into the back of a 56 Town and Back bus. The taxi driver behind him blasted his horn and gave Jonny a solid middle finger for extra measure.

Jonny pulled off down Fiskerton Drive, a quiet side street just off a main stretch of road that led towards town. He needed to get out and reset. There was a single row of detached houses and he parked up in the first spot he could and jumped out feeling like he was about to paint the road with his breakfast and black coffee.

The air was thick with cold, the fine morning rain even colder on his face. A cooked breakfast his nose enjoyed but his stomach didn't rode over from one of the nearby houses. He planted his arms on the roof of the Crossland and breathed heavily through his mouth.

In and out. In and out.

Jonny closed his eyes as he did, listening to the steady hum of the morning traffic he'd left behind.

With his head bowed, Jonny spent a minute or two spitting strings of phlegmy saliva onto the road. He checked on Eevie in the back. She looked at him with that same befuddled look she gave everything.

Then he was caught off guard. A weak hand tapped him on the back of his shoulder. Jonny, scared stiff, wheeled around to face two elderly women, one with a shock of pink hair and the other a tidy nest of white. They'd both managed to meander up the street in near silence. Apart from the hair, the two of them looked so alike. Jonny passed them as sisters, both in looks and how they dressed, both thin and frail in their thick trench coats and calf-length skirts, pushing their tartan-patterned trolly carts.

They'd caught Jonny mid-spit. The one who'd tapped him apologised for shitting him up — their words, not his — before reprimanding him for his bad habit. The other also didn't mind telling Jonny that he didn't look so peaky.

"This is a private street, you can't park here," one of the ladies said.

"I'll be off in a moment."

"Not been drinking, have you?"

"No," Jonny replied, not looking at either one of their faces. "Just a headache."

"Oh, hold on. I might be able to help with that."

The woman with the shock of pink shuffled around in the huge handbag that she perched on the handles of her trolley. She pulled out a packet of Nurofen.

"Never go anywhere without these."

She popped Jonny two capsules and forced a bottle of water into his hands. Jonny insisted he was fine. Nurofen could fix up most things but wouldn't help him with his problem. The two ladies were having none of his refusals, insisting they wouldn't leave him be until he had washed those capsules down.

"Stop messing about. We've got a bus to catch."

After Jonny had done as he was told, the woman with pink hair snatched her bottle of water back and off they were on their way as they tottled off to the bus stop at the top of the street, leaving Jonny there alone soaking up the crisp autumn air and the spitting rain.

His dad's reproachful voice echoed in his mind.

"Call yourself a man? A McIntyre."

Whatever that meant.

As a boy, Jonny would have had his ass whooped — whether his dad was sober or not — if he'd done anything to piss on the family name that Jonny's dad was so tribal over. Ironically, Jonny had never known his aunties, uncles, cousins, or grandparents. He'd known their names but could pass them on the street and wouldn't be able to tell a fellow McIntyre from anyone else.

As much as he hated his old man, Jonny often thought of what he would think of him now — his shortcomings as a father and husband over the last few months. The fact he'd been a shell of the man — the McIntyre — he once was. Jonny knew full well that it was only Elizabeth, an inducted McIntyre, who'd held the family together, doing everything while he hid down in the garden shed he'd built, playing old video games to escape his reality.

He couldn't stand seeing his own reflection and wincing as he heard his dad reprimanding him in his head. He told himself that as he caught Eevie gazing at him with innocence and confusion.

He couldn't go on like this.

Jonny knew that.

Baby steps, as Elizabeth had reminded him on numerous occasions. Baby steps.

Those baby steps started with picking up essentials at the local convenience store.

As Jonny parked the Crossland outside the front entrance, he took a moment to gather himself, observing others entering and exiting the store with envy.

How the trivial and mundane for them felt like a challenge wanting to put Jonny in his place.

Inside, the store was quiet. The aisles were tight, and he navigated down the ones that were absent of others as he hauled Eevie by his side and a small basket in the other hand.

Here we go.

Jonny whizzed around collecting what Liz had instructed him to, sick with the familiar sense of dread. His eyes remained largely on the floor. He didn't see faces. Instead, he saw shoes. And when he did, he quickly backtracked or skirted on by picking up his pace, circling back to any aisles he needed later down the line if necessary. Everything on Liz's list got mentally checked off in 10 minutes.

Compared to recent outings, Jonny could even say that the excursion had gone smoothly. Even Eevie had played her part, quietly taking the store in; its bright colours, the lights, smells, the coolness from the fridge.

He reached the checkout and unloaded the basket, chucking a Galaxy bar on at the very end for a job well done and a packet of spearmint Extra gum he'd keep in the shed. An over-enthusiastic dot of a woman called Joy welcomed him, proudly displaying her name badge below her left shoulder, which beamed with the words *Happy To Help*.

But Jonny didn't want help. Jonny wanted silence as he clumsily loaded up two bags as fast as he could while keeping Eevie balanced. But Joy was someone who wanted a life story, warts and all, as she went about her duties. Jonny offered a minimal amount. Answering questions, asking none of his own.

Eevie started to get fussy as they finished up. Jonny needed her to remain calm for just a little longer. He dug out the soft mermaid toy Liz packed away before they left. The current flavour of the month. Eevie grabbed at it gleefully and began to suck on its head.

Joy took this as an invitation to talk about her grandson. Troy, his name was. Only two years old, a little over a year younger than Eevie.

"Cute as a button, he is. Well, they all are when they're at that age, aren't they?" Joy said. "Even when they've got the grumpies on."

Eevie was getting less and less patient. Shopping falling out of the bags. Joy's incessant chatter. Machines beeping. People waiting. Eyes undoubtedly watching. Jonny nodded along, wishing the exchange away.

With the shopping clumsily packed, Jonny prepared to pay. At that moment, there seemed to be a lapse in time. Joy had stopped talking, her machine had stopped beeping. Jonny waited for the card reader to instruct him it was ready to take his money.

But it continued to hold him against his will — the only thing preventing him from getting the hell out of the store and back to the car.

"Everything ok?" he asked.

There was no answer from Joy but the card machine kicked into gear and he paid.

He looked up — just a glance. The least he could do was wish Joy a good rest of the day but his words were sucked out of his mouth by the two black holes staring right back at him. The old woman's thin smile was flat and intimidating. Jonny turned away, shook his head.

"Nope. Nope. Nope," he whispered.

He powered towards the exit with the words "Sir, you forgot your receipt," chasing him behind.

Once out of the doors, Jonny didn't look back. He wasn't thinking about anything else other than getting back to the car and didn't notice Eevie drop her mermaid outside the store entrance.

By the time he was back in the safety of the Crossland, Eevie was making strange sounds crossing between a cry and a squeal, similar to the way she did as a six-month-old seeking attention.

Jonny hoisted her up, gently bouncing her on the spot as she nestled her cheeks into his jumper, sucking on the fabric.

"We did it, baby girl," he whispered to her.

Doing something so trivial felt so monumental at that moment. His emotions poured out in big pushes of air and a fair few whispered fucks. All that remained was the journey home.

First things first. Jonny strapped Eevie into her chair. It was only then that he noticed the mermaid toy was nowhere to be seen. Liz would have his guts for garters if he came back without it. He frantically searched around the wheels and the boot to no avail.

He stuffed the shopping in the boot, all while still looking out for Eevie's missing toy. Eevie had become restless again, her moans veering dangerously towards tears. Jonny attempted to tease calmness out of her with other toys, a dressed-up bunny, a Minnie Mouse, and a parrot puppet that had been at the back of the boot for years. But she wasn't interested. Not in the slightest. Nothing measured up to the damn mermaid.

The worst-case scenario ran through Jonny's mind. The damn thing was back in the supermarket, wasn't it? Worse yet, right by Joy's checkout. The thought of going back sent shivers crawling over his skin. But there was no way he could leave it behind.

It was then he spotted it, the grape-coloured mermaid's tail standing out against the wet tarmac leading to the entrance. His shivers turned to relief. Jonny scooped the mermaid up. Eevie snatched it from him with both hands and plunged the poor mermaid's head back into her gob.

Her satisfaction — if that indeed was what it was — made Jonny smile. For the first time since leaving the house, any feelings of dread dissipated. As he made his way to the driver's side, Jonny saw a flier. Wet, a little torn, trapped under the wiper and whipping in the wind.

It promoted a Breakfast with Santa at Lepping's Farm.

RHYS

Lying on the bed, Rhys idly scrolled through the seemingly bottomless pit of songs on Spotify.

He had exhausted his favourite playlist. He'd grown fed up with listening to the same songs and needed something fresh, possibly entirely different from his usual choices.

He scanned the new albums, but none took his fancy. He checked the new singles and eventually landed on a new release from Billie Eilish — *Everything I Wanted* — and tapped play.

Rhys gave a song five seconds to leave an impression on him. He'd give most things a try — well, except for that Screamo rubbish. Once that brief window was up, the song would either be cast away into the endless abyss of songs, never to be played again, or find a spot in one of Rhys' many genre-specific playlists.

Rhys liked the beat of this one. He rested the iPod on his chest, lay back with his hands snugly tucked under his head and the top pillow. As the music played, his thoughts drifted to his mum, crying in dad's arms. His dad had tried to hide it away from him, make out it was no big deal.

But Rhys knew. He hadn't seen her cry like that since...

A wave of guilt washed over him. He knew he'd been awkward recently, keeping more and more stuff from her, shielding her away from what had been going off recently.

But in doing so, he'd played a part in what had unravelled. He convinced himself it had been the right thing. But now, doubt crept in.

Rhys made the silent decision he'd talk to her later that night.

Once things settled and Eevie lay tucked up in bed.

He wouldn't tell her everything. He couldn't. But he'd crack the door open a bit.

Just enough to begin to let her in again.

After the premature end of the school trip, Annie had been the only other thing to occupy Rhys' thoughts.

It wasn't like he had tried to block her out or how mad he was at her. He'd tried all the usual things to distract himself. He'd played on the Switch, drawn, tried watching TV and videos on YouTube, scrolled through social media.

But none of it worked. He couldn't let her go. Annie's face gnawed at his mind's eye, begging him to pay attention. So much so that he'd almost forgotten that he'd nearly drowned earlier that day!

The gentle beat of the Eilish song finished, leaving a momentary hush in which Rhys tuned into another sound nearby.

A faint tap, tap, tap.

At first, Rhys had thought it'd be his mum knocking on the door. Up to check on him. Good timing, Rhys thought. But as he waited, she didn't poke her head in as she usually would.

The door remained closed.

It was only when Rhys removed his headphones that he realised that the light, irregular knocking came from his window.

His bed creaked softly as he jumped off to investigate.

It turned out the tap tap tap was actually a peck peck peck.

A blackbird stood jabbing at the wooden frame as though it fancied itself as a woodpecker. It stopped what it was doing as Rhys drew near and held a steady gaze, its glossy pupils reflecting his bedroom light.

The radiator beside the desk cast a comforting warmth through Rhys' joggers as he leaned toward the window. As he did, the blackbird's beak opened, and its wings unfurled wide, the same way Rhys had seen swans do down at the park when they felt threatened.

Fixing its eyes on Rhys, the bird took two small steps back toward the frame's edge before leaping into the deep indigo sky, disappearing as its dark form melted into the gathering twilight.

Disappointed, Rhys surveyed Sandon Mount — a swift glance up and down the road for no reason at all but to just be nosey. Nothing stirred tonight. Nothing but a growing wind.

But that was about to change.

Two sounds followed, one after the other.

The first came from the stairwell.

The other was another squeak from Rhys' bed.

"Wha... what you doing here?" Rhys stammered.

Annie sat perched on the edge of Rhys' bed. Her legs swung back and forth playfully, like that of the young girl she appeared as. She scanned his room, her eyes settling on the wardrobe and the accumulating pile of clothes waiting to be re-homed.

"Nice room. Hasn't your mum asked you to sort that pile out, though?"

The comment made Rhys suddenly self-conscious. Why was he so bothered? So bothered that he walked over to stand in front of the pile.

"No need to hide it on my account," Annie teased.

Rhys stood disappointed. He didn't — couldn't — mask his feelings. "Is that it? Is that all you've got to say?"

An awkward silence lingered between them. Annie smiled. Rhys didn't. He noted the sound of the toilet flushing across the landing.

They weren't alone.

"What's wrong?" Annie finally asked.

"Are you kidding me?" Rhys replied in a harsh and frustrated whisper. "What the hell was that today?"

Annie looked bewildered. Like she had no idea what Rhys was talking about.

"What you did to Conor. It was so messed up. It's like... it's like you were possessed or something."

Annie lifted herself off Rhys' bed and levitated just an inch or two over the carpet, a small reminder to Rhys that she wasn't human at all and was capable of the wildest and scariest things imaginable. Rhys took a step back. His anger slunk back.

Annie's feet settled onto the carpet. "Are you scared of me, Rhys McIntyre?" Her voice was soft, playful, almost theatrical, as though she was performing in a pantomime.

Are you scared of me? Oh yes, I am!

"Wouldn't you be?"

"I suppose."

Rhys pursed his lips. He willed himself to ask the questions he'd been dying to since she disappeared by the lake at Hilltop Adventure Park.

"Why'd you do it?"

"Do what?"

"Come on. Don't play dumb. Conor?"

"I had to show you something."

"Show me what?"

At that, Annie smiled. "To show you that, sometimes, bad things happen. Things that are... totally out of our control. Like your sister, little Eevie. It was a terrible thing, right? A terrible accident. For months, though, you have blamed yourself. So has your dad. You've both been sinking in this sea of self-loathing. You needed... an intervention."

"My dad?"

"Hush. Just listen. But when these bad things happen, we all still have a choice," Annie said, flowing into a monologue. "We have the choice to hate, be angry, blame the world, or even blame ourselves — as you've done. We also have the choice to pick ourselves up. Be better. Rhys, after what happened on the beach, you'd taken a dangerous path. One that would have spiralled and spiralled had you stayed on it. Just as Conor has."

Annie closed the space between her and Rhys as she continued. "What you don't know is that Conor also has had some really bad things happen to him. Horrible things. And for the past year now, he's taken that anger, that resentment, and that fear out on the people around him. You weren't the first, Rhys, and you wouldn't have been the last. He had a choice. He had been warned."

"I don't understand," Rhys said.

"Because you too are in pain. A happy kid who had shut himself off from everyone because it was what he thought he deserved. You became the school loner, the boy who'd sit in the library with his colouring book, the kid that took crap from other kids, like Conor, because it felt like a perverse sense of justice."

Annie's pupils glossed over with a shimmering black.

"And today you had a choice," she said. "Out by the lake, you had the choice to let your pain eat you. You could have let all that bad consume you, all those months of misery Conor has inflicted on you. You had the chance to show him how much he's hurt you. But you didn't. You chose to do the right thing."

Another question hung on the tip of Rhys' tongue but he didn't get the chance to ask it.

ELIZABETH

She was still sitting at the dining table, basking in — unbeknown to her — a final moment of serenity.

Beside her, Eevie sat peacefully in her high chair, still captivated by the kitchen lights and engrossed in the growing collection of bubbly drool forming between her lips.

Elizabeth sighed and shook her head. She couldn't help but smile. "What we going to do with you?"

Eevie paused her raspberry-blowing for a moment. Her enormous eyes. Her beautiful brown eyes that used to sparkle were now glazed and vacant. Eevie's lips separated, pushing a line of drool to the corners as they curled upwards. Slightly, ever so slightly, but enough.

A smile.

Whether it was intentional or not, who knows? Elizabeth had been told from day one never to read too much into what Eevie did or did not do. Elizabeth had found moments like this difficult. She still wanted to believe everything Eevie did was intentional, that she was smiling now because she was happy and wanted to show her mummy that was the case.

There was no other way of communicating it, whether Elizabeth was doing a good enough job. And there most likely never would be. That didn't stop Elizabeth from clinging to the thought that even the slightest of smiles were intentional.

But as quick as the curls had risen had they relaxed. Eevie's body swayed, out of control, and she returned to blowing bubbles in blissful harmony.

Jonny would be hammering down the stairs soon to wash up the remaining dishes. After that, he'd probably head back down to the shed, wanting to play his games. Usually, she'd let him go. Let him have that space. Tonight, though, she wanted to curl up and feel close to him. She wanted to do what they used to, watch Emmerdale, maybe reboot where they'd left off with *Orange Is the New Black* before retiring to bed. Together.

As she waited for him, she pulled out her phone. There were a few notifications: a couple from Facebook, one from Instagram and Spotify, and three new emails. She glided over them to the bottom, her eyes only interested in the missed call she had.

From Walter Demick. He'd left a voicemail, too.

Elizabeth felt the usual flutter of excitement or anxiety in her chest. A concoction of both, perhaps. She thumbed over to her voicemails. It was short, only 10 seconds. She hit play and listened while she kept her eyes on the hallway.

"Hey, Elizabeth. It's Walter Demick calling. Can you give me a quick call back when you get a moment, please? I've got some news for you that you're going to want to hear."

News.

So vague. Could be good. Could be bad. But it was something nevertheless. Elizabeth thought his voice sounded like it was good news, though. Kind of upbeat. She *needed* to know more. Imagined varying scenarios he'd share.

She prodded the call button and brought it back to her ear. The thumb on her vacant hand also came up to her mouth and she began to nibble on a nail that was already short and didn't have a lot to offer in the way of comfort.

The phone buzzed and buzzed but there was no answer.

Typical.

Elizabeth didn't leave voicemails. She was a texter and quickly brought up her messages.

Sorry for missing your call... give me a buzz back when you're free.

Short but sweet. Also doesn't sound too desperate. Elizabeth left the phone screen facing up and her brain drifted into thinking what news Walter could have for her.

TWO MINUTES LATER

Jonny had finished up in the bathroom when he heard Rhys' voice pierce out onto the landing.

It was hushed, deliberately so. As if he were engaged in a secret conversation, making a conscious effort to keep it from reaching prying ears.

Jonny stood and listened, wondering if Rhys was on a game, something online like Fortnite or Rocket League, perhaps.

"Are you kidding me?" Jonny heard him mutter, a pinch louder.

The frustration in Rhys' voice was obvious. At first, Jonny smiled wryly to himself. Rhys always had been a sore loser. Jonny thought back to a year ago last summer when he'd told Rhys off for getting so angry at a game that he broke his Switch controller. Snapped the thing in two, he did. The insides spat out onto his bedroom floor. It was hard for Jonny to be too mad. Heck, he was just as bad when he was a boy.

But as Jonny continued to listen, anticipating a mini meltdown, he began to doubt his initial assumption.

"Annie, what the hell was that today?"

Annie? Who the fuck's Annie? Had he missed something and Rhys had a friend over from school? Jonny had been so disengaged that he didn't know an Annie.

Wanting to make sure everything was ok, he knocked on twice.

Didn't wait to be welcomed in.

Whatever question Jonny was going to ask got caught in his throat.

Rhys wasn't talking to someone.

But something.

And once Jonny saw the black shape standing in the middle of the room, he lost control.

"Rhys, get away from that Thing!"

"Dad. . . I. . . "

"Now!"

Jonny leaned in and yanked Rhys out to the landing by the wrist, never breaking eye contact with the Thing Rhys had been arguing with.

"Storm's coming, Rhys. I'll see you soon," Annie said. She tapped her nose with the inside of her index finger. Once. Twice.

Torn between deciphering those cryptic words and maintaining balance, Rhys skidded across the floor in his socks.

Down in the kitchen, Elizabeth dropped her phone on the table, alarmed by Jonny's panicked shouts.

What on Earth?

"I'll be back in a moment, sweetie," she said to Eevie. She planted a soft kiss on her daughter's head and hurried to the bottom of the stairs.

"Get away from my family?" Jonny shouted at the Thing, securing Rhys tightly against his chest.

"Dad, wait," Rhys protested.

But it was in vain.

Rhys couldn't move. His dad strapped him tightly to his chest. Something else caught his eye. Another lady, further down the landing by his mum and dad's room. He'd never seen her before, but knew instantly that she was one of them. Karma. This one had long dark hair that draped across her shoulders and ended with a shock of blue at the tips. She held up her hand and waved.

Amidst the chaos, Elizabeth climbed the stairs.

Jonny needed to get himself and Rhys away from the Thing. He heaved Rhys up to carry him and darted for the stairs.

Elizabeth reached the top.

She didn't see Jonny coming until it was too late.

Nor did Jonny see her coming.

But Rhys felt it. Felt something bump into his back.

All that remained were a sickening couple of seconds filled with thuds and bangs.

Rhys didn't need to see any of it to know.

An eerie silence gripped the house.

Rhys felt his dad's heart pound into his chest.

He craned his neck, looked down at his mum crumpled in a heap at the foot of the stairs, her body shooting in all different and uncomfortable positions.

"Liz..." Jonny whispered. His soft mutter pierced the stillness.

Jonny's mind cleared of everything else. He released Rhys and galloped down the steps, taking them two or more at a time.

As fast as his body could take him.

"Mum," Rhys whispered.

PART THREE

I'M NOT — I CAN'T — WAIT ANY LONGER

JONNY

Only a few months after hunkering down in a hospital waiting room, the McIntyres found themselves back again.

Only this time it was the much more familiar Kingsmill ICU waiting area.

The last time Jonny had been here was when his dad died a couple of years back. Before that, it was the same hospital where both of his kids had been born.

A place where time stands still.

It felt like it had again as Jonny cradled a soundly sleeping Eevie on his chest, her rhythmic snores providing a stark contrast to the tension enveloping the family. A nurse had draped a clinical, bright white blanket over Eevie, a futile attempt to provide some semblance of comfort. Jonny buried his head into Eevie's tangle of hair and closed his eyes, wishing this was all some horrible fucking nightmare.

Footsteps, a sound of flip-flops in the distance, gradually got closer. He lifted his pleading eyes, hoping to see Doctor Jammerson heading his way, returning with another update.

Not this time. It was just another couple of the docs, decked from head to toe in overbearing blue overalls. Jonny's eyes followed them as they disappeared through a set of double doors, clinging on to slim hope that they might turn around and realise they do have an update after all.

They didn't.

He checked the clock in the far corner of the room, above the vacant reception desk. It was nearing 10:30. He, Eevie, Rhys, Nellie, and Ron had occupied a line of chairs against the back wall for the last three or so hours.

Or so Jonny thinks.

However long it had been, Jonny was feeling that time in his ass which had taken the brunt of the uncomfortable chair he'd been glued to since Eevie had conked out. His shoulder blades nagged him from holding Eevie in the same place for the last hour without shifting weight.

He'd take the temporary aching for her to be at peace. Beside him, Rhys rested his head against the wall, eyes glued to the ceiling.

Nellie and Ron, who had grown increasingly silent, hadn't spoken to Jonny since he recounted what had happened back at the house. Jonny had left out the obvious details. And while neither Nellie nor Ron outwardly said anything, Jonny could feel their deep-seated resentment, that they probably blamed him for their daughter being in hospital.

Just another reason for them to hate his guts.

Jonny wasn't daft. As much as Elizabeth had always tried to reassure him that what happened all those years ago was water under the bridge with her adopted parents, Jonny knew the wounds were far from healed.

That they'd never let it go.

They thought their daughter deserved better.

His mind replayed what happened back at the house: Elizabeth knocking into him, falling down the stairs as though in slow motion. The blood pooling under her neck, him begging for her to wake up, pleading with some operator at the end of his 999 call for help, standing back helpless and terrified as the flashing blues cut into the hallway off Sandon Mount.

Maybe Nellie and Ron were right. She did deserve better.

The wait went on.

Over an hour had passed since Doctor Jammerson told them Elizabeth went for a CT head scan, and they hadn't heard anything since.

The waiting area had increasingly thinned out. Fewer people were milling around, fewer patients came in and out of the doors, fewer beds were being wheeled from one ward to the next.

Jonny noticed Ron out of the corner of his eye, rising with a sigh, approaching him with hands nestled deep in the pockets of his camo trousers.

"I'm heading over to the vending machines, old boy. Come and give us a hand," Ron invited.

Eevie had woken up just a couple of minutes earlier. Coincidence? Jonny didn't think so. He asked Rhys to watch his sister, to bring a few of the toys over from the corner to keep her occupied in front of nana Nellie.

He chucked his half-empty cup of tea in the bin and followed Ron. The vendors weren't far, just through the double doors where they hugged the wall to the right.

Aside from a cleaner mopping the floor a little further down the well-lit corridor, the pair of them were alone. Jonny went to dig out his wallet from his back pocket, but Ron put a silent hand on his arm.

I've got this.

Ron began feeding coins into the machine, squinting at the letters and numbers as he did so, just as he did when he was trying to figure out his next move on a sudoku puzzle. He was too proud to admit his eyes were failing him and he needed glasses. A real man's man. Ron reminded Jonny a lot of his father, albeit a much better version of his old man.

The machine clicked into gear, and it quickly became clear that Jonny hadn't just come along as an extra pair of hands.

"Me and Nel think it'd be best if the kids come back and stay with us for a few days," Ron said.

Jonny stood with his back to the wall, letting the words wash over him. Ron fed more coins into the vendor and punched in a couple more buttons.

"Jon?"

"No, you're right." He pinched his top lip with his teeth until it hurt. He knew it was the right thing to do. Jonny needed to be at the hospital with Liz and he didn't want the kids going anywhere near the house without him there.

"We'll swing by the house on our way back," Ron said. "Pick some bits and bobs up for Eevie."

"Haven't you got enough of what you need to see you through tonight at least?" Jonny said. He hoped to divert Ron away from needing to return to Sandon Mount.

"Not meds, no."

There was no way around it. Eevie needed those meds.

"And you know where they are?"

"Still top shelf of the cupboard in Eevie's room?"

"That's it."

"What's going off, Jon?"

"Nothing. It's just getting late and I don't want to keep them up more than necessary."

"Sure, sure. I'll text you tomorrow and we can work out a time to bring them both back up here tomorrow."

The machine finished up and Ron emptied a sugar sachet, then another. Nellie always did have a sweet tooth.

"She'll be alright, Son. You'll see," Ron said.

Jonny didn't know what he'd do if the outcome was any different.

The only spare hand Ron had actually needed had been for Jonny to hold the door for him on the way back through to the ICU waiting area.

As Jonny secured the heavy door, his attention shifted towards Nellie, engrossed in conversation with Doctor Jammerson, a feat or two away from Eevie and Rhys sat on the hard floor. Eevie gleefully smacked Lego bricks together, while Rhys' attention split between playing with his sister and discreetly listening in on what the doc was sharing with his granny.

Jonny let the door go and it swung back hard, within inches of leaving Ron wearing a couple of piping hot teas. Doctor Jammerson held a set of folders tightly to her chest and did all the talking. Nellie nodded attentively, hanging on every word.

The doc was midway through whatever she was explaining when Jonny cut her off.

"What's going on? Is Liz ok?" he asked.

Doctor Jammerson was all eye contact and smiles. She turned to Jonny and pushed a stray lock of her black hair behind her ear. Jonny met her gaze, daring to engage, and thankfully found only kindness in her eyes.

"I was just telling Nellie that there's nothing to worry about. We have managed to stabilise Elizabeth."

"Ron, our Liz is doing ok," Nellie said, jutting her head to the side to see past Jonny as Ron steadily returned to them.

"What a relief. Wonderful news. Take this tea off me, will you, love?"

Jammerson continued after paying Ron a pity laugh. "As we spoke about a little while ago, Elizabeth had some nasty swelling at the back of the head that we needed to get checked out before we did anything else. Thankfully, the results of the CT scan haven't shown anything that we need to be concerned about."

"She's a tough nut, that one," Ron said.

Damn right she is.

"So, what happens next?" Jonny enquired.

"Now we wait. Elizabeth is heavily sedated right now so she can get the rest she needs and we can get that swelling down. We'll keep a close eye on her tonight and she's booked in for another scan tomorrow afternoon — really, just to double check we haven't missed anything. All being well, though, I see no reason she shouldn't be awake and able to see visitors tomorrow night."

The relief whooshed out of Jonny's mouth as his hands clamped around the back of his head. Hot tears burned the corner of his eyes. He turned away from everyone, brushed them off with the sweep of a hand. He didn't want anyone to see him like that.

"Thank you. Are we able to see her now?" Jonny asked. "I'm planning on staying, but the kids are going home with the grand-parents tonight and they'd love to see her before they go."

"I don't see why not."

There was that smile again. "Let me drop these off at the front desk and I will come back and get you all on my way back up."

And Doctor Jammerson was off on her way. Nellie pulled out her phone, the old Doro she refused to part with for something a little more modern, presumably to share the news with Esme. Ron took a seat beside her, taking a swig of his tea, while Jonny took the seat nearest to the kids.

"Dad?"

Jonny looked down at Rhys, fiddling with a Lego block between his fingers. His face was weighed down by worry that carried through in his soft voice. "Is mum ok?"

"She... she's going to be fine, bud. Doc says she needs rest but she's going to come back and take you and Eevie through so you can see her. After that, nana and grandpa are going to take you both back to theirs."

"But why can't I stay here?"

"Because it could be a few days before your mum is allowed to come home and you'll be bored out of your skull," he said, attempting to suck the seriousness of the night away. "That, and your sister can't stay here. She still needs her routine."

Rhys nodded sulkily. Jonny knew his boy wouldn't be thrilled by the thought of staying with his grandparents. Until the summer, he'd been protesting for the last couple of years that he was old enough to stay at home on his own on the rare occasions he and Liz were both out.

They looked at each other in solemn silence. What happened back at the house hadn't been spoken about. Like each was afraid of what the other would say. That their version of events wouldn't match up to the other. Rhys' next question meant it became unavoidable.

"Why can't we stay at home?"

"Because..."

The understanding on Rhys' face meant nothing else needed to be said. But before Jonny could dig out the words to try and talk about it, the familiar clapping of plimsolls echoed, and through the double doors emerged Doctor Jammerson.

RHYS

The first thing Rhys noticed when his nana opened the door to 25 Sandon Mount was the blood — just a few drops, but unmistakable if you knew where to look.

Returning home felt peculiar. As if he were stepping into a crime scene or a forbidden place. The warmth inside enveloped him and fought away the mid-November cold. He'd not worn a coat to the hospital, and the chill had bitten right through his jumper and left his teeth chattering.

Rhys had left the house amid chaos: paramedics running around, the blues of the ambulance lighting up the hallway, Eevie crying from the kitchen, dad caught up in it all. His own mind going a million miles an hour. Looking around the house, though, everything still looked normal. The heating was on, the lights around the house blared, whatever was on the TV at this hour chirped on a low mutter, and the shoes and coats of its occupants hung on their hooks after another long day. Everything was as it should be. Well, aside from drops of dark dots of blood smudged at the bottom of the stairs.

Now, an unnerving silence draped over the house, concealing the haunting memory of what had occurred just five hours ago, leaving the house lived in yet vacated all at once.

A hand on Rhys' shoulder shuffled him along, encouraging him to not stare at the red-coloured elephant in the room. It was his grandad's hand. "Go on, laddy. Go and grab some bits and bobs you'll need for tonight and tomorrow. It's getting late, so let's be out of here in 15 minutes, yeah?"

Rhys complied. Out of habit, he kicked his shoes off and took the steps two out of time. His nana had, inevitably, mentioned needing to make a pit stop at the loo after leaving Kingsmill. She followed him up, but her spindly legs were much slower up the stairs, and that gave Rhys the head start he wanted.

He didn't know what to expect when he pressed his bedroom door open with tentative fingers. Maybe Annie was still there, swinging her legs back and forth, as though she'd been waiting for him to return the whole time. He'd scanned the landing for the lady, the one with hair that flowed into blue tips. The lady he'd never seen before. But she was nowhere to be seen.

Rhys poked his head into his vacated room. Again, he scanned, just to double-check. Annie had a history of showing up out of nowhere. But she was nowhere to be seen.

Was he disappointed? Relieved? He wasn't sure.

From behind, he could hear that nana had finally caught up with him. She gave him an awkward smile, clicked the bathroom light on, and went about her business, leaving Rhys to get sorted.

He yanked his small suitcase out from the depths of his wardrobe, through the line of clothes that clung on to the damn thing. He set about packing the 'bits and bobs' his grandad had told him to gather: socks, pants, a couple of t-shirts from an untouched clean washing pile, one jumper, his favourite jeans, and his thickest pair of grey jogging bottoms.

It was only when he was ready to seal the case up that he spotted the corner of a piece of paper peaking out of one of the pockets. He pulled it out, it was the drawing he'd started and never finished from the trip to Lizard Point.

How he'd do anything to go back in time. Back to that day. Back in time and make sure none of what had happened since ever occurred.

Rhys scrunched the sheet up and tossed it towards the bin — of course, he missed — and once his suitcase was zipped up and by the door, he packed his school bag with the essentials: his Nintendo Switch and a few art supplies, checking items off in his head as he went along.

And that was that.

Or so he thought.

He glanced around his room again, unsure of when he'd be back. Whether a day would turn into days, whether days would turn into a week, whether a week would turn into weeks.

Just as it had in the summer.

He remembered how uncomfortable his grandparents' pillows were and so he snatched the biggest one from the head of his bed and lobbed it onto the pile of belongings to go with him tonight.

"You getting on ok? Need a hand?" Nana said, poking her head in.

"Nah, I think I'm about sorted. I'll be down in a minute."

She gave one of those big nana smiles and tottled off back downstairs where Rhys could hear his grandpa coughing away again.

Rhys lugged the strap of his backpack onto his shoulder and just as he was about to heave up his tiny suitcase, he felt a compulsion to stop, a strange sensation from deep within. Like nothing he'd ever felt before. He turned on the spot, perhaps expecting that Annie would be right there.

His eyes smothered every inch of the room, waiting for something — anything — to move or stir and explain this random vibe he was getting.

"You're still here, aren't you," he whispered.

But there was no answer.

ELISA

Credit where credit's due. Walter had done a fine job.

One folder in particular, crammed with information, notes, dates, and records, stood out. As soon as I got home from his hotel, I spread it all across my coffee table. My entire life laid bare, sheet after sheet.

Part of me felt a flicker of annoyance at how easily Walter had pieced together every detail since I boarded that boat to Ireland. How he managed it in just a week was beyond me. Figuring out his methods could be useful down the line, but I guess I'll never know.

Still, now I knew why he'd been searching for me. Walter had left a paper trail for everything. He even had the original email from Elizabeth and a full transcript of their first meeting at a library outside of town.

That girl knows how to spin a tale as good as any you'll find on a library shelf.

The last bit of red wine I opened when I got home was calling me. I finished it off before heading to bed. Like they say, it'd be rude not to.

Anyway, it was anyone's guess as to how long it would be before Walter's body got found. I'd checked the local news a few times, but nothing yet.

I'm not here to do anyone's job. I've got my own shit to deal with.

This, there was a similar vibe to what happened with Alfred all those years ago. The night that started everything.

On that, though.

First Alfred, back at the orphanage. Then Gregor a few years ago. And now Walter.

According to Google, I'm officially a serial killer now.

WEDNESDAY 13TH NOVEMBER 2019

JONNY

But for the Crossland dashboard, Jonny wouldn't have had any sense of what time it was as he pulled up on the McIntyres' pebbled drive.

The clock showed 1:23 in the afternoon. Yet outside looked the same as it had when he'd first roused awake from a broken daze by Liz's bedside earlier that morning. The same unnerving thick layer of mist drooped beneath a familiar grey sky, blotting out the day's sun. It was a mist that dampened and clung to everything it came into contact with, the type that filled your lungs with cold air and hung solid on your breath.

Jonny hadn't returned home out of choice.

Doctor Jammerson had sent him away. He'd resisted leaving Liz's side, expressing his frustration to the point of attracting awkward glances and hushed murmurs on the ward. Only when Jammerson suggested that it would be a good idea for him to gather some of Liz's essentials and a few fresh pyjamas that he'd softened.

"The latest scans are looking as we'd hoped. The swelling has reduced overnight, so, yes, we're going to try to wake her, see how she responds to that next."

"What comes after that?"

"Let's not get too ahead of ourselves."

Jonny made Jammerson promise to wait for him before doing anything. And satisfied as much as he could be, he bent down to Liz and delicately folded a stray strand of her blonde hair behind her ear and whispered, "I'll be right back. You hear me."

He kissed her cool cheek, told her he loved her, and left. His gaze lingered on her until the door closed behind him.

Back at home, the first thing that hit was that it wasn't much warmer inside than it was out. It was one of the few issues Jonny had noticed with the house on Sandon Mount during late autumn and early winter that first year they'd bought it. The chill had a way of permeating if the heating hadn't been on for a while.

Standing with trepidation, Jonny's eyes got drawn to the foot of the stairs. Visions of Liz lying there in a sickening heap resurfaced. Someone, likely Nellie, had tried to clean the blood up while they were in the house last night. Just like red wine, blood was a bitch to get out of fabric and there remained a faint smudge that would need further attention.

That was a future Jonny problem.

His only priority was getting back to Liz's side.

To get the essentials she'd need, Jonny had to go upstairs.

He held his breath, putting all his focus into listening. Trying to make out even the weakest of sounds that might indicate he wasn't alone in the house.

The oppressive silence did nothing to put Jonny at ease.

He took the stairs cautiously, treading one creaking step at a time, ears on full alert, neck angled so he could see as much of the landing as possible. Nothing stirred, and so Jonny set about getting what he came for.

In their bedroom, he discovered the old overnight bag Liz had used when she had been induced with Eevie. He ripped through the drawers, tossing in her favourite PJs and underwear. Enough for a few days. There was the paperback on her bedside table that he tucked away with her iPad and charger. From the bathroom, he bagged up her toothbrush, paste, shower gel, and shampoo. Liz had a tub full of lotions and potions — enough for a house full of women — stowed in a basket in the corner of the shower. The bottles were sticky, and the lids clogged with gunk from whatever shit it contained. Undoubtedly, there'd been something in there Liz would class as essential. That she'd curse his ass for forgetting.

At that thought, Jonny smiled.

That was everything from upstairs. There were still some bits he wanted to get from the kitchen: a couple of cans of Fanta, bottles of her flavoured waters, and a bag of sweets. He bundled everything up from the bed and made his way out to the landing.

That's when he heard it. A creak. The subtlest of wheezes.

But it was enough to stop Jonny dead on the spot.

There was another squeak, enough to cement in Jonny's mind that it was coming from Rhys' bedroom.

With caution, Jonny proceeded, ensuring that he took each step with care as he nuzzled open his son's bedroom door. His exhaled breath made a soft whistling sound as he cautiously peered around the doorframe, mentally bracing himself for the worst.

That he wouldn't like what he saw on the other side.

To his relief, the room appeared vacant. He scanned the landing — you know, just in case — but again, there was no one.

Nothing.

The first thing Jonny noted was that while the rest of the house was cold, Rhys' room was even fucking colder. A slight crack in the window above the desk on the far side allowed the chilly breeze to seep in.

Jonny set down Liz's things and padded over to pull it shut, giving it a good heave before pulling the latch down.

Under him, on Rhys' desk, a crumpled sheet of paper lay, but it had been straightened back out.

One of his Rhys' drawings from the holiday. The memory came flooding back of the day at Lizard Point.

He picked it up, smoothed it out, and held it closer to take it in.

It was then he noticed there was something on the back

Jonny turned it over. On the other side was a picture of a girl with two big black circles for eyes.

Just like the ones that followed him wherever he went.

RHYS

There was a knock on the bedroom door, and nana Nellie let herself in.

"Thought you might be hungry, laddy?"

In she came with a plate of cheese and ham sandwiches. Sat atop it was a packet of ready-salted crisps and a spoon. She placed them at the end of the bed — his mum's old bed.

"What's the spoon for?" Rhys asked. Although he already knew the answer.

"Crumbs. I would have forgotten."

From her deep cardigan pocket, nana Nellie pulled out a small yoghurt pot and an angel slice, presenting them with a flourish, like she'd just pulled out a rabbit out of a hat instead. "Ta-da!"

"Thanks, but don't you want me to come and eat at the table?"

"No, you're ok. Just this once, though, and don't tell your grandpa. He'd lose his teeth if he knew I gave special privileges."

Rhys pulled the imaginary zip across his lips. He could have done with a literal one as a yawn escaped no more than a second later. The result of a crappy night's sleep.

"Sorry," he muttered.

"And so you should be. You wait until I tell your mum."

Rhys knew she'd regretted the words the moment they left her lips. The smile from her face was gone as quickly, and a subdued mood fell over them.

But she didn't let the tension fester for long.

"I've called the hospital."

"And?"

"No big change. But they are goin' to try to wake her a little later."

"Are we allowed to be there?"

"Of course. I need to ring your dad to find out his plans and get Eevie sorted, but I'm thinking we can leave here around 3:30ish."

Rhys glanced at the old alarm clock in the corner — his mum's old alarm clock. That was only three hours away.

"Parking during visitor hours is a nightmare," his nana went on. "But we should just miss it... if we leave on time," she finished with a raised eyebrow.

"Ha-ha." The response drew out one of nana Nellie's weak smiles.

She shuffled the plate of sandwiches closer to him and got back to her feet, holding the bottom of her back as she did so. "Righto then. Get that snap down you and maybe even try to get your head down for an hour. One of us will come up and wake you around 3ish. Yeah?"

"Sure." But there was no way he was going to sleep.

Nana Nellie's frail legs slowly took her to the door, but before she left, she turned back to him.

"She'll be ok you know, laddy."

Try as she did to reassure him. All he felt like he was doing was trying to reassure her.

"I know," he responded with a smile of his own.

ELISA

"Hey you. How're you getting on?"

I wasn't in the mood for this. Not today. Every time I pass the reception desk, it's always the same.

"How was your weekend?" *Not bad, ta.*

"Get up to owt much fun?" *Not really. Just the usual.*

"Happy Wednesday." *Is it?*

"You got any crazy plans this weekend?" *If only.*

That first question, it's like a piece of cheese sitting in a mouse-trap. If you're a mouse, that takes the bait and asks a question back, that's it. The trap snaps. She's got you. I learned that lesson very early on.

"Not bad, thank you," I replied, trying to move on. My eye caught the day's newspaper next to an empty breakfast bowl. The headline stuck out as though it lifted off the page.

MAN FOUND DEAD IN HOTEL.

"You want to have a read?" She asked, noticing my interest.

"That's ok,"

"It's fine. I'm done with it, anyway."

With the paper added to my arm, already full of folders, I was nearly away. I was so close. But she said something that caught me by surprise.

“Don’t run off just yet. I’ve had a call this morning from a Nellie Woodley. Rhys McIntyre’s grandmother.”

“Oh...”

“Yes, she phoned to let us know Rhys wouldn’t be in for the rest of the week, said his mum was in hospital.”

“Really? What happened?”

“I didn’t ask. Terrible though, isn’t it? Like that boy hasn’t been through enough. I met his mum last week when she was here and she seemed so nice.”

Patty Maxwell. She thinks everyone’s nice.

She was still rabbiting on as I let the door swing behind me.

Time seemed to be dragging its heels.

Ever since I found out Elizabeth had gone to the hospital, the clock seemed to tick slower, almost mockingly.

I’d used my free periods to ring around the local hospitals. I made out I was Esme, hoping to get an update on Elizabeth’s condition. There were three hospitals around us that she could be at. I just needed to know which one.

It turned out to be Kingsmill, 10 minutes outside of town.

Parking up had been a bitch. People rinsed every last second they could with their loved ones before all funnelling out at the same time. I’d left work the very second I could, refusing to hang around for the latest meeting with Conor Wilkinson’s mother to discuss what we were going to do next with her son.

If everything went according to plan, I wouldn’t have to deal with that at all.

The wind lightly swayed my stationary car and made light work of pushing winter's soggy leaves across the car park. The entrance to the ICU loomed in my vision, its doors pulsating with people coming and going.

Were the McIntyres already there?

It didn't matter.

I've bided my time long enough.

I'm not — and I can't — wait any longer.

RHYS

"Ron, there's a spot over there. Right at the end. You see it?"

"I see it. I'm not blind just yet."

The car swung in, narrowly missing a Toyota on Rhys' side. He'd winced, fully expecting the scrape of metal on metal.

"Well, I don't think we could have timed that any better," nana Nellie said, either oblivious to how close they had been to hitting the car next to them or just not wanting to test grandpa's patience further.

Was this how it was when you got older? Rhys wondered. Cheap thrills from dodging the busy visiting hours, nabbing spots where no one else could saddle up to you, narrowly avoiding forking out for an expensive paint job down one side of your motor?

Rhys slumped back while his nana and grandpa slowly heaved themselves out of the car. He faced Eevie, whose arms were flapping as she focused on something in front of her that wasn't there, oblivious to what was unfolding.

Their eyes connected as Eevie's head lolled to the side. Her arms stopped mid-motion like someone hit the pause button on her. Her lips were moving, though. An unperfected sound slipped through her teeth as her mouth dropped and came back up.

Rer Rer.

Well, this was new.

Eevie did it again. Rhys felt overwhelmed, but he tried to keep his sister going. Nodding. Smiling. Encouraging her. "Yeah, that's right," he said.

He put a hand to his chest. "Rer Rer."

Then he pulled it away and placed it on his sister. "Ee Ee. Can you say Ee Ee?"

Of course, she didn't. Eevie's face displayed the usual befuddled look. But her jaw continued to move on autopilot, dropping and rising to release the same sound, chuntering a solo ritual.

Rer Rer. Rer Rer. Rer Rer.

Grandpa cranked Eevie's door open and lifted her out into the stroller. "You're getting too big for me, missy."

There was a knock on Rhys' window.

"Come on. Don't want to keep your mum waiting, do you?"

JONNY

Jonny propped himself up against the row of vending machines he'd told Nellie he'd meet them at.

He's stood smack bang in the middle of a T-junction corridor — the prime spot to make sure they didn't miss each other.

The main entrance, shops, and cafés lay straight ahead, Gynaecology to the right, and ICU to the left.

With Elizabeth's overnight bag slung over his shoulder, Jonny surveyed the corridors, picking his way through the small clusters of doctors, nurses, volunteers, and visitors. The majority with their heads down going about their business. He checked his watch. Should be arriving any minute. He took a big swig from the water he purchased from the machine he was lent against.

Then he saw them coming in through the main entrance. Jonny threw an arm up, splayed his fingers as if it was the difference between them seeing him and not, and began to wave.

Rhys saw him first. Ron and Nellie were too busy chatting away as they pushed Eevie along in her stroller through the spread of people that parted out their way. Rhys was pointing him out to them, tugging on Ron's sleeve. Jonny ruffled Rhys' hair as he lined up against his side.

"How're you doing?" Ron asked with a wheezy breath.

"Not bad. Everything fine with these two?" Jonny asked, looking from Eevie to Rhys. As he did, though, he noticed his son was gazing off down the corridor. Following Rhys' line of sight, Jonny discovered a short, stubby woman staring back at them, her eyes smouldering black.

"Jon?" Ron pushed.

"Sorry."

"It's fine," he muttered, though the simmering annoyance in his eyes suggested otherwise. "I said they've been good as gold."

"Goodo," Jonny responded, stealing another glance, but the woman had vanished.

"Have you heard any more?" Nellie asked.

"Nothing. I only got here five minutes ago myself."

From the direction of the ICU, familiar footsteps patted quickly past them. Doctor Jammerson, decked in the same light blue overalls, had her head bowed, charging to her next destination, flicking through sheets as she did so. Jonny called out to her, prompting her to pause and turn back.

"Sorry, I was in a world of my own there. How're we all doing?" Doctor Jammerson asked.

"Yeah, I think we're all ok," Jonny offered on everyone's behalf. "How's *she* doing?"

"Yep, still stable. There's no reason we can't press ahead with the plan."

Jonny felt Rhys cling a little tighter. Jonny knew he'd not shown his boy nearly enough affection over the last few months. He wasn't going to let him down anymore. Jonny held Rhys in closer and gave his shoulder a soft squeeze.

"Feel free to head on down now," Doctor Jammerson continued. "Her sister's beat you here and is already in with her. I'll drop these folders off and I'll be right with you, ok?"

And just like that Doctor Jammerson was on her way.

"Didn't Esme say she wouldn't be able to make it until tomorrow?" Nellie asked, leaving the question hanging.

ELISA

It'd been remarkably straightforward.

But then, I'd known I'd have no trouble getting into Elizabeth's room. The reality is hospital staff are just too busy to be checking everyone that comes and goes. Amid the chaos of their demanding jobs, verifying every visitor's identity is a secondary concern.

Their primary duty is saving lives, not doubling up as security.

Providing you knew who you were looking for, you could say you were family and you'd get taken at face value. No questions asked. You'd ask what room they were in and they'd guide you without a second thought. Sent on your merry way with a smile to go with it.

Now, in this case, I didn't have to lie. Of course, I am, indeed, family.

Just not the family anyone was expecting.

And there *she* was.

Isolated in a spacious yet unremarkable room, lit up by two strips of LED beams overhead. The pale skin I remember blended in with her sealed shut eyes. She always had been the palest out of the three of us. Tubes crawled out of her mouth. Thin white sheets tightly swaddled her. The machines above her bed beeped and safety barriers stood guard, limiting her movements and warding off any risk of a fall.

Heaven forbid.

This moment had occupied my thoughts repeatedly over the days, weeks, months, and years since I escaped Aston. Never once did I envision it unfolding like this. But then life is rarely predictable, nor does it live up to our expectations, does it?

I unwrap my scarf, take off my coat and gloves, and dump them on the lone visitor seat, creating a careless mountain of fabric. I have my bag as well, but that stays with me. I'll be needing that.

It's strange. Even after all this time, I thought I would feel more.

"Hey, sis. Long time no see..."

Almost right on cue, the sound of a tired trolley stops outside the room and a junior nurse enters. She's sheepish, innocent, and young, going about her afternoon rounds. A recent graduate, perhaps. At the beginning of her adventure to save lives and make that difference she's always dreamed of.

The same dreams I had when I lived in Lewisham.

But this is one life I know she won't be able to save.

"Sorry, I didn't expect anyone to be here," she said.

She hauls the trolley into the room behind her, anyway. It rattles along with fresh medication, packets of tablets, tubes, and all matters of liquid. Sure, she had a job to do, but, fuck, she was killing the moment.

"Actually, would you be able to come back in 10 minutes?" I said sharply, more so than I intended. "This won't take long."

I saw her reluctance. But you know the beauty of most young people? They don't have it in them to question the authority of an older, firmer voice.

"Um, yeah. I guess that'd be fine." She finished with an awkward smile.

Finally, she left us to it.

To ensure I wouldn't be surprised again, I paced around to the other side of my sister's bed, making sure I had a full view of what was happening both outside the room and inside it.

Now was my moment. I looked at her, ready to finally say what I wanted to.

But that's just it. Despite thinking about this moment for so long, I didn't know what to say. My mind was blank despite a thousand thoughts whirling around up there.

I stared at her for a little, concluded that this wasn't the moment for a planned script.

"After so much time to think about this, you'd think I'd know what to say. Truth is, I haven't got this huge monologue planned or written out. A lot of people in our shoes might've had a lot of questions for each other. I actually only have two. I'll save one for later and so I'll start with this... did you think about me at all, after what you did all those years ago?"

I got in close, right by her ear. Her eyes might be closed, but I wanted to make sure she heard me if she could still listen.

"After you left me to rot. All while you lived the life you dreamt of. What was it, sis? What was it that made you send Walter to look for me after all these years? Love? Guilt? Not knowing what happened after you left? I read his file. You tell quite a story. You really do. You even had me hooked. But you missed some pretty important details. I'm sure you didn't do that intentionally, though, right?"

I pull the folder out of my bag, open it up, and perch it nicely on my arm. Like a mother getting ready to read a bedtime story to a child.

"I mean, even right here, see," I pointed it out to her. "You talk about mum dying of an aneurysm. No mention at all of you causing it and killing her. No mention of the fact you had hit her over the head with the rolling pin. And over what? Some ice cream she wouldn't let you have? Fuck, you were my little sister. If I'd told everyone the truth, they would have split us up. The very least I could do was try to keep the three of us together. It's what mum would have wanted. And so, I lied... told them that our mum had fallen down the stairs earlier in the day, had been complaining of a headache after hitting her head. From shitty place to shitty place, we got sent everywhere after that. All because I lied. It always felt like it was us against the world. Well, at least I thought it was, anyway."

Another detail stuck out to me.

"And see right here," yes, again I show Elizabeth the file. "I didn't know what game you were playing until it was too late. It was clever really. When you told me that Ron had grabbed and hurt you. You knew exactly how I'd react. How it would look."

I look at her again, taking a moment to wonder how she'd react to all of this if she was awake. Would she still deny it after all these years? From under the bedsheet, I draw out her forearm and turn it over to reveal the tiny scar that stood out paler than the rest of her skin.

A permanent reminder.

"Ah, so it did leave a mark."

I never did forget it. Back at Aston. When we were alone in our room arguing. Things had gotten really heated as I called her out on what she had been doing, the game she had been playing. Elizabeth had done something that had completely taken me off guard and bit down on her own arm with everything she had. Her teeth had gauged into her skin and drew blood. After that, Elizabeth screamed and begged for help. Her accusations were pointing straight at me.

"That day... it was the beginning of the end for me, wasn't it? Back then, I thought we'd sort it. Blind and naïve enough to think we'd get past it. But you had other plans, other ideas. It was the final nail in the coffin when we were out in the park. You remember? Up on that big slide together. The three of us."

Just like the bite, she'd orchestrated it perfectly. Atop the slide, Elizabeth had placed herself behind me, asked me to go ahead of her, behind Esme. Esme was just about to go down and then came the shove in my back. So hard my neck had jolted but there was nothing I could do as Esme went off the edge and broke her arm.

"Never did tell Es the truth, did you? Not that it matters. She will know everything soon enough."

I'm forced to pause for a moment as another trolley rattles by outside. A silhouette passes the window, but this one disappears out of sight.

"After that day at the park, I was totally on my own. Left to fend for myself. I was the evil one, even in Ron and Nellie's eyes.

I don't get it, Liz. Did you hate me so much that you wanted to leave me in that place alone? With those people? Even after what I did for you after mum?"

I have to stop myself now. Those years at Aston flooded my memories like a picture film powered by a steam train. The nights alone, the beatings, the dirty old men that patrolled the corridors. Jessica Thomas. Alfred Mongan.

All of it.

"I went to Ireland, y'know. But hey, you can read that in the file when you're awake. Walter did a stellar job for the large part by the way. He really did. He tracked me from Ireland to here to London and back again. Worth every penny you paid him. It's a shame it's been a waste, though. The dead don't need money."

My fingers slam the folder shut and I stuff it back in my bag.

"Saying all that, there were some things he missed. Important stuff, too. Like the baby I lost. Mine and Jonny's baby. And, yes, before you ask, I mean *your* Jonny. Liz... social media is fantastic, don't you think? Even back then, even over a decade ago, I could find out everything I needed to know about you. All while you knew nothing about me. It didn't take long to get into Jonny's head once I came back. I thought I could take him away from you. Make you feel just a tiny piece of the pain you caused me. But still, the dumb fuck went and chose you when you found out. He left me. Left *us*."

Now that I thought about it, this was the first time I had spoken about the daughter I never had outside of a AA meeting. Talking about it now, I realise why I hadn't. My mouth felt dry and my breathing was all over the place. Tears were threatening to spill. I wiped them and the pain they contained away.

Liz didn't deserve them.

"There was a time I thought I was truly done with this. That I'd never come back. For a time, I felt at peace in Ireland but in London, when I met Gregor I thought I'd done it. I'd put everything behind me and moved on. I got married. I got into teaching. Had a nice apartment with lots of plants. But even then, even at the happiest point I can recall, you and everything that comes with you started to peck away at me again, begging for my attention. You're like a scab you can't help but pick and as soon as you do, the wound reopens."

My grip around my bag straps releases and I, instead, lean against the plastic barrier.

"So, that just leaves me with my final question. Why? Why did you hate me enough to do this to me? To abandon me and take everything away from me?"

At that moment, I could swear it. Liz's hand — or maybe just a finger — twitched. I take her hand in my own. She's cold, and I wonder in that moment whether all of this has been nothing. Would she even remember any of this when she awoke? Had any of it gone in?

It was at that moment that the door to the room was etched open.

RHYS

There she was again.

Annie.

Lingering against the wall, right on the lip of it before the turn into the ICU.

She looked at Rhys — stoic and emotionless as ever.

He distanced himself from his dad, who was engrossed in a puzzle with nana and grandpa, attempting to figure out who had come to visit mum.

"One of her friends, perhaps?" nana suggested.

"Wouldn't have thought so. She's not even been here 24 hours and I haven't let anyone know," dad had responded. "Unless either of you?"

By that point, Rhys was gone. He didn't hear the rest of the debate. Although he thought he had heard Eevie muttering *Rer Rer* again as he sloped away. Maybe calling after him.

Perhaps anticipating what was about to happen next.

Annie didn't hang around.

After Rhys had peeled away from his dad's side, their

movements became synced. He moved; Annie moved. She slipped around the corner, out of sight. Trying to keep pace, Rhys refrained from shouting after her and drawing unwanted attention.

Once he had followed her into the ICU, Rhys impatiently waited for the automatic double doors that led into the waiting area to open in their own time. He squeezed through at his first opportunity and spotted Annie making her way towards the ward.

She didn't break stride and was soon out of his eyeline again. Rhys broke into a jog, his backpack slapping his back and the hood of his coat bouncing with each step. He followed Annie past the main desk and down a tight corridor that split off like connecting limbs. Rhys slowed down, scanning each of them as he passed by, but Annie was nowhere to be seen.

It dawned on him that he was heading towards his mum's room. The corridor he was on ended at another T-junction. He stopped to let a nurse pushing a multi-coloured trolley pass.

And there she was again.

Annie.

Stood right outside the door to his mum's room. Gazing either straight at him or right through him. With her, there seemed to be no difference.

A door opened between them, temporarily hiding Annie from Rhys' vision. A rattling hand dryer ceased and an old man decked in his winters emerged, brushing and smoothing his palms together. When he closed the door behind him, Annie had disappeared.

Hunching over, the old man walked by Rhys and nodded, probably expecting that Rhys was waiting to claim the toilet he had just vacated. *Gross.*

Annie had to be in his mum's room? It couldn't be a coincidence.

Rhys walked on over and opened the door.

The last person he expected to see stood on the other side.

"Hey, Rhys."

Mrs Johnson's voice was gentle and as soft as ever. For a fleeting moment, Rhys entertained the idea that he might have walked into the wrong room. However, seeing his mum's face dispelled that fear.

"Miss?"

"The school told me your mum had been in an accident. There was no way I could have gone home tonight without making sure you were all ok."

Still, it felt a bit odd.

Rhys loosened his grip on the door and let it slip quietly shut behind him. He approached the bed slowly, still unsure and uneasy about the fact that his tutor was standing across from him by his mum's bedside. He hadn't forgotten about Annie either and subtly scanned the room, but she was nowhere to be seen. Padding over to his mum, he found her unchanged from the night before.

"You here with your dad, I take it?"

"Yeah," Rhys responded, glancing back at the door. "He should be here any minute with my nana, grandpa, and Eevie."

Mrs Johnson's lips widened into one of her signature smiles. She made her way around to the other side of the bed where Rhys lent. Rhys enveloped one of his mum's hands in both of his. He felt her chill cooling in the warmth of his palms. He wasn't looking at Mrs Johnson, but he could hear fiddling behind him and then the rustle of a coat. She moved behind him. A gloved hand cupped his shoulder.

"She'll be okay," she said in a lowered her voice. "She's got good people watching over her. People who will make sure she gets the care she deserves."

Rhys didn't let his eyes leave his mum's face. This was all still a bit strange.

He recognised the muffled chatter approaching from outside the room. He was relieved that his dad would soon be joining them.

JONNY

The first thing he saw was a gloved hand hanging on his son's shoulder.

The second thing was the cascade of flowing ginger hair.

The third was a face he'd never forgotten but had not seen in more than 10 years.

"Hi, Jonny," she said.

"Jessica," Jonny responded, flabbergasted. His throat tightened with an unexpected shock.

"Been a while."

"Dad?" Rhys asked, his innocent features etched with discomfort.

"Come on over here, bud," Jonny said uneasily. He didn't feel good about this. Why now? Why was she back after all this time?

Rhys moved to do as his dad asked, but Jessica seized a chunk of his coat.

"You stay right there, Rhys," she said.

"Dad?" His son's distress visibly dialled up.

Jonny raised his hands, attempting to soothe Jessica. He was still stood in the doorway and flicked his head to the right, looking down the corridor. Hoping someone — anyone — might help.

"Come on in, Jon," Jessica insisted. "Come and join us."

But Jonny hesitated for a moment too long. "Don't make me ask again," Jessica said, tilting her head to guide Jonny's eyes towards something. That something was a small knife, about five inches long, gripped in her other hand, hugging the side of her coat.

"Ok, ok, ok. Just... I'm coming... I'm coming."

"Bag. Over there," Jessica demanded.

He did as he was told and lobbed the bag stuffed with Liz's things into the corner, out of the way with his hands up, pleading for calm.

Pleading for Jessica not to do something rash.

He remembered well enough, even now, how easily she could lose her temper.

Before Jonny shut the door, Ron and Nellie had caught up to him.

"Jonny, what's going on?" Ron asked, sounding out of breath. In the pushchair, Eevie gargled familiar noises.

"Ron, go and find help," Jonny said in a hushed and tense voice. "Security. Anybody."

"What on Earth for? What's going on in-?"

Ron didn't get a chance to finish the question.

"Please. Just go and get some fuckin' help, will you?"

Jonny gently allowed the door to close.

Muffling Ron and Nellie's concerned voices. Neither of them had any clearer idea of what was happening inside Liz's room.

Jonny kept his eyes fixed on Jessica, his hands remained splayed as though he was under arrest or being held hostage. As though a gun was being trained on him. There may well have been no gun involved, but only one person was calling the shots.

And she held a knife close by Rhys' side.

"There's just fine," Jessica declared.

"Please... Jess. Just let Rhys go. Whatever's going on here... he's nothing to do with it."

Her lips curled into a dark and vicious smile.

The kind of smirk you see from someone who knows they hold the upper hand. All the aces.

"Jon, he's just as much a part of this as you are."

Jonny wanted to know if Liz was ok. From where he stood, he looked her way for the first time, watching as her chest rose and dropped in a steady beat. Her eyes were knitted shut. She was at peace, hopefully oblivious to the situation.

Safe in that knowledge, he looked back at Jessica.

"What'd you want?" Jonny asked. "You come back to get back at me? Is that it?"

This question appeared to irritate her. She threw her head back, almost in despair, and muttered something under her breath he couldn't quite make out. In those precious moments, she wasn't concentrating on him. Jonny ushered forward an inch, then another, sliding his feet forward.

But he took one step too many. Jessica caught him and snapped her head down, the knife pointing at him, commanding him to stop where he was.

"Na-ah, stay where you are. I swear to fuckin' god, Jon. Don't push me."

Jonny noticed a tear cut a thin line down her cheek.

Behind him, Jonny heard a commotion unfolding outside the room. Footsteps clapped quickly in their direction from down the corridor. The muffled voices carried urgency as they converged around the only door in and out of the room.

"Please. Jess. We can talk about this. Me and you. Ju- just please let Rhys go."

She snorted as her head shook. With her knife still pointing at Jonny, she afforded herself a look at Liz behind her. Jonny didn't dare attempt another step forward.

"You know... I was pregnant as well, Jon. I was going to tell you. That day at the Spaniel. On that night you picked her," she looked down at Rhys. "And him," she said, her voice harsh as she gave him a little shake. "God, he looks just like you, doesn't he?"

"Jess,"

"Oh, please, you're pissing me off now. Stop calling me Jess. Open your eyes for once. Look at her. Look at me."

And he did see it. A puzzle formed in his head and the pieces fell quickly into place. Elisa. The sister Jonny had heard only fragments about from Liz over the years. The sister Liz always evaded discussing, to the point that Jonny had given up prying too much into the part of her life many years ago. A sickness consumed him. That mistake he made all those years ago was so much worse than he could have imagined. He was angry with himself. Angry with her. How could she play with him like this? Attempt to tear his life apart?

Elisa brushed Rhys' cheek with the sharp edge. Jonny could see Rhys squeezing his eyes closed, trying to jerk his neck away to the side.

For a moment, Jonny lost it. "Don't you fuckin—"

Elisa retaliated by biting harder. "What, Jon?" Don't fuckin' what? Hurt him?"

There it was again. That smile. The one that said *don't test me.*

From behind, the door pressed into Jonny's back. A woman's voice followed it in.

"Mr McIntyre, we've called security. Is everything ok in there?" A walkie-talkie beeped and cracked by her shoulder.

Elisa's eyes glared at him, waiting for his answer. Jonny's mouth felt hard and dry, the moisture sucked away. He didn't know what to do. If he opened the door and let them in, what would the cost be? Did Elisa really have it in her to harm Rhys? He wasn't sure. His last mistake had caused irreversible damage, out on the beach. He wasn't going to take that chance again.

"Mr McIntyre?" he heard again.

The door pressed open another inch. But that only prompted Elisa to take a tighter hold of Rhys and pull the knife just below his chin. The panic burst out of Rhys in his tears and heavy breathing. He struggled futilely against the arm that held him.

"Please. Don't come in," Jonny said desperately. "She... she's got my boy."

Jonny could only watch as Elisa kissed Rhys on the temple and hushed him softly. The way a mother would soothe their child.

She looked at Jonny again. "I just know it. A little girl. That's what we would have had, Jon. Little Annie. That's what we'd have called her. The life we would have had."

"I... I'm sorry."

He remembered them — those being the last words he'd said to her when he ended things, alone in that booth all those years ago.

She sniggered. "Not as sorry as you're going to be."

RHYS

"Rhys. . . Rhys. . . buddy. Keep your eyes on me, yeah."

He did as he was told and kept his gaze fixed on his dad.

"Everything's going to be ok."

Was his dad telling him that or himself? Rhys wasn't a kid. He could see how scared his dad was, too.

Rhys had never felt so frightened in his life. He could feel his heart fighting to get out of his chest and couldn't get his breath back under control. He could feel the knife edge ticking his Adam's apple and above it, the lines of tears that cut tracks into his flushed cheeks. Snot now layered his top lip and he daren't wipe it away.

"Dad. . . " It came out so feeble.

Mrs Johnson — Elisa — hushed him again.

More voices and radio chatter filled the space outside the room. Shadows danced beyond the frosted glass. Rhys felt his body pulled away from his mum's bedside, out towards the back of the room. A fresh wave of fear washed over him. Tears flowed, and he saw the same anguish mirrored in his dad's eyes.

Rhys attempted to struggle, to wriggle, but Elisa was too strong. She continued to wrestle him toward the window, his trainers screeching across the shiny resin floor. The knife pressed firmer against his neck, its silent warning unmistakable. Don't fight back.

She used the blade to tilt his neck up and expose his neck.

This was it.

I'm going to die. I don't want to die.

"Dad! Please!"

His dad edged closer. Just a step. But stopped again. Their eyes locked together, desperately meeting in search of a shared crumb of comfort.

"I want you to take a good look at your son, Jon."

Rhys burst into tears and began to grapple with Mrs Johnson's arm again. "No, no, no. Please. No!"

"Please, I'll do anything," his dad said. "Anything you want. He's just a kid."

"Why does it matter? Life doesn't always give us what we deserve. I was just a kid, too. I attempted to let it go, to forgive and forget what she did," Elisa said, briefly moving the knife away from Rhys to gesture toward his mum and then back at his dad. "For years, I've had to witness her moving on with her life as if I didn't matter, as if I didn't exist. Meanwhile, you built a family, all after I lost my own. You, her, all of it. None of you deserve any of it."

At that moment, the lights above began to flicker.

The knife at his neck moved to his cheek. The cold steel nipped his skin, forcing Rhys to yelp under his breath.

Then the strip of lights burst. Glass rained around him and Mrs Johnson. She staggered back and Rhys nearly lost his footing as she tugged him with her.

Without the light, the room relied on the gloomy yellowy-white of the moon that cast his, Mrs Johnson's and his dad's silhouettes across the floor. But in the corner, right by the overnight bag that his dad had lobbed over, another emerged.

It wasn't a silhouette, though.

His dad saw it too and sidestepped a couple of inches away from it. Just as he did back at the house, he only saw a threat. Something out to cause him harm. But Rhys, Rhys knew different.

It moved directly into the light. The same pose. Eyes a deep, never-ending black. Rhys felt Elisa's grip loosen.

Annie.

She smiled at Rhys. She tapped her nose twice. Just as she had done back at the house.

Then she looked over him at Elisa. Her feet lifted off the floor. Her eyes closed.

"No..." Rhys heard Elisa croak.

Annie flew towards them, right through Rhys.

Mrs Johnson's grip released.

Or got ripped away.

It was over in a flash. Just as it had been when his mum had fallen down the stairs.

He didn't see what happened. But he heard it.

The smash of the window.

The howl of the wind sweeping into the exposed room.

The scream.

His dad swept him up in his arms. His fingers pulled through Rhys' overgrown curls as he held him tightly to his chest. Rhys watched as the room flooded with nurses, doctors, security, and then nana and grandpa, pushing Eevie in on her stroller.

In amongst the feet was a single lotus.
Bright and alive, caught in the moon's ray.
Right where she'd stood.
Before it was crushed and died under a swarm of feet.

EPILOGUE

THREE MONTHS LATER...

JONNY

"How would you say things are going?" Dr Nielson asked, his leg resting in its usual place, exuding his typical relaxed demeanour.

"Ok, I think," Jonny replied, but uncertainty hovered beneath the surface.

With each passing day, things seemed to be on the mend and getting easier. He was back working at GW Construct with the boys. Liz was home. Things were better with Rhys. Eevie... well, Eevie was Eevie. A pain in the ass and sweetheart bundled into an adorable toddler that kept you on your toes. From the outside looking in, you could say a version of their new normality had been poured and had, finally, started to set.

But outside perceptions were often deceptive. Jonny still had bad days. Most of which he still kept to himself. He still thought back to that day at Porthcurno Beach. Often at night. Sometimes he would just look at Eevie and get transported right back there.

The guilt would almost swallow him whole.

Jonny wasn't sure he'd ever truly be able to forgive himself or forget it. But by spending time with Nielson, he had accepted that he couldn't allow himself to be chained down by it.

The past is a dark place for most of us to live in, Nielson had said. *In one form or another.*

It was those chains that had held him back, preventing him from being the father, husband, and friend he'd once been.

Jonny glanced over at the clock that ticked in the corner. Only a few minutes remained of his last session with Nielson.

"And what about the eyes? How are you coping with that?"

Yes, Jonny had told him. Nothing had changed. Those eyes seemed to be part of his life now, just as much as sleep and the need to eat and drink were.

Sometimes they still caught him off guard. Only the day before, he'd been pushing Eevie in her stroller as they made their way into town. He'd turned a corner, only to be faced with a blank face and those piercing eyes outside the bakery. They still shit him up. But Jonny had adapted and found a way to coexist with the bizarre and unexplainable. Those eyes were no longer a paralysing force, but rather an odd connection between him and Rhys. A shared understanding, an inside joke only they comprehended.

"I get by," Jonny said, responding to the question.

It'd only been recently that Jonny had found the courage to let Nielson in on the secret.

Nielson found it fascinating ever since. Jonny wasn't sure if Nielson truly believed it or whether he was just indulging him. Nielson was the only other person in on the secret and Jonny sat here now, looking at the clock, harbouring an itch to find out what Nielson truly made of it.

"Doc, I'm sure I'm not the only person you've spoken to over the years who has told you they see things."

"Sure," he said, gesturing for Jonny to continue.

"Do you believe it?"

"Don't beat around the bush, Jonny. You want to know if I believe you?"

Jonny did.

"Does it matter to you what I believe?"

"I guess not."

"For what it's worth, yes. I believe you, Jonny. Just as I believe your son does, as well. Just because I can't see what you see or even experience what you experience, it doesn't mean it's not real. There's a lot of mystery in this world and who am I to say what is and isn't real."

Jonny sat flummoxed. He'd not expected this answer or the unexpected sense of validation it came with.

Nielson continued. "Let me ask you this, have you ever seen a ghost?"

"What?" Confusion weighed down on Jonny's brow.

"I appreciate it's a strange thing to ask but, come on, pander to me for a moment. Have you ever seen a ghost? In-person, of course. Not on one of these documentaries or videos you see on the internet."

Jonny threw his hands apart. "No. Well... I don't think I have."

"I have."

At first, Jonny smiled. He was unsure of where this was going or whether Nielson was having him on.

And Nielson saw straight through him. "Honestly. No word of a lie. Back in my University days, I offered a lift to an old woman walking down a busy road that had no pavement. Bucketing it down with rain, it was. Anyway, she wasn't a big talker. Just said she was going to see her daughter in the next town over. And I mean it was a fair old distance. She asked me to pull over about a mile outside the town. So, I obliged after making sure she was ok and pulled off. I took a look back in my mirror and I swear on my mother's grave, she was gone. Disappeared into thin air."

"And there was nowhere for her to go?"

"Nowhere. But a few days later when I was driving back that way, I came across a bunch of flowers in the same spot I'd dropped her off at. Curiosity got the better of me. I parked up a little out the way and checked it out and, Jonny, they were all for her. For an anniversary. Turned out a woman had been killed in a hit and run on that stretch while she was cycling a few years back."

Jonny felt a lump in his throat and didn't know what to say. For a moment, the ticking of Nielson's clock filled the silence.

"I don't want to fixate on that for too long, so let's bring this back. What I'm trying to get across is that our world is one full of unknowns and full of people who experience and see things that simply can't be explained. I'm a man of logic, but science and maths can't always give us the answer. I've seen a ghost. You haven't. You see these black eyes and shadowy figures. I haven't. It doesn't mean neither exists. It's important to have an open and curious mind."

RHYS

"Come on now, your dad will be out soon. Let's wrap it up."

Rhys did as he was told. He flicked his Switch into rest mode and secured his headphones around his neck. Up front, mum finished up with what she had been doing as well, stowing the phone she had been scrolling through for the last 10 minutes into her handbag. Rhys watched her as she drained the last of her coffee — properly tipping it back to get every last drop — before returning it to the cup holder.

To Rhys' right, Eevie stirred, rousing herself from a nap. A newspaper lay between them. The front page was about the floods being caused by Storm Dennis. Above that, there was a bright red banner warning of something called COVID-19 that was spreading across Europe. Rhys' mum inquired about Ralph's arrival time through the rearview mirror.

"Think he said 4ish. Could be a little after. Depends what time he gets back from his gran's."

Rhys couldn't be more excited. He and Ralph had gone over to each other's houses a few times since Christmas, once things had settled down. But this was the first time either would be spending the night over. They were going to play video games and D&D. Mum promised she'd order pizza. Maybe they'd stay up to watch a movie, a scary one. The beauty of half-term was that there was no alarm clock ready to beat their asses out of bed. Tomorrow would be cool, too. Dad was going to drop him and Ralph off over at the water park.

After a minute or two, Eevie had properly woken up. Her arms did a little dance in the air. Her face was a picture of confusion, like she had no idea why her arms were doing what they were.

"How's she doing?" mum asked.

"Yeah, ok I think."

Eevie faced Rhys, and she began blowing raspberries. It didn't take long for the line of drool to thicken under her lip. Rhys copied her, doing so until he too went too far and needed to wipe his collection of spit from around his chops. Eevie just kept going, though. She didn't care that the slobber ran down to her chin. Rhys laughed at her. His mum smiled, before asking him to make his sister decent again.

After he did so, Eevie's arms stopped flailing. She stared past Rhys, out of the passenger window and into the car park.

Rhys tracked her gaze. A boy, around his age, he thought, stood sheltering under a tree. The boy waved the usual wave, and Rhys waved back. Rhys had got used to seeing *them* now. Each time, he'd thought of Annie.

He did again now.

Rhys had sent her a message on ChatterBox a couple of days ago. Her faceless avatar was the same dull grey and offline. ChatterBox reminded him constantly that she had not been online since that weekend before the night at the hospital — a night that hadn't been spoken about in months but still sometimes hung in the air like a bad smell.

Rhys still took comfort in talking to her online. Even if she wasn't there. For Rhys, it was the better alternative to writing in the journal that his nana had bought him for Christmas. The one that was still in his bedroom unopened and wrapped up in its plastic packaging.

He told Annie about the *others* he saw. He told her about his mum and dad and Eevie and what they got up to from time to time. He told her about school and how much better things were. More than anything else, he talked to her about Ralph.

Rhys was brought out of his distraction by Eevie.

"Rer Rer," she cooed.

He turned and smiled. She smiled back. Eevie was doing that a lot more now. She began to bounce her arms again and Rhys copied with his hands.

"Here he is," mum announced up front, buckling her belt. She booted the Crossland up. Ready to make a move.

Rhys watched his dad jog across the gravelled car park that surrounded the Evolve Therapy Centre. As he did so, Rhys also caught his dad flick his head off to the side, towards the boy under the tree. Rhys knew he saw him, too.

In he climbed. He and his mum lent in for a quick kiss. He shuffled in his chair, turning to face Rhys and Eevie in the back.

"How're you doing, kiddo," he asked.

"All gravy." It'd become the standard response between them.

"All gravy? What does that even mean?" Mum quizzed mockingly.

"You're just all gravy, aren't you? Means you're all good," Rhys said.

"If you say so. Speaking of gravy, though, we going to get some grub?"

"Aye, I reckon so. What you think, Ee? Some chicken strips at The White Bear sound ok?" Dad asked, waiting in anticipation.

Eevie's only answer was to pad her hands against her tiny thighs and look perplexed.

"It's as good as a yes."

The gravel crunched as the Crossland hit reverse. They pulled off towards the gate and the boy under the tree watched them take their leave.

He waved again, his mouth curling into a kind smile. Rhys waved again through the back window and their connection remained until the Crossland swung left onto the main road and left him behind.

ELIZABETH

"Here, take the key and let yourself in. I've got to grab some stuff out of the boot," Elizabeth instructed Rhys as she removed the house key, wedged among her collection of club cards and key-rings.

Rhys did as he was told, taking the key she held over her shoulder with pinched fingers before sliding out onto the gravel drive.

"And make a start on getting that room tidied," Elizabeth shouted, her words trying to catch Rhys as he ran for the door.

"Yeah, yeah, yeah," he replied, fobbing her off. As usual. Elizabeth was in no doubt she will have to tell him again. Jonny remained where he was. Elizabeth could feel him tracing her face.

"Give the lad a break, will ya," he said.

"And let him pick up your bad habits? I don't think so."

Jonny chuckled. She did, too, before the Crossland rested into silence. Her looking at him, him back at her. Their heads rested against the fabric of the car seat.

"We should talk later," Elizabeth suggested.

"Yeah? What've I done now?"

"Nothing... this time. I just..." she hesitated, trying to rearrange her words.

Over the last few months, they'd both avoided the conversation about what happened at the hospital, but also all those years ago. Elizabeth could see the cloud of guilt in his eyes, the change so instant, at the very mention of *her* name. "I don't know. We just never really talked about everything that happened. And—"

Jonny stopped her, shaking his head. "Liz, you don't have to."

"I think we should. We've come so far over the last few months, but I can't help but think this thing is like a cloud hanging over us. I want to move on from it. Properly."

Jonny looked out to the window, out to the house, perhaps thinking of another excuse not to drag it all up. This wasn't the first time Elizabeth had mentioned it. She'd been patient and she would continue to be if he wasn't ready. She didn't want to undo all the progress he'd made in becoming the old Jonny again. The Jonny that she knew.

But he nodded and said ok. Not with acceptance, though. With defeat.

"I love you, y'know. I'm sorry I don't tell you enough," Elizabeth said. "We'll be ok."

She meant it.

"I love you, too," Jonny said. Eevie gurgled, providing a timely distraction.

"Go on. You get her in. I'll be right behind you," Elizabeth said.

While Jonny took Eevie inside, Elizabeth made her around to the boot. She ferreted around, moving the bags for life and coats aside from a pile nestled in the corner. Under, there were more bags. Two for Eevie. One packed full of clothes and books. The other had a couple of Rhys' birthday presents in — a D&D expansion pack he'd asked for and a framed concept art from some game he'd been playing called Ichigo.

Elizabeth reminded herself that she needed to check in with Ralph's dad to make sure he was free for the party next weekend. Another thing to tick off on her mental to-do-list.

Before she closed the boot, her eyes landed on another bag. This one was full of clothes she needed to donate to the charity shop. On top of the pile was a cashmere scarf.

Not hers.

Elisa's.

Elizabeth thought back to that night at the hospital. Hearing everything but seeing nothing, as she lay incapable of doing anything about it. Her sister's words had played on a loop in her memory ever since, reforming a cloud of regret she had been seemingly running away from her whole life.

Everything Elisa said, it had all been true.

Elizabeth had been responsible for what happened to their mum. It had been an accident. A tantrum that had gone too far, one in which she'd picked up the closest thing around her, a rolling pin they'd been rolling Play-Doh out with, and swung it. It had smacked the back of her mum's head. Elizabeth remembers the instant and overwhelming regret. The flood of tears that had followed. Her mum had seemed fine and reassured her she was ok. A few hours later, she collapsed at the bottom of the stairs.

Nobody but Elisa knew — not even Esme.

But, yes, while Elisa had lied to keep them together, she had tarred Elizabeth and made sure she never forgot what happened to their mum, why they were in the care system, that she had needed to lie to keep the sisters together.

And Elizabeth couldn't take it any more.

She saw a way out with Nellie and Ron. A way to escape her past and the constant reminders.

And she took it.

The truth, though, was that she had never escaped it. Elisa's voice had always followed her. Still did, even though she was gone.

It was this that she needed to tell Jonny about and let him in.

She stopped herself looking at Elisa's scarf, grabbed the two bags full of Eevie and Rhys' things and slammed the boot down on the rest.

Elizabeth fumbled with her keys and locked the Crossland. From behind, the rough bark of a dog stole her attention. She glanced out down the drive, onto Sandon Mount.

At the bottom, a woman stood facing her. Legs shoulder width apart. Arms down by her side. Ginger hair draped like a curtain past her shoulders.

A look she recognised until she saw her eyes.

The two black, never-ending, holes that replaced the green she'd known growing up with.

Elisa.

ESME

"You sure you're not coming, Es?" Leesha asked, shouted up from the bottom of the stairs.

"I'm sure. I've got to get caught up with work stuff," she responds.

But Esme wasn't catching up with work stuff. She simply couldn't afford the regular nights out anymore. Ever since moving into the new house share, her weekly wages seemed to vanish quicker than a puddle on a scorching summer day.

There at the beginning of the month, gone the next on extortionate rent, a silly, expensive phone contract, and the other subscriptions and outgoings she purposely organised to come out at the beginning of every month, leaving her with barely enough until the next payday.

Truth was, living in London meant she had never had a lot to play with after payday, anyway. But since moving into her house share, her outgoings surpassed her income, and her overdraft was nearing its limit. Though she had never considered credit cards or payday loans, recently, she found herself exploring these options on Google, feeling increasingly tempted. It seemed more like a matter of when she would take one out rather than if she would take one out.

After closing the door to her studio room, Esme settled on the edge of her bed and sipped water, contemplating her situation. Another matter weighed on her mind.

From her bedside drawer, she pulled the letter out again. She'd read it most nights over the last three months when she felt alone and she was going to read it again now.

Esme hadn't told Elizabeth, Nellie, or Ron about the letter — nothing since she had discovered it waiting at her work desk as she swept in on that unseasonal warm Friday morning in October, no doubt thinking more about her plans for the weekend rather than her tasks that day. All of that disappeared as Esme opened that letter.

Realising very quickly who it was from, she'd taken herself off to a booth for privacy.

Esme had read the letter twice that day, absorbing every word, her eyes damp with tears. It was a handwritten note from the sister she never really knew and would never meet. The sister who had been a vague childhood memory. This letter was the closest she would get to understanding Elisa — learning about her life, her struggles, her losses.

Esme still thought about that night Elisa had died at Kingsmill Hospital. Nellie had phoned and in that awkward way she always approached any difficult conversation with her, she had jumbled her way through it.

But Esme had already known everything by that point, had done for a couple of weeks.

Not just about Elisa, but also about what Elizabeth had done. The lies she'd told her over the years.

Questions gnawed at her — what else had her sister hidden? What else was she capable of?

And as Esme sat there again reading Elisa's letter, grief for the sister she would never know wrestled with anger and resentment for the one she thought she had known so well.

Esme had grown to hate her sister and she wasn't sure what she would do with those feelings.

One thing was for sure, though.

She wouldn't be able to let it go.

ACKNOWLEDGEMENTS

It was a surreal moment, writing this acknowledgements page.

For a long time, I have described this book as my greatest experiment — one that started way back in 2019. I'll let you in on a secret. . . When Karma Comes Calling, originally, was supposed to be a horror story! I quickly realised when I started that this wasn't going to be a scary story. In fact, it wasn't very scary at all!

Writing is a cathartic exercise for me and after I stopped pretending to be something I wasn't, I recognised that my story was going to be one about forgiveness and the chains of guilt that can sometimes cripple us as humans. I truly believe they are feelings that we all experience at some point in our lives, and I hope I did a decent job of conveying that in this story and the parallels of them.

This book finally came together after four years of writing, editing, rewriting, and more editing. And seeing this story that has lived rent free in my head for so long out in the wild is one of the greatest achievements of my life.

But things like this don't come together without having great people around you.

I'll start with a thank you to Christian Storm for your incredible work turning my idea into a finished product. I came across Christian via Reedsy and knew after a brief conversation that he was absolutely the right person to collaborate with on the cover and visual concepts for When Karma Comes Calling. Your work is stunning and I look forward to working with you far more in the future.

Thank you to my friends and colleagues that have cheered me on from the sidelines and constantly asked me about this book. There are so many of you to mention that I would need a book to name everyone but just know I'm grateful to each and every one of you who has been invested in this journey.

Several authors have, unknowingly, inspired me on my way to this point and the eagle-eyed readers among you may have spotted references to them throughout this book, starting with the Kings in the Prologue! I do want to give a special shout out to Gabrielle Zevin, though. Her book Tomorrow, Tomorrow, Tomorrow remains one of the best I've read in recent years. I loved it so much that I included one of her fictional games, Ichigo, into my story. Thank you, Gabrielle, for letting me steal your fictional game during an author signing session in Nottingham. You possibly won't remember the meeting but believe me, it meant everything to me.

Thank you to my mum, dad, brother, and grandparents for your unwavering support. I sadly lost my grandad in the lead up to the publication of this book. He passed on so much wisdom to me in the 31 years I had with him and I hope some of that has been reflected in this story.

Thank you to my wife and first reader, Natalie. I couldn't ask for a more supportive, loving, humble, and generous partner in crime. Your feedback has been instrumental in the final version that is out in the world today. Thank you also to my son, Lewie, for always keeping me on my toes! The two of you are my world and biggest inspiration. I love you both and this first book of mine is dedicated to you.

T.T.A.

My last thank you goes to you, my first readers, for choosing to spend time with this story. There are millions of ways you could have chosen to spend your time and millions of other books you could have read. I'm grateful and honoured that you chose this book.

Hopefully, you will join me for the next one.

Until next time.

ABOUT THE AUTHOR

Tom Bestwick is an East-Midlands-based writer, who has spent his career up to now working in public relations. When Karma Comes Calling is his first novel and will be accompanied by three novellas: The Crash, Black And Blue, and Keep On Digging.

TOMBESTWICKAUTHOR.COM

Printed in Great Britain
by Amazon

51643075R00240